OATH & HONOUR

ANTHONY LASCELLE

AuthorHouse™ UK Ltd.
1663 Liberty Drive
Bloomington, IN 47403 USA
www.authorhouse.co.uk
Phone: 0800.197.4150

© *2013 Anthony Lascelle. All rights reserved.*

No part of this book may be reproduced, stored in a retrieval system, or transmitted by any means without the written permission of the author.

Published by AuthorHouse 06/14/2013

ISBN: 978-1-4817-9741-2 (sc)
ISBN: 978-1-4817-9742-9 (hc)
ISBN: 978-1-4817-9743-6 (e)

Any people depicted in stock imagery provided by Thinkstock are models, and such images are being used for illustrative purposes only.
Certain stock imagery © Thinkstock.

This book is printed on acid-free paper.

Because of the dynamic nature of the Internet, any web addresses or links contained in this book may have changed since publication and may no longer be valid. The views expressed in this work are solely those of the author and do not necessarily reflect the views of the publisher, and the publisher hereby disclaims any responsibility for them.

BOOK ONE
BAD BLOOD, NEW BLOOD

1 "TWO TIMES" VALONE

A COLD WIND BLEW THOUGH THE YARD, aggravating the prisoners that had taken up the option of outside exercise. Most had taken refuge in the gymnasium or rec-room. Groups huddled in their own cliques, smoking and taking surreptitious nips from contraband flasks. There was no interracial fraternity, despite the best efforts of the state governor and prison wardens to iron out the last remaining taboo in the correctional systems.

It was a period of halcyon progress throughout New York State's correctional system. A new order had been instilled in the consciousness of inmates and the public alike. The introduction of work-share programs, were examples of the modern age of reform. Inmates who had shown an exceptional level of good behavior were found day release jobs in local businesses, which helped them to slowly adapt to release and allowed the outside public to gain a confidence in the system, which in turn helped to bestow a certain respect upon both parties.

Five Points correctional facility was one of the pioneers of the new philosophy and was also a forerunner in the import of new skills for a new world. Computer training, internet skills, communication philosophy, emotional response linking. For the average inmate, who had committed violent crimes against individuals and society this could have been construed as insulting. Yet, most took to the programs with relish and found a freedom from the daily drudge and weariness of living in seclusion.

Five points was primarily a transfer prison. All inmates were of high risk category, but had shown an enthusiasm and aptitude to reform. They wanted to get back to the world and to leave the past behind them. That is what they had led the authorities to believe. In effect, Five Points to the inmates, represented easy time and every inmate wanted easy time. It was the reason that Serge Valone had worked hard for the last five years to earn a transfer to Five Points, but had succeeded only in being granted one a year and a half before his release.

He had kept his head down since his transfer and somehow managed to stay neutral. For this fact he was respected, by the blacks, Hispanics and whites. He was viewed as a figure of worldly knowledge and was seen giving counsel to any faction that sought it. Even the guards from time to time asked his opinion on certain matters.

On that cold afternoon as the wind blew down from Canada, across Lake Ontario and into the yard and through the inmates of Five Points, Serge Valone sat on a bench alone. His prison issue wool coat done up tight and a black woolen beanie pulled over his greying hair, his face buried in a book. He had one month to go.

A convict named James ambled over to him and sat without an invite. He lit a smoke offered one to Serge, who shook his head.

'You okay?' said James.

'Yeah. What's up?' Serge replied, closing his book.

'I need some advice.'

'Shoot.'

'What d'yer make of Jorge?'

'Why you asking me that?'

'Can he be trusted?'

'We're convicts Jimmy. You can't trust anyone in here. You know this.'

'Yeah. But since I lost my last supplier I've been scratching around to make a living. He says he can get more stuff in, but I ain't sure about him.'

'From what I seen of him, he looks like a stand up guy,' said Serge. 'But you know; you gotta make your own decisions. If I was you, I'd make it easy time. You got what, a year left?'

'Yeah.'

'Then stop screwing around with that shit. See it out, then you can walk. You know they're gonna fuck you, you get caught. You get a transfer outta here, back to some shithole like Green Haven or Attica. Serious fucking hard time, sentence increased and for what. You're short brother. Stay that way.'

James thought about it, the way Serge had put it. He looked around the yard, took a puff from his smoke, nodded.

'I guess you're right. I wish I was as short as you.'

'Yeah, well, it took me ten years to get this short. Eight years of hard time,' he said with a leaden smile.

'Whachyer gonna do when you get back?' James asked.

Serge shrugged.

'You going back in?'

Serge shrugged again.

'How do you manage to stay calm, after what they did to you?'

'What you talking about?'

'They put two hits on you Serge. Don't tell me that don't make you pissed.'

'Costello's gone now, so it don't matter.'

'Why didn't you turn?'

'You fucking serious? I ain't a rat. I got my honour. Through life, things get taken from you, some you just piss away. You make bad choices, live with it. I made an oath and all I got left is my honour. Ain't fucking nobody and I mean nobody gonna take that away from me and I ain't never gonna give it away. They wanna put me in the grave, so be it. But I won't go in it, without my honour. I'm fifty one now, I got no wife, no children, I don't know what's waiting for me when I get out. Life is a long shot, that's all I know. You know, everyone in here comes to me for advice, but I don't know shit. I ain't no wise man with any answers; all I do is show people another way of looking at things. Am I mad at the borgata? Yeah. If I could hit someone, would I? Yes. But Costello is in his grave, there's a new order and I'm just a forgotten man. The best advice I can give you is this James. Don't be foolish, don't think you're above the law and always watch your back. Because in this thing of ours now, you ain't got no friends.

'I was lucky to survive the two hits in Green Haven, I know that. They sent cowboys. They thought I was gonna roll over. I'd do life and wouldn't roll, because what honour is there in that? But by the same token, what honour is there on their part. Whacking guys because you think they're gonna roll. All they've created is anarchy. Now, you get banged up, you gotta assume they gonna hit you. The paranoia has created a lack of trust now. I look at the way things are and I see a barely functional organization. The Commission, allowing the spics, Russians and niggers to sit, it was a mistake. Don't get me wrong, at the time, well, it seemed like it was the only way to keep everyone in control. You gotta question why though. We were the mob; nobody could do anything in this country without our say so. Fuck, we even elected and ejected a president from office, it makes you think.'

'I thought we were forbidden to talk about that?' said James, through inquisitive eyes.

'Yeah well, what they gonna do, hit me?' said Serge with a smile. 'Give me a cigarette.'

'Sure,' said James and fumbled around his pockets for the pack. He slid it across to Serge.

'The decline began with Costello,' continued Serge. 'You look at how fucking strong we were. It makes you think. Costello abused his position on the commission. That fuck wanted us to change into this mutated version of globalization. Inviting outsiders to sit on the commission. He should have been hit, for that alone. Now look at us. The Colombians with all their wild west ways. They don't respect anything; they don't play by the rules. You can't deal with these people. You got the Russians, another bunch of terrorists. Gang-banging black street hoods, who seem intent on taking us back to the days of the twenties. What Luciano and Lansky had the foresight to build, that prick gave it away.'

'We ain't finished yet,' said James, trying vainly to lift Serge's mood.

'Maybe not. I see some hope in D'Angelo.'

'You think he'll be good for the family?'

'Maybe. But he hit Costello without a commission sanction. So what's that tell you?'

'I don't know?'

'It means he broke a rule. What I'm curious to know is, did he break the rule because he just doesn't give a fuck and wants to be the boss or because he didn't believe he needed an okay from people who shouldn't be on the commission anyhow?'

James shrugged and lit another cigarette.

'I'm hoping it's the latter. Then maybe, we can go back to the days of real *Cosa Nostra*.'

James took a long pull from the cigarette while thinking on what Serge had said.

'What's it mean for guys like us Serge. If it's the latter?'

'It means we're going to war.'

'Forget about it.'

'What you afraid of?'

'I ain't afraid Serge. I just don't like the idea of a war.'

'I don't blame you. It ain't pretty. Sometimes though, you gotta draw parameters. Sometimes you gotta have separation, which is what that fuck Costello could not see. You cross over and deal with these people, but you don't invite them into our thing. It ain't all Costello's fault. We brought a lot of this shit on ourselves. When the government began with their witness protection program crap, we did nothing to take that power away. Instead of assuring a guy his family would never have to want and his kids would be taken care of and if he just did the fucking time, he could come out financially made, everything would be okay. What did we do though? We drove our guys into the program by whacking out anyone who we thought would turn. We forgot loyalty and honour.'

'Hey Serge, it's no good locking the stable after the horse has bolted. They were just protecting the interests of our thing.' James flicked the butt into the grass.

'Not always James. Me for example. They hit me after I'd been in for a year. I didn't roll after that, so they hit me again. Consider it this way? If

I'd had children, I might have. Once you start whacking people because you think they're gonna roll, then you've breached your own defences. You've created a boomerang and the government plays on this. We survive by our loyalty and rules. The rule is you talk you die, not you get banged up, you die, 'cause we think you might talk.'

'I see that.'

'I'll give you some more advice Jimmy. You ain't made yet. When you get outta here, get out of our thing, unless you see a major change in attitudes.'

'You serious?'

'You bet your fucking life I am. You get all the training you can get in here, get whatever qualifications you can. When you go out them gates, relocate to another city, get yourself a job that pays thirty forty grand a year and forget about this shit. You're a young man, don't give your life to this if it ain't gonna give you nothing back. I might be wrong; maybe things will change, but take a closer look. You can be a gangster anytime, but once you're in there's only three ways out. The grave, the WPP or retirement,' said Serge counting them out with his fingers. 'And how many men can you count who have successfully retired?' he asked of James.

'One or two,' replied James.

'Yeah. You do the maths.' With that a horn sounded across the yard. 'Time for chow,' said Serge. 'Come on, I'm buying.'

'Comedian.'

That night in his cell as Serge lay on his bunk reading his book he was disturbed by a guard. The guard spoke through the slat.

'How you doing Serge?'

'Fine. Yourself?'

'Can't complain. What you reading?'

Serge sat up and showed the book to the guard. 'Nietzsche. Beyond good and evil.'

'You sure do have some strange tastes.'

'So I've been told.'

'Well, you've got a date with the warden tomorrow.'

'Yeah. What's that about? He gonna throw me a farewell party?'

'Nah,' said the guard with a laugh. 'It's protocol. You know, you down to a month. Part of the reform process, you get offered a short course of re-assimilation. '

'I heard about that.'

'It's a good course. It helps you to manage your stress and conquer your fear.'

'I ain't got any fear.'

'That's what I thought. It's not just that. They put you in contact with groups and counselors, so you got easy access to help once you back in the world. You might consider taking it Serge.'

'I'll think about it. Thanks.'

'No problem. Sleep well,' said the guard and drew the slat shut.

Serge got up and stretched his back and rubbed the back of his neck, sighed with agitation. The last few months had been harder than the first few. Serge viewed all the reform programs with disdain. He had built up a philosophy of contempt against the government. He felt it was just another way of keeping the criminal imprisoned; to induce them with a freedom and a false belief that they could be a functional member of society.

Serge knew where they failed in their vision, certain individuals, just did not want to be an integrated part of society. Some were so full of hate they would refuse society and its values until they died. Others just wanted to be gangsters; to live in that alternative society, with their own rules and liberties. Serge was one of those people. Always would be.

2 TEN YEARS GONE

CANADA THREW DOWN SNOWS FROM THE NORTH the next morning, filling the inmates with a sense of despair. The chill factor made it impossible to stand the outside and the authorities prohibited all outdoor recreation. A vexation ran through the prison. Inmates needed to get out into the air. The yard was the nearest they could get to the outside, the yard were they could forget for an hour or two, that they were locked up. It was there, that most of their business was conducted. Being cooped up inside only served to inflame their senses. Recreation time had to be staggered, so as not to cause overcrowding in the rec-room, gymnasium and library. This added to the inmate's perverse sense of injustice. They were used to recreation time at a set time and now their routine was all out of focus.

For Serge, it was a welcome liberty. After breakfast and his meeting with the warden, he decided to just see out the day in his cell. He was short and full to the brim with prison life and inmate problems. His self imposed solitary helped him to focus on his sketches. When Serge grew tired of drawing images from prison life, he turned to reading. These little hobbies helped to maintain his focus, so that he could deflect his mind away from the few weeks he had until release.

In the ten years gone, Serge had witnessed many short timers go crazy in the last days. It was if a spring within them finally uncoiled after the years of constant pressure. All the hard work they had weaved to secure their release was undone in a moment, and it did not take much to trigger the explosion. A curt remark, an imagined slur.

Serge had seen some of the toughest and wisest men throw it all away in an instance of insanity. Release revoked, sentence increased. Stir crazy beyond repair. It was the fear that had got hold of them. The phobia of actually being free. An absolute terror of learning how to live in the outside once again. The inability to control the fear which led to their irrecoverable emancipation.

So to keep it at bay, Serge kept busy and played a confidence trick on himself. He kept repeating, he had another year to go. The subconscious began to believe it.

Serge had become adept with the pencil and had sketched many images. When his concentration could not hold the book, he took to flipping threw his vast portfolio. His collection did not include the many he had given away as gifts to fellow prisoners or those that the guards sometimes bought from him, for a pack of cigarettes or some illicit liquor. Even so, what he had kept hold of was a vast array of prison imagery he had been unfortunate to witness.

During his stay at Green Haven, he had seen a riot between blacks and whites. The depictions were real enough, capturing the violence and hate on the faces. Some drawings were just simple outlines of prison life. A pair of inmates talking outside a cell on an upper walkway, viewed from floor level. Others were portraits. There was one of Seth Hudson. An unfortunate who had suffered severe head injuries during the Green Haven riots and was destined to spend the rest of his life in a vegetative state. Serge had drawn him in his infirmary bed. Eyes black and vacant, spit rolling down his chin, his body contorted in uncomfortable seizure like committal.

Leafing through them, Serge was hit by the magnitude of his time in incarceration. He came across a portrait of a haggard old man. Hair long and pulled back into a ponytail. The eyes were weary, defeated. Prison had taken all his smiles and lines of deep frown had carved their way into the skin. The man was Peter "Petey" Maxwell. He was a lifer in Green Haven and Serge had become great friends with him. Petey had helped to keep Serge on the straight and narrow during his first few years and his sagacious talk turned many a fraught moment into one of hope. When Serge won his transfer to Five Points, leaving Petey was hard on both men. Petey died six months later. As Serge held the portrait in his hands a tear forced its way out and landed on the paper. Serge swallowed hard, refusing to allow anymore to fall. He sucked in a large gulp of air and put Petey to the back and out of his mind.

There were self portraits. Some were contrived of the aspirations that Serge had decided to pursue upon his release. In one view, he was sitting at an upstate river, fishing, draped in a poncho and a muffler hat. He is alone and the trees are almost wrapping him in the comfort of seclusion. It was a place where his dad had taken him as a boy. A time when his father had been a specialty, before he took to the bottle and beat his wife and decided he did not really want to be a husband and father. Serge had not seen him since the age of thirteen and doubted if he was still alive.

Following his father's disappearance, his mother went to pieces. Because of loneliness, she took up with any man who showed an interest in her. None of her romances worked. Some of the men his mother dated seemed intent of being nasty to Serge. But by that time Serge was a child of the street. He had learnt the basics and at fifteen had busted one of his mother's so called suitors across the mouth with a metal pipe, knocking out six teeth, breaking the jaw, severely lacerating the tongue and giving the man a lifelong speech impediment. Juvenile hall beckoned and Serge tasted incarceration for the first time.

Fate would not be halted. Serge had a taste for delinquency. He spent the next three years in an out of various institutions. He had begun to build up a reputation, inside and out. His mother despairing and somewhat incompetent finally disowned him and Serge took it on the chin. Years later his mother tried to find her way back into his life, but Serge had become indifferent. He did not even attend her funeral.

So seeking a family Serge found himself in the clutches of a small time outfit. Stealing cars and robbing stores. He understood it was small time and had enough sense to realize that there was better money to be made in the Big Apple.

Fate once again put him on a collision course with the mob. While trying to offload a truckload of designer wear he came into contact with Tony "Bughouse" Zinardi. It just so happened that the truck he hijacked had already been hijacked and was en-route to a secure location.

Serge, being what he was, full of a dreadnought quality walked into the clubhouse of the local villain, who was "Bughouse" Zinardi and offered him the load. "Bughouse" had already received the call from a frantic associate about the audacious stunt and was none too happy.

When the kid before him was offering him back his own swag, Tony Zinardi could do nothing more than sit in his chair and laugh in hysterical disbelief. "Bughouse" took an instant liking to Serge, gave him a pass on his indiscretion and took him under his wing.

What made their friendship were the certain parallels in their family life. Tony Zinardi had also had a problem with one of his mother's boyfriend's. Whereas Serge had knocked out a few teeth and left a man talking funny, Tony had gutted his like a fish and also a friend of the man's who just happened to be with him. He was twelve at the time and spent significant years in a mental institution, though in his eyes, he was as sane as the next man. That was how he came to be known as "Bughouse".

Tony was a mover and shaker and he certainly shook up his crime syndicate, climbing the rungs with a speed unheard of. Before he was thirty five he was a capo in the Cuccione family. Being a capo was not what he wanted. He wanted his own family and broke away from the Cuccione's. To stave off an all out war, the Commission sanctioned his breakaway. It was at the time of change, when the Colombians and Russians and other outsiders were invited to sit on the commission. They didn't need the distraction or the aggravation and wanted to represent a house in order. So Tony Zinardi got his own family and the Cuccione's were forced to eat humble pie, much to their chagrin. Not only did this move annoy the Cuccione's, other families had the bit between their teeth, but they knew an all out war would be devastating and peace was what they needed to make money. Politics would always override a personal affront.

And so it went. Serge became a member of the Zinardi mob and was soon making his way through the ranks, becoming the number one enforcer and negotiator in the family. Serge had found the family he desired.

In less than ten years the Zinardi family would be blown to smithereens. Serge was indicted and convicted on conspiracy to defraud. When the first hit come down on him, his family would be taken apart, piece by piece. Tony "Bughouse" Zinardi would find himself outnumbered with a RICO statute about to be hammered upon him. He went into hiding and acquired more fame by being placed on the FBI's ten most wanted list. Their docking and trucking interests were carved up by the other factions and once again Serge was an orphan.

Serge survived another hit and would acquire the sobriquet "Two Times", which would replace his original, "Walk and Talk". That label was bestowed upon him because of his proficiency in negotiations.

Serge became tired of looking over old memories, put the drawings away, lay back on the bed and stared at the ceiling. For a moment he almost allowed himself to have imaginings about what was waiting for him back on the streets. He jumped off the bed and decided to join the general population. He could not allow himself to think about the outside.

He stood on the walkway and looked over the preserve. From out of the next cell came Russ Geeenbaum; a monster of a man, with thick black hair and full beard to match. He reminded Serge of some throwback to ancient Greece.

'What's up?' he asked in his deep growling voice.
'Nothing. Just taking in the view.'
'Here's your book man,' said Russ holding out a worn paperback.
'You finish it?' Serge questioned.
'Nearly.'
'What the hell you giving it back to me for then?'
'Thought you'd want it back.'
'You keep it.'
'You serious?'
'Go ahead.'
'Thanks man.'

'Just finish the fucking thing Russ.'
'Sure. You want a smoke?'
'Thanks.' Serge took one from the packet and tucked it in his top pocket.
'Same old shit eh,' said Russ.
'Same old shit,' replied Serge.
'I'm gonna miss you man.'
'Don't start in with that.'
'You been a true friend.'
'Russ, you ain't got any friends in here. I told you that a thousand times.'
'I know.'
'Then remember it,' Serge regretted being curt with Russ and immediately tried to rectify it. 'Listen. Don't you get thinking that you won't make it when you get out? When you're out, you forget about this place and the people in it. Ain't none of these mutherfuckers in here care a damn about you. You find that job, be it working in a gas station, stacking shelves in Safeway or mopping out toilets. Don't ever think you're below anybody. All you gotta do is stay clean and stay outta here. Too many people die in here, don't you go fucking up.'
'I won't Serge,' said Russ with a trembling voice and a shake of the head. Though he was three times the size of Serge, he was terrified of him. Serge had been a guide to Russ, just as Petey had to Serge. It was the way prison life revolved. Ninety percent forgot it all once they got out and became repeat offenders, but it never stopped them from trying. Russ in time would be a mentor to someone.

3 RELEASE

THERE WAS MUCH TO DO ON THE penultimate day. Serge made his rounds, saying farewells and handing out various possessions to whom he chose. His fellow inmates were all smiles and full of praise for him. Though there was envy, they were genuinely happy to see a con get out.

'Hey Serge, go find my old lady you wanta good time. She been screwing everyone in my neighborhood, tell her I sent you, you might get it at discount,' joked a con.

'Nah man. I already been there. She ain't all that,' Serge returned the joke.

'You take it easy brother,' said the man and they shook hands.

'You bet. You stay outta trouble.'

'You tell trouble to stay outta me.'

'Okay.'

Serge found James in the yard. Sitting alone at a bench table. He took the ribbing and cajoling with ease as he walked through the yard. Giving it back just as good.

James gave a smile and Serge sat with a sigh, setting a grocery bag on the table. No words were spoken for a long time. They both smoked and looked around the yard. It was a day full of sunshine, a perfect blue sky, though a light breeze spoiled the pretence of the coming season.

'Summer's coming,' said James.

'Yeah.'

'You'll be chasing skirt all summer long I bet.'

'I'm too fucking old for that.'

'You ain't never too old to chase pussy.'

'You'll think differently as you get older. Women are like the government.'

'How's that?'

'You can never escape them and you can never beat them.'

'You one cynical old bastard.' James laughed.

'It's what the joint does to you. Remember what I told you.'

'Yeah yeah yeah. I know.'

'I'm serious.'

'Don't worry 'bout me. I'm gonna be fine.'

'There's some stuff for you,' said Serge pushing the bag across to James.

'What's this?'

'Some books, music tapes. A carton of Luckies.'

'*Grazie paesano.*'

'*Prego!*'

'You want me to walk you out tomorrow?'

'Nah. We'll say our farewells tonight. It'll be easier on both of us.'

'I wanna thank you brother.'

'You don't have to thank me. Just do what I told yer.'

'You watch out for yourself,' said James with a melancholy air.

'I intend to. Let's go play some hearts before this conversation gets any more morbid. Gresso's got a game going.'

'Sure,' James said grabbing the bag.

'And don't be gambling those smokes away. You're the worst damn gambler I ever seen.'

'I learnt it all off you.'

'That right,' replied Serge and they broke into a playful fight.

Serge found very little sleep that night. He sat for many an hour smoking and flipping through a few magazines. Agitation pursued him no matter how hard he fought it. Less than eight hours to go before he could walk the streets, go to a bar and order a beer. Sit down in Battery Park; watch the tourists catch the ferries to Liberty and Ellis Islands.

Serge had always loved Manhattan. The teeming multi-ethnicity always managed to heighten his senses. It made him think about the mass migration between the late nineteenth and early twentieth centuries. The time when the first of his blood family arrived after an arduous and gruelling voyage. His ancestors, like many others found a haven in the burgeoning Lower East Side, where an intense melting pot of immigrants huddled together for safety and out of necessity. Little Italy, Chinatown, the Jewish section, literally pulsated with the sheer proportions of immigrants. The enclaves had clearly defined borders and tensions were always rife. The melting pot became an infamously tough place to live. It bred violence and crime, the squalor and overcrowding feeding those who wished to prey on the weak. It offered a haven for criminals from the old countries, who began to resurrect the memory and embellish more misery on their fellow countrymen. Most, quickly moved out after grasping basic English and Serge's grandfather, Luigi was no different. He did not stray far though, just crossing the East River into Brooklyn, where he eventually founded Valone Ice Cream, a company that prospered for five years until the Wall Street crash of twenty nine.

Undeterred and without bitterness he found a labouring job in the garbage industry and within three years had set up Valone Carting Company. He married his sweetheart and she gave birth to healthy boy, Serge's father. But luck seemed to be against him constantly. The carting company was put out of business in the late fifties, simply because Luigi would not join the new Garbage Executive. A sinister organization set up to control and enforce contracts on the companies and industries that relied on waste disposal. Luigi Valone was forced out. Locked out of negotiating for tenders he wound the company up, taking a net profit of five thousand dollars after selling his premises and trucks.

Serge was two when his grandfather, grandmother and uncle were killed in a house fire. Probably started by one of his grandfather's cigarettes.

He was a constant smoker, sometimes forgetting where a cigarette was left burning. So Serge never knew his immigrant grandparents except through the snippets of information his own father had gave him, before he lost a handle on life and abandoned Serge to the vagaries and chance of New York city.

It would have been sadly ironic to Luigi Valone to know that his own grandson had found his way into the menacing elements of Italian-Americans, and would at one time be the head of Waste & Trade Management. A syndicate, responsible for keeping certain carting cartels in line and preserving the status quo of an extortionate rates system.

For Serge, the history of New York was ironic. He could not imagine living anywhere else in the world. The Big Apple had offered him a bite and he had taken it, delighting in the fertility it offered. Everything was possible; anything could be taken care of in NYC. Serge laughed to himself when he thought on the twenty four dollar purchase of Manhattan from the Indians and how the enterprising organizations were now raking in over five billion dollars a year, albeit illegal.

Serge Valone wanted his slice of that vast capital returned. What was waiting for him on the streets, he did not know. There was a new order settling across New York with the slaying of Costello and the emergence of D'Angelo, but Serge had the nous to take money from the streets and he would, whether they sanctioned him or not. Besides, he was too old to do anything else now.

A cold sunshine filled morning greeted Serge and his heart palpitated with anticipation. The process of release took too long to his mind. A guard led him through the corridor and out into fresh air. Through a chain link fenced walkway up to the inner gate. Once opened they waited for a few minutes until the door to freedom was unlocked and Serge Valone walked out, with a nod to the guard, who wished him the best.

In New York City, in the private social clubs and coffee houses of the mob, the talk about "Two Times" Valone was the topic of choice.

4 SIT DOWNS

NEW YORK CITY AWOKE TO SUNSHINE AS the first days of spring pushed out winter. By the time Gus Shapiro arrived in Manhattan rain had moved in, souring the earlier spirit of New Yorkers.

As his car pulled up on Fourth street in the East Village he jumped out, then leaned back into the car to talk to his driver, slammed the door closed then trotted through raindrops and into the sanctuary of the Friends of Naples social club.

'Look at this shit,' he said to anyone who would listen while shaking himself down. There were only two other men in attendance, which was strange to Gus. 'Where the fuck is anyone?' he demanded.

'Gone to the races in Jersey,' replied Philip Gialcone. He stood up and slowly walked behind the serving counter to prepare coffee.

'It's getting like a fuckin' boy scout club around here.'

'You organized it.' Philip busied himself with the coffee.

'Is that the thing?'

'I'm just saying.'

'Forget about it.' Gus sat at the table and spoke to the other man. A young man in his early twenties, with classic Mediterranean looks. 'How you doin'?'

'So so.'

'Why ain't you in Jersey?'

'I needed to see you.'

'What about? Your fuckin' late vig,' said Gus with a raised voice.

'No,' said the man and pulled out a wad of money and placed it on the table. Gus picked it up and counted it.

'Good,' he said, satisfied. 'So what's on your mind?'

'Valone. He gets out today.'

'What are you the Post? Everybody knows this, so?'

'I didn't know you knew.'

'You done?'

'Yeah.'

'Then fuck off to Jersey or go make some money.'

Once the young man had exited Philip brought over two espressos to the table.

'Can you believe that *cugine?*' said Gus, randomly turning the daily news pages.

'He's a good earner,' said Philip.

'He's a fuckin' sycophant. You know what that is Phil?'

Philip shrugged.

'It's a guy that uses flattery to achieve an end. I don't trust him.'

'You don't trust anybody. But, he is a good earner.'

'Yeah well.'

'Every one is talking about the Valone situation,' Philip said.

'The fuckin' Valone situation!' exclaimed Gus with arms and hands.

'Could be a problem.'

'Fuck him. We should be worried, right?'

'Perhaps nothing will happen.' Philip lit a cigar.

'Perhaps nothing will happen,' repeated Gus with incredulity. 'What the fuck is gonna happen ? The guy's been away for ten fucking years. Zinardi's gone the whole fuckin' crew has been assimilated. Where's he gonna go?'

Philip said nothing.

'Where's he gonna go?' repeated Gus.

'He's got nowhere to go.'

'That's right. So fuck him. I'll give him some work if that's what he wants,' Gus said in jest.

'The thing is, I mean, if someone takes him on. It's a difficult period now. We're in transition. Off the record. I don't like who we got.'

'Oh, is this somin' I should be amazed at? You think I like the fuck we got now? You think I approve of the hit on our boss? Whack a boss without a Commission sanction, I tell you we got some hard times coming' down. He's gonna restructure the whole landscape. Off the record, I could do without him. If I could get to him, I'd whack him. But he's insulated himself. You know that fuck is bringing over Sicilian zips. I tell yer, he's rebuilding. I seen the fuck what, four times in the year since he came to the throne. I gotta go pay homage to that prick, I gotta sit with him and talk, I gotta talk 'cause he don't. He listens, he don't speak. He's said all of fuckin' thirty words to me in a year and I'm a capo. But where's the commission in this? Not a fuckin' peep. Nothing. And look at us, talking about Serge Valone getting out. The real fuckin' problem is D'Angelo.'

'Take it easy. Drink your espresso, ain't nothing we can do at the moment, we just gotta roll with it,' Philip responded.

'Forget about it. You wanna play some chess?'

'Whatever.'

QUEENS NY

Roberto Marco D'Angelo, the new head of the Cuccione family was in a meeting with his under boss Silvio Dalla Bonna and *consigliere* Joe Piemonte. They had finished the main meal and now eased themselves into the evening with a large selection of cheeses and red wine.

Roberto D'Angelo was simply known as Robbie to his friends. His mob sobriquet was the name he had inherited as a child. *Il Agnello,* which translates to English as the lamb. So he was known as Robbie "The Lamb" D'Angelo. The name was born out of his quiet nature and in western culture it is an almost derogatory term. The Chinese however, believe the Lamb the be bestowed by good fortune, one who possesses an unforeseen inner strength.

It was true that Robbie was quiet. At a certain time in his childhood he had been afraid of everything, until the day he had overheard his father speaking a quotation from an infamous New Yorker.

"The man who say's the least is the most powerful," said his father and the quote was attributed to Carlo Gambino. The quote is a variation of Plato's, *"Wise men talk when they have something to say; others because they have to say something."* The young Robbie began to understand that to be a sheep did not mean he was weak. He began to see the world in a different light. He saw empty words behind bravado and strong instincts behind silence. He began to understand the streets, not through any violence he could put out, but he learnt how to play them. When he had no other choice to fight, he did so, but by his rules.

Robbie secured his name into mob folklore by masterminding the JFK airport hijacking of the century. A hundred million dollars. Currency being returned from overseas armed forces bases and confiscated currency from the banks of Nicaragua.

That made Robbie D'Angelo and soon he was a capo. Now he was boss of the most powerful crime family in the city. He was still young, forty two. He was blessed with good looks, tall, slim and wore his hair short in the vogue of the times.

To stave off the unrest that his wrest of control would cause, he granted his capo's a three month grace, where all tributes were suspended. It was unheard of and gave him breathing space to solidify his position. D'Angelo made Silvio Dalla Bonna his second and retained the sixty eight year old Joe Piemonte as his advisor.

Joe Piemonte had been counselor to the Cuccione family for three decades, serving Salvatore Cuccione, the recently deceased Costello and now D'Angelo. Joe Piemonte had seen it all during his forty four years in the mob. He had a knack of getting into the character of his bosses, so as he could nurture their path safely through the minefield of illegality. With Robbie, he sensed that there was an undeniable will coursing through the young man, a steadfast desire to re-write history. He quietly doubted if he could serve the young man with proficiency.

Silvio Dalla Bonna was an altogether different character to D'Angelo. Throughout the five boroughs he was widely known and feared. During the troubles with the Irish mobs of Hells Kitchen he was responsible for twenty or so murders; including the disappearance of Seamus Gerhaty who was the toughest Westie ever known. Legend has it that Dalla Bonna stuffed him into an oil drum, alive, and then tipped it into the Hudson River. The truth was even more bloodcurdling.

Seamus was shot in both kneecaps, and then driven to a local butcher. He was boned and gutted, alive until his body gave up the fight, and then chopped with a cleaver. His body bits were then driven to Nassau county, Long Island, where his remains where given to a mob controlled company of crab fishermen, for bait.

The brutal and disrespectful demise of Seamus Gerhaty would not have happened if he had not resorted to the kidnapping of mob men, then torturing them for ransom. He would have received a bullet in the head, and achieved a burial in honour, if there could ever be an honourable end. Such is the way of life in the gangster underworld and the perverse mentality that inspires their violence.

Silvio had been briefed about the night's proceedings. Robbie would not lock out Silvio from anything, he had complete trust in him and Silvio had complete confidence in Robbie's judgement.

Robbie topped up the glasses after opening a fresh bottle of wine, then sat and decided to get directly to the point.

'How do feel about retiring Joe?' he said.

Piemonte rubbed his nose then lit a cigarette. Picked up his wine and took a sip.

'You moving me out Robbie?' he asked with a serious air.

'You did your time Joe. You got ideas about Florida, sunshine, the easy life with your family.'

'You need a good *consigliere* Robbie. I know the ground better than anybody.'

'I know that Joe. It's out of respect that I'm offering you this.'

'Grazie,' Joe said, continued, 'I need to be frank with you Robbie.'

Robbie gave him a nod of approval.

'I don't approve of the way you took control of this *borgata*. And believe me when I say you are a lucky guy to still be alive today. The Commission didn't move against you, for reasons best known to their selves. In truth you should have gone. You violated the most basic rule of this thing of ours.'

'Joe. Costello had ripped the heart out of this thing of ours. We're supposed to be enclosed, we're meant to be at the head of the table. Costello violated a rule by allowing stranieros to sit on the commission. He waned our power.'

'Robbie. You have got to look at the future. We can no longer survive in this country just by being *wops*. The Colombians, the Russians, the Blacks, the Chinese, have organizations to equal us. Don Costello knew this; he had a vision to tie up this country from the east coast to the west. The days of us being an enclosed society were long gone before Don Costello came to the throne. What he set out to create was a unified countrywide syndicate. A cross town traffic business, which had the simplicity to work because it threw a line to everybody. When Luciano and Lansky set up the new order they were working on the same premise. The country has gotten bigger, business has gotten bigger. The government is fighting a war against terrorism and they put us in the same barrel, they're utilizing resources to fight us that have never been seen before. Don Costello wanted to expand our government to make it more intricate, to capitalize. How many young Italian-Americans are coming through the ranks now? Very few. Because they know they can earn bigger money with legitimate skills. Some of our soldiers can earn less than an educated person in computers where they don't run the risk of life imprisonment under a RICO conviction. Don Costello saw that legitimate business was progressing into globalization and he had the balls to take us into the future. In my mind Robbie, you're gonna tear this thing apart because your thinking is *anitquato*.'

'That's the way you see it Joe. Take your retirement. Let me worry about the future.'

'If that's the way it's gonna be then so be it. If you need me to consult from the outside I'll always be available.'

'I appreciate that Joe. Thanks.'

'Is this move affective immediately? I mean, have you got a replacement lined up?'

'Yeah Joe, but I ain't gonna reveal his name.'

'I understand. Before I officially retire I'll give you this for free. You done okay up till now, but you got capo's who are still loyal to Don Costello, and they're dissatisfied. They could move against you.'

'I appreciate the advice Joe. You want a refill?' asked Robbie picking up the bottle.

'Nah. I'm goin' home to break the good news to my wife. Finally I'll succeed in putting a smile on her face.'

Robbie and Silvio laughed and Joe joined them.

'You need a cab or you okay to drive?'

'I can drive. I drunk better wine than this and drove before,' said Joe aiming a Parthian arrow of derision at Robbie.

'Okay,' said Robbie disguising his detest at the slight. He got up and embraced Joe, kissing him on both cheeks, which Joe returned with equal, but reluctant respect.

After Joe had departed Silvio poured more wine, cut himself a slab of French Brie and spread it over broken bread.

'Tough day?' he said.

'It's difficult, removing a man who's been around for so long. '

'Forget about it. You did it with respect; he walks away free and clear. We move on.'

'Shapiro's gotta go.'

'I agree,' said Silvio, his mouth full.

'You got any word on Valone?'

Silvio "The Pistol" swallowed his mouthful and washed it down with a gulp of wine. Nodded.

'See him soon,' said Robbie.

'For sure.'

MULBERRY ST, LITTLE ITALY

Gaetano Corsini was the highest ranking capo in the Cuccione family. He had a free license to operate outside of the Family. In effect, his crew was a separate family. This was because he was head of Murder Inc. A dark organization thought mainly to be a myth and widely believed to have been disbanded after Albert Anastasia's fatal visit to his barber many years earlier.

This merry band of hired killers was still used extensively by the mob families throughout the United States. Corsini had developed the importation of gunslingers from Sicily for certain contracts, shipping them back immediately after the deeds. It worked perfectly. If the hired guns were ever nabbed, they could tell very little because all they really knew was who to hit, not who had hired them. To date, none had been caught.

Gaetano "The Archangel" was having a difficult day. A foul mood swept over him, the rumour mill was grinding his ego. Like Gus Shapiro, he too felt locked out of Robbie's new order. He was a deeply paranoid man, which did not help his reasoning. Because of his prevalent paranoia he had for years forbade any family talk to be conducted within his club, much to the chagrin of the FBI who had been bugging him for the past year. All they ever picked up were conversations about football, baseball and the state of the country's politics.

Corsini was on a walk and talk with his number two Ritchie.

'So what's it gonna be?' said Gaetano with a growl.

'Search me.'

'I tell you this, there's a lot of unrest. That cocksucker, sitting in Queens, building a fuckin' regime with old country guys. What the fuck's that about?'

'I don't know.'

'He's too fucking big to come down to the old neighborhood now. Not one visit, not even to come down here and have a demitasse. Is that respect?'

'It's bad.'

'You're fuckin' right its bad. Every boss and I mean every boss does the rounds. Am I right?'

'Yeah G.'

'And what's with the lockout. This is still the fuckin' Cuccione family, right?'

'Yeah. You spoke to Shapiro?'

'I don't have to speak to him to know he's as pissed as us. Everyone's pissed.'

'We got beefs to settle.' Ritchie kept the pace.

'Yeah right. I'm in a beef with the fuckin' Colombians over that incident uptown. It's gotta be straightened out. I can't even get an audience with him. I'm a fuckin' capo.'

'Whatchyer gonna do!'

'*Minghia*! Forget about it. ' Corsini nodded his respects to various people during his walk. He stopped for a minute to talk to an old lady and offer assistance in anything she needed. Then they were walking again.

'Where he's taking us is anybody's guess. I'm betting on war. The peace is over.'

'You really think so?'

'Fuckin' right I am. Too many cracks are developing. There's gonna be a reaction. That you can bet on. I gotta go uptown, union business. More headache.'

'You got time to stop in Umberto's.'

'Yeah, I'm fuckin' starving.'

'It'll help you wind down.'

Gaetano decided to have a full three course meal. Union business could wait. To ease his digestion he took a large brandy before his coffee. A considered mood overtook him and the random speech throughout the meal dissipated. In fact, he was tired of talk and entertained the idea of blowing out his union meeting.

'You feeling better?' said Ritchie.

'One hundred percent.'

'You want me to drive you uptown?'

'Nah. I wanchya at the store.'

RED HOOK, BROOKLYN

Vinnie Marranzo, Cuccione skipper was tired of all his crew's bullshit. They were the least powerful, compared to the Shapiro and Corsini regimes. The Marranzo crew was tightly knit though. They were a family concern, in the truest sense of the word. Vinnie was surrounded by his two brothers, Tommy and Paulie and of the rest; thirty percent was made up of their cousins.

The Marranzo's were in the same amount of dark as everyone. Uncertainty caused fear and uncertainty was always rife when a boss got clipped. Vinnie Marranzo had enough savvy to know that change was inevitable. He knew, like everyone else D'Angelo was rebuilding.

Despite the dubious vein which ran through the underworld, business was good, money was pouring in and the high life continued.

Today was a beef day. Where the soldiers came to air grievances to their immediate boss, Vinnie. He was almost indifferent that morning. The whispers were growing louder on the street; the nerves began to affect the mind.

Vinnie fidgeted in his chair as his youngest brother Paulie got his turn.

'I wanna know why the fuck we ain't doin' nuttin wid 'dos outlaws who took two stops outta F.D.?' F.D. was the abbreviation for the Financial District. 'We ain't had a talk in a month wid 'dos fuckers and you know dat dey were s'possed to get back to us.'

'We've been through this Paulie.'

'Yeah, well we'll go thru it again.' Paulie could never control his temper. This latest episode with an outlaw garbage hauler was just another catalyst to light his short fuse. He had got into a lot of trouble in the past with his mouth. He would never get away with talking to a capo in that fashion, but he was lucky enough to have his older brother in that position.

'Can you just drop it, bring me somin' that don't bore me,' said Vinnie with a scowl.

'I'm ready to whack out the fuckin' cocksuckers,' shouted Paulie across the table. The raising of his voice killed off the other chit chat in the club and brought Vinnie across the table to land a sound slap across Pauline's face. It sounded throughout the place and wiseguys in attendance averted their eyes.

'You ain't gonna whack nobody unless I say so. I'm the fuckin' skipper and I told youse a million times to drop it and youse will fuckin' drop it. You hear me ?'

'Yeah,' replied Paulie in a quiet defiance.

'When the time comes the time comes. I decide, not you. I don't care if you have to keep goin' back and back again. You will get them to the table. That clears enough for you?'

'Yeah,' said Paulie and got up from his chair so fast he knocked it over and walked out of the club like a tornado.

'You got anything to say about this?' he said to Tommy, the middle brother. Tommy shook his head.

'Good,' Vinnie said and rubbed his temples with his thumb and forefinger.

'He'll be alright, he'll calm down,' Tommy added.

'Like I could give a fuck. Charlie,' he called out.

'Yes skip?'

'Bring me a brandy.'

STATEN ISLAND

In New York, the Cuccione's were easily the strongest outfit. Genaro Costello, now in his grave was the chairman of the commission, the government of the mob clans. Since his slaying the commission had convened once, to inaugurate Robbie D'Angelo as head of the Cuccione family.

In any power house, there has to be an entente to allow its basic function to prevail, to allow it to pursue it aims. Without it, it becomes a game of chance. Robbie's unsanctioned hit on Costello had thrown challenges into the system.

A cordial dislike, unspoken, sullied the respect shown to Robbie. With his actions he had broken a cardinal rule and committed a mortal sin. Corruption can easily be thrown to the wolves and Robbie gave the first insight into his cunning and tactical skill. During his explanation, he implied that other families had unofficially given him the nod. It immediately created a divisive suspicion within the commission and gained him more time to construct his new order.

Uncertainty had always been a keyword in Robbie's thinking. Now he had delivered it, causing as schism within the commission. The Italian families immediately began to distrust each other, the Colombians who distrusted everyone, did so more. The Chinese began to take on a stronger mantle of withdrawal and employed a laissez-faire policy. The African-American mobs, shrugged their shoulders, spat a little, and once again realized what they had always known; that they just couldn't trust white people. The Russian mob suddenly had their paranoia ignited again and withdrew to regroup, thinking they would be the scapegoats. The Irish wanted affirmation did not get any and secretly smiled at the end of the proceedings; they were hoping the *guineas* would wipe themselves out.

Angelo Gigante was most displeased with the whole contrivance. Gigante was the sixty nine year old head of New York's Badalamenti family, second most powerful family in NYC. Between these two families existed five decades of hate. A hate born out of the fact that they were once the same *borgata*.

Feuds do not wane easily in the world of the Mafia. Through generations the story gets passed down and each time a little gets added for effect. It seems perversely important to keep the history of blood feuds firmly ingrained in the psyche.

Divisions occur frequently within the Mob, mostly they are stamped out at the beginning, those that are not become all out violence, where people disappear and are found in shallow graves or trunks of cars. Others happen without the outside world being aware. The Badalamenti- Cuccione war made everyone aware in New York. It made front page news, was recorded as the most vicious period of American *Cosa Nostra history* and made the establishment gasp with wide eyed astonishment.

The war became a devastating one of attrition between Nunzio Badalamenti and his underboss Salvatore Cuccione. Soldiers were blown away at will in public, in restaurants, in parks, on sidewalks. The death toll reached sixty and lasted four months before Meyer Lansky decided enough was enough and stepped into the fray. "Lucky" Luciano exiled in his native Italy, took a secret flight to Cuba to meet Meyer. Their talk, with the other chairs of the nubile commission lasted only two hours. The Badalamenti family would be split and Cuccione would be granted his own family. From that day on, whacking each other on the streets was considered a no-no. It had catapulted the Mob back into the public eyes, which is just where they hated to be. They wanted anonymity and demanded it to work their black magic. No family could pursue an inner war without first sitting with the commission. No boss could be removed, without a democratic vote at the commission. New York now had five families and it was decided that three families would have permanent seats on the commission. Those were some of the fledgling rules marked down that day in Cuba.

Nunzio Badalamenti accepted the decision with detest and through hurt pride and lack of judgment put out a contract of Salvatore Cuccione. The commission got wind of his plan and Murder Inc was invoked against him. It was the first time that subterranean organization was used against a boss from the powerhouse of New York.

It was an irony that the same thing would happen to the Cuccione's decades later, when Tony Zinardi was granted a breakaway and for a brief time, the city had six families, and now the Cuccione family had lost a boss, although for different reasons.

In underworld mythology, it is normal practice to retell the story with the emphasis on a false thread of the calamity. The war began because Nunzio Badalamenti wanted to move his brother into a position of underboss and undermine Salvatore Cuccione's power. In truth, nothing could ever seem more ridiculous than the facts.

Nunzio Badalamenti was caught having an affair with Salvatore Cuccione's mistress, which in Mafia circles is an odious act having the qualities to imbue hawkish rage. So New York suffered it most vicious war, because of a woman and one man's lust.

Angelo Gigante was a young man during the troubles, just on the fringes on the Mob. The families at war were desperate for new blood and soon Gigante was indoctrinated and proved himself to be a proficient hitman. Ambitious, strong and embellished with a wicked streak he was soon Christened "The Black Angel".

After the truce his natural progression was to Mob enforcer and anyone who had "The Black Angel" on his back knew they had serious trouble. Now he was the head. At sixty nine, he had no health problems, was super fit for a man of that age. He swam for an hour a day, walked in the parks for two hours and lived a life of luxury on the profits of his vast criminal empire.

The old man, who stood at five foot, four inches, was stocky with the slightest of paunches, had balding grey hair and wholesome olive complexion, a fearsome reputation and was held in the greatest respect; he had been a Mob man for five decades had spent a total of thirty months behind bars. Nothing would stick upon him.

Through his conspiring and cunning he had enforced the Badalamenti family back to a major force, after years of being weakened by internal strife and being chipped away at by the other families.

After Costello was gunned down, he fully expected to be installed as chairman of the commission. What he did not foresee was Robbie D'Angelo's trickery of the mind.

'So what's the word on the streets?' he asked of his consigliere Joe Cirello, in his slow gruff voice.

'D'Angelo's insulating himself. His captains are not contented. It won't be long before something erupts.'

'And what of the other families?'

'Not a word. They're lying low. It's definite that none of them quietly backed him.'

'So then he conspired with outside factions. This D'Angelo has a gift for artful deception. Maybe he did not consult with another family; maybe he makes us think like that, so we do not make a counter move. Who has the most to lose from D'Angelo's rise?'

'In his own family or the others?'

'Both.'

'In his own family the capo's Shapiro and Corsini. Outside, maybe all of us.'

'He won't be able to upset the families, he'll have to keep us at bay, but he must keep the peace. But what is his planning? What is he aiming for?'

'It's one of two things. To overhaul the entire New York families or too exhort himself to chairman of the commission.'

'He will never be chairman. Not while I'm still alive. I will use all my powers to veto that; even it causes that which we do not seek.'

'He's a difficult man to get to at the moment,' advised his consigliere.

'So we wait. But while we wait we conspire. He wants to gain time and so we'll use that time. We must have a meeting with either one of his discontented capos, both if possible.'

'I'll get on it.'

'And I need to speak to our old friend in New Orleans.'

'I would advise against that.'

'It's important to play a deep game.'

'But to bring him into affairs on our own turf, it would be seen as undermining ourselves.'

'Maybe, but D'Angelo is flooding his own courtyard with Sicilians. He is building and a man that builds has some aim. I don't want to seek out any of the city's families. Let them to their own ploys. We will have to insulate ourselves too. It's important that we make our own strong undercurrent, in case the waters grow too high.'

'I understand, but I do not trust Sartois and his organization.'

'He is a strong ally, which is what we need. If everything goes sour, we will need to be stronger.'

'And what of the commission?'

'Screw the commission. Right now it's an invalid. Tonight I want to see Gaspare. We will need to get the word out to the captains. I plan to fly down to Orleans tomorrow, make the arrangements.'

'Certainly.'

In the evening, the old man counseled with his underboss Gaspare and Joe Cirello. He informed Gaspare of their moves and told him to make sure that the captains and their soldiers played low key. Gaspare was to watch the store while he and Cirello were away. When his guests left, he went with his wife for dinner at his daughter's house. He enjoyed his family and felt a pride that he had kept both his sons out of the murky business where he plied his trade. For himself, he had no desire to get out.

Angelo Gigante did not harbour any dreams of retirement. In his blood family, he was the father that had given his children everything. Good education, money to start their own ventures, freedom to be whoever they chose to be. He was the grandfather that loved with a passion, who would side with the difficult ones against their parents. He was the man that would tell his grandchildren they could be anything they wanted to be, just as he had told his children. His blood family made life everything to him, it made his heart jump and caused his blood to stay young.

Gigante's criminal Family was his true passion though. It was this other life that aroused every sinew in his body to repel death. Power is everything to a man who refuses to be a nobody. Power is respect. Respect is what makes a man of substance. A man without respect is living a life of degradation. He is the man who has to wait in line. The one in the cheap seats, existing hand to mouth, day to day. Who, works hard for other people and gets laid off at the drop of a hat. He is the man who lives in poverty come old age and looks back on a life that just passed him by. He is the man betrayed throughout by governments who extort him with constant taxes and tell him he should work harder. He is the man owned by banks, for life, with their tricks of ascending credit limits. A man who saves and saves into schemes that are suddenly worthless when needed most. He's the man robbed of proper medical treatment, because he was sold a lousy health policy. The man who watches the killer of his children serve an unjust prison term, because certain forces wish to experiment with some spurious philosophy. He is the man who reaches his finality with no conclusions and too many questions.

Angelo Gigante could never be that man. He wanted respect like a child needs candy and respect is like the chalice of ego, it can never be filled. Respect is a constant hunger. At sixty nine, he was still feared and deeply respected. A man who had been a boss for twenty years and had spent more time on public transport than in jail.

For Gigante, to know that his soldiers, who he never saw or spoke to, were out there making money, added to his sense of power. To know that they would kill for him, with a word, that out in that vast metropolis they were scheming and angling for high stakes and kicking up to him massive tributes gave him the feeling of being a president. Beside all that though, what gave him greatest pleasure and pride, was the fact; that of all the five Families, since he had been on the throne, his family was the only one never to produce an informant for the government.

The aging, but very healthy and astute boss had no plans to retire and was determined to die as head of the Badalamenti Family. In fact, he felt the Family should now take his name.

NEW ORLEANS, LOUISIANA

A claustrophobic day of humidity blanketed the south, which caused Angelo Gigante to sweat, despite the air conditioning in the car. Cirello did not find it as stifling, but he was tired. The last few days of talks had wearied him and now they had more talk, with Pierre Sartois, a man he distrusted, but in whom, Gigante had much faith and years of dealings.

Pierre Sartois, a Cajun from Grand Isle, who was at the head of an organization known as Les Blues. His organization was a mixture of Cajun natives and African-Americans. Pierre was in his late fifties, a small squat powerfully built man, with a face of a boxer, crumpled nose and puffy eyes, which were a Caribbean blue.

His main interests in the underworld were the docks and harbours that littered the southern sea board. His hand of corruption stretched to include freight hijacking and the extortion of the fishing industry, through tribute taxes.

He was a major player in the French Connection conspiracy when he was much younger. With ties to the Marseille and Corsican mobs which were strong, he was still a major importer of the white death. His distribution network coursed through the Deep South and reached as far north as Arkansas, Tennessee and North Carolina. No further east than Louisiana, but it hit the north of Florida, as far as Jacksonville. The rest of Miami was out of bounds. Illegal gambling in the same jurisdiction was also one of his major profit industries.

Sartois had many legal enterprises. The grandest being a legal liqueur spirit distillery which produced that renowned drink as supermarket own brands. He had contracts for a home based chain as well as a major European chain. That business alone made him close to three million a year.

Despite all his wealth, Pierre Sartois dressed like a swampland dweller and had no refinement in food tastes. He had rarely ventured out of his home state and could not abide any other food than that which he was brought up on. To look at him you would think that he had less than twenty dollars to his name. He was always dressed in baggy cotton sweat pants and age old espadrilles. Always a white t-shirt or bare-chested. The only time he wore suits was at weddings, funerals and of meetings with his political friends, who were firmly in his pocket. To his close friends he was known as Pierre, *Parran*, or simply Pappy. Throughout the underworld he was "Little Napoleon."

The call came in that Gigante and Cirello were on route from the airport. Sartois had already instructed his kitchen staff to prepare a magnificent spread and they were busy at work. Some of the soldiers that were hanging around his old French colonial mansion, he sent away. He waited for his eldest son, Jean-Louis to make his appearance. Jean-Louis was the heir to his throne. His youngest wanted nothing to do with him. His wife was long gone, but he did not fret, there were enough pretty young ladies willing to entertain him throughout Louisiana.

He busied himself in his courtyard, eyeing and fingering the young ivy that was creeping upwards of the old surrounding wall.

Suddenly he felt a sharp pain behind his knee.

'*Cho!*' he called out and turned around while reaching for the pain. He saw the instrument of his pain lying close by, a small wooden dart. He looked around for the culprit. A bush close by rustled.

'Bebette!' he shouted. 'Come, come.'

The young Plains Indian crept out into view, a villainous smile etched on his face, blow pipe in hand. 'Papere. *Te en colaire?*' he said.

'*Alohrs pas,*' Pierre said and held out his arms. His young grandson ran into his arms and his grandfather picked him up and planted loving kisses on both cheeks. They shared some quiet talk as Jean-Louis revealed himself. Then Pierre put the boy down and he ran past his father into the vast mansion to seek out his grandfather's treat.

'He grows big,' said Pierre to his boy.

'*Weh*,' said his boy and embraced his father.

'*Mais*. Ready to *vay-vay* ?'

Jean-Louis nodded and lit a cigarette with a serious air. 'What for our New York friends?'

'*Ha!* Up the bayou, be *buljoos* problems.' Jean-Louis said nothing and his father took his arm. 'Come come.'

When the car rolled into the grounds, Pierre waited with Jean-Louis on the front porch, and then made his way down to the car. As Gigante stepped from the car Pierre held out his arms.

'*Bienvenu my podna*,' Pierre stopped and waited for Gigante to come to him.

'*Bonjour Pierre. ça va ?*'

'*Bien*. Good trip ?'

'Yeah.'

'*Mais, entrer.*'

Gigante and Cirello shook hands with Jean-Louis, then Gigante and Pierre linked arms and walked up the stairs and into the house. Jean-Louis and Cirello followed, making polite small talk with each other.

In the large opulent study which was furnished with antique leather couches from France and writing bureaus and other assorted teak furniture the men sat. Pierre opened the large French windows to allow airflow and the Louisiana weather entered gently into the room.

Gigante took out his handkerchief and wiped his brow. He was adjusting to the change slowly. He shifted his body to get comfortable, and then helped himself to a cigar from the table.

'What you drink?' asked Pierre.

'Do you have amaretto?' Gigante said.

'I have everything.'

'Good, then I'll take an amaretto.'

'Me too, please,' added Cirello.

'*Bon*. Jean?'

'Brandy, *papa*.'

'*Mais podna*. What can I do ?' Pierre sat next to Gigante.
'New York is troublesome. I fear for the future.'
'*Co faire* ?'
'This D'Angelo.' Gigante pursed his lips and fell silent.
'He is a man, hungry, yes ?'
'He is a man without honour.'
'*Mais*, you are strong.'
'Maybe, but this man is like a politician.'
'*Weh* ?'
'Umm. As cunning as a fox, as dangerous as a scorpion.'
'What would I do ?'
'I have to know that you're my friend.'
'*Mais, jamais d'la vie* ! Why would you ask me that ?'
'*S'excuser* Pierre. I need all my friends now.'
'*Maudit* ! That D'Angelo, *fils de putain. Defan*. That *gallette il faire embrasse mon tcheue !*'
'No need to curse Pierre.'
'What you do ? A *cunja* for him.' Pierre got up and began to pour another round.
'If what I think will happen I will ask for your strength to help me defeat this *cattivello*.'
'I am countable. *Fuh shore*.'
'*Grazie*.'
'*Bon*. For you I hope that this will pass. You have hunger ?'
'Yes my friend.'
'*Bon*. Come come. I have a grand spread of Cajun goodstuff.'

Pierre told no lies about a grand spread. On the long table in the dinning area waited a fabulous display of delicacies. Crawfish Etoufee, Bayou baked Red Snapper, Shrimp Creole, Catfish Court Boullon, boiled crabs and fried oysters, Alligator Sauce Piquante. For those that did not like animals from the water, they could feast upon Sugar Steak, Chicken and Sausage Jambalaya. There were red beans and rice, baked vegetables and the obligatory Gumbo. Blood sausage. Deserts were Beignets; Creole doughnuts and a home recipe of bread pudding.

'My friend, your generosity is beyond comparison. One day you will come to New York and eat with us,' said Gigante.

'My eye! I never wish to leave my place.'

'One day you will leave this state, I promise.'

'*Jamais d'la vie*. To be here is everything I need and wish for.'

'You fuckin' ol' Cajun, you'll never change.'

'*Fuh shore.*' Pierre laughed aloud.

During the meal they continued to discuss the problems of New York. Gigante made it clear that he wanted Pierre to do nothing to the various businesses that D'Angelo's family had going in the south until he gave the word. Pierre understood and confirmed that he would be willing to help his old friend in the south, but that he would not get involved directly with matters up north. Gigante agreed that he would never ask for that favour.

Pierre dipped his fingers into a bowl of warm water then dried them and wiped his mouth with a napkin. He eased himself back into his chair, full. Down the front of his white t-shirt, laid evidence of his slobbish eating habits. He called upon one his waitresses to bring Cafe au lait Luzianne, then passed around cigars and another waitress went around pouring brandy. There was much of the food uneaten, but it would stay there until Pierre called for it to be taken away, until he was sure that everyone was completely finished.

'*Mais, bon?*'

'Superb,' said Gigante then a ruckus happened as Pierre's grandchild ran into the room, shooting everyone with a toy machine gun.

'*Maudit!*' shouted Pierre.

'No no. *Vous peeshwank*,' said his father Jean-Louis and raised himself from his chair and caught his son by the arm. 'Come come.' He led the boy from the room. '*Pardon!*' he added. Pierre raised a hand to signify the unimportance.

'Children. They grow too fast these days,' said Gigante with a laugh.

'You know what I find with children this today's?' said Pierre.

'What's that?' asked Cirello.

'We give too much. Appreciation they have not.'

'It's natural for us to spoil our grandchildren. It's what we work so hard for,' Gigante said.

'*Fuh shore. Mais.* Tonite, you wish for the French quarter. I have a special place with young beautiful women. What's your pleasure ? Creole ? Caribbean ? French ?'

'No Italian girls ?' said Gigante.

'Only beautiful women my friend.'

'You son of a bitch,' replied Gigante, smiling.

CENTRAL PARK

Serge Valone sat on a bench throwing handfuls of feed to the pigeons. To be in the open without the stifling constrictiveness of walls or razor wire and the suffocating closeness of inmates gave him a sense of enlightenment. There was pleasure in feeding pigeons, in people watching, sitting on his own time.

It was his third day of freedom. He was living out of a second rate hotel, but he did not mind. He had his state handout which was nearly gone and he had walked the streets of his villainous past and drank in the bars. He was recognized by a few people, but there was no fanfare, which suited him, fine. He blew a great portion of money on a fine Italian meal the night before and then spent the evening working his way through two bottles of red wine, while listening to opera on the radio and watching television shows of his choice.

Word on the street did not take long to wire its way through to those who needed to know where he was and he was given word that people wanted to see him. He prepared for his agreed meeting and went out the next morning and bought a cheap piece. He still had enough street smarts to get the necessities.

Now he waited. While he enjoyed the freedom of the park, he kept a watchful eye. If it was to be his time, he would go out taking a head count. He put his hand in the pocket of his overcoat and run his hand over the gun; it had been so long since he had felt the inanimate cold steel in his hand that he couldn't be sure he had still had the skill to handle it correctly. Doubt began to eat away at him and for the first time ever, he wished he could truly be free of the mob.

His breathing became difficult as his chest constricted and he could feel his heart beat against his ribcage. A panic set in, the vast arena where he sat offered him no comfort now. In his neck and shoulders he could feel a stress, as if somebody was twisting every sinew and the strings that held his body were a regime of dictatorial magnificence that he would have to dance to. He shook.

From the corner of his eye he saw a figure heading towards him. His hand gripped the gun tightly. He turned his head to get a better view. He knew instantly that it was Silvio "The Pistol" Dalla Bonna. Then he relaxed. He knew that he was not going to get hit. An underboss would never be sent, alone, to clip anybody. Serge let go of the gun and took his hand out of his pocket and returned to feeding pigeons.

Silvio sat next to him.

'How you doin' Serge?' he said, coldly.

'As good as I can.'

'Robbie wants to see you?'

'D'Angelo wants to see me? Should I be worried?'

'Whatchyer got to worry about? You'd be gone already youse were in trouble.'

'I guess. Where?'

'I'll pick you up outside your hotel at eight. Okay?'

'Okay.'

'Don't worry about nuttin.' Silvio stood up and offered his hand. Serge accepted it, and then Silvio was walking away. Serge watched Silvio for a few seconds, and then went back to feeding the pigeons.

5 STREET LIFE

LITTLE ITALY

GAETANO CORSINI, WHO WAS PLAYING CARDS IN his club on Mulberry Street and in pleasant mood, got a whisper from one of his crew members. He turned to face the man.

'Is he fuckin' serious?' he exploded.

'That's what he say's,' said his man with a shrug.

'Mutherfucker,' he shouted and threw his cards on the table, springing out of his chair in one motion. His breathing was heavy but he moved with the grace of a ballet dancer as he pushed past the messenger and out of the club.

'What the fuck's goin' on?' asked his lieutenant Ritchie, of the man.

'It's "Frisco Joe", can't make it today.' The man gestured with a hand and a grimace.

'Terrific. I spent a day getting him calm, now Frisco's gonna get him all riled again.' He shook his head, threw his hand in. 'This game's over guys,' he said, then left the table and walked to the window, checked out what he needed and went behind the bar and poured himself a large whiskey and topped it off with cola.

Corsini had dodged his way through the traffic to a phone booth across the street. Filled it with change and banged the digits on the number board. As he waited during the dial up he lit a cigarette.

'Hello,' answered the voice through the receiver.

'Never fuckin' mind hello. Where are you?' he shouted with menace.

'I'm at home,' replied the voice with a nervous laugh.

'Ain't the fuckin' question. Where you supposed to be?'

'I told er...'

'Don't give me that fuckin' shit. I don't care who you told. You tell me where youse supposed to be.'

'Well, I was to come see you, I know that but....'

'Listen to me.' Corsini's decibel had lowered and his talk had slowed. 'I don't give a fuck if your mother is dying in the fuckin' hospital, if your wife gives birth to a still born or you gotta be in fuckin' court. When youse are supposed to be where youse supposed to be, you fuckin' be there.'

'I understand G, but....'

Corsini raised his voice again, so much so that a passer-by might think he was connected to the other side of the universe. 'Don't you fuckin interrupt me. You listen. Don't you be a fuckin' example. If I have to make you a fuckin' example I will, don't you fuckin' push me to make you an example. Two fuckin' weeks now Frisco. You hear this good, you got till tomorrow. If you don't show, then you forget about it, you understand you cocksucker?'

'Yeah, yeah sure. Thanks G.'

'Fuck your thanks. Show. Tomorrow,' Corsini slammed the receiver on the hook, took a lungful from his smoke then flicked it into the gutter, danced back through the traffic to the sanctuary of the club.

'Okay?' ventured Ritchie as Corsini returned.

'Yeah,' he replied, agitation stretched across his face.

'Have a drink.'

'Fuck it. I won the hand right?'

'Yeah,' said Ritchie, fixing a drink. The others in the game got up from the table, leaving the money where it was. They knew better to leave well alone. Aggravation over a late vig payment on a loan; one of the easiest ways to rile a gangster.

RED HOOK, BROOKLYN

Vinnie "Big M" Marranzo parked his Lincoln outside the Vesuvio Social Club. Vinnie was wearing dark pants, black t-shirt and a leather lounge coat. Shades sat over his eyes. He made no point of locking the car and nodded hello to a few soldiers sitting at the table outside, who were doing nothing but shooting the breeze.

Inside the club, music was too loud for his liking, he immediately turned it down.

'You guys deaf?' he said.

'No,' replied one.

'Youse will be you keep having' it that fuckin' loud.' He went and sat at the bar and Tommy "Machine Gun" his next in line brother poured him a beer. Vinnie lit a cigarette and picked up the paper.

'What's new?' asked Tommy.

'Same old shit. You seen Paulie?'

'Nah. I heard he was at Lou Lou's last night.'

'What is it with him and them pole girls?'

'They got great bodies,' Tommy sighed and leaned on the bar.

'You have to buy the cunt twice over before you can lay it. Don't make economical sense to me.' Vinnie took a sip of beer, and threw the paper behind the bar.

'Let him alone, while he's fucking he's quiet.'

'Glad to hear it.'

'You see Mikey "Black" and "Family Man" Pete outside?' Tommy continued.

'I passed 'em didn't I?'

'They got an armored truck score on. They want your okay.'

'How many dimes?'

'Hundred to you.'

'Risk?'

'An inner s.u.'

'Here?'

'Virgin country.' This was code for Queens.

'Tell 'em to attend mass.' This was Vinnie's code for a blessing. Tommy nodded and went outside to relay the message. Vinnie finished his beer.

When Tommy returned Vinnie questioned him about the recent hassle Paulie was dealing with.

'Any word from those outlaws?'

Tommy shook his head whilst pouring another beer for his older brother. 'They won't move.'

The "Outlaws" as Vinnie called them were a legitimate garbage collection firm that had taken two stops from a Mafia affiliated company by underbidding them. Vinnie was head of Disposal Waste Corporation, an illegitimate organization that controlled a section of the garbage industry. This organization managed bids and ensured that the Mafia kept control of the garbage industry and kept the prices over-inflated, which in turn lined their pockets with huge cash amounts. So, every garbage company in the New York City and the outlying metropolitan areas that wished to tap into the huge profit margins of the garbage industry had to belong to a management company. There were about eight of these organizations that enforced the rules, operating in strict jurisdictions. Any independent company that operated outside of a Mafia controlled management was an outlaw. To get the cream contracts, you had to join, there was no way they were going to let legitimate cash of those proportions slide away.

'Okay. Send 'em a message.' Vinnie gulped down his beer.

'Yeah. You takin' Vicky out tonight?' Tommy asked.

'It's Friday ain't it?'

'I got this new broad; I thought we could hook up.'

'After the shit Marie gave you, I thought you were straightening out.'

'I've been on parole with her for three months now. She loves me again.'

'I'm taking her to Manhattan Joe's. Don't tell Marie you're out with me though. She'll fuckin' call Andrea and then we'll both be tumbled.'

'Working around wives is worse than dodging the feds,' chuckled Tommy.

'They're the same fuckin' breed that's why. Meet me there about eight; I'll call ahead, get a bigger table.'

'Okay, bruv.'

'See you later.' As he walked past the men at the table he made of point of telling them to keep the music down. When he pulled away, Tommy turned the volume up.

Twenty four hours later the *outlaw* company had a brand new truck firebombed, they decided to go to the table.

EAST VILLAGE/NEW JERSEY

Gus Shapiro and Philip Gialcone were driving out of the East Village, heading toward the Lincoln tunnel through to New Jersey. They were heading for a meeting, where someone was offering a proposal to make more illicit money. Gus was annoyed at the fact that he had to check this out himself. But Philip told him the man they were meeting only wanted to deal with the organ grinder.

'What's this guy's name?' said Shapiro.

'William Bennett.'

'You sure this guy's clean?'

'I checked him out. He's a whiz with computers. He say's he's got this scheme to make many dimes, he needs front money. I'm telling you what I know. As far as I know, he's clean.'

'Who put us on to this?' Shapiro persisted.

'Skinny Mario,' answered Philip.

'You know I think it's outrageous I gotta go to Jersey to meet wid dis prick.'

'He's adamant. He won't come to the city.'

'If he's wasting my fuckin' time, he's gonna go.'

'Well, he's serious. Skinny put it to me, I checked the guy out, and I put it to you. Give it a chance.'

'Forget about it. I hope for his sake he ain't dickin' us around.'

William Bennett was waiting for the men at the chosen diner. Typically, he was nervous. Asking an accommodation from gangsters has that effect. The scheme that he had been engineering needed people with the financial muscle and the protection he imagined would shelter him.

Shapiro and Gialcone stepped into the diner, which was quiet and suited both parties for a meeting, *sub rosa*. They recognized him through the description they had been given and he made troubled eyes toward them.

'Hello,' said Bennett with a shaky voice and held out a trembling hand. Gialcone offered his in return, Shapiro sat and a waitress sprang upon them. They ordered coffee only.

Shapiro poured sugar into his cup and stirred it briskly, while looking at Bennett, sizing him up.

'I don't appreciate being dragged across the river if this is bullshit,' he said sternly.

'I apologize. But you must understand I'm very nervous about this.'

'Really. You done any time?'

'No, no never.'

'And why you so eager for us to get involved in this?' added Gialcone.

'Look, I don't know you guys. I was talking with a friend about this; he put me into contact with Mario. He said he didn't have the money to back it but he'd see about setting me up with someone else. Then I have to meet you guys.' Bennett fidgeted in his chair.

'So you told a friend, he told Mario and now who knows how many fuckin' people know about it,' said Shapiro with disgust.

'I couldn't help that. Look, I was just talking and before long it was spiraling out of my control.'

'Alright, forget the bullshit; just tell me what you got.' Shapiro leaned back and lit a cigarette. Gialcone studied every inch of Bennett's face while he spoke.

'Okay,' begun Bennett. 'The internet is a world wide maze of information and disinformation. You can buy anything you want in cyberspace, get a wife, hire a prostitute, book a vacation, anything you need is...'

'I know what the fuckin' internet is. Get to the point.' Shapiro showed his impatience and displeasure at being spoken to like a moron.

'Right, right,' continued Bennett and lit a cigarette. 'I figure you set up a legitimate company, a porn site. You build up your subscription base, people pay with their credit card, and it's amazing. Once you've been running it solidly for about six months, you hit every card you've got in one complete move. Now, you set up an account in the Cayman Islands and I've got the routing system all mapped out where the large amount worms it way through the banking system for a week before it reaches the Islands. Then you go down, withdraw the money. You walk away; they're looking for a company which has disappeared.'

'That sounds too fuckin' simple,' said Gialcone.

'It is and that's the beauty of it.'

'How much research you done into this?'

'I have been working on it for six months. I've built the site already and I'm just waiting for the backing to launch it and set up the company.'

'And how much you looking for, to set it up?' said Shapiro, leaning forward.

'A hundred grand and I also need a complete identity, social security number, false driving license and tax returns to set up a company bank account.'

'A hundred grand?' asked Gialcone incredulously.

'Yeah, I've got to rent premises for the duration and money is required to set up the offshore account, basic running costs.'

'You know credit card fraud and interstate transferring of illicit profits are serious crimes? Not to mention setting up a company for an illegal venture. You get caught you looking at serious time.' Gialcone finished his coffee, still peering into Bennett's face.

'I know, I know. It's worth the risk.'

'What are we looking at?' asked Shapiro.

'Based on research, about two and half, three million. After the money is washed, you come out with around a million, one quarter.'

'And you make what, a million?' Shapiro said.

Bennett nodded.

'Why a porn site?' Shapiro added.

'Because it's simple and addictive. People will pay up easily to jack off.'

'I understand that, but where you gonna get enough material to keep these losers interested?'

'That's simple. I'm an expert a creating and re-modifying images. I can take a film and turn all the white bitches into black. I can totally alter anything, so even if they've seen a film a dozen times, they'll think they're watching a new movie, its magic.'

'It's fraud and copyright breech too?' added Gialcone.

'So in effect we're committing a crime before we get any money.' Shapiro leaned back into the chair.

'Look, trust me, this is gonna make a lot of money,' Bennett said with haste, trying to sell himself.

'I'm gonna think it over. Leave your number,' Shapiro said.

Bennett scribbled his number down and Gialcone took it.

'Now you can go,' said Shapiro with menace. Bennett left the table without a word.

Once the waitress had refilled their cups Gialcone asked the question.

'Wanda think?'

'Don't know,' said Shapiro with a sigh. 'It's always a sure fire hit wid dese pricks.'

'Want me to check him out some more?'

'Yeah. See if he's into any shylocks for dough, what debt he's got, if he's married, got kids. I need a bit more security before I give that cocksucker a hundred.'

'Sure,' said Gialcone with indifference.

LITTLE ITALY

Gaetano Corsini was placing bets with his bookmaker when a soldier asked for an audience.

'I'll be with you in a minute.' He waved the man away. It was a bad day, he was already fifteen grand down, most of his horses were still running after the track had closed and his college basketball team let him down too. He slammed the phone down then motioned for the man.

'What the fuck's wrong wid you? Can't you see I was on the phone?'

'Sorry G. I got a truck load of designer dresses and I can't get hold of Jake.'

'Are you fuckin' serious? Take it to Fred "The Fish" you fuckin' idiot.'

'He won't handle it unless you give me an okay.'

'Unbelievable. Where's the truck?'

'I got it down the street.'

'And you come here with it? The feds could be watching this joint and besides, what did I tell everyone about talk in this fuckin' club? Store the fuckin' truck some where's else.'

'I'll take it to him now, can you call him?'

'Get the fuck out. And don't forget to bring some back for my wife, she's a twelve, I think.'

On top of his betting losses Corsini had been shown disrespect by a member of his crew. "Frisco Joe" did not show as he was supposed to, did not call and succeeded in setting off the belligerent trigger in Corsini. He had sent Ritchie to Joe's house and Ritchie had phoned through with the bad news that he wasn't home. Corsini had told him to wait there all day.

Ritchie phoned through again.

'Yeah.' Corsini adopted a terse manner.

'No show. I heard he's in Newark,' Ritchie said, just as terse.

'You got an address?'

'Yeah.'

'So you're Jersey bound then.'

'Yeah ?'

'Yeah. He's gotta go to confession,' Corsini said in anger.

'You sure?' Ritchie asked for confirmation.

'Yeah, he's in overtime.'

'Okay,' said Ritchie and hung up.

BROOKLYN

Paulie "Pazzo" Marranzo found his best friend Al Bondini at the bar in one of their favourite haunts. Paulie was tight with Al, since they had been children. Whereas Paulie was a typical wiseguy, Al was not. Paulie did not care who knew he was mobbed up, which had been a constant irritation to his brother and captain Vinnie, but blood is thicker.

Al Bondini was a thief and connected, but he was not made. Most of the scores he took were breaking and entering into warehouses and stores, he knew how to pick locks and beat alarm systems. Recently, he was part of the gang that ripped off an armored car. It was his first armed robbery. He had other problems on his mind though.

Paulie put an arm around Al's shoulder as he took up the stool next to him.

'How you doin' goombah?' he asked and took a swig from Al's beer.

'Awe, fuck it,' said Al, he looked distant. He ordered another round.

'You make out okay?' Paulie pressed, in reference to the armored truck score.

'Yeah.'

'Good. So everything's *kosher*.'

'Yeah.'

'Come on, liven up. What the fuck's wrong wid you?' Paulie lit a cigarette, even though all bars were now non smoking establishments. He didn't care. It was a wiseguy joint and woe betides anyone who complained.

'That fuckin' bitch is acting up again,' said Al with restrained anger.

'She didn't show again?' Paulie asked taking a gulp from his bottle.

'Three weekends on the bounce now.'

'That crazy bitch. You been round there?'

'She's taken out a restraining order now. Say's I'm causing disturbance. Can you believe that?'

'I'd cause a disturbance if some cunt stopped me seeing my kid. I tell yer, dese fuckin' women,' said Paulie shaking his head.

'On top of it all, I went back the other day and her new fella fronted me.'

'For real? What you do?' Paulie dropped his smoke and crushed it under foot, more angry than Al now.

'What could I do? Smack the guy in front of my daughter? Just make matters worse.'

'Fuck him. One thing you don't do is get between a father and his kid. Right?'

'Awe, you should of seen this prick, acting like a big man, telling me to stay away while standing behind that bitch and she giving me this smug look, as if she's daring me to start it up. I been wound up all week.'

'Who wouldn't fuckin' be? So fuck him, he wants to be a big man? We'll take care of him.'

'Yeah?' asked Al and looked at his friend.

'You know it. I got your back. Always. We'll take this fuckin' guy off the street, see how fuckin' big he is then.'

'Thanks Paulie.'

'Anything for you. You know that,' Paulie put Al in a headlock and kissed his forehead. 'Ain't staying here all night. You wanna go into the city ?'

'Yeah,' said Al, his spirit uplifted.

Steve McNair had managed to finish early for the day. A good mood swept over him, he was looking forward to the evening, to seeing his new girlfriend, he was eager to give her the present he had bought her, a gold bracelet and he was smiling inside at the anticipation of the sex, which was the best he ever had. Life was good, apart from the recent trouble with her ex, but he had taken care of that. Stand up to these people and they melt away, he had always told himself that and throughout his life it worked. He had never been bullied and delighted in his ability to take care of himself. His philosophy initiated the desired effect again; there had been no trouble from his girlfriend's ex-beau since he had told him straight. Three weeks without a word. Steve McNair had certainly taken care of that.

He made his way through the traffic, music turned up, driving on autopilot, unaware of anything out of the ordinary. There was no notice of the car following him.

Al drove and Paulie rode shotgun. They both smoked and said little. Paulie slid further down into the seat, keeping his eyes trained on the road.

Al chewed the inside of his mouth, his eyes were narrow and his breathing was long and deep. There was a standard modus operandi for dealing with these situations and they were breaking all the rules. They were showing themselves, putting their faces in the frame.

They tailed McNair to his house with ease. He was a civilian and did not know how to clean a tail. As McNair stopped at his house, they drove past, made a u-turn and parked out of sight, then waited. Anyone walking by would notice two men sitting in a car, anyone who wanted to play a good citizen would memorize their plate and model of the car and get a good description.

Evening set in, then dark before McNair showed again. He was still unaware of the tail. He stopped at a liquor store to buy some wine and they observed him talking on his mobile phone, presumably to Al's ex.

Al and Paulie had said nothing for ages. They were in a zone, psyching themselves up for the violence ahead. Trying to keep their nerves in check. McNair was of big build, he had a construction worker physique, close cropped hair. An ex soldier air about him.

When he drove off and turned onto a main road, they made their move. They would take a shortcut to where he was going and they reached McNair's destination a full five minutes before him. They parked and got out, each carrying a weapon. They anticipated he would park in the residents car park, which gave easy access into the apartment complex where Al's ex and his child lived. McNair did not disappoint them.

Steve McNair, in happy mood and oblivious to all around him got out and leaned back in to grab the grocery bag of wine. Behind him, someone said, 'Hey.' He turned around.

Al Bondini unleashed a backhand as McNair turned around. The twelve inch metal pipe he had in his hand crashed into the nose and mouth of the man, shattering the bone instantly and causing a temporary blindness. McNair in reflex dropped the bag of wine which shattered and put his hand up to his face. He still stood but not for long.

Instantly Paulie slammed his aluminum baseball bat into the knees, which made a sickening sound as the kneecaps splintered into pieces and inflicted compression wounds on the cartilage and ligaments. There was no support for McNair's weight and he buckled and hit the tarmac with a thud, he could not scream, not for the pain, not for help, because his throat was filled with blood from his broken face. As he lay incapacitated Al rained a blow down across his skull. Cerebral hemorrhaging began instantly.

'Big fuckin' man,' said Al, contemptuously.

Al and Paulie were both breathing heavy and fast. Paulie squatted and rifled through McNair's pockets, taking his wallet, mobile phone and keys and gold chain present. He turned off the phone, took the money out of the wallet, pocketed it, gave the chain to Al then opened the trunk of McNair's car. He threw in the wallet, phone and bat, Al threw in his metal pipe, and then they picked up McNair and dropped him in. Al gagged the lifeless body, bound the feet and hands, then closed the lid. Paulie tossed him the keys.

'Stick to the speed limit,' he said, all business. Al nodded, got in McNair's car started the engine, and then followed Paulie out of the car park.

As he drove, Paulie counted the money he had taken from McNair and smiled, turned on the radio and lit a cigarette. Fifty minutes later they pulled into an auto wrecking yard. Paulie talked to the owner.

'That red Chevy out there, it's a ghost. Here's a grand,' he said, handing over the money he took from McNair.

'Sure thing Paulie,' said the owner and counted the money. Paulie walked out of the office and got back into his car.

'Everything okay?' asked Al.

'Yeah. Just wait until we see the fuckin' thing go.'

Ten minutes later the car and McNair were gone, compacted, removed, unknown history.

'Let's get a drink,' said Paulie as he backed out.

'I certainly need one.'

'You did fine. Easy ain't it?' said Paulie with a smile.

'Yeah, it is.'

Al posted the chain to his ex and two days later got a call from her, asking if he wanted to see his daughter. Of course he wanted to.

Paulie, always eager to make money was beginning to embark on his own enterprise, without the blessing of his brother. The street life he lived endeared him with a sense to sniff out the big bucks and he was making new associates, outside of both families. Without the knowledge of his brothers or Family connections, or even his best friend Al, Paulie was branching out into heroin. Nothing new to the Mafia, but he was a member of the Cuccione Family and was going outside of their sacred circle. Fate had dealt him a hand and he had played it. It was through chance that he met two brothers from Afghanistan, who had already begun to route the drug from their homeland, through Iran and across to Oman. The vast quantities of the drug departed from Oman onward to Madagascar, where it was smuggled onto world cruise ships as bona fide provisions. The chefs and porters were the protectors of the white gold as it sailed from the Indian Ocean, into the Atlantic Ocean, making its sightseeing tours of the Caribbean until finally reaching its offload point, Miami.

It was in Florida they encountered their problems. They had the knowledge to import it but not to move it and Florida State was like the wild west. Without protection, no entrepreneurial faction could survive. They got scammed numerous times, first by the Colombians and Cubans. Then the Mexicans and Jamaican Yardies and when they tried to move it through Georgia, Alabama, Mississippi and Louisiana they encountered Pierre Sartois, "Little Napoleon" of the southern underworld, who was not about to relax his grip on the business of importing the white death and would absolutely not allow any competition in his own back yard.

In New York, while weighing their options they stumbled across Paulie Marranzo. They were selling nickel and dime bags out of a nightclub and Paulie found out. Enforcing another law upon them, he came to learn that these brothers were not average street dealers.

He listened to their story, sized the profits up in his avaricious mind and agreed a cheaper than going rate price per kilo with them. Paulie set a condition, they must get the loads further north, to Virginia and he would take it home, to crime city New York. The tills were ringing up in his mind's eye. The brothers, desperate to get their hands on cash and in fear because of what they owed to the terrorists who were at the head of the snake, took the short end money, although it was more than they dreamed of.

Paulie knew it was a death sentence, if caught, and he was moving around with caution as he put the final touches to his clandestine operation. He sought out street gangs in the Bronx, Albany, Jersey City and Newark and before long the network was in place. There was a simple method to his planning. Get the stuff in and offload it instantly. The gangs were crying out for the goods. Paulie needed help and he decided to reveal all to his best friend Al Bondini.

Al was half asleep the morning Paulie knocked him up. He made a pot of coffee and smoked.

'Jeez man. Where'd youse go last night?' said Paulie observing his friends disheveled look.

'Nowhere. Just stayed here, drank a shitload, watched cable movies all night.'

'Oh yeah, jacking off,' said Paulie while imitating the action and laughing.

'Fuck you.'

'I ain't into that.'

'What the fuck you doing here, this time anyhow?'

'Business.'

'It's too fuckin' early for business.'

'Not if you want to get super rich,' Paulie offered, lit a cigarette.

'Whachyer got?' Al poured coffee, gave one to Paulie, lit a cigarette, even though he had one burning in the ashtray.

'White powder, lots of it.'

'Coke?'

'Naw.'

'*Babania*?'

'Yeah.'

'You're a mad man. Your brothers know?'

'Fuggedaboutit.'

'Paulie. What's the matter with you?'

'What? Fuck 'em. I gotta make some serious money. I'm tired of being hired muscle.'

'There's enough dealers in this city and not enough turf.'

'I got it all figured out, I got the connections to move it in and out fast. Don't sweat it. You in? I promise you big dollars.'

'I don't know Paulie.'

'Come on man. I got everything covered. I promise you. I need you with me, you're the only person I completely trust, I need you to watch my back.'

'They'll fuckin' kill us they find out.' Al had a depressed look.

'Take it from me, they ain't gonna find out. Would I fuck you up?'

'No.'

'Come on then, say yes, let's get rich.' Paulie was smiling, with a face that drew Al into his web of deceit.

'Okay, fuck it.'

'Good. Get your shit together, 'cause we gotta be in Virginia tonight.'

'Tonight,' repeated Al.

'Yeah. First shipment tonight.'

'Who you getting this stuff from?'

'Don't start with the fuckin' questions.'

'Look Paulie, you gotta give something I'm gonna come aboard.'

'Two fuckin Afghan brothers. They bring the shit in, can't move it, that's where we come in. All we gotta do tonight is pick up the stuff, which is in a rental car parked in a motel car park, bring the shit back offload it to my connections, drop the car off to the rental office. Running water.'

'Okay. You picking me up?'

'Fuck that, I thought we'd spend the day together, get out of the city.'

'Fine.'

'Don't go naked either.'

'Thought you said it was running water?'

'Will be, just bring a piece,' Paulie said impatiently.

6 PROPOSAL

SERGE VALONE DELIBERATED MANY HOURS OVER WHETHER to meet with D'Angelo. Since his release he had been vacillating over many aspects of his life. Part of him wanted nothing more to do with the Mob and that life, part of him missed it. Serge wanted money, not the kind working as a stiff in a job set up by the system. The plans he formulated in prison were born out of a desire to be independent, the necessity to live free on his terms. To make money for his own pocket.

Valone agreed and made contact with Dalla Bonna, they arranged the meeting and now he was on his way. Curiosity reigned over him. He drove carefully in his rental. It had been too long since he had been behind the wheel and the last thing he needed was to be stopped by some over zealous cop. Even in his heyday Serge had hated driving in Queens, in fact did not like one inch of Queens. It was a borough that never sat well in his heart, he never felt safe there and it depressed him. Maybe it was his family past that made him feel that way, but Serge never delved into the reason. He hated the place and that was all he needed to know.

He found Robbie's house and was amazed to see it was nothing ostentatious. An average sized early century house which just blended into the neighborhood. Some of the capo's had swankier places of residence. As he parked he noticed a couple of men come out from the side of the house and head in his direction, by their motions, he could tell they were armed.

Serge slowly got out of the car and waited for them.

'Hello,' said one of the men, with a thick Italian accent.

'Hi. I'm here to see mister D'Angelo.' Serge did not move and watched them as they spoke quietly to each other. He immediately picked up their Sicilian dialect.

'You are meester Valoni?' the first one asked.

'Mister Valone. Yeah.'

'Okay, you coma dis way.'

'Ain't you supposed to check me?' Serge said. The men spoke between themselves for a few seconds.

'You no hava gun.'

'How do you know?' Serge persisted, testing them.

Both Sicilians gave him an inquisitive look. The first man smiled then spoke to the other, both laughed.

'Dis way.' He walked off. Serge looked at the other man who nodded, then followed as Serge stepped in line.

Inside the house the men waited with him until Silvio Dalla Bonna appeared. They slinked away, back to their guard duties. Dalla Bonna held out a hand.

'You okay?'

'I'm fine,' replied Serge as they shook hands.

'Let me take your coat.'

'Thanks,' Serge said as he slipped it off. Dalla Bonna took it away then come back and instructed Serge to follow him.

In the large lounge room Dalla Bonna offered Serge a drink.

'I'll take a scotch.'

'Anything with it?'

'Just ice.'

'Okay. Robbie won't be long.'

As they sat Dalla Bonna made talk about prison. Serge played along even though he really did not feel like talking about it. Then D'Angelo entered and saved him. Serge stood up.

'Hello mister D'Angelo,' he said offering his hand. D'Angelo took it.

'It's Robbie. No need for formality here.'

'Okay.'

'Sit, please.'

'You want a drink Robbie?' interjected Dalla Bonna.

'Yeah. Pour us a whiskey, thanks.' He sat, opposite Serge. 'Good to be out yeah?'

Serge nodded and looked at the glass in his hand.

'Did you eat yet?' Robbie continued.

'Yes. Thanks.'

'You sure, I could rustle you up something.'

'No. I'm fine.'

Dalla Bonna took the drink to Robbie, and then sat next to his boss.

'So Serge. What you planning on doing now?'

'Haven't had time to think about it.'

'Really. You know there's been a lot of talk. People are worried you're looking for revenge.' Robbie carefully watched Serge.

'I ain't looking for revenge. Besides, who would I take it from? The people that did me wrong are gone.'

'Yeah and all your organization's been carved up.'

'Look D'Angelo. I ain't out for revenge. I'm too fucking old, too tired. What I want to know is; can I make my own moves without you on my back?' Serge looked D'Angelo straight in the eye.

'Is that what you want?'

'I gotta live ain't I?'

'Sure. How would like something else, something more secure?'

'Like what?'

Robbie looked at Dalla Bonna. He got up and walked to Serge, took the glass out of his hand and went to refill it.

'I want you to be my *consigliere*.'

Serge's color drained from his face and he looked from D'Angelo to Dalla Bonna. His forehead was taught with perplexity.

'You fuckin' serious?' he managed finally.

Robbie moved his body, his face like stone. 'Of course. Would I waste your time otherwise?'

'I'm sorry.' Serge was awed at how much respect D'Angelo commanded. His presence made him realize that D'Angelo had an undercurrent of power that was covered lightly by the soft external mannerisms. Serge understood that Robbie D'Angelo was a throwback to the true men of honour.

Dalla Bonna brought him the refill and Serge took a gulp, then asked if he could smoke.

'Of course. Look Serge, I know you just got out and I obviously know the problems you've had. You know enough about me through the street wires. You never rolled. I need a stand up guy to be my left hand. Silvio's my right hand. You've been out there, I know your moves, I know you got the mind to guide me and I know you'll be loyal. You got the same ideas as me about this thing of ours.'

'I thank you Robbie, but I'm not sure I could do it.'

'Yes you can. You've seen what's become of us; you know what a mess the commission is in. I'll ask you a question. If you was in my position which capo would you clip, right now?'

Serge's eyes narrowed and his mouth became tense through tension. In his mind he worked out the answers and settled for honesty.

'In my opinion, you gotta whack two out of the three most powerful you got,' he said.

Robbie smiled and looked at Dalla Bonna.

'Which two?' he asked and looked back to Serge.

'Shapiro and Corsini.'

'Why?'

'They're the ones with the strength and they most likely think they owe Costello a debt. They won't take kindly to me taking this position.'

'Good. See, you're a natural.'

'Your biggest threat outside the Family will be Gigante,' Serge continued.

'He's been in New Orleans lately,' said Dalla Bonna.

'Then he's making his move against you. Gathering his allies.'

'The last thing we need is a war,' D'Angelo said.

'Then and I don't know how, but you are gonna have to strengthen your side.'

'That why I'm going to Chicago this week. I want you along.'

'We're gonna need more than Chicago.'

'I know. Chicago is one key to many locks. I'm gonna rebuild the commission. All the outsiders have gotta go.'

'Jesus. Robbie. The Colombians won't stand still for that.'

'I got my plans for the Colombians.'

'What's that?'

'I'm gonna give them to the government.'

'I wouldn't go down that road Robbie.'

'Why is that?'

'We can't trust those fucks. Look at that mess with Kennedy. They left us out to dry.'

'We don't speak about it,' said Robbie sternly.

'Apologies, but how you gonna play both sides?'

'That new head of the Organized Crime Task Force.'

'Rushdie. What about her?'

'I used to date her.'

'Get out of here.'

'On my honour.' Robbie held up his palms and smiled with devilish glee.

'How's that enough to get her on our side?'

'Pictures. Of her having dinner with me, going to the theatre with me. Won't go down too well with her boss if he was to find out she was cavorting with organized crime figures. Would it?' Robbie laughed.

'How did you work that?'

'She was a girl I saw in at a bar. I genuinely got a hard on for her, so I buy her a drink, we hit it off. She calls, we see each other. I find out she's working where she is, I figure an angle. Use my charm, date her a while, get what I need then drop her. She works her magic and now she's where she is, I'm where I am.'

'Will she play ball though?'

'She's a careerist. She'll put away some big players. The further she gets in the harder it is for her to fight us. It's a shame, because she's a good girl and we could've had something great, but…'

'That's crazy.'

'It's magic,' added Dalla Bonna.

'Anyway, that's for the future. Back to present business. The other families in this city haven't got the muscle to fight us and they won't ally themselves with Gigante. We know he's made his move with Sartois and I figure he's gonna tap himself into our capos. If there are no objections, I think it's time to call time on Shapiro and Corsini.'

'Sooner the better,' said Dalla Bonna.

Serge nodded and realized that he already accepted D'Angelo's proposal. He was back in the Mob unable to escape the clutches and the temptation. He was a major player in the street politics of New York, once more.

More drinks were poured and Serge felt an affinity with D'Angelo and Dalla Bonna. They were another substitute for family. They talked about personal matters. He deduced that Robbie understood enough about the life he chose to never take a wife or have children. Dalla Bonna was a typical hood. He had a wife and three children, two girlfriends on the side, various ex-girlfriends that he had forced to have abortions; bringing disrespect upon his wife would never do. Dalla Bonna's reputation, Serge knew about. If Serge had figured anyone to take over the Cuccione Family, it would be Dalla Bonna. Not Robbie, who had always kept himself out of the limelight, out of prison and surprisingly out of the mouths of most of the street hoods, who liked to look up to the loud tough brash guys. D'Angelo had slipped though that net and installed himself at the throne. He didn't have respect from all the soldiers, but he had respect from Dalla Bonna and now Serge. He was building and to survive a boss has to build.

For Serge, Robbie was a saviour. He treated people with respect, looked at the world as one big scam, but didn't think it was there for his own personal gain. He wanted their thing to survive and he wanted it to be the major player again. Serge felt pride swelling within him again. It was a long time since he had felt pride in being a part of the Mob.

So through the night they set out their strategy. The players they were going to take out, who they would be replaced with. How to bring aboard the powerful heads of other crime Families. They knew things might turn bad, even with intricate and careful planning, nobody could foresee the future in its entirety. Obstacles would turn up out the blue, unaccounted for, which would cause a cog to seize-up and filter into the other cogs. As they talked, the triumvirate considered Pierre Sartois to be one such obstacle. They knew the size of his organization and the ruthless nature of his soldiers.

Robbie had his own legion now though. A legion of pernicious violent assassins from that island in the Mediterranean, from where the whole concept began, some four hundred years ago.

Sicilians have a curious streak running through their blood. Blessed with an amiable and quiet nature, they are prone to bouts of melancholy and paranoia. They have a gift for the dramatic, the romantic, yet can be nihilistic and caustic. It is said, that if you fight with a Sicilian, it is to your advantage to kill him that day. For a Sicilian, honour is everything and to impugn it, is to sign your death warrant. A fierce pride of heritage adds to their mystique and their legendary secretiveness has built up an indomitable legend.

Robbie had a hundred of these tough Sicilians around him now. All loyal to their new boss, who had opened up the locked doors and brought them to the land of riches and the land of possibility. A few were even veterans of the Sicilian troubles, twenty odd years past. A time when the Families of Sicily fought a war with their own government; assassinating judges and officials sent from Rome and turning themselves into a group so hated that the Carabiniere and soldiers were instructed to shoot on sight.

These were men that shrugged their shoulders at death and had no concept of fear. Some of them had been to America before, hired by Murder Inc to hit some poor unfortunate. This time, they were living the dream. They marvelled at the magnificence of the city. Enjoyed the nightlife, with its cosmopolitan bars. And they loved the eager ladies with all the passion that they loved their homeland. They sent home pictures of themselves, standing at the Statue of Liberty. They desired to go to Little Italy, but were barred by Robbie. He did not want their profile to be too high and they obeyed him, because he was the boss. As much as they loved it, they were sensible enough to not be corrupted by it. They were Sicilians after all and they would not jeopardize their new life and lose their honour. Robbie knew that if a war did come down he had an elite army.

Robbie's concept of an imported army was not original. It had been used before in history, but Robbie was the first of the modern day bosses to deploy the tactic.

Silvio "The Pistol" Dalla Bonna was instructed by Robbie to begin the tasks when he and Serge were in Chicago.

'Also, I want you to visit the Marranzo's. If we're gonna keep them on board, we should put them into the picture a little bit,' Robbie said, finishing another glass of scotch.

'They'll play ball. They ain't got the strength to resist and they don't fuckin' care for Shapiro or Corsini,' Silvio said.

'That's because our last boss kept them under. He didn't treat his capos equally.'

'Which is something I don't understand, because those Marranzo's are fuckin' good earners,' Silvio continued.

'Ain't that the truth... Now, about Sartois. Serge. How far in with Gigante do think he is?'

'To be honest, I couldn't say. But he's notorious for taking care of his own back yard only. I doubt he would directly involve himself up here, but that all depends on what Gigante has offered him. Gigante might think he can still be chairman of the commission, perhaps he would have offered him a seat.'

'That's crossed my mind too.' Robbie thought for a minute. 'Okay. Silvio, send twenty of our Sicilians down there, just to keep an eye on our interests. That way we'll be showing our muscle and it'll let them know that we know. It might give Gigante a reason to think again.'

Silvio and Serge nodded in agreement.

'Okay gentlemen, I think that's enough talk for tonight. Serge, you be ready tomorrow for about ten.'

'Sure Robbie,' he stood up with Robbie and Silvio and the three men shook hands.

Once home Serge could not sleep, his head was in oblivion at the position he had been handed. He understood that Robbie did not care what rules he broke. Robbie D'Angelo had a vision and to set it into reality, he would remould or break whatever got in his way. Serge could only admire the man.

7 CHICAGO

AS THEY EASED THEMSELVES INTO FIRST CLASS Robbie set out to learn more about Serge Valone. Robbie was contented with his appointment. In his heart he felt the right choice was made, he knew that Serge would be loyal, that his integrity could not be questioned. Valone was a stand up guy and he had old time qualities, it was a substance that was dying throughout the ranks of the Mafia.

Robbie, like many other mob bosses knew they were under siege. They had suffered too many set backs in recent history; informers, undercover agents who had managed the unthinkable and penetrated into the heart of their society; new immigrant criminal gangs that were uncontrollable and had the fearlessness to confront them. The halcyon days were like a setting sun. Robbie dreamed of returning the American-Italian Mob to the feared heights from where they once ruled. He knew it wouldn't be easy and he knew it might be impossible.

'You never wanted kids, Serge?' Robbie asked after Serge had talked a while about his time inside.

'Not for this life. I know guys who teach their kids this way of life from about the age of ten. What kind of sick mentality is that? I was realistic to know the uncertainty, but hey, it's the life I chose. I always loved it, but I could never see myself with kids, not exposing them to this. I'd hate for my kid to be told by his mother that I weren't ever coming home or I was in jail for life. That's fucked. Okay, I'm a mob guy, if I fuck up my life, that's my choice, but fucking up the life of a child of mine, forget about it. Just 'cause I'm a hood, don't mean I ain't got a sense of morality.'

'I understand that.' Robbie poured more coffee.

'What about you?'

'Children. No. For pretty much the same reasons as you. Besides, I'm a selfish prick. I ain't got enough time to bring up children. There ain't enough time.'

'Not for a wife either?'

'Same again. What kind of life is this? It better to have girlfriends; try to avoid the emotional entanglements. There's always women. My mother and sister wish I would settle down. They don't understand this life. They know what I am of course, I guess they're like everyone else, they just want what's best for kin.'

'I appreciate all this Robbie.'

'I know. You deserve it. You got a rough deal. Costello did you wrong. You gotta forget all that shit now. You are were you are 'cause I trust you. We're gonna return Cosa Nostra, to where we belong.'

'Do you think Chicago will go along?'

'Yes. See, the thing is, we've been drifting apart. Chicago has taken care of the mid-west, we take care of the east, and out west the Lonardo's have been isolated. We've forgotten how to interact, like we were supposed to. All these *stranieros* have begun to muscle us out. Costello fucked up, now we gotta put it right. We got twenty three families in this country, if we can't get it together, forget about it.'

'I understand what you mean Robbie, but these others, they're all established now.'

'I know. Look, they ain't gonna be wiped out, I know that. But they ain't gonna sit on our fucking commission and when they operate in our territories, they gonna pay. We'll make 'em like affiliates, like franchises. But they are gonna play to our tune.'

'There's gonna be tough times comin' down,' said Serge with a thoughtful look.

Robbie nodded. 'Yeah. It's gonna be some head count.'

They rented a car and drove directly to Ancello's mansion in the suburbs. It was just the kind of opulent place that typified the brash way of the Chicago mob. Nothing was ever done quietly in the windy city.

Ancello made them wait. It was his way. He had never respected New York. Ancello hated the way these New Yorkers always seemed to self appoint themselves as the head of the Cobra. Ancello was king of his city, had been for many years, was now sixty and was not about to allow this new upstart D'Angelo dictate to him.

Eventually he hosted his guests, with false greetings and empty handshakes. He had a showman's demeanour as he insisted on taking them about a tour of his mansion, dressed in his three thousand dollar suit. When they exited into the grounds, he walked his dog, a two year old white English bull terrier.

The trio walked. Robbie and Serge holding a glass each, Ancello holding the leash. The Chicago mobster talked incessantly about the renovations done on the grounds, about his plans for renewing his overwhelming lawn, big enough to play two football games simultaneously. After an hour of this facade Robbie had had enough.

'Look, mister Ancello. I didn't come here for a real estate tour,' he said politely and firmly. Ancello seemed to ignore him and bent down to pet his terrier, unhook its leash and allow it to roam free. Excitable as it was, it jumped up the legs of both men. Ancello didn't command it to stop, then the terrier went in search of something new about its vast home. Ancello rose, his back straight, in iron like manner.

D'Angelo and Ancello stood facing each other, both sets of eyes locked upon the other. Serge scratched his cheek and turned his back on the men, taking a slow stroll away.

'I don't appreciate being treated like a jerk Ancello,' said Robbie, his eyes a steely focus.

'And I don't appreciate your condescension in my home,' replied Ancello.

'I came here for business and you agreed to see me for that reason.'

'Yes and this is Chicago, my town. I agreed to see you because it's obvious you're a very serious man, but don't make the mistake of thinking you can tell me when we talk. We will have our sit down and I'll listen to what you have to say, when I'm ready. Understood?'

'Okay.'

'You need a refill. Let's go back to the house.'

Robbie nodded. The two men had done a little dance, to feel each other out. As they walked Robbie believed he was in for a long evening.

Ancello had a light meal served on the patio deck. They took in the evening sun with their meal and wine and when finished were joined by Ancello's underboss and his counselor. He made a point of pouring the brandy himself.

'Now let's talk business.' Ancello sat back in his oversized chair and placed a large cigar in his mouth, the underboss lit it.

'You're aware of the trouble I got in New York,' began Robbie.

'That's your business,' replied Ancello, coldly.

'It's all our business.'

'New York is New York.' Ancello added a wry smile.

'Our thing is our thing, in whatever city. You sit on the national commission mister Ancello; you're bound by honour to protect our society.'

'Are you saying I'm not loyal?' the old mobster shifted his bulk to sit up.

'Not at all. But we got a divisive element running through the commission now.'

'A divisive element created by your departed boss. It was your family who opened up our world to these outsiders. I sit on the commission, but I don't respect it no more and I'm not alone.'

Serge contorted his face as he took in these words, but he said nothing.

'That's why it's important for us to regain the respect again, to rebuild. To make the commission worthy of itself, to re-establish the necessity for which it was created. We got twenty three families in this country mister Ancello. We can pull all of those resources to regain our hand.'

'With you as chairman of the commission,' stated Ancello with a solemn voice.

'That's one of the problems with the commission isn't it? The fact that we have a permanent chairman.'

Ancello smiled and puffed away on his cigar, allowing D'Angelo to continue. His Underboss and counselor behaved as Serge. They listened, said nothing.

'That's why it's time to change. We need to scrap the permanent position and replace it with a more democratic form. I propose we adopt a notion like how the Europeans work their parliament. They have rolling presidency that lasts for twelve months. We could incorporate that into our system. That way no family will feel inferior.'

'Wait a minute. You can't have some cowboys like the Gerrado's out of Denver sitting at the head of the table. That just ain't gonna work,' Ancello said with disgust.

'Of course not. At first it will be only the most adept and powerful families. The others will have to bring themselves into line, clean up their act. Once they've done that, they will be given a chance at the twelve month presidency. If we don't reorganize now, we're in danger of being thrown back to where we come. No more than street gangs, incapable of survival. With all respect mister Ancello, even you can see this.'

Ancello leaned forward and crushed his cigar in the ashtray. 'Pour some more brandy,' he said to his underboss with a hand gesture. 'And what happens when you're at the head of the table? I mean what concessions do you get?' Ancello took his glass from his underboss and took a sip, staring D'Angelo in the eyes once again.

'Well for one you draw a tax from the other families for that duration,' said Robbie, to which the old man's eyes lit up. 'And you get to determine which beefs are worthy of commission ruling, which are not. You get to sanction the usual, which families need to be disciplined. Of course, it will still be important not to interfere with a family's personal problems unless that family insists. Mostly the president will be responsible for keeping the peace and keeping outsiders in check.'

Ancello nodded, the machine of his brain working in silent tandem with his vision of the future. 'It will make us strong again.'

'Yes. Also there's something else.'

'Go on.'

'The dismantling of Murder Inc.' Robbie lit a cigarette in the silence. Serge looked at Robbie with surprise and Robbie returned him a slight shake of the head.

'How do you figure on implementing our justice without it?' Ancello asked.

'Once again that will have to be shared out. We'll hand out contracts to a family of the presidents choosing. Murder Inc makes everyone nervous, especially because it's based in New York under my family's jurisdiction. It has to end. It's too independent and almost uncontrollable.'

'So now we come to it. What do you need from me D'Angelo?'

'I need you in unity. I believe Gigante will move against me. He desires to be head of the commission and I suspect he has sought the backing of New Orleans.'

'Sartois?' said Ancello, then added incredulously, 'What the fuck is it with you New Yorkers and outsiders?'

'Bad judgment,' said Robbie in a light air to try and diffuse the old man's disgust. Ancello nodded approvingly. He motioned for more drinks to be poured and lit another cigar as the night drew in and air grew cold.

'Okay. I'll come along with you, but I'm getting old. I don't want to be waiting too long to serve at the head of the table.'

'I understand. You have my word you won't. I'll need you to use your influence over the Milwaukee, Cleveland and Detroit families. Convince them to shut out Gigante if he seeks their hand.'

Ancello nodded without a word. Then he got up and Robbie did likewise, they embraced and kissed each other's cheeks.

Alignments were formed to a tune of wonderment and a quiet sense of foreboding.

Ancello offered them the hospitality of his city and instructed his underboss to drive them into the city and show them around to his various nightclubs and bars. Robbie was relaxed and glad to be forgetting business for a while. Ancello's underboss took them to a popular haunt of Chicago wiseguys then had two of his lieutenant's watch out for them for the rest of the night. He did not want to play chaperone, he had his own life to attend to.

It was cabaret night and Robbie and Serge felt at ease. Their bodyguards kept a safe and secure distance from them.

'Robbie are you sure that blowing out Murder Inc is a wise move?' asked Serge.

'Yes. It's redundant now. The animosity it creates is not good for any of us. We can't allow it to operate and hope to maintain any sort of peace. It's far too strong. Corsini is unaccountable no longer, the family within is our enemy within. Corsini doesn't want to relinquish his power and why should he and so I figure if Angelo Gigante approaches him, he'll turn that axe on us. Corsini is a *Barese*, in his mind I'm unworthy. The organization he heads strikes fear throughout the land. It's hated and it's the misfortune of this family that it's under our control. On that basis that means I'll be hated. It's gotta go, be buried, be wiped from our future. You got no problem with Corsini going, have you?'

'Of course not. I hate that cocksucker. How you gonna fill the gap though?' Serge rubbed his hands together, and then picked up his glass. 'Is there anyone in his crew that can be promoted?'

'I doubt it. I might put them under the control of the Marranzo's.'

'Well. That makes sense, but once again it could cause divisions. Could Vinnie handle the expansion?' Though Serge knew he should be offering advice, he thought it better to do it by way of delving questions, to let his boss speak and outline his plans. Serge felt that Robbie had worked out all the equations and knew in his thinking what directions to take. Serge was just a support mechanism at the moment.

'Vinnie's a good captain. A good disciplinarian and his crew earns. From his camp there have been no murmurs of discontent. Uncertainty maybe. Give a guy like that a break and he won't forget.'

The two men took in the show and enjoyed the gratis drinks which arrived at their table in a constant flow. Serge had a niggle that kept taking little bites out of him, finally he decided to ask Robbie straight out.

'Robbie. How come you don't hold against me the fact that I was part of Zinardi's crew when the breakaway occurred?'

'That's history. These things happen. I didn't think it was such a good move for the other families to keep hitting on Zinardi. The commission sanctioned his break from this family and it should have been left alone. The talk on the streets about me not respecting the commission, it's all bullshit. They gave to Zinardi then proceeded to take away, it's all bullshit, they never wanted six families and Costello was never gonna forget it.'

Serge said nothing, took a drink.

'You know where Zinardi is?' Robbie said with an air of indifference.

'No.'

'Well, I know where he ain't.'

'Yeah?'

'Yeah. The witness protection program and I'll drink to that,' said Robbie in dry humor.

'Yeah,' Serge laughed.

Once Robbie was done with their private talk he invited over the men assigned to look out for him. 'Sit down.'

'Thanks Mister D'Angelo,' one of them said.

'What're names?'

'I'm Jack,' said the higher standing Chicago mobster. 'This is Phil.' Phil nodded to Robbie and Serge.

'I guess you're the big enchilada in New York,' said Jack.

'I am?' Robbie said with a lopsided smile.

'Everyone in the country knows you're the top man in that city.'

'Well, you shouldn't believe everything you hear on the streets.'

'It's been a long time since a boss of Costello's standing has been whacked,' Jack was desperate to hear about the hit from the horse's mouth. Robbie deflected him.

'It's the life we choose. Could happen to any of us. I know you don't want to talk about such matters though.' Robbie delivered his sentence with the ghoulish grace of a command. Jack did not reply. 'You know of any games going on tonite?' Robbie continued.

'You wanna lose some money?' Jack answered with mirth.

'Win some,' Robbie joked back.

'You can't win in this town. They take outsiders to the cleaners.'

'I'll take my chances.'

'I could take you to Zeeks. They have always got a game on. Cost a grand to get you in though.'

'Yeah.'

'Yeah, but don't worry about it. I'll take care of that for you mister D'Angelo.' Jack was quick to bestow a favor.

'Thanks. I appreciate that.'

'No problem. I'll just go and call. Tell 'em I'm coming in.'

'Good.'

When Jack and the other man left the table, Serge said, 'He's a smart one.'

'Yeah, but he ain't right.'

'No?' Serge looked at his boss quizzically. Robbie shook his head. 'What's the matter with him?' Serge said.

'He's too confident for one thing.'

'Let's go back to the hotel then, blow off the game,' Serge suggested.

'Yeah.'

When the men came back, Robbie informed them he had a change of mind. Jack and Phil looked at each other.

'You sure. I just got the okay, they're expecting us,' Jack persisted.

'I'm sure. You go on. We're gonna finish our evening here.'

'Okay. Have a good evening. It's good to meet you mister D'Angelo.' Jack had a look of disappointment in his face.

Robbie nodded, 'You take care.'

Jack and Phil nodded back then walked away.

'You figure he's setting us up for a hit?' Serge said.

Robbie grimaced. 'I wouldn't go that far, but he definitely ain't right.'

8 SILVIO'S DIRECTIVE

MANHATTAN

WHILE ROBBIE WAS AWAY SILVIO WAS BUSY. He had a directive and it took planning and he had limited time. He had sent out spotters, to gather "intel" on his prime objectives. For a whole day the spotters had been watching every favorite haunt in the city of the targets. Silvio knew their basic daily routine, but he never underestimated the unknown. It was important for everything to run smooth, it was important to implement a clean cut. A clean cut makes it easier to stitch up afterwards.

He was a universe of energy, drinking endless cups of coffee and smoking prodigiously as he and his ten prime batters waited for word. They were shacked up in a lock-up unit in Manhattan, him, five of his own crew and five Sicilians. Outside, the streets were in a state of calm and unknowing.

The Sicilians played flip a penny against a wall and Silvio's crew watched them with curious eyes, while playing Double Rum. There were no stakes, because they knew they could move at a moments notice, they did not want to get into it over the pot if time was called. The nervous tension was not unique to Silvio, everyone had it, but unlike Silvio they did their best to keep it at bay.

Silvio "The Pistol" was known for his jobs. They numbered well into the thirties. At twenty his first job came through and he delivered and kept delivering. Nerves were isolated from him, he felt nothing. Silvio Dalla Bonna was the personification of a true stone killer. These jobs were different though. It was his first directive as under-boss and the killing did not bother him but the necessity to do it right, to deliver, because he was ultimately responsible now. This operation could not be compromised. It was these factors that caused him anxiety.

LITTLE ITALY

Gaetano "The Archangel" Corsini had surprisingly had a good day laying bets. He had taken two bookmakers for a total of forty five thousand and they had just come by to pay. His crew had just made a hole in one with the rip off of a truck load of high quality stereos which put another fifteen grand in his pocket.

Ritchie kept pouring drinks and a high stakes poker game was in process. The pot was up to twenty large. Corsini was in high spirits. Others not playing the game, sat around enjoying their loud entertaining boss.

'Hey, Ritchie, you remember that broad I was banging from the Bronx, the one with the red hair, body like Brigitte Bardot. What the fuck was her name?'

'You was banging her '

'I know that. What the fuck was her name?'

'You can't remember?' said Ritchie astounded.

'Would I be asking if I could?' Corsini shouted rhetorically.

'Sandra, ain't a hard name to remember, you're goin' senile.'

'Fuck you. Sandra. So, I'm lying in bed with this broad and she tells me she's got a thing for men in uniform, especially cops. So I'm listening, you know, tryin' to figure where this is going and she tells me she wants me to go to this party with her, like a fuckin' fancy dress party and she wants me to dress up as a cop.' The crowd laugh. 'Yeah, for fuckin' real. So she keeps on and on and to get some fuckin' peace I agree. Come the day, there I am all dressed up. Yeah, in that fuckin' blue suit, full works nightstick, cuffs, the whole she-bang. Picture that right.' More laughs. 'Now she's dressed up as a hooker, a total fuckin' tramp and of course with a body like hers she can only look doable right? Right. So we go to this place and what the fuck is it?' The crowd look puzzled. 'Her old man's retirement bash and what is he?'

'A cop,' someone answered.

'You fuckin' bet your life he is.' The place erupts. 'So I'm fuckin' surrounded by New York's finest, I'm the only one in that silly fuckin' suit, I'm screwing his daughter who's dressed like, well you know and these guys are looking at me. She's downing drinks like there's no tomorrow, acting up and it's getting tense. So I figure I should go and talk to the old guy, try to diffuse the situation. I barely get my name out and he say's to me and this is for real, "Are you gonna book her or bang her." ' The place erupts. 'And I'm choked right, 'cause the old fuck has just leveled it right out. It turns out they got this father daughter conflict goin' on and she does this crazy shit to try and get his goat.'

'So what happened?' someone asked.

'What happened? I'm there all night getting drunk with her old man and his buddies, listening to their stories of the streets. Me, a wiseguy, dressed as cop, banging a cop's daughter and surrounded by cops. I tell yer. Do your research on a bitch, no matter what kind of body she got and how good she lays.' More laughter.

'So what happened to the broad?' someone asked.

'I put her on the game,' replied Corsini and the place erupted once more.

And then Corsini struck it three times lucky. He laid a straight and won the hand, another twenty thousand dollars. His star was shining. After the game a lull occurred. Crew members went on their way, some stayed to indulge in nightcaps with their boss, put forward scores, but he wasn't interested. It had been a good day. He poured out more drinks until the last of them left, until it was just himself and Ritchie.

'You don't get too many of these fucking days in your life,' Corsini said and puffed in exhilaration.

'Every day on the outside is a good day,' replied Ritchie.

'What are you now, the fuckin' Dalai Lama?'

Ritchie gave him the brush off. Corsini looked at his watch and sighed.

'Three. You wanna go down to Umberto's, get some chow?'

'Yeah, I could eat.'

'You buying?'

'Fuck you yer cheapskate,' said Ritchie.

Corsini laughed. 'Come on, I'll treat yer.' He downed his drink. Ritchie grabbed his

coat then turned off the lights and Corsini walked out and waited for him.

A spotter had phoned Silvio to tell him that Corsini's crew had been locked inside the social club for two hours; they did not appear to be moving. Silvio went with five Sicilians in three separate cars and they waited close by. He was still weighing up his options. During the waiting time he got another call, which relayed to him that Gus Shapiro was visiting his girlfriend, without back up. After the call he phoned the lock up and gave them the go ahead. The spotters at both locations disappeared into the New York night.

Dalla Bonna waited in a car with one Sicilian zip; they made light talk and shared each others cigarettes. Dalla Bonna attached a silencer to the Walther 9mm he carried and checked the clip once again.

The two other cars were parked thirty meters from his car. One up the street, one down. The early morning was quiet, a truck drove past them and they watched the driver pull up to an automated newspaper stand, get out and switch the stock, and then drive away. The sky was clear and full of the galaxy's shining outposts. A definite air of approaching summer hung over the city.

All six men kept their focus on the social club. They watched a group of Corsini's crew exit and depart their separate ways. Dalla Bonna flicked his cigarette into the tarmac. Minutes slid past agonizingly, then they saw Corsini exit. He pulled down the shutters then lit a cigarette and stood waiting. The Sicilians from the other two cars got out and walked down the street towards the club.

'Let's go,' said Dalla Bonna. He got out of the car, gun to hand. He had the shortest distance to walk. He was upon Corsini who was checking messages on his mobile, without a sound.

In the quiet street, the sound of midtown traffic drifted down. Distant engines and sirens were broken, by the effects of an audible that resembled a single wave crashing onto shingle.

The single shot carved through the skull of Corsini and exited his face, blowing out his left eye, shattering his cheekbone and forcing his weight to crash against the shutter; the noise reverberated along the street. Corsini hit the pavement with a lifeless thud. From inside Ritchie called out, 'Okay, okay, I'm coming you impatient fuck.'

Dalla Bonna was already walking back to the car. He got in and started the engine, shifted to drive and eased the car across the road. The five Sicilians set themselves. Ritchie had a limited view of the street, because of the shutters, but he did not expect anything out of the ordinary. As he came out of the door the shooters opened up on him, taking no quarter, they pumped at least twelve shots into him.

Gun fire sounded off like fireworks for about ten seconds. Dalla Bonna pulled up to the kerb, got out and opened the trunk. Both bodies were picked up thrown in along with the wiped down untraceable used weapons, lid closed. Two Sicilians got in and drove away. Dalla Bonna went with his Sicilian *compare* in another car, the other two in their original car and followed the car with the corpses. Dalla Bonna was on his way to somewhere else. They crossed Broadway into Tribeca, where Dalla Bonna got out and transferred to his car. The bodies in the car were driven across the Queensboro Bridge and parked long term close to La Guardia airport.

Dalla Bonna drove home and made himself a pastrami salad sandwich and washed it down with a can of cola. After, he sat looking at television waiting on words of confirmation.

At the other operation the five gangsters waited in their positions. One had crept around the outside of the house, spying on the unprotected capo Shapiro, who was having rough sex with his girlfriend on her couch.

The spy enjoyed the scene. He continued to spy on them while Shapiro lay watching a movie, as she blew him. He carried on watching as they finished and continued to drink hard liquor until they finally fell asleep, drunk and exhausted. The hitter walked back to the cars.

'He's ready,' he said. Three of them got out and went to the house. Around the back one of them took out his pick set. It was dark, but he knew his tools, he put the tension wrench into the key-in-knob then slid in the Snake Rake pick. He closed his eyes and concentrated on tension in his left thumb and raked the pins with the pick between his right thumb and forefinger. It made a little noise, but not discernable enough to drunk and sated people. It took a few minutes for the lock to give way; he pulled out his tools and pushed the door open slowly.

The gang of four filed into the house silent, until they stood overlooking Shapiro and his girl. Two of them took out claw hammers from their jackets. Simultaneously they slammed them into the sleeping heads. The girl let out a gasp as her breath was taken away. Both received about five blows. Another man went back to the kitchen took out a carving knife from the selection holder. He slit Shapiro's throat deep, so deep the blade touched the neck bone.

When it was done they pilfered his clothes, took his money and driving license, then in a quiet staged act, turned the place upside down and stole some jewellery to make it look like a robbery-homicide. The killers left the house and drove to an all night diner, where they ate large breakfasts. One of them called Dalla Bonna.

Dalla Bonna picked the phone up on the first ring.

'Yeah,' he said.

'Morning. I need you to come in, we're short today,' said the voice on the other end.

'You got the wrong number asshole,' Dalla Bonna said and hung up. He turned off the television and lights then went upstairs. After looking in on his children he took a piss and brushed his teeth, undressed, climbed into bed and pushed up against the warmth of his sleeping wife, who murmured but did not stir.

Throughout the streets during the day there was talk, confusion and fear. Shapiro and his girlfriend had been discovered and the fact broadcast in radio bulletins.

In Brooklyn at the Vesuvio club, Vinnie Marranzo listened as a reporter on the scene relayed the scene.

'Police are still conducting forensic tests on the house where the bodies of Gus Shapiro and his girlfriend were found dead late this morning. Now the police are not releasing too many details, but they have said that the reputed mobster and his girlfriend were killed by multiple blows and that Shapiro, also known as Garry Shires had his throat slit. Earlier I asked Detective Berendt if this was a gangland hit. He refused to comment but independent experts say Shapiro; whose death comes just a year after the slaying of Andello Costello, was probably a contract killing as a power struggle grips the Cuccione family. Shapiro who was a high ranking captain in the family was probably executed so as to get rid of any bad blood that was lingering since the death of Costello; who we all remember was gunned down last year in the middle of Manhattan along with his underboss.'

The radio host cut in. 'Julie, are the police looking for anyone in particular, do they have any suspects?'

'No they don't Bill. The police are conducting house to house enquiries but it seems nobody can offer any information, I managed to speak with one neighbor earlier and he said he was up most of the night with his sick wife and he didn't hear a sound, so it seems this one will go into the history books as just another unsolved mob slaying.'

'Okay. Thank you Julie. Julie Parker there at the scene of the murder of mobster Gus Shapiro. I'm sure that story will run for a few days and we'll keep you posted on latest developments. Top of the hour and your listening to WSNY, I'm your host Bill Nichols and next we're talking with Professor Rupert Mattel on the state of the economy, right after this commercial break.' The program cut and Vinnie turned off the radio.

His brother Tommy said nothing whilst placing a coffee before him. Crew members came in, bringing tribute taxes to Vinnie or wanting to talk scores. Vinnie was in no mood, he told them all to get out and make some money.

'This is the beginning then,' Tommy said.

'No fucking kidding. Where's Paulie?'

'I don't know.'

'Well get a hold of him. Tell him to get his ass over here.'

'How bad do you think this one will be?'

Vinnie shrugged and gave his brother a look of disgust. 'How the fuck should I know?'

'What are your plans?'

'Will you stop with the fuckin' questions. Just get a hold of Paulie.'

'Okay. Jesus!'

'I'm going through to the back room. I don't wanna be disturbed,' Vinnie ordered.

The quiet solitude of the back room offered Vinnie a sanctuary of sorts. He drank his coffee, smoked a cigarette, his mind whirled across the scenarios, deciphered the angles. He titled his head back, moving it from side to side, trying to work out the tension from his muscles.

'Fuck,' he said in realization of the probability that he would be whacked too. Vinnie would have liked to go somewhere, to get away from the city while the streets were uncertain, but he was a realist and he knew there was nowhere to escape the heat. Vinnie had suspected for months that something was coming down, it was the way the mob worked, a new boss would cull the old flock. Power was not in Vinnie's hands though, he would just have to wait and watch the pendulum swing.

*

Throughout Gaetano Corsini's crew there was much panic. Their boss and his number two were nowhere to be found in the city. Also some of their hardest and most feared killers had disappeared. Murder Inc had been ripped apart. Crew members hung around the club on Mulberry Street all day, waiting for word. Talk was mostly of what would happen next, no one said it; but they knew Corsini and the others had been blown away. There were no tell tale signs on the sidewalk. The street cleaning truck, hired by Dalla Bonna had done a thorough job. Soldiers knew the streets and knew what Corsini's no show meant.

*

Dalla Bonna awoke to the sound of his children causing a ruckus, his wife's voice shouting at them to hurry up and move or she would wake their father. He listened to the door slam shut, the opening and closing of car doors, the engine start and the car back out of the driveway.

After showering, he grabbed a coffee, and then dressed. A dark suit and black roll neck top gave him the look of an executioner. He waited, smoking a cigarette, then heard a car pull into the driveway. He walked out of the house and got into the car, driven by Salvatore Grecco, one of the toughest imported zips. Dalla Bonna had more errands to run, but he only needed Salvatore as back up this time. They nodded to each other without words then Salvatore backed out and they were on their way.

Salvatore parked outside the Vesuvio in Red Hook. Dalla Bonna lit a cigarette.

'Wait in the car,' he instructed Salvatore.

'Sure boss,' said the Sicilian.

Two of Marranzo's crew were sitting outside, upon seeing Dalla Bonna they stood up, both wore a countenance of worry.

'Hi, Mister Silvio,' said one of them anxiously.

'Yeah,' he replied with a serious air and walked right past them into the clubhouse. The two soldiers walked away, fast.

Tommy Marranzo was locked into the news on the television. He heard the door open but did not turn around.

'Vinnie ain't seeing nobody. Don't you guy's fuckin' listen,' he called out.

'Yeah well he'll see me.'

Tommy turned around in recognition of the voice and stood up. 'I'm sorry Mister D. I

didn't, I mean we weren't expecting you.' He turned off the television.

'He out back?' Dalla Bonna said all business.

'Yeah.'

'Tell him I'm here.'

'Sure,' Tommy managed then walked out back.

'What is it?' Vinnie said to his brother in annoyance.

'The Pistol's here.' Tommy's voice was panicked.

'He's here. Now?' Vinnie was caught off guard.

'Waiting out there.'

'Fuck.' There was a silence as he thought. 'Fuck,' he repeated. He pushed his hands through his hair. 'Okay. Send him in and bring us some coffee.'

'Sure. You gonna be alright?'

'Well we'll see, won't we'

Dalla Bonna pushed open the door and saw Vinnie sitting behind the desk.

'Hello mister Silvio.' Vinnie stood up, came around the desk and held out his hand. Dalla Bonna took it, a firm handshake followed, then and embrace and a kiss. 'Please, sit down.'

'Thanks,' Dalla Bonna said. There was a knock on the door and Tommy entered with a tray. On it stood a pot of coffee, sugar bowl, two cups, single serve cream pots and a selection of Italian biscuits. He set the tray down.

'Keep everyone out of the store,' instructed Vinnie.

'Sure Vinnie.' Tommy then walked out, closing the door behind him.

Vinnie poured.

'How do you take it?'

'Two sugars, black. You seen the news?'

'I heard.' He handed a cup to Dalla Bonna, who proceeded to stir it vigorously, for what seemed an age to Vinnie. It was the only sound in the room, metal against china until Vinnie lit a cigarette. He offered the pack to the boss, who shook his head, then waited.

'You caught a break Vinnie,' said the Pistol and looked Vinnie directly in the eye. Vinnie had been hiding the fear well, but when he heard those words, the muscles in his face relaxed and he began to breathe more easily. He said nothing.

'What's happened has happened. Corsini's gone too.' Dalla Bonna continued. 'Ain't had no beefs from you or your crew, you earn, never talk out of school. As of now Corsini's crew and Murder Inc are finished. There's gonna be a transfer. Half that crew's gonna be under you now, you been recognized, you been moved up. You know what that means right?'

'Yeah.'

'Good.' Dalla Bonna finished his coffee, and then stood up. 'I'll send over your new soldiers today. In a few days there'll be a meet.' He offered his hand to Vinnie, another handshake, Dalla Bonna saw himself out.

Tommy went into the room the minute the boss had left the club.

'Everything okay?' he asked of his brother.

Vinnie smiled. 'You bet you're ass.'

'So what's the deal?' Tommy held out his hands for an answer.

'Changes.'

'And us?'

'Forget about it. We're climbing the mountain.' Vinnie was still smiling.

'For real?'

'For real.' Vinnie went to his brother and embraced him in a victory hug, then pulled away. 'We got new crew coming later today. Go and get us some breakfast.'

'Sure bruv. What do you want?'

'Everything.'

'You got it.'

Dalla Bonna rolled into Little Italy with Salvatore. That famous enclave was alive with excitement. Inside and outside the club of the disappeared Corsini there were many soldiers. Speculative talk filled their hours along with the usual scheming to make money. Just because the immediate boss was gone, organizing scores did not stop.

Dalla Bonna and Salvatore parked a few blocks away and walked the streets. "The Pistol" smoked and moved with an arrogant and fearsome march, as if propelled by a manifestation of pent-up violence. His countenance had changed into a granite impression of gravity. Energy emitted from him, sending out a pulse which threatened the universe, silently. His eyes were full of fire, which bored into anyone who dared to make contact.

Salvatore the Sicilian, walked in time with his boss. He was taller, less powerfully built but assured. He too wore an exaggerated fearsome tone, indicating to the world that it would be foolish to mess with him. His eyes were unseen, covered by sunglasses, which added to his ferocity. Civilians moved out of their way on the sidewalk, such was their energy.

As they approached the club, soldiers outside anxiously moved and stopped their talk. Very few made eye contact.

'Everyone inside,' ordered Dalla Bonna. The soldiers obeyed without a question.

There was no structure, soldiers who were higher ranking tried to assert themselves during the morning, but nobody was about to back down. Now they had Dalla Bonna before them, one man, a powerhouse who they feared. Quiet talk filled the room until Dalla Bonna spoke up.

'Your skipper's gone. Nobody knows anything, so don't ask. You're the Cuccione family, so you don't worry. As from today, this crew's finished. You're gonna be restructured, some of you are gonna be put under control of Marranzo, the rest are going with Salvatore here. Is that clear?' Dalla Bonna kept up his fearsome attitude during his terse speech.

'Good,' he said in reply to the lack of questions. 'I'm deciding who goes where and I wanna make it short and sweet. So be quick with your objections, if you have any. I'll set up in back. Someone bring me a coffee.'

Once he had finished with the business in Little Italy, Dalla Bonna went on to deal with Shapiro's crew. They were in the same amount of confusion and disarray as everyone else.

Philip Galione was taking counsel, doing his best to assure the troops that there would be no need to go to war. Asserting his authority was harder than he expected. When he was directly behind Shapiro, it had been easy, because he was Shapiro's muscle. Now he had to stand alone, for how long he did not know.

When Silvio Dalla Bonna arrived, Galione was quick to disperse the crew. He expected the worst and did his utmost to be cordial. He offered coffee, but Dalla Bonna refused, he was full of coffee and tired of talk.

'I ain't staying long. You got upped Phil. It's your crew now. You keep your side of the street clean. Corsini and Murder Inc are finished. Marranzo's gonna be the top capo now, but you know the drill. You can handle it?'

'Yeah.'

'Okay. Robbie's calling a sit down, some time this week. Apart from this ain't nothing changed. You're crew is your crew. You still got your respective territories. You got any questions?'

'What about a number two, do I get who I want?'

'You got someone in line?'

'Yeah.'

'Then it's your decision.'

'Thanks Silvio.'

Dalla Bonna nodded. 'Right I gotta get back. You pull in your crew and give 'em the good news.' The two of them embraced and shook hands, then Dalla Bonna walked out to the car and Salvatore drove him back to Queens.

9 IRISH REBELLION

THE WESTIES HAD ALWAYS HAD A LOATHING for the Italian mob. Business had been done between them for decades, but it was always a precarious arrangement. The Italians had never really respected the Irish and in turn a tempestuous love affair had existed.

After the violent demise of Seamus Gerhaty the New York Irish could not organize and rouse themselves into a collective strength. A power struggle occurred within and their grip on power slowly waned, until the Boston mobster Dawson Culpepper intervened and asserted his authority, bringing a state of calm and prosperity.

Dawson Culpepper ran Boston with autocratic violence. His hegemony ensured that from his Boston power base his web stretched throughout Massachusetts and into Connecticut and Rhode Island. He considered getting his feet under the table in New York and a seat onto the Commission as his greatest achievement. What cemented his position, along with his violence, was his proficiency in corrupting politicians. Two successive governors had been firmly planted in his domain, along with various police chiefs and a district attorney.

Dawson Culpepper was a curious character though. He was a fiercely proud Irishman. Flew the tri-color from his house and his various bars throughout Boston, read Irish history prodigiously and celebrated St Patrick's Day with a vigor that would put any native of that Emerald Isle to shame.

Yet his Irish ancestry was questionable. His family history could not be traced and there was no evidence to suggest that he grew up in an Irish community, even though he insisted he had.

If his heritage from Ireland was in doubt; his history as a gangster was not. He had first shown up on Boston police files at the age of sixteen. Arrested for demanding monies with menace and robbery with violence. At twenty he was collared again for armed robbery, but beat it. Then for murder and beat that. Throughout Boston he was known in the Irish mob and by the Italians. At thirty he had risen to a high ranking member and made his first million by selling guns to his supposed Irish brethren who were fighting the British government. He made strong connections with the mobster gangs in Ireland and provided safe havens for some of their heavy hitters.

He was thirty five when he took control of Boston, supplanting the ageing mobsters with a tighter and more violent ethic. He fought a war with the Italians to a stalemate and effectively constructed a cordial where the two factions would never cross. As with any business though it came to pass that eventually they buried their differences and carved up Boston equally. The Italian mob, as is common with them set off on a self inflicted inner war and as they waned, Dawson Culpepper grew stronger until Boston became effectively, his.

After his working over of politicians he managed to have his history wiped and became in the public eyes, a respectable businessman, in which his many interests included the construction of shopping malls, a bar and grill chain called Dublin Fare, which stretched throughout New England and a highway roadwork maintenance company that made fortunes because of his political corruption. Illegally, money came from drugs, gun running, hijacking and the usual conspiracies.

Dawson Culpepper was unhappy with events of the last year in

New York. He knew Robbie D'Angelo was turning back time, that the Commission would be ripped apart and he knew it could mean war.

He was approaching sixty now, a multi-millionaire, legal and could walk away clean, but with any gangster they are governed by ego and he decided he would take on D'Angelo. He called New York and told his man to come to Boston.

Dawson Culpepper was determined to have his say in the politics of the crime syndicate and to make a point decided upon sending Robbie D'Angelo a message. His face in New York was John O'Neil, a graduate of the Boston crime school and loyal member of Culpepper's mob.

'That fucking guinea D'Angelo, he's causing a lot of headaches. He thinks wops have got a divine right to run everything in this country. He wants to send us back to the last century, keep us down. He giving you problems in New York?' Culpepper sipped his Bushmills.

O'Neil shook his head, lit a cigarette. 'Nah. He's fighting his own people.'

'He's rebuilding. Once he's settled, he'll begin ripping into us. I ain't gonna allow him to keep us out in the cold. I want you to deliver him a statement of intent. He ain't gonna keep us off the Commission.'

'You wanna go to war with him?'

'Fuck a war. I want you to hit some of his people. Some of his capo's. He ain't got the time for a war at the moment. He's gotta consolidate his position within his own family, then he's gotta work the Commission. This is the right time to give him a wake up call. The Irish don't lay down for anybody, especially some fucking upstart wop who thinks it's his world. Fuck him. You cause as much mayhem as possible. Keep him on the back foot. I should've moved sooner against this prick, but it's my sense of objectivity that made me delay. I thought he would be a reasonable man, but he's shutting us out. We'll move against him first, once we do, the Colombians and everyone else will. He won't be around for long.'

'I ain't got the muscle in New York to fight him,' O'Neil protested with impassioned oration.

'I'll give you more soldiers. Ireland's full of young men, desperate to make it in the new world. You'll get enough muscle.'

O'Neil nodded.

'Why the pensive look?' asked Culpepper of O'Neil.

'I'll never question your judgment on anything boss. But are you sure this is the right thing to do? Our organization in New York is the most solid it's been for years. The wops don't bother us; we're raking in vast money. If we do this, we could set off a chain reaction that will get out of control.'

'You're Fighting Irish. What the fuck you worried about?' Culpepper poured another whiskey with a contorted aggravated face.

'Nuttin. New York is different to here, that's all. I know we fucked the Italians here, but we got five families down there and as much as they despise each other, they grow into one in the face of an outside threat.'

'That's bullshit. These greasers ain't as tough as everyone imagines. Costello knew it, that's why he restructured the Commission. They've been getting slowly fucked by the government and other factions. They've had their fucking day. You got so many nationalities in this country, all with their own mobs. Their time is at an end. Nobody fears them like they used to. If you ain't got the stomach, you can come back up here, I'll give it to a new guy.'

'I've always been loyal. You don't have say this shit to me.' O'Neil said with a frown.

'I'll say whatever shit I want to you John. I put you in New York as my face and you done a good job, but don't you go fucking questioning me.'

'I apologize. I just want you to send me some reliable people. I don't need any thick Mick's. I want proper hitters to do this right.'

'I ain't gonna leave any man of mine alone, pissing in the wind. You'll get the right back up.'

O'Neil stayed in Boston for a night, getting drunk with his boss. He also gave him fifty grand. Peanuts to a mobster, but it gave Culpepper a nice weekend out, in the finest restaurants and top seats at the Celtics. O'Neil held back twenty grand for himself, skimming from his boss, but that was the gangster life. Scheming and ripping off everybody was normal. Culpepper suspected it happened but he turned a blind eye. Like all other bosses, he would murder anybody that was found out, but he became blind because he understood his soldiers had to live too. As long as it was kept quiet and he wasn't embarrassed, Culpepper would allow its continuance.

O'Neil knew he was dicing with a bad fate and kept his cards close to his chest. In turn, he knew that soldiers underneath him never squared up a full end; it was a continual money-go-round. Now, he had greater problems. It vexed him to be put in this position. Inside he felt this move by his boss was wrong. To stir up the hornets nest in New York would be injurious. If they left the Italian mob alone and let them do what they were doing, when it all settled, they would still be in a strong placement.

It would be impossible for him to play truancy. If Culpepper wanted this to happen, then he would have to go along. So as he whiled away the hours with his boss, his mind worked over how to stall, without bringing down the wrath on himself. The mobilization that was happening throughout the ranks of the different organizations indicated the certainty of war.

When John O'Neil returned to New York he was thrown into the pain of another headache. Two of his soldiers had started a fight in a bar and put a guy in hospital. The injured party was a made man in the Marranzo crew and they wanted the men that committed the offence. O'Neil was cited for a sit down.

O'Neil was distraught at the incompetence and gave out verbal to some of the crew.

'I been away two fucking nights and I gotta come back to this crap. Where are those idiots?'

'Hiding out,' said a man sheepishly.

'Hiding out. And now I gotta go sit down with those crazy wops, I gotta chew the fat and let them lay it down. What were they thinking?'

'Hey John, those greaseballs were on our turf in one of our clubs. They were acting like the degenerate pricks they are, telling jokes about the Irish, being assholes. The guys asked them to leave and one them took his cock out and pissed up against the bar. That ain't right, John. The fucking pricks got what they deserved.'

'We got fucking channels. The last thing we fucking need is to get into a beef with these people. If there's a problem, it comes to me, I go to them and we straighten it out.'

'That give 'em the right to disrespect our neighborhood?'

'You don't fucking listen, do yer. What has happened in the last year in this city?'

'I don't see how that has got anything to do with it.'

'Listen; don't go getting smart with me. While they've been doing their business they're leaving us alone. We're making more money while they've been occupied, now the spotlight's on us again. If they tell me to give the guys up, what I'm gonna tell em?'

'Tell 'em to fuck their self.'

'You go over there now and tell 'em, right now. See how fucking far you get,' O'Neil began to shake with rage and bit the inside of his mouth. The sound of his teeth clinking together could be heard and his jaw was visibly tightened.

'John, this ain't right. Why the hell we gotta defer to them anyhow?'

'Because that's an arrangement. We don't touch their guys, they don't touch us. You want that psychopath Dalla Bonna on your ass 'cause I don't. Fuck it. Call up Vinnie and set it up.'

Vinnie Marranzo requested to see O'Neil that day and John drove over to Brooklyn, alone. He figured it would be an act of faith to appear without back up. He knew Vinnie well and liked him; they had done business together on numerous occasions. He was glad that it was with Vinnie that this entanglement had occurred. O'Neil had always seen Vinnie as a reasonable man.

Vinnie respected John for coming alone and they shook hands and shared a bottle of wine. Vinnie's brother Tommy sat in.

'We gotta get this straightened out John,' Vinnie stipulated, giving very little room for John to manoeuvre.

'I understand your position Vinnie, but my guys were on the defensive. Your men were acting up and being disrespectful.'

'That ain't the point John and you know it. I can't allow any member of my crew to be worked over by outside factions. These are made guys, it just don't wash. You know where your guys are?'

'No.'

'Come on John, we go back a while, don't fuck me around. Something's gotta be done.'

'I can't give 'em to you Vinnie. You know that, there's gotta be another way.'

'Well they can't be seen to get away with it. Lay a tax on 'em.'

'Your guys will agree to it and it'll be dropped after.'

'I'll tell my guys that's the way it is.'

'What you figure on Vinnie?'

'Twenty five grand a piece. I'll give twenty each to my guys and I'll take ten for the insult.'

'That's fair enough.'

'You tell 'em they got two weeks grace, after that I'll take the leash off and there'll be no negotiating.'

O'Neil nodded but inside he was seething. If there was an insult laid it was by the Marranzo crew.

'You wanna stay on for some dinner?' Vinnie asked.

'No. Thanks. I gotta get back.'

'Fine. I'll see you soon.'

On the drive out of Brooklyn O'Neil's demeanor changed. He decided to go all the way with his boss' mandate. His body was quivering with anger and he stopped at a bar and had three large whiskeys to enable him to complete the drive.

Back on home turf, with an emotion of boiling fury, he threw all but two people out of the bar he owned. He ordered his bartender to serve him a pitcher of beer and a bottle of whisky.

Mickey Conway, his lieutenant set up a table for the both of them. Mickey had seen this mood in John before and knew it meant trouble. Mickey was a native of New York and when John O'Neil first arrived from Boston he felt disgruntled at being overstepped. O'Neil had done his homework though and wasted no time installing Mickey as one of his top men. They were now close friends and Mickey Conway had become O'Neil's most trusted man.

Mickey poured the whiskey as he sat at the table. John had his head tilted back and a cold damp towel across his eyes.

'It didn't go well then?' Mickey said.

'Ugh, those greasers. Their attitude is always the same. I thought Vinnie was different, but when it comes to it, they're all the same.' John took the towel off his face and flung it across the room at the bar. The bartender picked it up and continued with chores. The bar was dimly lit, fashioned in a nineteenth century saloon from the old country. Pictures of Dublin and Cork hung about the walls, along with paintings from amateur Irish artists, sent over by relatives and tourists.

'How was pepper?' said Mickey.

'Ugh. He ain't happy. He's got his serious head on.' John gulped down a whiskey and coughed, followed it with a mouthful of beer, straight from the pitcher, then filled two glasses. 'Wants us to send that D'Angelo a message.'

'We ain't got the muscle for that.'

'He's sending it.'

'He's gone nuts. Why's he wanna start that up?'

'All this bullshit with the Commission. I don't get it at times. Always playing at politics like some goddamn insane government.'

'Everybody wants to be president.' There was an ironic tone in Mickey's wording.

'I don't know. When he told me, I tried to tell him that they were leaving us alone, let them whack each other out, you know, business is good for us at the moment. After that meeting with Vinnie though, they just get my back up. On the drive back I was just itching to start it up.'

'We ain't gonna get close to D'Angelo.'

'Ugh. He wants us to do some of his capos. After that bullshit I just went through I'd be happy to go ahead.'

'He got you riled eh?'

'It's the fucking way they talk to you. Like you're a kid.' John shook his head and swallowed another whiskey. 'They talk about respect all the time, but they're mighty slow at giving it out.'

'I didn't think I'd see anymore bullshit with the wops in my time.'

'Ugh, those greasers, bullshit's their middle name.'

Vinnie had a card game going. It had been active all night. The sun would be up soon and his back was aching. He stretched in the chair and rolled his head, cracking the vertebra in his neck. It was drawing to a close and only Tommy and another soldier remained, having the stamina. He knew he would lose this hand, he had kept in, just bluffing, but now he was up to eleven grand and in the back of his mind he thought there was a chance. There wasn't. Tommy won and the other soldier cursed in Italian, gave Tommy the *Malocchio* then left, disgusted with his luck and his inability to call it quits earlier.

'He's a bad loser,' Tommy said with a laugh.

'So would you be if you'd just gone on the streets for the money.' Vinnie stood up.

'He borrowed.'

'Yep, off Didi.'

'Fucking degenerate.' Tommy began to collect the notes.

'I'm gonna make coffee. You want one?'

'Yeah. You gonna take me home?'

'Where's your car?'

'I gave it to cousin Joey earlier.'

'I don't understand how you let anyone drive your car.'

'It was a favor. You know what that is?'

'There's favors and favors. You don't know what the hell he's doing with it.'

'He's taking some broad out, no big deal,' Tommy said unconcerned, still gathering the cash and folding it.

'All I know is; you don't lend your car.'

Vinnie began to feel the effects of the hard living as they sat with their coffee. His eyes grew heavy and were sore from being cooped up in an enclosed smoky space. The conversation had run dry.

'Come on, let's get out of here.' Vinnie took out his keys and threw them to his brother.

'I'm driving?' asked Tommy annoyed.

'Yeah. You take me home, and then take the car. Pick me up later.'

'What was all that crap you gave me just now then?'

'You're my brother, that's different. Go start the car, get it warm. I gotta take a piss.'

'Yesir masser.'

Vinnie leaned across the bowl, propping himself against the wall with one hand. His head hung and his eyes were closed as he urinated. He grunted through tiredness. After he zipped up he pulled the chain and the place rocked. He stumbled against the wall, not knowing for a second where he was. In his ears there was a pop and a high pitch noise as if the whole of his inside was being sucked out from the small orifices. He covered them with his hands and his face contorted. He was in dark. Electricity had failed.

For a minute he tried to regain his balance, feeling like he was drunk or had been hit across the skull. Finally he found poise and with composure opened the door that led from the toilet to the club room.

It was pure devastation. The front of the building was opened up, glass and fragments of metal were scattered everywhere. Chairs and tables were gathered at the back wall as if someone had pushed them in fury to that position. Drinking glasses and cutlery were spilled about the floor. The bar along with its coffee machine, bottles of spirits, beer cooler were in a state of disorder and the air was a choking dust filled enigma.

Vinnie could smell a high tone of sickly burning rubber and down at his feet a wheel was smoldering. The sense knocked out of him, he still could not figure what had happened until finally the flames from outside registered in his vision. He rushed through the bombed out club through the new opening into the street, where his car was a contorted hellfire wreck, lying on its side. Vinnie tried to get close, but the intense heat pushed him back. He called for Tommy in desperation, knowing the reality, Tommy was gone.

Exhaustion finally swamped him and he sat on the curb stone, staring in disbelief at his brother's tomb. He gasped for breath and felt his eyes grow heavy once more, then slowly slipped backwards until he could feel the cold stone against his head. He looked up at the stars that filled the New York night, smoke drifted across his vision and the sound of sirens arrived from all directions.

The bombing sent more confusion throughout the ranks of the Cuccione Family. Silvio Dalla Bonna was one of the first to arrive at the hospital. He was greeted by the "Crazy" Paulie Marranzo. They embraced and kissed each other on the cheek.

'He's gonna be okay,' said Paulie. 'He's just suffering from shock and smoke inhalation.'

'That's good,' Silvio replied and put an arm around Paulie and lead him out of the hospital.

Outside they smoked. There were too many police and FBI inside, all wanting information.

'Any news on the street?' Paulie asked.

'Nothing.'

'I want these fuckers. I want them carved up for fish food.'

'You just calm yourself. Nobody knows anything yet,' said Silvio looking Paulie directly in the eyes.

'It's gotta be the remnants of Corsini's crew.'

'Nobody knows nothing yet and you'll keep yourself in check. I got enquiries going on now; you just calm that temper of yours. You keep holstered until Robbie or I say different. You hear me?'

'Yeah.' Paulie had a florid face and intense rage in his eyes.

'You stay with your family, they need you now. How's your mother?'

'She's a mess.'

'Well that's more of a reason for you to stay harnessed. You let us figure it out. You'll get your revenge. I'll send flowers, you need anything else, you call me.'

'Okay. Thanks mister Silvio.' The two men embraced again and Dalla Bonna drove to the airport to meet Robbie and Serge.

'We're gonna have to move fast on this. I don't want this family to begin in-fighting,' Robbie said as Silvio weaved through lanes of traffic. 'Bring in all the captains tonight.'

'Our sources will give us details of the bomb as soon as they know,' said Silvio, driving with one hand and lighting a cigarette with the other.

'What do you think Serge?' Robbie asked.

'Too early for Gigante and his Orleans friend. I doubt if it's any of Corsini's crew. Colombians maybe.'

'They do like car bombing,' Silvio said.

'Those fuckers wouldn't try it on here. But I hope it is outsiders. If it's one of our own, it's gonna weaken us. I knew something like this would happen. I wanted to delay it for longer though, the last thing we need is to be caught up in a war. I gotta keep an order or we can forget about it.'

'How was Chicago?' Silvio asked.

'We got the old bastard. He's gonna deliver Milwaukee, Cleveland and Detroit. We gotta quell this crap before I can proposition the families here.'

'I don't think you'll have a problem. The Molina and Sciorfa families have been losing too much power to the *stranieros*. The Gennazo's will do anything to keep the peace, they've always been weak.' Serge offered the truth.

'You're right, but if Gigante has already worked 'em over with his tongue. It's gonna be problems.' Robbie lit a cigarette.

'To be honest Robbie. I think Gigante's looking out for himself. If he can keep them in the dark, he will. Once he brings them in he's got to offer them something and then he's got to deliver. He wants everything. He'll keep them out.'

'I just hope it ain't the Colombians,' said Silvio.

'You really don't like them, do yer?' said Robbie.

'No I don't. They'll turn this city into Beirut. Just like they did Miami. They're animals.'

'They speak highly of you too,' Robbie joked.

'Fuck 'em. I'd be happy to send those fuckers back to Medellin.'

'Forget about them for now. We'll deal with them when the time comes.' Robbie tossed his cigarette out of the window.

That night, most of the Cuccione Family captains gathered around Robbie and he instructed them he would not accept civil war and told them not to worry because they were the Cuccione Family, the strongest and most feared, that he would guide them into a new age and as they in return offered their loyalty, three soldiers were gunned down in the city in a bar in full view of the drinking public.

Word came through of the massacre just after Robbie had sent his *capos* home. The news incensed him and for the first time he openly showed his rage.

'I'm gonna put a lot people in the fucking ground for this. Whoever's pushing is gonna suffer. If I turn the Sicilians loose there's gonna be no hiding place for these fuckers. It makes me look like a prick to my skippers. I can't have it.'

Serge said nothing, Silvio poured drinks. Robbie drank his in one go.

His face had transformed into an alabaster quality and the vehemence made him shake.

In west Manhattan, in a small Irish bar, the mood was adrenalin filled one. John O'Neil and Mickey Conway greeted the news of their first strikes with double shots of whiskey. Within the space of two days, John O'Neil had changed from a wavering mind back into the avid street soldier who killed without questioning. Inside he had rediscovered that surge of feeling that gives killers their high sense of emotion. Life in the Big Apple had been good, but it had been stagnant. Now the adrenalin was pumping once again, he had been a cold killer of his adversaries; he had ignited the touch paper of Dawson Culpepper's order and set New York ablaze.

John knew that missing Vinnie Marranzo could be seen as failure, but it did not matter, he had taken out one brother. Tonight he had managed to blow away three soldiers. No Irishman had achieved what he had against the Mafia in so short a time. There was no thought of the backlash, just of the continuing stealth strikes. Culpepper was good on his word, had sent the bombers and they had done a good job. Vinnie had taken the luckiest leak he would ever take in his life. If he had not felt the need to urinate, he would have been laying next to his brother in the mortuary. John did not dwell on it; he would go after Vinnie again.

Silvio received a call from his contact in the echelons of the legal world. They had identified the bomb. Semtex was the explosive proponent. It had been fixed onto the fuel tank, then wired into the ignition, once the ignition was engaged it sent the required electricity to the charge causing the devastating firestorm.

'So?' Silvio asked, looking for more information.

'The Arab terrorists use it a lot now.'

'Well it ain't Arabs,' said Silvio impatient.

'The Irish Republicans used it for years, were probably the first in the field. Of course they got an accord now with the British government, but there's still three tons of the stuff unaccounted for. The Republicans say they have disposed of it, but there's been no verification. I would say it's the Irish. You got problems with them?'

'Fuggedaboutit. I'll see you get what you need in a couple of days. You hear anything more I wanna know.'

'You got it.'

Silvio replaced the receiver then dialed Robbie.

'Robbie, I just got word.'

'Bad?'

'Bad as it could be. Something we didn't see.'

'Okay. Come over. I'll get a hold of Serge and Salvatore.'

'What about Vinnie?'

'No. He just got out of the hospital; we'll keep him in the dark for a while.'

Silvio arrived last. Robbie was already serving food, fried sausage and meatballs in a rich tomato and basil sauce along with gnocchi.

'Sit down, let's eat and talk,' instructed Robbie. Salvatore tucked in without further invite and Serge followed suit. Robbie handed a plate to Silvio and filled it. 'So what did you get?' Robbie asked before filling his mouth with a fork full of food.

'Well it was Semtex and it points most likely to the Irish.'

'The Irish.' Robbie repeated without emotion.

'Now the other day there was a beef with them and some of Vinnie's crew. Vinnie had a sit down with O'Neil. Apparently it was all straightened out.' Silvio talked with his mouth full.

'What was that crap over?'

'A bar fight, a nothing, not to warrant a car bomb anyways.'

'O'Neil's from Boston right?' Serge asked.

'Right.'

'And O'Neil is Culpepper's face here,' added Robbie.

'So this is about the Commission,' Serge continued.

'Serge, do you think Culpepper's zipped in with Gigante?' Robbie asked of his counselor.

'Can't see it. I would bank on Culpepper making this move alone. He's another outsider he's got an idea you're gonna cut loose.'

'A guy with his fucking millions. You'd think he would shuffle off into retirement,' Robbie said with a shake of the head.

'Last thing we need is bombs going off around here,' Silvio added.

'It's a message. He knows we can't fight a war right now. It's a smart move, he's telling us not to forget he's a major player,' Serge said.

'Get word to him, quell this,' said Robbie.

'Giving him a pass?' Silvio asked.

'For now but O'Neil's gonna go. It's only right the Marranzo's get their vengeance, not until I give word though. Any objections?' Robbie continued to eat, nobody disagreed.

Alone that evening Robbie struggled to find some relaxation. The events with the Irish were more debris he had to somehow configure. The pressure of juggling each of the factions, keeping the New York families from becoming aggravated and beginning a war, stabilizing his own Family so as there would be calm was taking a toll on his nerves. He drank a glass of wine and analyzed his decisions over the last eighteen months. The miscalculation of the Irish aggrieved him. In his reasoning though, he knew it was impossible to think of every eventuality. On the streets he knew that he didn't have the full trust and respect from all the soldiers, but his displacement of the old guard and installation of new captains was the correct action to take. Throughout the country, the dismantling of Murder Inc was greeted with relief. It was an antique which just did not sit well in the new age. The appeasement of Chicago was necessary, but Robbie knew time was short. Soon, people would want to be heard and the Commission could convene and order his hit.

Robbie was tired of male company. He had been surrounded twenty four hours a day lately and now there was a need in him for the touch of a woman. Compulsion and urge overtook the repressive emotion and he picked up the phone and dialed Angela.

Robbie and Angela had been having a stop-go relationship for four years. Robbie could never commit to her and she never tried to force him. Angela knew Robbie was a mobster, he never told her, but she knew, it was obvious. Deep inside her the pulse of love raged for Robbie and if she didn't see him for months at a time, when he called she exploded with joy and dropped whatever plans she had to see him.

10 COMFORT

ANGELA'S APARTMENT WAS AN HOUR DRIVE FROM Robbie who could not face it, so one of his Sicilian bodyguards drove him. Salvatore, until yesterday was Robbie's personal bulldog, but now he had been promoted and had a crew to run. The Sicilians that surrounded him closely, numbered four. They lived at his house and accompanied him around the city. A back up car followed him.

The street in uptown Manhattan where Angela lived was quiet. The cars toured for a while, cleaning themselves and checking out any potential threats. Nothing suspicious caught their eye and Robbie made his way to Angela's apartment block. The Sicilians stood around and smoked, conversing, but with a considered watchfulness.

Robbie pressed the intercom.

'Hello,' Angela's voice came through, crackling as if charged with static.

'Hi babe, it's me,' he said leaning into to the speaker.

'Who's me?' she asked.

'Come on, you know.'

'Hush. Could be anyone. What's that code?' she said and giggled.

'Come on Angie. It's gonna rain.'

'That ain't it.'

'You gonna make me say it?' Robbie asked with a sigh. He turned around to look at his garrison, who had noticed his delayed entrance and mobilized. Robbie held up his hand to indicate it was nothing and they went back to their talk.

'You don't get in otherwise.' Her giggles followed. Robbie shook his head and cleared his throat.

'Mary had a little lamb with fleece as white as snow, everywhere that Mary went the lamb was sure to go.' The words were recited in a staccato tuneless way. 'You happy? Open the door.' The buzz filled the doorway and Robbie pushed the door and entered.

Angela was waiting for him at the door, her smile radiated warmth which flowed throughout the corridor and Robbie returned her smile. She was wearing a towelling robe and her hair was wet and she cheekily opened it to give him a glimpse of her body, then pulled it tight around her just as quick. Robbie shook his head at her antics and once within distance pulled her to him and their mouths locked together. Angela pulled away, her breathing was heavy.

'Where you been stranger?' she said, looking up at him with dark eyes that emitted lightning.

'Work, you know.' He immediately went to his vague act.

'I won't ask, just as long as it ain't another woman.'

'Come on, that ain't me.'

Angela smiled and looked at him in a way that made him feel like a priceless piece of art.

'You gonna invite me in or we gonna stay out here all night?'

Angela took his hand and walked in, Robbie closed the door with his foot.

Angela went to get dressed and Robbie poured himself a coffee from the fresh brewed pot. While she dressed she talked from the other room.

'So what you been up to?' Her raised voice travelled through the place.

'Not a lot.'

'Yeah, that's fascinating,' she called ironically. Robbie furrowed his brow. 'You taking me out? I sure hope so,' she continued. Robbie screwed his face, he had not anticipated this. He wanted to stay out of the public as much as possible. Then he thought on it for a few minutes.

'You hungry?' he shouted back.

'I could eat. Sure.'

Robbie nodded and took the phone from his pocket, pressed through the phone book and hit the dial button. He listened to the ring and got through.

'Reggia di Calabria. Tony here,' said the voice along with background music.

'Hey T, it's Robbie.'

'Eh Robbie. *Come sta?*'

'*Bene*. How's business ?'

'Business is okay. Not so good tonight. When you coming to see us?'

'Well I was gonna come tonight.'

'You are, great.'

'I'm bringing Angie.'

'Hey no problem. I got two sittings that will be finished in about an hour. I'll close after that, we'll have the restaurant to ourselves, you, Angie, the family.'

'That's great T. Thanks.'

'No problem. Stella will be happy.'

'I'll bring her some chocolates.'

'No chocolates Robbie, she getting fatter everyday.'

Robbie laughed. 'I'll see you in an hour.'

'Okay.'

Robbie pressed end call and shouted to Angela. 'I'll take you to the Reggia. We'll have a good meal with T and his family.'

'Cool. I love their food.' She walked out from the bedroom and into the kitchen. Robbie looked at her. Angela had put on a tight black dress, which finished just above the knee. It perfected her figure. It was sexy, but not too revealing and Robbie knew she was not wearing underwear. She wore classy sling back shoes with a long pointed toe and stiletto, which accentuated the shape of her legs. Her long hair was pushed up tight and secured with a band; the long loose strands gave her a classic Italian look. Her eyes still shone.

'You look great,' he said.

'Well, you're worth the effort.' She flashed him a tantalizing smile. 'You gonna pour me one of those?'

'Sure. You want something stronger?'

'Not yet. I wanna remember tonight.'

'I'm sorry babe but all you get tonight is a fine meal and a good night kiss,' said Robbie with a seriousness and turned his back on her to pour coffee.

'Is that so?' Angela replied and leaned against the doorframe with folded arms and sad eyes. Robbie turned about to hand her the cup.

'I suppose I could fit you in for an hour or two,' he said and smiled.

'An hour or two ain't gonna cut it,' she took the cup.

'Okay, I'll stay,' he said, resigned.

'Is it such a chore?'

'There's a good fight on cable tonight.'

'Bastard.'

Robbie leaned into her and kissed her lips, which brought back her smile and joyous eyes.

When they exited the building Robbie motioned to his sentinels to take one car, he would drive with Angela. Once in the car Angela lit a cigarette.

'Who are those men?' she said, curious.

'They're friends.'

'Are they joining us?'

'No.'

'Robbie. Why do you need to travel with four friends?' she looked at him as he started the engine.

'They're just looking out for me. No big deal.' As Robbie pulled away Angela turned around briefly to see if the men were following. Robbie said nothing.

'It makes me nervous.'

'You got no reason to be nervous Angie.'

'Normal people don't go around with four bodyguards.'

'It's not …' Robbie sighed. 'It's my business Angie. In my line of work I make a lot of money for people. I'm susceptible to being attacked. My business demands I have protection.'

'And what is your business again?'

'I told you. I'm a corporate stock broker. I'm vulnerable in the outside world.'

'Robbie. I love you and you don't have to lie to me.'

'What do you mean?' he asked, turning to look at her.

'Robbie. I know you're a gangster. I'm an intelligent girl.'

'Gangster.'

'I don't care. I just want you to know I don't appreciate the lies.'

'Angie. Look, okay. I am what I am. But I lie to you to protect you. I keep you at a distance because I don't want you to have this kind of life. You seen just how worn out wives and girlfriends of mob guys look? It's a life of constant pressure and worry.'

'Are you telling me that I will never have a part in your life?'

'Yes. No. Angela. I'm in this life, forever. You don't get out. I'm trying to make it easier, more isolated and secure. It's gonna take hard work, but eventually I'll be there, then there'll be time for us to share a life.'

'And how long is that Robbie, ten, twenty years. We ain't getting younger Robbie.'

'And?'

'I might want children Robbie, a family.'

'I don't want to bring children into this life.'

'Then get out Robbie.'

'I told you,' said Robbie with a serious and iron voice. 'Nobody gets out.'

'Forget it.' Angela did not hide the annoyance.

'Come on. I thought we were gonna have a good night.'

'You just don't understand how I feel about you.' She stubbed her cigarette out in the ashtray furiously.

'I do babe, just don't ask me to do things I can't.' He reached for her hand. She did not pull away. 'Be patient, it'll work out.'

Reggia di Calabria was owned by Tony and Stella Agostini. In New York it was a well established restaurant. Their silent partner was Robbie but he was more than a partner to Tony and Stella, they looked upon him as family. Years back, Tony had borrowed money from a loanshark to fund a refurbishment. Tony found trouble in repaying the extortionate vig and the loanshark assumed a fifty percent partnership. That was the beginning of the real trouble for Tony. The loanshark would entertain wiseguys without paying a single bill, running up huge debt for Tony.

Robbie who had eaten there since forever and become a good friend listened to Tony's troubles one day. Robbie told his friend not to worry. Then one day, just after his famous Kennedy airport score he waited in the restaurant. When the loanshark came in for usual free ride he immediately saw Robbie and went over to be cordial. Robbie told him to sit down, he wanted to talk.

Robbie told the loanshark that the partnership was dissolved, he was going to be the new partner of Tony, he made a mental calculation of an amount he thought fair to pay off the outstanding loan, without any interest and insisted the man take it. The loanshark protested that this was not the right way to do things and Robbie once again insisted he take the deal, because to do things in a friendly manner was easier than doing it by violence. The loanshark succumbed finally and took the thirty thousand that Robbie placed on the table.

So Robbie had a piece of his first legitimate business and treated his partner fair. He never took more than twenty five percent of the profits and never abused his standing in the way of running up huge tabs and allowed Tony to pay back the loan over an extended period with nil interest. Tony and Stella loved Robbie and treated him as a son; Robbie treated them in the same fashion.

Upon arrival Tony, Stella, Robbie and Angela embraced and kissed each other, then Tony poured a round of drinks, the table was already set and Stella was doing the cooking. The pleasant varied smells wafted through the air.

'It's great to see you,' said Tony in high spirits and a genuine smile. 'And you Angela. How are you, why don't you come see us more often?'

'It's work, I'm always busy.'

'You young people, it's all work and no play. You need to enjoy yourself more.'

'That's what I keep telling Robbie,' she said and snuggled closer to Robbie.

'Awe. He's business business business. When you gonna start a family, you two?'

Robbie shook his head and Angela laughed.

'Never mind.' Tony turned in his chair. 'Stella,' he shouted, 'Leave the cooking for a while, come and have a drink.'

Stella appeared from the kitchen with a towel in hand. 'You want the food burned you crazy old fool?' she emphasized the point with hand gestures.

'Come and have one drink.'

'*Santa Maria* !' she exclaimed.

Robbie noticed that Simon their son was not present and asked about him.

'He has a new lady in his life. He might be around later,' said Tony.

'Huh. Always women with him, *per amor di Dio*. He thinks he's some kind of *donnaiolo*.' She threw her arms up in exaggerated emotion. Robbie and Angela looked at her quizzically. 'A lady-killer. He thinks he's a lady-killer,' she said sternly.

Tony smiled and took her hand. 'Times change,' he said.

'Huh,' Stella huffed and got up to return to the kitchen. When she was out of earshot the trio shared laughter.

Stella cooked too much food for the quartet and a good deal lay untouched on the table. Wine and cheeses followed and Tony looked at the food and sighed, he always hated to see good food go to waste.

'I've got four men outside who wouldn't turn their nose up,' Robbie said.

'I'll set them up a table,' said Stella.

'No, you don't need to trouble yourself.'

'Nonsense. They can sit down the back, it's quiet. I'll cook fresh pasta.'

'No Stella, you've done enough,' Robbie protested.

'It's no trouble,' she said, and it really wasn't.

Robbie went and summoned his men and Tony led them to a table, out of sight and earshot. He opened a bottle of wine and poured the first four glasses. The men began on the bread rolls and soon Stella brought out a big bowl of fresh pasta.

Stella made sure the men were comfortable then joined the others, she finished off her wine.

'I don't want you doing anything else tonight Stella,' said Robbie. Stella held her hand up and brushed his words away.

'Hey Robbie, we're going on vacation this year,' Tony said, getting the conversation started again.

'It's about time. How many years since you last had one?'

'Six years,' Stella said and raised her eyes while giving her husband a devilish look.

'Six years?' Angela said with astonishment.

'Well, it's been a busy period, you know, it's hard to just close down the restaurant and Simon ain't up to it. What can you do?'

'So where you going?' Robbie asked.

'Europe, for a month.'

'That's good.'

'Yeah. We start in Rome, go down to Naples and Sicily, then fly to Cannes, from there to Barcelona and Madrid, Paris, London and home.'

'You got room for one more?' Robbie said.

'Come if you want, the both of you,' said Stella.

'No. I'm kidding; I got too much to do.'

'There he goes again. He's all business. Angela, you better finda way to nail him down,' Tony joked.

'I'm working on it,' she said and clasped a hand over Robbie's

'You have to work harder. I want to go to a wedding soon,' Stella said, making Angela blush. 'Who wants some chocolate cake?'

'No,' said the others collectively.

'Okay, okay. I'll make coffee.' She walked to the bar and set about her business.

'Always on the go that woman and she chastises me for the same thing,' Tony gestured with his hands and lit a cigarette.

'I hear you, you crazy old fool,' Stella shouted from the bar.

Another couple of hours passed with the imbibing of coffee and amaretto until the pleasant evening drew to an end. Robbie's minders thanked Stella for the meal and she waved away their thanks but accepted their kisses. Robbie then embraced his hosts and they kissed Angela and told the both of them not to take so long to make another visit.

Outside Robbie spoke quietly for few minutes with the zips. He instructed them to follow him back to Angela's apartment, and then wait a few hours before they drove home as he was spending the night there. They asked if he was sure it would be safe, but Robbie insisted it would be fine.

The night was mild, sending out the message of approaching summer and when they got back to Angela's, she opened the French windows allowing the sounds of the New York night to fill the flat.

'You want coffee?' she asked.

'Something stronger.'

'Good, because I'm going to have a vodka.' She kicked off her shoes.

'You got any scotch?'

'Of course. You want Canada dry with that?'

'Yeah, please.' Robbie walked to the windows and stood at the railing guards, then took in the sight of the illuminated skyline. He lit a cigarette, lost in thought. Before him was a city that cried out to be loved and offered vast riches in return. A city that insisted you walk the tightrope between lawlessness and dogmatic law, the only centre ground was the organization. The Organization, a society built within a society. It had territories and laws and punishments. It had its soldiers, its politicians and businessmen. It had its history and its wars. Taxes, corruption and secrecy acts. What it did not have was a president, but Robbie knew that one day it would and the structure would be stronger, the foundations would be dug deeper and the fear would once again course through the legitimate society and maybe hold it to ransom, to secure its future. The magnitude was almost unforeseeable, but Robbie knew it was possible. His hallucination was broken by Angela, who slipped an arm around his waist and held a glass before his eyes.

'Thanks babe,' he said taking it.

'A penny for them,' she whispered into his ear.

'Just admiring the view. You got a great apartment.' He took a sip.

'Well, it costs enough,' she sighed, then broke away from him to get her drink.

'You need money?'

'No, jeez. I don't expect you to sort my problems out. I do work you know.'

'No need to get strung out Angie.'

'I can take care of myself,' she said, walking back into the room.

'I just offered, ain't no big deal.'

'I ain't a freeloader Robbie. I got a career and I make my own way,' she took a gulp from the glass looking at him with serious eyes.

'Forget it.'

'I'm sorry. I don't mean to snap, I'm just independent where some things are concerned.'

'It's forgotten about. Come over here,' he commanded.

'Why?'

'Coz I want to give you somin' good.' He had a peremptory manner in him. Angela walked slowly over to him and when she was in distance, he grabbed her waist with his free arm and pulled her to him. 'You are one sexy woman,' he said, then laid his mouth upon hers. They remained locked in that passion for ages, searching out each other, his hands running over her buttocks and she rubbing the front of his trousers, feeling the strength of his desire. Robbie broke away, took her glass from her and set it down along with his, then dragged her to the sofa, threw her upon it and pulled her dress up, exposing her bare haven to the cool night breeze; he wasted no time in reacquainting himself to her with his tongue. Angela gasped in passion.

Their intercourse moved from the sofa to the bedroom and when they were sated, they lay locked within each other, listening to one another's breathing and feeling the pulse of each other. Nothing outside mattered to them, just the short time comfort they shared.

11 STREETLIFE 2

DURING THE NEXT WEEK ROBBIE GOT WORD to the Boston mobster Culpepper; that he was willing to talk. It bought some time and insured them against further attacks. At the end of the week Tommy "Machine Gun" Marranzo was to be buried, or at least what could find of him. Robbie addressed the forthcoming funeral by paying all the expenses, which touched the Marranzo's. Two days before the funeral Vinnie was summoned to see Robbie.

'How you feeling?' Robbie asked sincerely.

'I'm fine.'

'I'm sorry for your loss. When we lose one of our own, it hurts us all.'

'Thanks boss. And thank you for all your help, you know with the funeral and everything.'

'Don't mention it. I know this ain't the best time to meet and talk about what we got to talk about but I've kept you in the dark the last week or so.'

Vinnie looked at Robbie, Silvio and Serge quizzically.

'We thought it best, why you were getting right,' added Serge. Vinnie nodded.

'I'll get right to the point. We know who it was,' said Robbie.

Vinnie moved with agitation, anger was evident as color drained from his face. Robbie acted to nullify the emotion.

'You will get the go ahead to take your revenge, but for now, you have to let it slide and it's important that you keep your brother on the leash. I know he's insane now and fiery at the best of times, he has trouble with his temper. We all know this, but you must keep him in check now, it's important to the Family.'

'I understand. Who?' Vinnie said, the thirst to know evident.

Robbie looked at Silvio and Serge, they both nodded.

'The Irishman, O'Neil.'

'That cocksucker, over that fuckin' small beef with some of my crew,' Vinnie scowled and lit a smoke.

'It goes deeper than that Vinnie. I ain't gonna tell you everything just yet, but it's a commission problem, complicated shit. The Boston Irish had a hand in it but that's my problem. O'Neil and Mickey Conway are yours; you do with them what you please. But not...until I give the word. You clear on this?'

Vinnie nodded. His eyes were still glazed with rage, 'Yeah,' he said through gritted teeth.

'I'll give you my apologies now Vinnie, 'cause I can't make it to the wake. I'll be at the funeral, pay my respects.'

PAULIE & AL

Two days after the funeral of his brother, "Crazy" Paulie Marranzo and his best friend Al Bondini were taking another drive down to Virginia, to hook up another shipment of heroin bound for New York. Paulie was uncommunicative, which put Al on edge. He smoked and drove on automatic. Finally the silence broke him.

'You okay?' he said.

'Yeah, I'm okay. For a guy that just buried his brother.' Paulie lit a cigarette, with vacant, cold eyes.

'I'm sorry man. I'm just a little worried about you.'

'Awe, fuck it. Life goes on right. Tell you the truth, I'm tired of these trips and I'm running out of excuses to cover myself. I can't stash any more money in my garage. I didn't think I'd ever say I had that kinda problem with money,' he chuckled.

'We maybe oughta think about banking it?'

'We need connections for that, quiet ones. They find out about this junk money, they ain't getting an end, forget about it, I'll see you in hell.'

'There's gotta be a way to wash it.'

'There's loads of ways, I just don't have any connections that ain't mobbed up. Any ways, I was thinking we should bring in some other guys.'

'You serious?' said Al.

'We can't keep making these trips, we gotta find someone else. We need someone unconnected, clean, though. You know anyone?'

Al looked at Paulie. 'No one I trust enough.'

'You know who'd be good for this?'

'Who?' replied Al.

'Your cousin, the boxer, what's his name?'

'Gary. Give me a fuckin' break.'

'He can handle himself; he ain't making out too good in the fight game is he?'

'No, that's beside the point. It means I got to bring in someone from my family and even that ain't enough for me to trust 'em.'

'He'd do fine. He can handle himself, he knows you're connected. He wouldn't fuck us over.'

'He might not fuck us over with money and shit, but I can't vouch for him keeping his mouth closed if he got pinched Paulie. You're asking a lot.'

'I suppose. We gotta find someone though. Now Tommy's gone it's gonna be harder than ever to get away from the store.'

'It'll work out.'

'Find a place to eat, I'm starving.'

As they sat tucking into their food Paulie smiled at Al. Al motioned with his chin a question.

'You know my big brother's a top man now?'

'Yeah, everyone knows that.'

'He knows you're my guy, I vouch for you. You made some good money for him. You got respect, people like you. When they open up the books, I'm gonna put you forward.'

'Jeez Paulie.' Al put down his knife and fork. 'I really appreciate it.'

'You might not get it. He's a capo, he's got considerations himself, but I'd fucking do it for you.'

'You're a fucking crazy man. I know what it takes, thanks bruv,' Al showed a tearful smile and they shook hands across the table.

'You are my brother, not just my friend,' said Paulie.

'Always man.'

BROOKLYN

In south Brooklyn area on the edge of Jamaica Bay, a car drove through Canarsie and came to a halt near the curb stone. The four men were from Salvatore's new crew. From across the street they looked at the house in question.

'That it?' said the driver; a scar faced stocky built man.

'Yeah,' answered the passenger. The two men in the back lit cigarettes, said nothing.

'You're sure?' said the driver.

'Yeah, that's it. That's where the Colombian mutherfucker lives.'

'And you say he's got a quarter mil stashed in there.'

'That's the info I got.'

'Tell me from who again?' the scarred one persisted.

'Fuck Pete, I told you three times. I did a deal for some funny money with this spic, it went sour, but he put me onto this. The guy that lives here is a coke dealer and the money is there.'

'But what I'm saying is this. Your man didn't come through with the other deal, how can you be sure he's on the level?'

'I gave the prick a beating. He ain't gonna lie to me now.'

'And there's no security?'

'He's got three pit bulls. He lives here alone, he's very low key. No wife, no kids, a girlfriend that comes and goes irregularly. And he's down in Florida from tomorrow.'

'He's got no crew?' Scarface lit a cigarette.

'He's got a big crew, but he don't do business here. He ain't a usual flash spic; he keeps out of the light, does his thing very quietly.'

'So how does your man know the money's there and why ain't he doing it?'

'Look Pete. The guy looks after the dogs from time to time. The last time he was there, he found the money while looking for dog food. It's in the pantry, hidden in one of those big bags of doggie dry mix. He ain't got the balls to pull it off.'

'And how much he want?'

'Fifty grand, but he ain't getting it, 'cause I'm whacking him out after. I don't want this jackoff on the streets with my name on his tongue.'

'That's good. If we do it and the dough's there, that's fifty each for us and fifty for Sally. Okay?'

'Fine with me,' said the passenger. The two in the back nodded in agreement.

'Who's feeding the dogs this time?' Pete continued.

'His girl I suppose. I don't know.'

'We don't know the money's there for definite.'

'No. Do you ever on a score like this?'

'Point taken.' Pete looked across at the house again. 'Nice place.'

'Yeah,' said one of the men in back.

'Okay, fuck it. Tomorrow night, we're on.' He turned the ignition and pulled away.

A heavy rain came down the night of the heist, which gave the thieves an added sense of security. Pete, pulled over near the house and killed the headlights and engine. One of the men in the back took out a gun and screwed in a silencer. They got out and quickly got off the street into the vicinity of the house. The house had a shingle stone drive, but the rain masked their footsteps.

Because the house was set back from the street, they decided to go in through the front. One of them took out a crowbar and pushed the flat edge into the doorjamb near the deadlock, he exerted pressure and part of the wood splintered and came away. Again he repeated his action and split the doorpost along a seam. After he slipped in the bar using the other end and pushed in the opposite direction, the casing for the strike plate gave same play, noise was made, which the night rain covered. The man continued to manipulate the deadbolt, until the force caused the lock to pop from the housing, the pressure of the now misaligned door caused the hinges to twist and all the man did to gain entry was slip an old credit card between the latch and strike and slip the lock. The whole process took about eight minutes. The men entered.

The house was silent and the water dripped off them onto the wooden floor, an upstairs light, left on, gave them some vision. One had a flashlight and switched it on, using it like a searchlight to scour the place. Then the house filled with sound, they heard the furious patter of paws rushing out toward them and the menacing deep throated growl as the three pit bulls came at them like a furious tornado.

The man with the silencer equipped gun blew the first dog away with a single shot; it slid across the wood floor and crashed into a wall. The second shot hit the next dog in side, the dog let out yelp as the breath was knocked from him, the legs went from him and he lay splayed out breathing heavily. The third dog managed to get to one of the men, but it was his misfortune to choose the crowbar wielding thief and the metal slammed into his jaw knocking out several teeth. The dog let out a sound which resembled the call of a wolf; he was quickly silenced by a bullet in the head.

The wounded dog lay looking at the foursome with pleading eyes of mercy. His labored breaths filled the open plan hallway. The man with the gun went over to him and pointed the gun at him then stood as if frozen.

'Kill him,' said Pete.

'I can't,' said the shooter.

'Whatta fucks the matter with you? You just blew the other two away.'

'That was different, they were vicious. He's just lying here, suffering.'

'Well put him outta his fuckin' misery.'

'I can't do it.'

'Give me the fucking gun,' said Pete pulling it from the man's hand, who instinctively looked away as a silent shot ended the grotesque episode. 'Some fucking wiseguy you are,' said Pete emotionless, handing the gun back to him. 'Come on.'

It took little time for three of the men to find the pantry. One of them stayed near the door, at the scene of the massacre as lookout. The three men tore through the cupboards until they found the bags of dry mix, they pulled them out and found one tucked away at the back, already opened. Upon pulling apart the re-seal they looked at each other. The flashlight illuminated a stack of money. One of them let out a slow whistle.

'There's more than a quarter mil there, I fucking know,' said Pete.

'I reckon about six hundred,' added one. Then they smiled.

'Yeah. But it was two fifty, right,' said Pete, confirming that that was the figure they would claim. Salvatore, their new captain would get his end of fifty grand, nothing more. The two others nodded in agreement.

'Let's get the fuck outta here.'

As they walked back towards the exit, the posted sentry, standing among the corpses of dogs asked how they did.

'We did great. Come on, let's go.'

SUGARLAND BAR & GRILL

Sugarland was a frequent haunt for New York mobsters, especially those from the Cuccione Family. When the quartet from the Colombian score walked in a few hours later they were confronted by a sea of mob guys from the Sciorfa Family. Only a few Cuccione soldiers were in attendance. The Sciorfa soldiers were celebrating the release from prison of one of their captains. Freed after a four year stint on appeal. They were in high spirits, loud, rowdy and an air of arrogance hovered over them.

Pete and his three comrades pushed through to the bar, nodding hello, now and then shaking hands with gangsters they knew. There were no civilians present, the atmosphere was too intimidating.

At the bar they found "Mickey Spats" a respected Cuccione soldier, sitting alone.

'Hey Mickey. What's up?' said Pete putting his arm across Mickey's shoulders.

'Petey "Two Cents" how you doing?' replied Mickey.

'You know me, ain't got two cents to rub together.' It was his line and from where he coined his street sobriquet.

'Ain't doing too well eh?'

'That's what I said. What the hell is all this?' he asked and tried to summon the overworked bartender with a wave of the hand.

'Sonny Milan, got out today. He's over the back there, telling his fucking war stories,' explained Mickey in a lowered voice.

'They let that prick out, they should have thrown away the key,' said Pete.

'Hey, keep it down.'

'Fuck em. Why ain't they in one of their streets?'

'What can you do?'

'Look at this. I gotta wait on line.' He gave a shake of the head as a Sciorfa man brushed against him, without the offer of an apology. Mickey put a hand on Pete's back and patted it.

'Let me get this drink,' said Mickey.

'Sure. Fuck em' right,' said Pete, loud enough for some of the opposition to pick up. They looked at him and he returned them a hard look. For a while a tension of testosterone charged the air between them. The three men with Pete moved closer to back him up and the stand-off went cool.

Sugarland Bar & Grill was owned independently but Cuccione members made it a place of their own. The owner was on good terms with them, he let them run up tabs. Never hassled them and there was a genuine respect for him, they paid their tabs eventually and he allowed them to go about their business unmolested. At times he bought stolen goods from them and once he threw a gratis engagement party for a soldier. It helped to keep on their good side. It was a known Cuccione Family establishment and rarely do opposing Family soldiers mix.

Mickey, Pete and his *goombatas* sank many drinks. The score did not get a mention, because even though Mickey was a family member, hoods didn't discuss recent take-downs, not until months, sometimes years later. They didn't have too, because the kick-up of dollars to the boss done their talking. What they did talk about was politics, street politics. Recent hits and promotions. Murder Inc being consigned to the history books was a big topic. Nobody expected to see it in their lifetime.

'I didn't like D'Angelo. I mean at first, but you gotta hand it to him, he's got balls,' said Mickey.

'Yeah. He's a mover and shaker. It's good to see this Family strong on the streets again. The old fuck was all big business; he didn't give a fuck about us on the street.' Pete drained his glass. 'Same again?' he asked of Mickey.

'Thanks,' Mickey nodded.

'You three having the same?' he said. The three men, in their own conversation stopped and responded.

'Hey Nicky,' he called to the bartender as he passed.

'I'll be with you in second Petey,' replied Nicky.

'Fuck these hard-on's, serve the regular clientele first.'

'What's your fuckin' problem pal?' said a Sciorfa partisan close by.

'What?' said Pete with violence as he turned to the man.

'You heard me.'

'I did, then how come I'm asking again? Perhaps I'm stupid. Is that it?'

'You been making disparaging remarks all night pal. We're a little sick off it.'

'You are. Well I tell you what, you line up and we'll line up, if that's the way you wanna go, I'll phone my bookie and lay the bet that after, the only guys left standing in here will be us. This is our place. You come down here, mobbed up and give us shit, but we're standing here and we're gonna keep standing here and I'll say whatever I like and don't ever think you can tell me different.' Pete stared the man until he broke.

'Fuck it,' said the man. Around them the talk had died as they all listened, the beef filtered back to Sonny Milan and he made his way over.

'What's the problem?' he asked. Sonny Milan was an imposing figure, he moved through life with a typical gangster air.

'Hey Sonny. I was just telling your man here to show a little respect. After all it is our place,' said Pete, in a friendly but steadfast manner.

'Petey "Two Cents." How you doing?' he held out a hand, Pete took it. 'We don't want any aggravation. We're just celebrating. What you drinking?'

'That's okay. I'll buy this.'

'Come on, let me get it.'

'Sonny, no. You just got out you're in our place, I'll get it.'

'Okay. Life's too short though, what do you say. We ain't staying long anyways. We're going to that new strip joint uptown. Come along.'

'I might.'

'Good. You come to me you got a problem with any of my guys. Okay?'

'Okay, Sonny.' They shook hands and Sonny walked back to his table.

JFK AIRPORT, QUEENS

Billy "Diamonds" picked up the truck from a lot in Forest Hills. It was plain white, not sign written and had false plates. The cargo space was empty, apart from a box which contained three uniforms and three temporary magnetic strips, which had the name of a bogus company embossed on them. Billy put two signs on each side panel and one on the hood, and then quickly changed into one of the uniforms. He opened the dash compartment and checked the paperwork, made a call on his mobile. After a short conversation he drove away, heading for Howard Beach. There he made a rendezvous with Tony "The Wop" and Joe "Grease". All three, Marranzo crew members. Tony and Joe were cousins of the Marranzo's, both in their late twenties and both tough street hoods. Billy "Diamonds" was unrelated by blood in his late thirties and was known as a good thief. He had many connections at JFK and the surrounding airfreight industry and because of this had made stealing from the airport an art. JFK was a gold mine and very little risk was involved.

'Check that paperwork out,' he said to his passengers after they had changed while driving along the Southern Parkway.

'Looks good to me,' said Tony. Joe "Grease" shrugged.

'Of course it looks good. It's genuine.'

'So what we getting?'

'Computers fresh in from Korea.'

'You got this place sewn up alright,' said Tony.

'Most of it. You gotta get in with the people; treat 'em right. Like the guy who's arranged this, he's getting two grand and for what, pulling off documentation. He gets a bigger bonus for that than his company profit share. You take care of the people and they do this shit all year round.'

'It'd be cheaper to just hijack a load,' suggested Joe as he lit a cigarette.

'It would eh? Well go and do one then, see just how much profit you make. You wanna be smart you gonna work the airport. Too many guys screw up being stick up men, end up with a truck load of shampoo or tampons, and see how much dough you get for that crap. You gotta work this place like a snake. I know exactly what's coming in, what I want, what I don't. What I can move, what I can't. You know so better, go show me.' Billy looked across at Joe, but he did not respond.

'Yeah. Shut up Joe, listen and learn,' Tony said aggrieved.

'Fuck you.'

'No fuck you. Always a wise ass.'

'Both of youse shut up or I'll crack your skulls together,' Billy ordered.

Joe sighed with nonchalance.

'We'll be there in two minutes. Act like you know what you're doing, don't be standing around waiting for me to tell you what to do.'

'I know what to do. Ain't the fuckin' first score I been on,' Joe responded.

'Well see.'

Tony gave Joe a surreptitious nudge in the ribs. Joe gave one back.

Billy "Diamonds" turned into an industrial area and slowed his speed as he pulled up to the Transway Express terminal. He turned around and reversed up to the bay. A night worker came out with a security guard and the three men jumped out.

Billy lifted himself up onto the bay.

'How you doing chief?' he said, addressing both men.

'What you got for us?' asked the night worker.

'Nothing. I'm collecting.'

'Yeah. Didn't know we had anything going out,' the man looked puzzled.

'I was supposed to be here before five. Got jammed up with a late delivery upstate.' He handed the man his paperwork. 'Yeah, we been on the road since six this morning.'

'That's a pisser,' replied the worker looking at the paperwork. 'Awe, there's been a screw up here.'

'What's that?' Billy leaned in to look at the paperwork.

'This stuff ain't meant to go till Monday.'

'You're kidding me. You mean I drove all the way out for nothing,' he shook his head and looked at Tony and Joe, to gage their reaction. They were keeping their nerve.

'Nah, it's gonna be alright, it's just we got it right at the back of the unit, we're gonna have to move a lot of crap to get to it. Might take forty minutes or so.' The man handed the paperwork to the security guard for booking out.

'That's alright.'

'You guys want some coffee, there's a machine in there, takes quarters. If you want something to eat, there's an all night burger stand just up the road, they do good food and there's a nice piece of skirt that works there,' the worker smiled.

'We'll take the coffee, pass on the food, I want these kids to work tonight, you know how they are, a piece of skirt and balls full of cum I won't get a cents worth out of 'em,' he smiled back.

'I know what you mean. I got a few like that here. The machines just in there to the right. I'll get started on it for you.'

'Thanks chief,' said Billy.

'No problem.'

They waited on the bay, sitting, drinking coffee and smoking, listening to the sounds of aircraft engines from the airport and the various noises of airbrakes from the eighteen wheelers rolling in and out. Shouts and laughs from night workers and high volume music form some nearby unit. Forklifts moving pallets. An industry, legitimate and alien to them. The night was balmy and they enjoyed the wait, without the nerves of a usual heist.

Billy pulled up the roll shutter on the truck as the first of the five pallets was delivered to the bay. Tony tore off the shrink wrapping and they formed a chain and loaded the big boxes quickly. They finished before the next pallet arrived. In all they collected one hundred and fifty home computers. They were a full package, monitor, keyboard, tower, speakers, and mouse, originally destined for a store in the city. Now they were headed for the streets, to be sold at half the price, but one hundred percent profit to the pirates.

As they finished loading the last pallet they had worked up a sweat. Billy was out of breath. The night worker laughed at them as he piled the pallets up.

'Tough eh?' he said.

'I work too many hours, there's got to be a better way to earn a living,' Billy said.

'Don't I know it,' agreed the man. He walked over with the paperwork and handed Billy a pen. Billy signed and printed a false name. Then was given a copy, then the man signed Billy's paperwork and took a copy, handed the rest over.

'Thanks chief, have a good night,' Billy said.

'That's impossible here. I could think of a thousand things I'd rather be doing,' he joked.

'I got a thousand and one,' Billy said and they shared a laugh.

'Drive safe.'

'Will do, see ya around.'

The man held up a hand as he climbed back on his forklift, took the pallets away and closed the shutter. The trio of thieves got in the truck and drove away. Billy immediately made a phone call to his fence.

'I got a hold of the Jap,' Billy said.

'He got the tickets?'

'Yeah.'

'Okay. When?'

'About an hour,' Billy said.

'See you then.'

They hung up.

After the carve up, minus expenses for the buying of certain necessities, the kick up to their capo, the trio would clear about seven and half grand each. It was peanuts considering that they had just stolen over a hundred thousand dollars worth of computers. Put it into context of a few hours work though, it equates to a baseball players wage and on the street, money is king.

VIRGINIA

Al pulled into the Arbour Motel, Paulie was asleep, so he woke him.

'What?' he said, his voice heavy with tiredness.

'We're here.'

'Yeah,' he rubbed his eyes and sat up to eyeball the parking lot. The switch car was there with two men sitting inside. Paulie got out, looking around as he walked over to them. Al, stepped out from the car and leaned on the door, watching. From the switch car the driver got out and greeted Paulie. They went around the back and opened the trunk. Paulie looked inside for a few seconds, slammed the lid shut. The passenger got out and the trio walked over to Al, who followed the lead, went to the back of the car and lifted the lid. All four stood together at the trunk and one of the men lent in to check what he wanted. He came back up and nodded, then Paulie exchanged ignition keys, the men shook hands and dispersed their own ways. The transaction proceeded smoothly, as it should, but drug deals sometimes go sour resulting in violence and death. Paulie and Al were aware of the risks, and so far had had no problems. But Paulie was becoming aggrieved because each time he made the transaction it turned out to be different people. His thinking turned to imagination of a situation where he could get jacked one day, simply because the people he was dealing with were getting richer and more powerful. They were refining the smuggling and importing more kilos per month. Paulie knew they would soon demand more money or employ a cowboy who would get greedy and cause a problem. It was part of the reason he wanted another party to carry out the switch over. He wanted to insulate himself, not only from his Afghani connections, but from the Family. The dealings were unsanctioned and he was withholding kick up money to his captain, his brother. If it was discovered he could hit.

Business on the streets was a twenty four hour industry, it never stopped. It was one constant turning mill of scams and heists, raking in a collective fortune for the mob and causing misery for the average citizen. The younger generation of mobsters was part of a new culture. They were imbued with the pizzazz of modern brashness, devoid of the secrecy for which the mob was known. A recklessness ran through them and drugs were increasingly becoming a part of the culture. They were an MTV generation, using drugs because it was a fashion requirement.

It was one reason why Robbie D'Angelo had began to build a family with a backbone of Sicilians. They had hard old fashioned values, understood respect and honour and they thought that most of the Americans were too spoilt and soft. Robbie D'Angelo thought this way too and eventually would use his Sicilian cousins to clean house.

12 THE SICILIANS

SALVATORE GRECCO WAS BORN IN PALERMO, TO a father who was a butcher and mother who mended clothes for a living. He had three brothers and two sisters. His family name he changed when he was eighteen. His father had disowned him when he found out he was involved with the Mafia, that ancient society that brought shame to their beautiful and tragic island.

Salvatore's father did not try to rescue his son from the clutches of those talons, he outcast him, to save his own family name from being blemished and dishonored. Salvatore changed his name partly as a measure of respect to his blood and as a severance of finality from them. He had not spoken to any of his family from that day forward. During the following years he knew his parents had died, had seen his brothers and sisters around Palermo from time to time, but never felt a need to contact them.

Mafia wars were a constant in Sicily but none more so than the turbulent past times, when the violent Corleonese began to embattle the Palermo family when Salvatore was a well known trigger man within the Palermo faction. But like so many soldiers, he could not seem to get the recognition he deserved and the outbreak of war gave him an opportunity to move. He joined the Corleone faction and become one of their most vicious murderers.

He was a main instigator in the plot that resulted in the bombing of Judge Falcone's car. It was the height the Corleonese reached, their tentacles throwing out punches at the Government as they slipped into the depths of insanity, transiting themselves into terrorists and causing public outcry and disdain the length and breadth of that booted country. Not satisfied with the bloodletting they turned inward to fight among themselves as paranoia of informers and overthrow took hold.

The madness became too much for Salvatore when the Corleonese murdered a suspected informer and slaughtered his whole family, including a child of five years. Salvatore, sickened by this lack of honour deserted and hid in a monastery at Menfi, working on the farmland for the monks of the St Francis order.

For Salvatore it began a year long period of contemplation. His philosophical side arose and he began to question the motives for the man he had become. Remorse entered him one night and did not leave for six months. A need to apologize gripped him until he resisted no more and travelled quietly to Palermo to visit the graves of his mother and father, where he laid a rose upon each and offered to them all that remained in him, his tears. Once he had purged himself and made his peace he came to realize the strength of the oath he taken, the life he chose was etched onto his soul. He was Mafia, until the grave.

During his year long exile the Corleone faction was smashed, the Palermo family took control and restored order, trying to repair the damage which had once again beset an island whose history was embroiled with invasion and turmoil.

Vendetta. The word could be unique to the island of Sicily. People do not forget in that sun soaked island. Any slight is ingrained into the next generation, like fairy tales passed onto children. The *lupara* is the justice of the land. Once a dishonour is served, that dishonour must be avenged, it is never forgotten. The context of this makes Salvatore Grecco and his story unique.

No vendetta was ever unleashed upon him by Palermo. It went against all reason that he should be allowed to live, but allowed he was and welcomed back into the faction he had deserted. His life had come full circle, back into the city where he was born and back into the fold of an organization where he would never be nothing more than a soldier.

Then America called. His first visit lasted four weeks to carry out two hits, the second, for two weeks for a hit that was cancelled. His third was to meet Robbie D'Angelo for a major hit. It was three of his bullets that put an end to the life and reign of *Don* Costello and helped make D'Angelo the boss. It was Robbie who persuaded him to stay and be his personal pit-bull and Robbie who had now made him a captain.

Now he was American, he held an American passport, social security number, driver's license. His heart and the blood that pumped through it would always be Sicilian and in most ways, his thinking.

For his trio of bosses; Robbie, Silvio and Sergio he had the utmost respect. They were tough, inside. They had a strong sense of reasoning and cunning likened to a Sicilian. But for the average American street mobster, he had nothing but disdain. They were too spoilt for his liking, they lacked control. He saw too much self destruction in their drug and gambling abuse and their recklessness reminded him of the Corleonese back in the old country.

He understood the problems Robbie was tackling. In Sicily, there were only Sicilians. In America, there was everybody. And in the street soldiers, he saw a problem the same size and shape as outside factions; which is one of the reasons he decided to make an example of a coke sniffing soldier under his command.

Salvatore Grecco, the Sicilian who had killed more than thirty people, who had found refuge and solace in a monastery, then his way back into the honored society, America, a new life and a position of standing decided alone on what justice to met out to insubordinates under his control.

At a gathering of his regime, he extracted the offender. A young man who was a good earner, through his coke dealing, but like so many others, had a liking for the Inca powder.

He made the man sit at the table and placed a kilo bag before him, sliced it open with his stiletto blade then had another zip put a gun to the man's head and ordered him to sniff. The young man, shaking with fear began, deciding to take his chances with the white powder rather than the bullet. He had four seizures and vomited three times until finally his heart exploded. It took a little under an hour for him to die.

'You deal the *cocaina*, thatsa fine. Nobody take it. You die. Capeesh.' Salvatore had laid down the law and shown them the penalty. Throughout the Cuccione Family other penalties would be carried out upon those who took drugs. The Sicilians would carry out the justice. They were cleaning house.

The Sicilians were ruthless, devoid of compassion, lacking remorse and stamping a fear into the hearts of the street soldiers. Within two months, a third of abusers had cleaned up their act and the Sicilians had enhanced their reputation to the point where they were more feared than the defunct Murder Inc.

It was the new order of Robbie D'Angelo, taking effect, dispelling complacency and ensuring his position at the head of the throne. New York was being remodeled into a new bastion of strength. The other families began to follow suit, clean up their soldiers and become what they once had been. The Mafia. The powerhouse of American organized crime.

Robbie had a strong backbone now. With Silvio Dalla Bonna as his underboss and the Sicilians as his enforcers, with Chicago and the outlying families as close associates he knew that Gigante and the Badalamenti Family would be outgunned. If Gigante made a move, it would be his doom.

13 POLITICS

SUSAN RUSHDIE PARKED HER CAR IN HER allotted space. She got out and leaned back in to grab her briefcase, locked the door and activated the alarm with the remote then arranged her suit, which was a maroon color, with a not too short skirt but enough to give her power. Her stiletto shoes gave her added height which magnified the power she now held.

Susan Rushdie had a strong structured face, prominent cheek bones and a mouth of authority. She had fashioned her straight hair so it was pulled back across her face, her forehead was strong and there was a tough bitch air about her.

Before going up to her apartment she walked down to the local store, to buy a ready meal and a bottle of wine. There was much paperwork for her to catch up on that evening and she did not have time for socializing. She was approaching her fortieth birthday, single, no children, a hardcore careerist. Throughout New York and Washington political circles she was affectionately known as "The Head-hunter." She had a big budget and free license to smash organized crime.

The night was warm, her day had been long and she walked slowly to the store with a vacant mind. At the store as she decided upon what to eat, her appetite deserted her so instead she settled on two bottles of expensive white wine. At the register she paid and had a friendly conversation with the store owner, then took her leave.

Back out on the sidewalk from behind her someone called.

'Susie.' The voice was distinctive and she whirled around catching a sight of a man she once dated and still had strong feelings for. For a second a smile formed, but she quickly buried it.

'Robbie,' she said astounded. 'Robbie?' she then asked, wanting confirmation.

'How you doing Susie?'

'What? What are you doing here?' For all the power she showed in her professional life, face to face with Robbie D'Angelo it cheated her. A feeling of vulnerability swamped her, making her feel like a child again.

'Let me take you to dinner. We should talk,' said Robbie as he moved toward Susan.

'I can't,' she hesitated, her mind full of conflicting emotions and unresponsive countermeasures.

'Yes you can.'

'I have work to do, I have, I've got too many things to do. I just can't drop my life at the drop of a dime. '

'Yes you can Susie. I noticed you couldn't decide what to eat, bought wine instead. That ain't no kind of sustenance for a hard working girl like you. Come on. It's my treat.' Robbie took her by the arm, gently shepherding her to his car. Susan resisted, and then broke away from him.

'I can't be seen in public with you Robbie. What are you thinking?'

'Fine, we'll go up to your place. I'll cook if you like.'

Susan stared into his eyes, shook her head, then looked around, to see if anyone was watching. Her face had turned a nervous alabaster shade.

'Nobody's watching. You don't have a thing to worry about,' Robbie said.

'Really,' Susan said with anger. 'You can come up, but I want you to leave when I ask you to.'

'You got it.'

Once in the apartment and on home soil, her nervousness did not abate as she had hoped; she was not in control of the situation and this made her dizzy.

'I need a drink.' Her voice was stern but shaky. 'You want one?'

'Sure.'

'Well, what do you want?' Susan sounded ridiculous the more she tried to convey control.

'I'll take a Jack and coke if you've got it.' Robbie lit a cigarette.

'Jack and coke,' she repeated emptily. She poured the drinks and they stayed in the kitchen, standing. It was her best effort to keep Robbie from entering her life any more than was necessary.

Susan drank almost half a bottle of wine before Robbie had finished his first Jack and coke. She chain smoked as her nerves dictated to her.

'What do you want Robbie?'

'I have to say I'm impressed with what you've achieved.'

'Oh fuck you. Tell me what you want or get the hell out.'

Robbie offered her a half smile which she did not appreciate. He helped himself to another drink, filled it with ice.

'Okay Susie. I know who you are, you know about me. I'm ready to do a deal with you, off the record.'

'I don't make deals,' she replied in fury.

'You're in politics, it's all about deals.'

'Don't try and compromise me by bracketing me in the same sleaze pit as other so called politicians. It might come as a surprise to you, but my department is not only charged with taking down organized crime, but corrupt politicians too.'

'Well it's about time.'

'You're a contemptuous bastard.'

'Why you getting so personal?'

'Because I despise you and everything you stand for,' she shouted in a fit of pique.

'And what do I stand for?'

'You stand for disorder, corruption. You have an apathetic dissolution for the laws of this country. You go through life unfeeling and uncaring about the destruction you bring to communities, you have no respect or regard for the suffering you impose upon people. That's why I despise you.'

'You know Susan, to hear you speak; I'd think you were prejudiced against Italian-Americans.'

'Fuck you.'

'Sure, fuck me. You know Susan for a woman with all these qualifications and an intelligence of understanding you really do not see the world.'

'No. Tell me then big shot,' she responded with a raised voice and poured more wine.

And Robbie unleashed his vitriol upon her.

'Does my organization have a C.I.A? People who play chess with millions of lives globally. Did we create a space agency that wastes billions of dollars on pointless explorations while children still live in ghettos in this fine nation? Do we create wars over oil? Elevate and dispose of despotic regimes in South America and the middle east? This government could wipe out the poppy and coca plant worldwide, but they don't. We've had Kennedy as a president, whose father was a bootlegger, Nixon who advocated breaking and entering. Countless administrations that have constantly raised taxes on hard working people which amounts to nothing more than legalized extortion. Other administrations who outlawed unions and showed no indignation about seeing the American working man exploited. We've got a welfare state that's dysfunctional, a healthcare system that benefits only the rich. A structure in place that pays sports men and women forty fifty million dollars a year and still advocates minimum wage for hard working people. Who allows sports manufacturers to exploit workforces in the far east and sell their wares on home soil for extortionate prices. Industry that was never backed and allowed to be wiped out by the Japanese and Koreans. We've got a society where directors and chief executives are paid millions for severance when they fail, but a labor force gets laid off with two weeks pay and a letter to say sorry. We've got a country so strict on immigration that turns a blind eye to the illegal workforce when it benefits the economy. Don't make me laugh Susie. What I stand for? I refuse to be lied to; I refuse to be a fool. So yeah, I live outside of your respectable society, simply because I don't see any respect in it. ' He drained his glass with anger, and then gave her a hard cold look.

'That still doesn't make you right.'

'I ain't trying to justify myself. What I'm saying to you is we can help each other.'

'How can you help me?'

'I can give you people.'

'You're a hypocrite.'

'Call me what you want. I'm trying to survive. You'll come out clean, you'll move up and I'll hopefully preserve something that I honour.'

'You talk about it as if it were a lover.'

'That's because I believe in it. It gives a sanctuary to people who do not understand your world.'

Susan rubbed her head, her eyes were shut and her face unveiled the strain. Finally she opened her eyes and looked at him.

'Why don't you come in Robbie? The program will give you assurance.'

'You're not listening Susie. I ain't giving up my own people. I'll hand you Colombians, Chinese, Russians, Irish. My name never appears anywhere. I'm a ghost.'

'And just how am I supposed to swing that?'

'You're the head of the O.C.T.F. You deflect the attention away from us, concentrate on the other organizations, convince your people that the *Cosa Nostra* ain't the threat we used to be. Everyone knows this anyway, what with your WPP and these new organizations, they suppose we're finished.'

'Really. After that stunt you pulled last year. Killing a boss in middle of Manhattan, you made front page news again. How the hell am I gonna convince them otherwise?'

'Take down Gabriel Vargas. That'll give you your headlines.'

'Who is Gabriel Vargas?'

'Exactly. To you he's nothing. In our world he's the cocaine king. *Reyes de Cocaina*. That's just how good your organization is. The C.I.A probably knows about him. They should, he helped to whack out Pablo Escobar. He lives in this country four months a year. He's a big name, you take him, and you'll be stirring it up. It won't be easy, but I'll give you what you need.'

'Robbie. You don't understand, I can't compromise myself.'

'You already compromised yourself, by opening your legs to me.'

'You bastard.'

'I didn't want to get hard on you, but you're fucking around with my world and I ain't gonna allow you to do that. So you're in Susie. You wanna play politics, this is it. It's dirty and immoral and the only way to survive it is by being dirty. I'll give you your filthy governors and senators too.'

'I'm saying no to you Robbie.'

'Then it's a tough road you gotta walk.' Robbie stared at her.

'You can't intimidate me,' she said, staring him back.

'I ain't trying to intimidate you. I'm trying to save you.'

'What's that mean?'

'It means Susie, it's outta my hands, if you don't play ball.'

'I want you to leave now.' She turned her back on Robbie, hiding her eyes, that were filling up with tears. Robbie put his glass down and moved behind her, put his arms around her and kissed the back of her neck.

'Why after all this time did you have to come back into my life?' she asked, shaking.

'You came back into mine Susie.'

Susan felt for him, finally allowing herself to remember pleasure and forget who she had become professionally. "The Head-hunter" became once more a woman whose needs for tactile communication outweighed practicality, a woman who needed to respond to the fire within that certain men ignite. In her case it happened to be Robbie D'Angelo, an entity on the other side of the boundary which divided them. An opposite to the world she somehow believed in.

They lay together in bed, smoking, Susan was restless. Robbie had no comfort to give her, he wanted to get out, but played out the farce.

'What if I can't pull this off Robbie? What happens then?' She said, shifting her body again.

'You will. Don't doubt yourself.'

'It's dangerous. I'm afraid.'

'Susie. A year from now, you'll be out, moving on to another department. Moving through your world.'

'And where will you be?'

'I'll be around.'

'You won't get out.'

'No. You don't get out of this thing, alive and with your honour. I'm in till the end. All I can do is make the best of it.'

'Will I see you again?'

'Stay smart, Susie.'

'I mean, like this?'

'It's a risk.'

'I suppose. Maybe you're worth the risk.'

'I'm not Susie. You just do your work and I'll get in touch, I'll supply what you need.'

'I want you to leave now,' Susan said in a soft broken voice, then turned away from him and wrapped herself in the sheet.

14 THE NEW COMMISSION

UNDERWORLD UNION IS NECESSARY FOR IT TO survive, differences will occur continuously, power will be sought, lost, business will continue. The twenty three Mafia families of America gathered for the first time since the Apalachin fiasco of the fifties. The bosses had accepted D'Angelo's offer and now they sat, as one unity to listen to a man who had murdered his way to the top.

There was a strange curiosity about them. In their minds they needed to understand just who this man was, what his proposals were. Some knew already. Robbie decided to have Ancello from Chicago chair the union with him. A move which added weight to his side.

The conference room was booked under the name of a legitimate company, in a Seattle hotel. Discreet, unassuming, it was the measure of just how meticulous they had become. The legitimate world was constantly watching and to gather like this needed shrewdness beyond that of the authorities.

A technician swept the room for bugs and gave it a clean bill of health. Once everyone was seated, bosses only, no second in command, no *consigliere*, Robbie spoke.

'Thank you gentlemen for accepting the invitation and I hope we can reach an agreement so that we can reconstruct this thing of ours into what it deserves to be. I like to see this as our last opportunity. The government, outside factions have been eating into us for far too long now. As much as we have tried to go legitimate and our efforts have been considerable and commendable, we have only succeeded so far. It's time for us to take back this country.'

To this there was very little response. Ancello stood up. Chicago was making a stand.

'Now I understand where the problem lies in this room. Most of us are, excuse me if this sounds like an insult, old men. We have seen a lot of change. I say this now and ask you as a friend, you all know me, give Mister Robbie a chance to express what he has to offer. I tell it straight. Chicago, Detroit, Cleveland and Milwaukee are firmly behind what he will propose.'

From down the table Angelo Gigante's eyes narrowed and he looked around the table as if seeking help. There was none. Gigante had not formed any alliances, only with those that were outside of the circle. He stood up and Ancello gave him the floor.

'You know me. I have to talk the truth here today and what I have to say might be offensive to some of you who sit here. I offer no apologies. So, I'll get right to the point. Mister D'Angelo is a son of a bitch.' Along the table, some bosses shifted uncomfortably in their chairs, some bowed their heads, others gave looks between D'Angelo and Gigante, who continued.

'He has us here today to try and nullify any opposition, consolidate his position. He'll have you believe he's acting with honour. But I ask you. What man of honour will kill the head of the commission? An unsanctioned hit on a man, a great man who had a vision to bring in outside elements, to make big money for us all. It's true this thing of ours has been weakened, but Don Costello, knew that we had to change. It's a global world now, global economy.

'So what's next? D'Angelo takes control of the Commission, pushes the old out, maybe, that's the cycle of life, but to let a man who has no honour, who plays by his own rules take control, simply because he showed a recklessness to whack his own boss. Where is our honour?' Gigante looked around at the faces and held up his hands, then sat.

Robbie stood again. He picked up his glass of wine and took a sip, put it down then lit a cigarette. He studied the faces looking at him, swallowed hard.

'It's true what mister Gigante says. I broke a rule; I organized an unsanctioned hit on a boss, not just any boss, the head of the commission. Why? Well I'll tell you. The commission was a joke. You had the five New York families permanently sitting on the board, and four other families. We've got twenty three families in this country. The Colombians have four, the Chinese sixty, the Russians eight. We've got Jamaican Yardies, Cubans, Mexicans, Puerto Ricans, Dominicans, the African American syndicate, the Irish. Added to that you got other samples of delights. This country is one big stew. But what have we got that they don't have? We have the organization. They are not organized. They are clever, big earners, but they ain't organized. This is why they needed the Commission. In all respect, Costello wanted expansion, but why not with our own? Why can't we have a syndicate of the twenty three families, who rule this fine land? We'll put the hammer on them; we'll drive them back to their fuckin' shithole countries; if they don't wanna play by our rules, they won't play at all. I look around and I see a collective strength. I see power. All our soldiers outnumber them. We work with them, yes, but like politicians do to their voting public, we fuck them, they pay us to operate, we tax 'em.'

Robbie was stopped by Gigante, who stood up again. He gave over to the old man but did not sit.

'It's good talk. It makes for a good film. Because let's face it, Robbie D'Angelo would rather be a film star than a gangster. Sure he made his mark, his big scores, the most public and reported hit in four decades. This is the man you would have to lead you into the future. He talks well about Cosa Nostra and outsiders. It makes me laugh. I hear no talk about the Sicilians he's surrounding himself with. Is this a man of honour, who builds a secret army?'

Robbie cut off Gigante.

'You talk about my army, while you make alliances with *Little Napoleon* in New Orleans. Yes, I have Sicilians in my quarter. They bring strength back into our thing. They have a schooling of the old country ways. They bring it to our streets, our soldiers are too soft, they like the junk too much, the easy life. You get too fat, you can't move; fast. So yes, I have my Sicilians, simply because of my desire to save this thing of ours. You think the other factions are just gonna accept what we lay down. They're gonna go for war. To win it, you gotta have hard hitters. I've never been opposed to drugs, it's big money. What we can't have is soldiers stoned out of their nuts. Too many of our soldiers are and so I needed to clean up my house. Evidently the other New York families agreed with this because they have followed suit.'

Around the table came nods of approval.

'What you say is immaterial,' Gigante said with a raised voice. 'If I had my way, you'd be whacked, for breaking a fuckin' rule. Am I the only one who can see that here? How you gonna trust someone like this, if our rules don't apply, how can you trust any new rules?'

Gigante looked around the table, he stood in the silence until he was convinced the point was nailed home, and then he sat, giving a strong look to D'Angelo.

Robbie D'Angelo offered a look in equal measure. He was still standing and brushed his left hand through his hair, picked up his glass with his right and took a sip, set it down.

'The real issue here is that Don Gigante thinks he deserves his chance at the head of the Commission. Maybe he does, he's next in line. So give it to him. Let him sit on that false Commission, that defunct system. I didn't bring you all here to discuss what should or never should be. I brought you here to offer something more. I want to propose a new beginning. Tomorrow still has its hand out. It's up to us to take it. That's all I can say. Now I'll let the respected Don Ancello talk.' Robbie sat, never letting his eyes move off Gigante.

During the course of Ancello's speech as he outlined the new concept, the rotating presidency, the need for every Family to get their house in order, the tribute taxes to the president of the commission, the nails they would hammer into outsiders so as they could operate at the top of the heap, Robbie kept his eyes trained on Angelo Gigante, head of the

Badalamenti Family. A man who believed in a divine right to sit at the head of something that Robbie was tearing down. A man who detested Robbie and had decided upon a personal affront.

What Robbie saw was an old powerful man turn white and crumble as he realized the portent of the proposal. And at the same time Robbie knew that Angelo Gigante would refuse. He would refuse because his heart was obstinate, he would refuse because his mentality was old fashioned and he could not give over to anew. He was an old man, steadfast in his desire to reach a pinnacle. It was being stripped before him, before an audience. Robbie understood the old man would fight against him, no matter what was decided that day.

Ancello, after delivering the proposal offered a two hour break, before they convened for the vote to either ratify of dispel the new order. The men of power agreed and filed out of the conference room. Some went to their rooms, others to the restaurant, some to the bar.

Robbie and Ancello stayed in the conference room. They had enough wine and enough peace to talk. Robbie was feeling the tension, his battle with old man "The Black Angel" Gigante had carved into him. He walked to a window, took a sip from his glass and sucked on his cigarette, looking out across a city he did not know. An overwhelming feeling took hold of him; stress began to creep into him.

Ancello's hand rested on his shoulder. Then words entered his ear.

'You did well. They saw what I saw, they heard what I heard.'

'And what's that?' Robbie asked.

'Strength, honour and truth.'

'Will that be enough though?'

'It was for me. I didn't like you Robbie. I thought you were another upstart when you came to see me. But you didn't lie. You offered something. Gigante don't see it. He will vote against and he'll put a hit on you. Don't doubt that.'

'I don't.'

'You'll get the vote. Then the new order will vote to clip him.'

'I ain't sure I want that. Maybe we can offer him retirement, something.'

'He won't retire. He'll have to go,' Ancello smiled, walked away. Robbie turned and watched him walk away. His eyes narrowed, he grimaced and turned back to the view of the city. Everyone was searching for an angle and Ancello was no different.

When the order reconvened, the vote came through for Robbie. Only three votes went against him; Gigante and the Tampa and Los Angeles families. Gigante found himself on the outside, outnumbered. A rage brewed within him and he stood up.

'Gentlemen, what has happened here today in this room is a disgrace. It sickens me to be here and watch this convergence. A wrong has been committed and you have turned a blind eye. I for one cannot stay to see anymore of this crap. I'm going back to New York and I want it on the record that I disprove and that this thing of ours is no longer filled with men of honour. My family will go along with the program under duress.'

As he walked from the room, the heads of the new commission watched in silence.

'We have our first problem to deal with,' said Ancello, asserting himself as the new president. Robbie stood up and thanked the board, then officially proposed Ancello as the inaugural president of the fresh order. The vote was delivered and then the order was given to the lesser families to get their house in order. Drug use among members was formally outlawed, punishable by expulsion or death.

President Ancello put forward the notion to execute the rebel Gigante. Surprisingly, Robbie argued against, once more suggesting an offer of retirement and insisting they give Gigante the benefit of the doubt. It assured a pass for "The Black Angel".

Certain other matters were dealt with during the next few hours, then the men celebrated the rebirth of their strength with cognac and cigars. At the adjournment Robbie left for his hotel where he met Silvio Dalla Bonna at the bar.

The underboss was squared up with the details over many drinks. Robbie felt an exhaustion which he could not hide. The lids hung heavy over his dark eyes and a weight made his face sag. He poured the last of a bottle of beer into his glass and lit a cigarette.

'Why don't you go and get some sleep,' Silvio said.

'I'm too fucking tired to sleep. I just feel like sitting here for a few hours, get wasted. You got plans?'

Silvio shook his head.

'Stay and have a drink with me then?'

'Sure boss,' he leaned over to Robbie and put a hand on his shoulder. 'You know, I think what you've pulled off is nothing short of spectacular.'

'There's still a long way to go,' Robbie said with a sigh.

'You'll make it.' Then Silvio held up his glass. To the new order, the rules and the future.'

'The new order and the future,' Robbie responded and they touched glasses.

'I gotta take a piss. Shout 'em up boss,' Silvio said as he got up.

'I gotta buy these too?'

'We're celebrating ain't we?'

'You're a cheap bastard.'

'I'm saving for my old age,' said Silvio with a smile. Robbie watched him walk away, then laughed, ordered more drinks.

They forgot about the business as the hours moved past and the alcohol flowed. They discussed sport, films, told jokes and talked intimately about their blood families. Two powerful men in an underworld of violence and decadence, two true friends bonded and travelling a road into a future of infamy.

15 DOMINANCE

THE NEW ORDER BEGAN TO SWEEP THROUGH the country with the power of a hurricane. Soldiers, strung out on drugs began to get clean, began to earn big again, did not hold out on kick up money. The consequences were nailed home; there were some still who thought they could buck the system, who thought they would never be found out. They suffered.

Mechanics were moving throughout the land. A storm front was closing in, about to encompass, strip out and purify any infection. The underworld and the authorities were unprepared for the magnitude of the new dominance.

Ancello in Chicago had given a special contract to the Cleveland mob. Their target was the Irish Bostonian, Dawson Culpepper. The Irishman was a gremlin in the works and would battle against the new order.

Cleveland sent out their top batsman. A man accomplished in the profession of human removal and was very secure in the Cleveland underworld. He was in his mid-fifties, bereft of any promotion desires. A heartless man who enjoyed his trade and was genuinely happy in his life, just so long as the work continued and the money flowed into his pockets. His name was Raymond DeVita and his CV listed forty two hits.

Raymond DeVita had the appearance of a gentle grandfather. His hair had grayed long ago and had grown fine, yet not thin and he wore it in conservative fashion. He donned soft rimmed glasses and his blue eyes were friendly and joyous. The killer was always clean shaven, he was a man who believed in personal grooming and it was reflected in his tailoring. He always wore suits, nothing expensive, but well cut designs, a shirt or polo top and soft leather shoes. The thick leathery skin that covered his face still held its olive complexion and had very few lines of age. In all his face conveyed a feeling of security, emitting out into the world which made people around him feel at ease. He rarely drank alcohol but was a prodigious coffee drinker and still managed to get through a pack and half of Lucky Strikes a day.

DeVita considered the contract after gaining all the facts on the subject. In his mind it was a shot to take out someone of importance. It had been a long time since he had whacked anyone of magnitude. In recent years it had been low level soldiers. The challenge was to his liking. The task would be difficult and would be made more arduous because he was working in an alien city. He saw his way through a pot of coffee and endless cigarettes before he agreed to take the contract.

Boston had advantages. It was easy to hide. He kept a low profile for a week while he accustomed himself to the city. He drove the roads for hours, until he was satisfied in his competence. The next week he began his surveillance of the mark.

Dawson Culpepper was a hard man to track. He had no set routines and he was always mobbed up. One morning he would go the offices of a legitimate business and stay there for a half a day. The next day he would go to Turkish baths or not even exit his home. Towards the end of the week he tailed Culpepper as he drove out of Boston. The man headed for Maine. DeVita drove back to Boston, checked in with Cleveland and told them the job would require patience. Cleveland responded by telling him it did not matter, just to make sure he got the Irishman.

Raymond DeVita did not know the length of time Culpepper would be away from Boston, but as he sat in his hotel room, looking over his notes and pictures, the idea of phone tapping came to him. He had used this ploy once in history, but it was fraught with danger. FBI, OCTF or the police could already have a tap on his phone. But Raymond DeVita needed more idea of the mark's moves. So he decided to go ahead.

For the next twelve hours he was tied up on the phone. Through his contacts at a phone company he got them to call the house and ask for the man in person. The maid who answered gave over the information that they required. Mister Culpepper was out of town for the next four days. He decided against having a phone company operative monitoring calls but had his contact phone the house again and explain in technical detail that the phone company needed access to the phone line to rectify a problem. The maid agreed and an appointment was made for the next day for an engineer to call. Raymond DeVita was in.

Back in his hotel room after fooling the maid with his ruse, he organized his technology. Any outgoing or incoming calls he could monitor. The first call came in that night. Raymond picked up the conversation, though he had to contend with a lot of static and squelch. The device was doing the job though, he had an insight now. The conversation was a personal one for the maid, from her sister. Raymond signed off, then took a shower and left the hotel for a night of fine food and a few sensible glasses of vino.

That night Raymond enjoyed a sleep undisturbed. He awoke at six, checked the recordings from his phone tap, which was empty, then indulged himself with a large breakfast. Now it was about time, about waiting, about true patience and professionalism. The contract killer has to vary his approach to appease his sense of stagnation. Not every hit can be carried out with a bullet in the head. Though most are carried out by associates, allowing them to get close to the target, the professional contact killer will have to snake his way into a victim's life. Raymond DeVita was such a professional. During his career, he had whacked guys he had worked with, strangers and even a blood cousin. To him it was a job. He had no remorse for his victims, they were his job.

DeVita had a redundancy of sense concerning humanity. His philosophy dictated to him that humanity was a waste, undeserving of a place on this earth. Often times he spoke about the ridiculousness of the human condition. When associating with mob guys he would talk them down in an argument about human existence and its failings. His intellectual capacity was above them. They were mostly street guys who would stay that way, DeVita was an avid reader. In his observance of the human race, he found very little to cheer his heart and consequently his heart hardened into an impenetrable fortress, were humanity could not enter and corrupt the purity of his philosophy. He had evolved into a separate entity.

While he waited on assignment he read. He walked the city, observing and his conviction that it was all a waste never faltered. Raymond DeVita was a living Lucifer. If the A-Bomb was about to be dropped, he would laugh and cheer. Compassion, faith, hope and charity were words banished from his personal dictionary.

During one night of waiting, DeVita read a biography of Robert E Lee, cover to cover. Tiredness did not hit him and he showered as the Sun arose over Boston. The phone was silent. It did not bother him; he had the stamina to wait and the control to maintain patience.

As he towelled himself dry the phone tap kicked in. Dawson Culpepper received a call from his dentist confirming his appointment for two p.m. three days onward. DeVita replayed the message and wrote down the name of the dentist and time and date. Then he dressed and got to work. Preparations had to be finely tuned and he had to scramble his resources.

During the course of the day he rented two cars, from two rival companies under a false name. As night fell he set about the essence of his mission in a quiet underground car park. After, he drove one of the cars to a location close by to Culpepper's dentist, parked it and took a taxi back to the hotel.

The following new day brought Dawson Culpepper home. DeVita waited. Culpepper called his dentist to confirm the appointment.

For the next two days DeVita made reconnaissance tours of the areas surrounding the dentist. There was a public car park close by and DeVita guessed that Culpepper might park there. He checked out routes into and out of the area, how close emergency services were, how visible the action would be. In other areas he tried to fathom if Culpepper would park somewhere else. He drove the various routes from Culpepper's house to the dentist, noting the time it took. Once satisfied in his mind, DeVita went back to waiting.

Come the day, DeVita waited in his car close by and when Culpepper left his house with two bodyguards he tailed them. He was proficient in tailing techniques and remained undetected. Just as DeVita hoped they parked in the public car park. He stopped at a safe distance; he observed Culpepper and one of his bodyguards walk in the direction of the dentist surgery. The driver got out and leaned against the car, lit a cigarette and began to talk on his mobile phone. DeVita drove around the car park until he was close then pulled into the free space on the right of Culpepper's car. As he got out the bodyguard turned to face him. DeVita locked the car and gave a nod to the man, who did not respond, being engrossed in his phone call. DeVita walked off and after about fifty yards glanced back. He was not being watched. He continued until he reached the other car. Once inside he opened the glove compartment and took out a small remote device, placed the device in the passenger seat, then lit a cigarette, opened the window and waited.

An hour later. Dawson Culpepper and his bodyguard came walking across the tarmac. He was wiping his mouth with a handkerchief and trying to speak. The driver saw them approach and opened the passenger door, started the engine. DeVita dropped another cigarette out of the window and picked up the device, pulled out the antenna and flicked a switch to activate the bomb.

As Dawson Culpepper walked between the two cars and was about to get into his, DeVita pressed the detonation button.

The rental car exploded in a fierce firebomb, blowing out the driver's door into Culpepper. His body was torn limb from limb. One leg flew into the car, along with shattered glass and shards of metal and impaled itself into the driver's side. Culpepper's right arm was thrown across the car lot and landed on the hood of another car. The right side of his body was opened up and blood and organs spilled out, some cooking as if being char grilled. The other bodyguard was tossed in the air effortlessly and came crashing down on his skull, which killed him instantly. The blast set off car alarms and blew out auto glass everywhere and the area become a fire storm as gasoline ignited. Smoke rose skywards, signaling a disaster to passer-by's.

DeVita waited a couple of minutes to see if there was any sign of life, though he knew it would be impossible for anybody to survive the wreckage he created. Satisfied, he turned the ignition then pulled out slowly towards the exit. On the road, he drove at a safe and indiscreet speed. He took a route into the heart of Boston. Wiped the car down and left it. The remote device he wiped, placed it in a grocery bag and threw it in a trash can. Then he called Cleveland from a phone booth.

'Boston's clean,' he said and hung up. At his hotel, he checked out, collected his car and drove away from the crime, back to his hometown.

Cleveland meanwhile phoned Ancello in Chicago, who congratulated them then relayed the news to D'Angelo in New York.

Robbie went to the refrigerator took out two bottled chilled beers, popped the caps and gave one to Silvio.

'The Irishman's gone,' he said.

'Good stuff. I'll drink to that,' he replied as they clinked bottles. 'I guess this means we can give word to the Marranzo's?'

'Sure. Call 'em.' Robbie sat and lit a cigarette, let out a smile.

The call was made, word passed down and within two hours, the Marranzo brothers, Vinnie and Paulie had the Westie mobsters John O'Neil and Mickey Conway, taken off the street.

O'Neil and Conway were taken to a lock up close to the Gowanus Canal. They had been worked over by the Marranzo crew and were strung up on meat hooks, suspended above the floor, tired, afraid and disorientated.

When the brothers arrived O'Neil and Conway desperately began to try and talk their way out of the situation.

'Culpepper's gone. He's barbequed, so youse two are all alone in this fuckin' world and it's right you should feel afraid, because tonight you pay penance for our brother. It's your last day in this world, 'cause I for one don't give a fuck for your words of pleading and apology.' Vinnie put a cigarette in his mouth and his young brother "Crazy" Paulie lit it. "Crazy" Paulie was charged with emotion, full of torrid vengeance. If Vinnie was to tell him to pull off the culprits heads with his bare hands, he would do it, so wired up was he.

'Mister Marranzo....' began John O'Neil.

'Shut the fuck up, you Irish scumbag. I ain't even gonna ask you why you betrayed my friendship. I'm gonna tell you what you get tonight,' cause I'm a man of honour. I'll give you a way out. Get 'em down,' Vinnie said to his men. The men acted and for the first time in two hours, the Irish gangsters felt ground beneath their feet.

'Now let them have one hand free,' Vinnie said. At that moment there was a bang on the shutter. One of the mob men opened the side door and a crew member entered carrying take out coffee. Vinnie took a cup, Paulie refused. Vinnie pulled off the lid and took a sip.

'It's gonna be a long night boys. Caffeine keeps you going,' he said and his crew laughed.

O'Neil and Conway were standing about two foot from one another, their right arms were chained up above them, and their left arms were free.

'You know what a great pastime is?' Vinnie asked of them. There was no response.

'Dog fighting. And since youse both act like fuckin' dogs, you're gonna entertain us.' He motioned with his head to Paulie, who pulled out two hunting knives from a bag. He walked to the captives and placed one in each of the free hands. 'Now fight dogs,' he said and walked away, taking up a position next to his brother.

'I don't see any action,' shouted Vinnie. 'Fight, the winner just might get to go home.'

With that Mickey Conway slashed away at his friend and boss John O'Neil. O'Neil tried to move away in his limited space but the blade caught him across the side of the head opening up a wound. O'Neil countered quickly and the blades clashed together and the sound of steel against steel filled the lock up. On the sidelines, crew members betted.

Conway moved back as far as the chain would allow him, trying to get a foothold and a sense of balance as O'Neil come at him. He moved quickly but could not dodge the incoming attack and the blade penetrated into his right shoulder, he shouted in pain but quickly countered managing to slice across the face of O'Neil, catching the middle of his nose and cutting to the bone. O'Neil moved away, tearing the blade out of Conway's shoulder, who gave another shout. Their Irish blood cascaded from their wounds, but they were fighting to live and the adrenalin of survival swept over the pain. The fury to survive grew greater and the two men forgot tactics, as pure will made them slash away at each other. Their bodies and blood became one as the combat became a frenzied close quarter stabbing horror. Then it ended quickly as O'Neil's blade found an artery in Conway. He dropped his knife and as his blood imitated a geyser the energy drained from him and he slumped, bent at the knees, the knuckles of his left hand touching the floor, held up by his chained right arm. The breathing in his body got desperate until finally the oxygen ran out. He gave a final gasp and his head fell forward and rolled lifeless about the neck.

On the sidelines a cheer went up from the winners. O'Neil, exhausted, dropped his blade as his body came to realize the damage and shake, he breathed hard. Vinnie Marranzo threw the rest of his coffee onto the ground. Paulie was smiling, his lust for blood and violence still rising.

'Okay O'Neil,' said Vinnie and walked over to him, trying to tread carefully through the blood puddles. He picked up the knife and put it back into John O'Neil's hand. 'You can have an ancient Roman death of honour. Open up your veins.' O'Neil wearily raised his head and looked Vinnie in the eyes. 'Fuck you,' he said in a tired defiant whisper. Vinnie nodded and took the knife out of his hand, walked away. 'Death by a thousand cuts then,' he said nonchalantly to his crew. 'When you're finished throw his body in a dumpster somewhere.' He put his arm around Paulie and led him from the lock up.

Salvatore Grecco began to manoeuvre his soldiers to carry out his mission. Personally he felt he did not have the complete trust of the American soldiers under his command. They feared him, because he brought the hammer down hard, but he was wary of pushing them too much. With his Sicilian counterparts he knew they would carry out his orders to the full and they were more experienced for the job he had been charged with.

He gathered five of the top killers and outlaid their mission. All six men would take part in what would soon be written into New York Mafia folklore. Salvatore had been handed the task because of his reputation and ruthlessness. What they were about to do was along the lines of how things were done back in the old country during the recent troubles.

After hearing Salvatore talk they all left in two separate cars, drove to one of the Family's social clubs and collected three Uzi's and three pump action shotguns. They indulged themselves by having a coffee. Mob men who were in attendance said nothing to them, mumbled among themselves speculation about who was going to get hit.

The band of Sicilians were quiet, said little to each other, chain smoked and in their faces was an austere taciturn look. Salvatore eventually ordered them on out, and they followed him. Then they drove away.

The advantage they had over their victims was their unsuspecting. They had no reason to believe that the Mob would be coming after them. In their daily life they went about conducting their criminal enterprises as normal. No state of alert was issued, they knew the Mob was having trouble and they did not care for the Commission any longer. They were building a circle of their own.

What they could not know was that surveillance had been carried out on them for the last two weeks and that they had an informer within the ranks, who was to be paid a king's ransom for spilling his guts and giving up his comrades.

The sextet positioned themselves, ready to perform a new music to fill the night air of the city. It was a quiet street, residential, very little traffic and the men blended in with the surrounding bushes and trees. The street lamps were energy saving and gave out a dim illumination, which aided the men. They carefully tracked the three armed men stationed outside the house. As they made tours of the house, they took them out of the game one by one, using garrotes. The lax security was erased and those inside the house were vulnerable.

Inside the house the gathering had finished the business in hand. Talk was finished and now they partook of fine food, expensive wine and the deep mysterious pleasures of young courtesans, with bodies of goddesses and looks of movie stars.

The only concern Salvatore had was if the targets departed in dribs and drabs. He wanted to get the twelve men in one clean sweep. The informer was attending the meeting and assured Salvatore that they would all be leaving together as he personally had arranged a celebratory party at his night club. Seven cars were parked in the driveway and Salvatore and one of his countrymen punctured the front tires on every car, ensuring that a quick getaway would be made difficult, if it so happened that way. For good measure they cut the phone line to the house.

In his pocket Salvatore felt his phone vibrate, he took it out and answered it. Listened to the informer inside tell him they would be coming out in five minutes. He signaled to his men and they quietly positioned themselves at the door. They were locked, loaded and psyched to massacre.

The door to the house opened and the sound of voices poured out from the men in high spirits. Salvatore moved out from the shadows stepping directly before the first man, who began to speak to him as if expecting to see an outside bodyguard. Just as the man recognized what was happening and his face contorted to terror, Salvatore sprayed bullets from his Uzi. The power threw the man back into the entourage behind him and in the pandemonium five other people took bullets, four girls and one gangster.

Salvatore was joined by the other Uzi toting killers who joined him in unleashing a flurry of bullets. They unloaded until they were empty. Inside, girls screamed, gangsters tried to take out their pieces, but bullets numbed their senses and when the Uzi's were done, the shotgun canister arrived upon them in a more measured and subtle touch. Some of the inhabitants had managed to crawl away, up the stairs, to other rooms. One gangster pulled a dead body on top of him, but there was to be no escape. Shotgun blasts filled the house as the killers took the time to be thorough. No one was to be spared and when the shooting ceased, the screaming and agonizing calls for mercy were silenced, blood was spilled across wooden floors and splashed across the walls, the informer showed himself.

He and Salvatore shook hands and as he walked out of the house alongside Salvatore, triumphant and gleeful of his elevation a Sicilian behind him raised a gun and fired a shot into the back of his head, opening his skull and spaying his brains onto the driveway. The Sicilians made their getaway before the police arrived, leaving behind them a carnage unseen in recent times and the Russian mob in demise.

The hit on the Russians was compared in the press to the St Valentines Day massacre. The police had no leads and the FBI were unwilling to comment. The Mayor assured the public that the war on organized crime would be won and chastised crime figures for their disregard for human life. The Russian purge, as it came to be known in the press made worldwide news. Days afterwards it was still being reported in full page spreads. Organized crime historians and experts wrote extensively to feed an eager public who still needed to be fascinated by gangsters. It was obvious to everyone a war was being waged in the underworld, yet nobody could quite grasp the intricacies. It was a puzzle to them, with many missing pieces.

This latest outrage caused more of a stir than the mid-town hit of Don Costello over a year ago, or the recent mincing of Dawson Culpepper in Boston. New York was compared to the Chicago of prohibition.

What effect the latest hits had on underworld figures was to give them a sense of awareness. Outside factions begun to hide. Except the Colombians, who went through life with an arrogance of invincibility anyhow. Others took stock of their lives, they stepped up their security and moved through their days with added caution. The massacre of the Russians sent out a message and the message was; a new age of the Italian Mafia was ascending.

16 BLACK ANGEL

ANGELO GIGANTE SAT ASLEEP IN A UNIVERSE of a leather chair. A breeze blew in through the open patio but gave no cooling effect to the sweltering heat that held New York in a vice like grip. Sweat run down from his head and dripped off the end of his nose onto his short sleeve shirt. It made no difference as the material was soaked anyhow. The heat done for him eventually and he awoke in an uncomfortable stickiness. Because of the closeness he found breathing difficult and raised himself with a great effort.

In the kitchen he filled a jug with fresh water and ice, poured himself a large glass. He gulped it down, then pulled off his shirt, drank some more as he overlooked his vast garden. The tiredness had not left him and his legs felt heavy, he pulled up a stool and rested his bulk.

The suffocating closeness of New York and life had begun to eat away at his energy and for the first time he had felt his age. Something else too had weighed heavy upon him, the new Commission. His years of experience had taught him about power shifts and now he knew his was waning.

The new order knew he was disapproving and would see him as a threat to the restructuring. Gigante expected to be hit and felt isolated. His only ally was far away in New Orleans and their combined forces were hardly powerful enough to take on D'Angelo, Ancello and the rest of the Commission.

On the outside, the Russians had been wiped out. No other factions wanted to try their luck and were lying low. Gigante knew the Colombians were strong enough but felt an impossibility to marry in with them.

For the last week, one idea run through his mind; to hit D'Angelo. He knew that even if he achieved this, it would not change anything now. Inside of his heart, the wrong that had been dealt gave him a pain of discomfort. Robbie D'Angelo was an acid causing a constant burn. A glob of bubble gum on the sole, a car engine running constantly in the quiet of night. D'Angelo was the irritation that denied Gigante peaceful sleep. Gigante wanted peace and he reasoned within himself that the wrongs of D'Angelo would have to be avenged to help him achieve that end. Fate had pitted the two men against each other and one, if not both would have to fall.

Angelo Gigante poured another glass of iced water then took a stroll around his garden. His upper physique which belied his years took in the rays of the hot sun easily. A good diet and moderate sun intake was a philosophy he had always lived by. The dark skin of his Sicilian ancestry did not feel any discomfort with the heat that beat upon it, but along with other combinations did not rest easy with the old man and by the time he reached his large pond he was breathless. He sat under the shade of a large parasol and watched his expensive Koi as they glided slowly throw the water. They gave to him a calm hypnotism and soon he was drifting off once more as the lids of his eyes grew heavy.

Gigante awoke an hour later, the heat once more disturbing him. The inside of his mouth was dry and he reached for the glass next to him, the water inside was warm and a couple of black fly lay drowned on the surface, he tipped it away, then moved to a storage unit nearby, took out a tube of pellets, shook out a handful and flung them into the pond, but the fish could not be interested. Gigante put the tube back then stretched in the baking sun and eventually walked back to the house, checking out his tomatoes along the way and a plum tree.

After a cool shower he went to the kitchen and poured a cup of freshly brewed coffee, then sat before the television and lit a cigar while he watched a soccer game from Italy beamed in by satellite. Somewhere inside the irritation continued. He turned off the television and decided to call his consigliere.

Jon Cirello's voice answered promptly.

'Afternoon boss. Hot one ain't it?'

'Sure is. I want you to book us two first class tickets to New Orleans for the end of the week.'

'Okay,' said Cirello slowly, giving his confirmation an added air of questioning.

'Come over tonight, we need to talk about certain aggravations I have.'

'Sure boss. You doing okay?'

'Yeah, apart from this fucking heat. I'll see you later.'

NEW ORLEANS

The east and southern states experienced a lingering heat wave during the next week and the constant heat, the travelling and the stresses of the underworld were taking their toll on old man Gigante.

Eyes, which normally held a fire, seemed dulled adding to his worn looking expression. Gigante's temperament became fractious and he took some of his irritations out on his *compare* during the trip. His slim frame moved with weary effort to the waiting car and he was grateful for the air conditioning into which he dozed as the car sped to Pierre Sartois' home and was awoken as they pulled into the courtyard.

Pierre was his normal cheery self and made all the usual fusses of welcoming. It did not go unnoticed to him just how tired his friend looked. He offered a room for recuperation to which Gigante refused, so Pierre took him by the arm and they walked slowly through the sunshine into the shade of a large canvas awning. Cirello followed and sat next to his boss. Pierre poured glasses of ice cold homemade lemonade, then sat and lit one of his strong smelling French cigarettes. The smoke lingered about, waiting for a breeze to dispel it.

'New York gives you much trouble, *non* ?' Pierre asked.

Gigante tiredly nodded. 'I'm finding enemies everywhere I turn.'

'Not here my *podna*. Only friends.' Pierre protested.

'I know, I know,' nodded Gigante.

'This is my country, this is your country.'

'*Grazie*. But I am isolated my friend. What I expected to happen has not. That bastard D'Angelo has made moves even I could not predict. I told you he was cunning, but his tricks would embarrass even a snake.'

'*Fuh shore*. I know he put his soldiers down here. I know them and I send them back to him.' Pierre's anger had risen up in his throat and he stubbed out his cigarette furiously.

'His organization is too big, he is too insulated now.'

'*Mais dit mon la verite monsieur* ! You knows anyone can be got, even that *salope* D'Angelo.'

'There's nothing that would give me greater pleasure. This new structure, this commission, if I went against it I would be signing my own death warrant. And that bastard has got away with breaking a rule and now he's a fucking hero.'

Pierre lit another cigarette. 'We will find a way to dispose of this *merde*,' he said with deep conviction. 'You rest. The day tomorrow we talk. Tonight I bring in a good Creole girl for you.'

Gigante smiled, wiped his brow with a handkerchief and finished his lemonade.

'Come come, I'll show you to your room.'

After he had settled in Gigante, Pierre took up his place under the awning and contemplated the troubling problem of D'Angelo. To witness the toll all the strain had taken on his friend perturbed him, that and the fact D'Angelo had placed new soldiers upon his territory. The underworld they resided in was always fraught with dangerous complexities. They trod though life on thin ice knowing that their fate was ultimately out of their control. Every underworld figure knew they had limited time and they were all fighting for self-preservation.

Pierre Sartois was no different, was wise enough to know his limitations. As the heat invaded the shade he admitted in his heart what he had been denying. He was in agreement with some of his old friend realizations. D'Angelo and his new order might just be too strong to reckon with now. Pierre poured himself lemonade and lit a fresh cigarette, but upon his first gulp the beverage had become warm and he spat it out. He was in need of something stronger anyhow so lifted himself out of his chair with a huff and labored into the house.

He returned with a pitcher of icy water and a bottle of absinth. Without diligence he poured a heavy measure and took a mouthful of the bitter drink. Little Napoleon had much to separate and negotiate within his mind and the murky underworld. Loyalty remained strong for his friend at court and it clashed with his intrinsic need to survive. Green liquid and heat conspired to deny him any pleasurable outcome, only to induce a headache. He took another large measure into his blood then made his exit from the courtyard into his cool dim study. He phoned a contact to order some girls for the evening frolics, then lay on his worn leather couch and closed his eyes and his heart to the world.

A drop in temperature combined with the flash of lightning moving in from the Gulf of Mexico awoke him. Pierre sat up, rubbed his eyes and took a few minutes to stare into the dark outside. Pangs of hunger griped in his stomach and he denied them with a cigarette then tuned his attention to the sixteenth century hand carved antique which cheerfully chipped away at the time. More flashes illuminated the courtyard and the first of the rain escaped from the storm. Marseille crashed into his thoughts causing him to consider a visit to that far off destination. Dragging heavily upon his cigarette, his eyes began to lose their glassy appearance and feeling better, he decided upon a shower.

After a light dinner with Gigante he dismissed his son, Jean-Louis, Gigante done likewise with his consigliere and the two of them walked towards the door. Jean-Louis stopped and suggested he take Cirello into town. Pierre looked to Gigante for his approval, who nodded.

'Jean-Louis. Get men on the grounds. We need much security.'

'Yes Pappy.'

'*Mais*. A brandy my friend?'

'Thank you Pierre. May I ask what time the girls will be arriving?'

'Sure sure. They will arrive soon. I hope you have the strength for these young girls, they are the finest in Louisiana.'

'I'm not too old to enjoy the pleasures of women. God forbid,' he said and crossed himself.

'Ah, the subtleties of young flowers. How they blossom and capture our desires. What fools they make of men and how weak we feel in our lust for *gallette*.'

Gigante smiled at Pierre's thoughts on women and drained his glass. The storm had cleared the heat, but now a new heat had formed in his loins. They would resume their business tomorrow, for tonight he wished to unleash his frustrations in a sexual nature and forget about D'Angelo and the commission.

Four young women arrived promptly. Pierre knew two of them intimately, having indulged himself in their bodies on numerous occasions. The other two were new to him. All four were no more in age than twenty five, all had hard bodies. They were a mixture across the board, one Cajun, one Mulatto, one Negress and one of Mexican origin.

The girls indulged in drinks and flirting with the men until there were clear lines on who would be going with whom. Gigante was openly playing for the black and Mexican girl, which suited Pierre fine, because his interest was in the two new girls.

As the drinks flowed and flirtations gathered pace, Gigante slowly dragged his chosen two off to his quarters. Pierre stayed in the room pouring more drinks. He handed them to the girls then made himself one, lighting a cigarette while studying them. The girls talked amongst themselves while Pierre thought about what he would enjoy.

Suddenly he called over the Cajun girl and as she approached he unzipped his fly and pushed her down on her knees, then he beckoned the Mulatto over and commanded her to kneel behind her friend. He took a gulp of his drink and puffed on his cigarette whilst looking down upon the girls. A wicked look formed in his eyes as he mulled on the sordid things he would do with these fresh newcomers.

Pierre satisfied himself until he had nothing left, then with a cold heart sent them away. But whatever degradation he had unleashed upon the women served no purpose in alleviating the magnitude of the problem that was now aggravating him yet again. Sleep would just not slither in and he found himself pouring another large spirit.

He settled in before the television, but constantly channel hopped, unable to find any release. Then he played some Zydeco records but became bored all too easy. Finally he walked through his large private library, eyeing and fingering various rare first editions, books he would never read, but which gave him a sense of comfort to know they were on his bookshelves. He moved away from the rare collection into the biography section and as he focused on the names he absent-mindedly scratched his genitals. He belched and took his cigarettes from his robe pocket, put one in his mouth but refrained from lighting it. He was suddenly aware of the peace, the storm had finished and the library became his centre of calm. Choosing a biography of Huey Long, he sat at a table, lit the cigarette dangling from his mouth and flicked through the pages.

Pierre did not concentrate on reading the words on the pages. They somehow filtered through though, because after an hour of continuous reading and chain smoking it became apparent to him that in order to survive the predicament he was facing he would have to evolve to something greater than a mob figurehead. He had confidence that he could take on D'Angelo but he understood the destruction it would cause and he knew he was too old to restructure even if he came out alive. He had commitments, deep bloodline commitments, to his son and grandson. He couldn't throw away their future; he would not ever sleep peacefully.

Yet what he was considering gave him a nauseous stomach. He did not feel comfortable with it and so mulled it over, while sipping alcohol and smoking his special brand French cigarettes. The deep loyalty he felt towards Angelo Gigante could not be compared to anything or anyone he had encountered during his criminal life. Not even within his old Marseille fraternity could he recall being as close to someone as The Black Angel. Not even his own brother, who he let go to his death during the battle for supremacy in days gone by. It was the first time in his life that he found himself questioning the path he had chosen and the first time in his life he considered playing at what he despised, politics.

Pierre Sartois had always been a man of iron will, he saw what he saw, he carved out life to his design, he never compromised. It was the same characteristics that he saw in Angelo Gigante and to which he was drawn. It was Gigante who provided his connections in New York during the French Connection days; it was Gigante who did not turn his back after the fiasco of the takedowns. It was Gigante who never asked for recompense after losing a million in finance and it was Gigante who always travelled to him and never, never demanded him. Angelo 'The Black Angel" Gigante was his brother, but he wasn't blood. Pierre's blood coursed through his grandchild now and Pierre wished for that blood to be purified.

So Pierre, after considering, realized he would have to play that role which disgusted him. He would have to become politician, he would maybe have to sacrifice some of his empire, but just maybe he could keep himself and Gigante alive. For all that to happen, he would have to meet with Robbie D'Angelo.

The morning was hard on Pierre. Gigante kept the girls around for breakfast which irritated Pierre. He wanted rid of them, he wanted to talk business. After they had finished eating and he had poured more coffee, he bluntly suggested that they leave. The girls got the hint after a word from Gigante and after kissing and giggling they left.

'What's troubling you?' asked Gigante, sensing the despair in Pierre.

'Our business is troubling me,' said Pierre with impatience.

'Our business? Our business is simple, we're gonna whack out that *puttana* D'Angelo.'

Pierre for a moment grimaced, and then composed himself. 'To hit the man might not be that easy. You said so yourself.'

'That was last night. Now it's a new day, I'm refilled with new energy. D'Angelo's gonna go.'

Pierre bit his lip as he thought about his response. He was playing a new field and needed time to adjust. He was not ready for his friend's new found resoluteness. Pierre looked for a way to deflect Gigante's emotion. He lit a cigarette and sipped his coffee, played with the spoon in the cup.

'Mais, I have an idea about how to handle D'Angelo,' said Pierre without looking at Gigante.

'So do I have an idea. We're gonna whack that cocksucker, bury him, so that I can have nights of peaceful sleep,' replied Gigante with a smile, fingering the newspaper before him. Pierre shook his head. 'What's the matter?' asked Gigante.

'You, I, we can't be connected with a D'Angelo hit.'

'I said it's a new day, I say fuck the commission, I say we show ourselves, give them something to think about. Show them the power we still have.'

Pierre shook his head once again. 'My *podna*, this is a time to lay calm across the land, to have a humble heart, to forget what happens up the bayou.'

'You telling me to forget about the indecency that has been happening for the last year or so?' said Gigante with a stern voice. He leaned forward across folded arms to look into Pierre. His eyes had narrowed and become obsidian marbles, inflexible and deathly. He continued, with a low pitch, 'You telling me that the disrespect that has been shown me is nothing, that the funfair that has been happening in my city is nothing?'

'The Irish are gone, the Russians too. You think he's gonna stop? You think he won't come down here? Fuck. He already has soldiers down here. You're a Cajun; you ain't a Wop, Pierre. You're an outsider. He ain't gonna deal with you; he ain't got no respect for you. You won't get a pass. Sooner or later, he's gonna come after you. We've gotta hit him now, we gotta smash this new commission.'

Pierre shook his head. 'Not yet. I understand I'm an outsider and my time could come. So I do like D'Angelo does. He brings in his friends from Sicily. I bring in my friends from Marseille and Corsica, best gunmen you ever want.'

'We build a secret regime.' Gigante said, nodding.

'*Weh*. We become quiet, ghosts. Eventually we get him.'

Nothing was said as Gigante leaned back and considered this.

'How long?' he finally said.

'One year, maybe less.'

'Let's make it less,' said Gigante in command.

Pierre shrugged, nodded.

At lunch, Pierre sat next to his consigliere Cirello. Gigante had his son Jean-Louis next to him. They discussed their plan. After explaining they asked for opinions. Both Cirello and Jean-Louis agreed, both with an air of reservation. They were unsure of where this would lead them, but knew better than to reject the proposal in the open. So they agreed.

In the courtyard Gigante and Pierre embraced, and then Gigante and Cirello were sped away to the airport.

'Papa,' said his son and put and arm across his father's shoulder. 'It will be okay, yes?'

'*Qui*. It will be okay. Now I have to speak with D'Angelo.'

'D'Angelo?'

'Yes. Gigante is my *podna*, he is a man with honour, but you know what I find? He is now a *tahyo*. He has a *boudé* heart with thinking *de pouille. Maudit !* I have to be a politician, I have to be a *grand merde*. D'Angelo has the power. D'Angelo has the keys to open new doors.'

'*Co faire papa ?*'

Pierre turned to face his son, then put his hands upon his face and looked into his eyes.

'For you, my grandson, for the name Sartois. They call Gigante, *The Black Angel*. I always thought he was a man of reason. Now he is a bitter man. His hate will not let him see anything but his enemy. We two are old men, we cannot battle forever. The risks we took when we were young, had the beans in our gut, we have no more. It has taken me a lifetime to get here. Soon enough I shall go. What can I leave you? War, destruction. *Non!* I want you to promise me today, here, right now, that when I get us out, you will stay out. Enjoy your time with your son and your wife. Promise me you will stay out of this life.'

'What will I do *papa* ?'

'I'll make arrangements. I'll legal our family name. Fishing interests, dock and handling businesses. You capable. I put my trust in you.'

'Okay *papa*. I promise. But what are you ganna do?'

'Go up the bayou. See this D'Angelo.'

'*Papa*. You gonna travel out the *français* country?'

Pierre laughed. 'I been from it before.'

'But not north. Not to New York.'

'Now I have a reason.' Pierre smiled, but it was a smile which veiled fear. 'Where's my grandson?'

'His mother will bring him here soon.'

'*Bon*. You wanta take your old man indoors and share a bottle of red?'

Jean-Louis nodded and linked his arm with his father's and they strolled across the courtyard.

17 ROBBIE & MARRANZO TROUBLE

PAULIE MARRANZO AND HIS BEST FRIEND AL Bondini were feasting in the city. The last month had been all profit. The consumption of New Yorker's for the white powder was of gigantic proportions and their importation business was lining their pockets with more cash than they knew what to do with. It should not have been a problem, but it was. Al was worried about storing so much money his garage. Paulie was sympathetic to his friend's fears.

'I don't know what to suggest Al. I don't know anyone who ain't connected that we can go through to wash it and if they ain't connected I ain't sure I trust them.' Paulie drank his beer, waiting for a suggestion from his friend.

'What about the Afghani brothers, surely they could put us in touch with someone?'

'I don't wanna trust them with our money. There's a law firm in Jersey that I know of. They do mob work, handling offshore trusts and stuff, but if we go to them, we gotta be fucking careful.'

'It's worth the risk Paulie. I can't keep another box of berries in my garage. I don't sleep well at night.'

'Okay. Ill set it up. Wouldn't think we'd ever have this kinda problem with money, would ya?'

'All this kale if giving me headaches.'

'It's a nice fucking headache to have though,' joked Paulie.

A soldier came to Silvio with the rumor he had heard on the streets. Silvio Dalla Bonna took it upon himself to do his own checking up, before he went public with it before Robbie and Serge. At first he could find out nothing within their own ranks, so he touched upon the unaffiliated street gangs. The scale of what he uncovered shocked him.

'How you doing?' Robbie greeted him with a handshake. Serge Valone was already in attendance; he poured out three cups of coffee and brought them to the table.

'So, Serge said you had some disturbing news,' Robbie casually said while dropping two cubes of sugar into his coffee.

'Yeah. Someone's moving junk, a lot of junk and its unsanctioned,' Silvio picked up his coffee and took a sip, searched for his cigarettes, lit one. Serge screwed his face up and chewed on the fat cigar in his lips.

'You're sure of this?' Robbie asked.

Silvio nodded. 'I found out about a week ago, checked around. All the punk street gangs are moving it.'

'What's the estimate?' Robbie asked.

'Around seven hundred and fifty large a month.'

Serge took the cigar from his mouth and let out a low whistle. 'How long's this been going on?' he added.

'Seven, eight months.'

'That's around six million dollars,' Robbie said with incredulity.

'And nothing in kick-up,' said Silvio.

'Not a fucking cent,' added Serge.

'Who?' Robbie said with a stern voice.

Silvio paused for a second, took a drag of his smoke. 'The Marranzo's.'

'How the fuck didn't we see this going down?'

'It's a smart operation. It's shipped in from down south, channeled through these street gangs. No made guys are involved.'

'How did you find out?' Robbie persisted.

'A low level soldier, he ain't hooked up in this thing.'

'How the hell did he find out?'

'It's the street Robbie. Things spill, leave a little mess.'

'Tell me if the soldiers are hitting the mud pipe with this shit.' Robbie said in a raised voice.

'Nah. The soldiers are clean. They know better to start in with that crap; there's been too many busted heads in the last year. It's just Joe public who's buying the dope.'

'Well. I gotta go to Brooklyn and speak with Vinnie. Serge you call him, tell him were coming over today. You mind the store, me and Silvio will sort out this mess.'

'I know you like him Robbie, but if he's been fucking us, he's gotta be clipped,' Serge said. Robbie nodded then finished his coffee.

'What else is bothering me is where it's coming in from. If they're moving it up from the south, how do we know they ain't dealing directly with that fuck Sartois?'

'Forget about it. They know not to tie in with outside factions, not after what you been setting up. Surely to Christ,' said Serge.

'But if they have. Were gonna look like fucking monkeys to the commission. These fucking pricks,' Robbie said in a dark mood.

BROOKLYN

Vinnie had taken the call from Serge and had cleared the Vesuvio club of those that need not be there. He kept his cousin Tony around as he was the closest thing he had to a second in command. His younger brother Paulie had pulled one of his vanishing acts again and Vinnie was becoming increasingly aggrieved with his attitude. Paulie's absenteeism had evolved to an act of misconduct, yet Vinnie could not get him face to face to discipline him. It bothered him that he would have to meet the boss without his brother, it showed disrespect and Vinnie was aware that Robbie did not make visits unless there was some serious concerns.

The Vesuvio had been refurbished after the bomb attack that killed the Marranzo's middle brother. It didn't take away the memory of that night and Vinnie still had nightmares about it. But the new look Vesuvio managed to ease some of the pain and on the east wall there was a shrine to Tommy. Pictures of him, with his brothers and crew and a plaque that was engraved with a poem, to commemorate his life.

Vinnie had a table set up and he waited at the bar, sipping a brandy. He mulled over the racing pages of the paper, picking out his days bets. When the car pulled up outside he closed the paper and threw it behind the bar, then got up and went to the door to greet his boss.

Vinnie could tell by Robbie's face that whatever issue was at hand, it was serious. He held out his hand and Robbie took it briefly.

'Would you like a drink?' he asked.

'I'll take a scotch and water,' Robbie said lighting a cigarette.

'For you mister Silvio?'

'Nah thanks,' Silvio said abruptly.

Cousin Tony poured the drinks as Vinnie walked them to the table. Tony brought over the drinks and Vinnie told him to wait outside.

'Would you like something to eat?' Vinnie asked.

'I ain't gonna be here that long,' Robbie coldly said. Vinnie put his hand to his chin and rubbed his bottom lip with his index finger. The silence was deafening. Robbie took a hard swig of his scotch, said nothing, just let the silence brew.

'I wanna know where the tribute tax is?' Robbie finally said.

Vinnie looked confused; his eyes darted from Robbie to Silvio and back to Robbie as a way of asking. He got no answers.

'I sent this month's end up last week,' he said with protest.

'I ain't talking about your normal delivery. I'm asking about the new venture you've had going for the last half a year.'

'I ain't got no new venture Robbie,' pleaded Vinnie.

'You gonna sit there and deny you know anything about hop being shipped in from down south.' Robbie stubbed out his cigarette, gulped down his drink.

'Hop? Robbie. I ain't moving in no junk.'

'Well, the word out on the street is that Grand Canyon type quantities are moving in and the Marranzo's have their finger on the pulse.'

Vinnie sat back in his chair with a furrowed brow as he tried to decipher what he had just heard. He gestured with his hands as he could find no words.

'Vinnie, why would your family name be used if you weren't connected with the story?'

'Robbie. I don't have an answer. I don't know anything about any hop being moved. I ain't involved with anything; I ain't making any money from it.'

Robbie looked at Silvio whose eyes told of belief in Vinnie.

'Okay Vinnie, but you got some problems with your crew. Someone is definitely moving stuff and you're the guy in line. I wanna know within two days who it is or the hammer comes down.'

'Can I ask how much you think has been moved?'

'We estimate about six million,' Robbie said.

'Six fucking million. With all respect Robbie, that just ain't possible.'

'Vinnie you fucking better believe it, because it's happening.'

'And you better find out who's been jacking us off,' added Silvio.

'You got two days Vinnie,' said Robbie as he lifted himself from the chair. He buttoned up his jacket and stood looking at Vinnie. Vinnie scratched his forehead with a blank look about himself, he nodded. He watched his boss and underboss exit the club then walked to the bar and poured a big measure of whiskey and whacked it down his throat.

On the drive back to the island Robbie asked Silvio for his opinion. Silvio explained to Robbie that he truly believed that Vinnie had no knowledge of the junk score, but felt that he should of.

'You're saying he ain't capable?' Robbie said.

'He should keep his house in order. That is all I'm saying.'

'If he has rogue elements, you can't blame him.'

Silvio looked across to Robbie, then back to the road. 'He's a capo Robbie. He should fucking know what's going on in his own family.'

'Just as we did. We just found out about this shit.'

'Robbie. Vinnie's a capo; he's close to the street, that's why we have them. We're dealing with higher plain shit, it's the capo's who have to keep an order at street level.'

'Maybe you're right, but he does kick up his tax without fail and his crew does earn. Why weren't his brother around?'

'That's been bothering me. If he has got problems in his crew, I pray that it ain't with his brother.'

Robbie thought for a minute. 'In finality, what's your opinion on the outcome?'

'It's true he's a good earner and in general his crew are straight. But he's got splinters. You've worked your arse off because you got a vision of how this thing of ours should be. You put yourself out on the line, followed up your beliefs with action. He is of our *borgata*, if he's got splinters they get under our nails and that reflects to the commission. My vote. He would go.'

Robbie looked across to his friend thinking about what he had just relayed, turned back to the traffic before them. He nodded.

Back home he discussed the events with Serge. Serge was steadfast in his opinion that Vincent Marranzo should be clipped. Robbie asked his council to leave and for what seemed the first time in an age found himself alone. Stress crept into Robbie and his neck and shoulders were tight. He picked up the phone to call Angela but midway through dialing he hung up.

Robbie knew that he would have to keep a lid on the development, but knew that if the streets knew already it would only be a matter of time before the commission got word of the problem. The idea of holding the warm flesh of Angela, getting lost in her soft dark hair gripped him once again, but he found reality within himself. Knowing that he would be of irritating company, he held back from calling her. Instead he called up Salvatore Grecco.

Salvatore had not seen much of his boss of late. He was keeping the leash tight on his crew, raking in vast profits and organizing more activities to boost earnings. He was more settled in his life, but a piece of his soul greatly missed the old country.

Salvatore greeted Robbie with a customary kiss on the cheek and his boss offered him a seat and coffee. Then Robbie explained the Marranzo trouble. Salvatore was shocked, simply because he had his ear close to the streets and had heard nothing.

'Thersa no problem in my crew?' Salvatore said with concern.

'No. There's no problem with your crew. You've got no concerns there. You do good work, but this problem with the Marranzo's, I want you to fulfill the contract on Vinnie but not until I give you the word is that understood?'

'Sure boss.' Salvatore took a fat cigar from his jacket, put it to his nose and sniffed in the unique aroma.

'You keep this conversation between us Salvatore,' Robbie commanded.

'Sure boss,' he replied with deep sincere eyes.

BROOKLYN

Vincent spent the rest of the day drowning himself in liquor. The hammer was raised above his head. He felt powerless to halt its fall. Several times he phoned his brother on his mobile, but his call went directly to answer service. Within himself he played over the conversation with D'Angelo and raked through his mind to find out who could be responsible. Patience was thinning in him and once more he phoned his brother. Once again he got the message service and in a fit of pique he threw his phone across the room, it bounced off a wall and exploded across the floor. Unfazed, Vincent got up and went behind the bar, picked up a fresh bottle of whiskey and cracked the top open, poured out a large measure and gulped it down. He began to feel sickly but conquered it.

Cousin Tony who had been sitting near the door of the club got up from his table, locked the door then walked over to Vincent.

'Vinnie. Take it easy with that shit,' he said.

Vinnie looked at him with glassy eyes. But the rage within was evident.

'Call my fuckin' brother. Find out where that cunt is.'

'Youse shouldn't talk that way about him Vinnie.'

'Yeah. Well since we buried Tommy he's been spending less and less time at the store.' He steadied himself with a hand upon the bar.

'He's just blowing off steam Vinnie. Tommy hit us all hard.'

Vinnie stared at his cousin, picked up his glass and drained it.

'He ain't taking care of business. He's my back door man. He ain't ever fuckin' here. He's neglecting his duties in our garbage industry, I'm minding the place on my own, this fuckin' crap with junk in our own ranks. Fuck. I've been made to look a mug, especially after Robbie put his faith in me.' Vincent took another gulp of whiskey and held it in his mouth, chewed on it before swallowing. His jaw muscles were taught and the anger stretched the skin. 'Call him,' Vincent commanded.

'Okay Vinnie,' Tony replied in a calm voice.

'In fact. Call everyone. Get fuckin' everyone in. We're gonna find out what's fuckin' what.'

'Youse should maybe sober up youse wanna get everyone in,' Tony said.

Vincent's eyes narrowed and his teeth ground against each other. In an instant he swung at his cousin, crashing the glass into the side of his head. The blow knocked Tony to the floor and he landed in a sitting position, blood streaming from the wound, down across face. He sat looking up at Vincent, stunned, in fear.

'Fuck it,' shouted Vincent with frustration. He put his head in his hands. Blood from his own wound mixed with his tears. He swallowed hard then removed his hands and moved out from the bar to his cousin, who backed away from him. Vincent reached down with an outstretched hand. 'I'm sorry,' he said and pulled Tony to his feet, then embraced him. 'I'm sorry,' he repeated in a whisper.

Vinnie helped to clean up Tony's wound, which turned out to be superficial and they spent the next few hours contacting the crew.

When all those that could be summoned put in an appearance Vinnie stood before them. He had sobered up sufficiently and gave a performance of a man in control.

'I thank youse all for coming. But we've got serious business to deal with. I know the weekend is coming up and most of youse will have plans but those plans are folded. Now someone in this fuckin' crew is dealing in junk without an okay. Nothing is being kicked up to **the chair**, and so I'm getting the shit. I promise that you if I go down some of youse are gonna go too. So I want youse all out there and I want answers before midnight tomorrow. I don't care if youse find out it's your son or your mother, I wanna know. There's gonna be no hiding from this fuckin' thing and if youse think I'm being a hard case on this, imagine Dalla Bonna or that crazy Sicilian fuck Grecco dealing with you. You fuckin' guy's have got an easy ride wid me. So I wanna know by midnight tomorrow. Now get the fuck outta here.'

After the crew had departed Vinnie sat with his cousin again. They shared a silence over cups of coffee.

'Youse did good,' Tony finally said.

'Don't matter if we find out who's doing what. You and I know D'Angelo's gonna hit me,' Vinnie said with resignation.

'The boss is the boss and mostly they are hard headed pricks, but D'Angelo is a reasonable man. You'll get a pass. He likes you.'

Vinnie made a sour-cum-smile.

'He likes you,' repeated Tony, to which Vinnie sighed. 'Wanna go to a club?' Tony asked.

'You kiddin me?' Vinnie retorted.

'Well then let's go get somin' to eat. I can't stay in this fuckin' place all night.'

'You buying?'

'I ain't flush.'

'You cheap bastard. How the hell did I end up wid youse as a cousin?'

'You got lucky.'

'I got lucky. Yeah right. Well you're fuckin' driving.'

'Come on man, I'm injured.'

'Fuck you, you're driving.'

Vinnie enjoyed a large feast accompanied with bottles of wine, which helped him to put to the back of his mind the troubles he had. He had still not heard from Paulie and decided that he would look for him after his meal. Vinnie knew he would have to discipline him, brother or not.

To finish off the meal Vinnie indulged in a coffee and brandy, then he sent Tony home, paid the bill and drove directly to Paulie's home. Vinnie did not find his brother there only grief from his irate sister-in-law. Vinnie did the best he could to deal with her, but ended up telling her to shove it and leaving in a hurry.

Next he visited some of the dancing clubs and talked with a few pole girls that his brother was seeing. None had seen him, but the owner did tell Vinnie to remind Paulie of his bar tab, which had not been paid that week. Vinnie paid the debt, just to get another point to dish up on his brother.

For the next two hours he trawled the clubs and bars, conducting idle chat with associates and accepting their drinks until he found himself in no fit state to drive. No one had seen Paulie, nobody knew anything and Vinnie was intoxicated with liquor and frustration. He took a cab home and before he went to bed poured a nightcap, then called Paulie's mobile one last time. It transferred to answer phone.

'You better listen good Paulie 'cause I'm on a short fuse wid youse now. You return my call by nine a.m. 'cause if I have to come looking for you again, youse better disappear for good. We got trouble and youse ain't where youse should be. Brother your list is mounting up and believe me the axe is gonna fall.'

The return call did not come with the morning. Vinnie showered, barely spoke to his wife and gulped down a coffee. He caused an argument by informing his wife he was taking her car. She wanted to know where his car was. He told her he would only have the car for two hours maximum. She complained about shopping and various other issues which he did not hear, then exited the house.

At the social club he instructed a cousin to go and pick up his car, bring it back to the club and then take his wife's car back to her. Just as his cousin went out his brother walked in.

'Morning everyone,' Paulie said with an air of nonchalance. He walked to the bar and ordered a coffee from cousin Tony. Tony looked nervously from Paulie to Vinnie.

'Never mind your fuckin' coffee, get your ass over here,' shouted Vinnie from the table he was sitting at.

'Can I get a coffee for Krissakes?'

'Fuck your coffee,' Vinnie shouted in higher decibel. The mob clientele cleared out from the club. Except Tony who stood frozen behind the bar. Paulie's reality kicked in and he sauntered over to the table.

'I ain't even gonna ask where youse been 'cause I don't give a fuck. I don't want your apology or your excuses. All I wanna fuckin' know is, do you know what your role is around here?' Vinnie stared at his brother with raging eyes.

'Come on bruv,' said Paulie.

'Don't even start with that shit. Do you know what the fuck is going on around here?'

'What?'

'D'Angelo and Dalla Bona have been down here because we've got someone in the family who's dealing in unsanctioned candy.'

Paulie said nothing, but his eyes could not hide his shock.

Vinnie keyed in to his brother's shock immediately.

'You know about this?'

'No,' Paulie responded, trying to compose himself.

'You don't know anything about this shit?'

'No.' Paulie shook his head but could not look his brother in the eyes.

Vinnie leaned on the table closer to Paulie.

'I'm gonna ask you for the last time. Do you know anything about shit that's being moved?'

Paulie knew that his brother only asked three times maximum. If you gave Vinnie the truth within that time you would get leniency, if anyone thought they could get away with it he would find out eventually and they could forget about leniency.

'I might know something,' Paulie said in a quiet voice.

'Something. What's something?'

'We moved a little stuff.'

Vinnie sat back in his chair heavily, a deep look of astonishment set in a grey concrete across his face.

'You moved a little stuff. What's stuff Paulie? Cigarettes across the border, whores from Jamaica. What?'

'H.'

'Fucking H without seeking an okay.' Vinnie leaned across the table and backhanded Paulie's mouth. Paulie instantly jumped up and backed away from the table.

'What the fuck do you want from me? I'm sick of dealing with garbage trucks and gambling packages. I tired of making fucking chump change; I work my fuckin' ass off. An opportunity to make some serious money come along and I took it, so fuckin' what,' Paulie shouted down to his brother. Vinnie stood up but stayed his side of the table.

'What the fuck am I? I'm your boss. It's about respect; it's about knowing what's what. Where I stand, where you stand. You don't know the lines anymore. You've made me look a prick and you've put me in range with your antics. You're a selfish bastard and you always have been. When I'm in a casket will you be happy then?'

'You got no right to talk to me like that.'

'I got every right. I'm your elder brother and I'm your fuckin' boss. I'm responsible for answering to the guy in the chair and you put me in a position where I can't answer. '

'So don't answer, tell D'Angelo to go fuck himself.'

'What the fuck is wrong wid you? This crew belongs to the Cuccione *borgata*. You wanna go up against your own blood, you wanna remember the old fuck we had before Robbie, we were fucking starving.'

'You remember it. All I know is this, the money I make is mine. Fuck all these tribute taxes; I'm tired of being squeezed. All these fuck bosses are no better than the government, taking our money, laying down bullshit rules. And as for blood, we ain't got Cuccione anywhere in our name. We're Marranzo and you wanna know that.'

'I know I'm a Marranzo and you're bringing disgrace on our name. If Tommy was here now he'd be as disgusted as me.'

'Don't bring Tommy into this he's dead and his opinion don't matter no more.'

'You cunt. Well I tell you somin' now. Whatever money you made you better bring me seventy five per cent of it and I wanna know who's in with you and your suppliers.'

'Fuck you. You're getting nothing from me. D'Angelo's getting zilch of my dough and you can all go to hell.' Paulie stood with a posture that told his brother he had snapped in his mind. The whole family had always called him crazy since he was a child, because of the stunts he pulled and his temper, but now Vinnie could see that his mind had crossed into madness, for what he was telling Vinnie was as good as signing his own death warrant.

Vinnie swallowed hard and tried to clear his mind.

'Is this the way you want it?' he asked.

'It's the way it's gotta be from here on in,' Paulie replied steadfast.

'Then I gotta turn my back on you,' Vinnie spoke softly.

'So be it,' said Paulie with no emotion and walked directly out of the club and his brother's life.

Vinnie replayed the conversation over and over again in his mind to try and find some reason. None come and finally he broke. He locked himself in the back room and cried as the reality of losing his two brothers within a year hit him.

The counsel Vinnie courted with Robbie was granted two days later. Vinnie was a nervous wreck, he knew he was walking into judgment and believed his doom was sealed.

Robbie was cordial, unlike the other day when his blood was hot and his anger prevalent. Silvio Dalla Bonna was his usual uncommunicative self, which gave the room a deathly feel. Serge Valone gave Vinnie friendly smiles and a warm handshake.

'You look like you could use a drink.' said Robbie.

'Yes. Thanks,' stuttered Vinnie.

'Scotch?'

'Vodka please.'

Robbie nodded to Serge and studied Vinnie closely, offered him a cigarette. Vinnie took it and Robbie lit him. Robbie sat close and waited for Serge to bring the drinks. Nothing was said. The silence became an extension for Vinnie's fear. He struggled to conceal his trembling. He got some relief when Serge handed him his drink.

'So do you have anything to tell me?' Robbie finally said. Vinnie nodded. Dalla Bonna lent forward in his chair, catching Vinnie's eye. Vinnie knew there was no point in prolonging.

'It's my brother.'

Robbie nodded. 'And you had no prior knowledge of this?' he asked in a stern tone.

'I swear,' Vinnie answered with a shake of the head.

'And where is he now?'

'I don't know. He's walked. He's beyond my control now Robbie.'

'I'm sorry to hear this. The money?'

'He won't give over a cent.'

'He ain't gonna make it. You know this, Vinnie.'

'I know. How do I stand Robbie?'

'To be honest with you Vinnie, the vote was two to one against. But I'm gonna give you a pass, because I believe in you. You fuck up again though, well I guess you know.'

'Thanks Robbie.'

Robbie nodded, lit a cigarette. 'I don't mean to be insensitive, but do you want to do it?' Robbie said this without looking at Vinnie.

'I don't think I could Robbie,' Vinnie said, choking.

'I understand.'

Vinnie was fighting against the tears as he thought about his next question, but knew he had to request it.

'Could he have an open casket?'

The question shocked the room. They just hadn't thought about it in that fashion. The question brought home the reality to Robbie, Silvio and Serge that when the Marranzo's buried Tommy there wasn't much to put in the ground. It seemed natural that Vinnie would want to attend his last brother's funeral with the respect of an open casket, so he could say goodbye properly.

Robbie glanced to Serge who gave a surreptitious nod. Then he turned to Silvio. Silvio shrugged with a perplexed look.

'Sure Vinnie. We'll accommodate you there. I wanna be the first to say I'm sorry. I wish it didn't have to be like this.'

Vinnie said nothing, stared into the glass in his hand and nodded.

'Now let us put this behind us,' he stubbed out his cigarette and got to his feet. Vinnie placed his glass on the table, got to his feet. Robbie opened his arms and Vinnie went into them, kissed his boss on both cheeks, then they broke and clasped hands. Robbie put his arm around Vinnie's shoulder and led him out.

The contract went out on Paulie Marranzo that afternoon. Vinnie found a place to hide for the next few days, that place was in the bottle. He took no audience and allowed cousin Tony to run the store.

The contract on Paulie was given to one of Salvatore Grecco's Sicilians, with the strict order that head and face were to be left untouched. Salvatore hammered the point home to his man, who understood the severity of screwing up the hit.

Paulie Marranzo continued to move more heroin in and made no bones about hiding his feelings for his former families. He was a man on a self destruct mission, whose only goal was money. His best friend Al Bondini caught the vapor trail of Paulie's mode and filled with fear, loaded an easy haul truck with as much cash as he could and disappeared. Paulie transformed into a crazed man, living up to his sobriquet. He visited a well known mob bar, was refused drinks and shot the bartender in the shoulder. He was not hiding and seemed oblivious to the fact he was going to die. Paulie was building his organization, employing the street hoods as his muscle, not just using them as his distributors. He even managed to upset his Afghani partners by paying them less than what he originally agreed for the goods. In his final month he became a whirlwind within New York City. Mobsters gave him a wide birth. He had moved out from the house he shared with his wife and found his usual comfort with pole dancers from the clubs.

It was a pole dancer who set him up in the end. She was his latest sweetheart and he roomed with her. After a marathon sex session, as he lay exhausted and deep in his sleep, she called the number she was given. She opened the door for the assassin and he went to the bedroom, put a pillow across Paulie's chest and unloaded the six bullets of his revolver. The girl was promised two grand and a plane ticket to sunny climbs. She did not need either, for she never left the house alive that night.

By that time, the mob knew his whole organization. They took over his routes and paid the Afghani's the original rate for the heroin.

Serge was left with the deed of informing Vinnie of his brother's demise. Vinnie had had time to adjust to the impending fate and took it calmly. Just as promised Paulie was allowed an open casket. Robbie intended to pay his respects.

18 NAPOLEON & THE LAMB

AFTER THE RECENT MADNESS OF PAULIE MARRANZO it was a welcome comfort to see a calm descend across New York. Robbie felt he was ready for a vacation and decided to surprise Angela.

The Cuccione family was now deemed unworthy of newspaper reporting and Robbie was happy to see the limelight taken up by a corruption scandal at city hall and the recent utilities mismanagement debacle that had led to a reported fifty percent drop in profits and also threatened a shortfall in supply.

The Marranzo trouble had passed without a hiccup within the commission and the vast profits of the new heroin traffic were bolstering the family's offshore accounts. So Robbie felt justified in deciding to take a break. The road he set out upon building nearly two years ago was snaking its way to completion.

Like any other business though, there are always unforeseen complications and mysterious depths that can never be plumbed. So when the word came through that Pierre Sartois was in town and requesting an audience with Robbie it mystified everyone. Robbie immediately called council.

Consigliere Valone suggested to Robbie that the captains attend. Robbie dismissed the notion, explaining that he did not want it leaked on the streets that Sartois was meeting with the family. The proposal might be auspicious and even though he distrusted Sartois he still had respect for him and would respect his need for discretion.

'I don't trust that old French fuck,' Valone stated with venom.

Robbie smiled. 'Let's hear him out at least. You gotta figure it's serious enough for the old bastard to come north.'

'Is he visiting Gigante first?' Valone asked in sarcasm.

Robbie scratched his forehead, but did not reply.

'It's interesting,' said Dalla Bonna when he arrived.

'What is?' Robbie said.

'The fact the frog is coming here without seeing his sponsor.'

'You know for a fact he ain't gonna see Gigante?' retorted Robbie.

'No I don't know, but what I do know is that if he doesn't then he is opening himself up to a reprisal.'

'Let's just wait and see what is going on. We gotta hear the old fuck out. Give him the benefit.'

'Maybe he's got the dog about the Marranzo business.'

'There was no evidence that he was involved with Paulie's H smuggling.'

'It's kinda strange he's coming to town now though. And we all know he was a major player during the French connection days.'

'Nah. That ain't important enough to drag him away from that fucking swamp he calls home. This is bigger.' Robbie opened a bottle of wine and poured three glasses. He handed a glass to Serge then Silvio then raised his glass. 'Salute. A la familia, e le nostri salvezza,' Robbie toasted.

'La familia,' said the *consigliere* and underboss in unison.

Robbie put down his glass and lit a cigarette. 'Now when Sartois arrives, I want you two to show him the respect he deserves. I know I shouldn't have to say this, but let's not forget he was around with a lot of the old timers and he done a lot of business with them. He might want to stay on that old cobblestone road, but we owe him the diligence to listen to what he has to say. In our time have you ever known him to leave his Cajun country?'

Silvio and Serge shook their heads.

'Me neither. So he is affording us a respect that he has not shown to our predecessors. So while he is on our turf we're gonna afford him that courtesy.'

Little Napoleon of the southern underworld arrived in New York with one of his most trusted enforcers. A man who had served him well for the last quarter of a century. Sartois had managed to keep him in the background, so his reputation was one of myth. Sartois' oldest friend in the underworld, even Gigante had only ever met the man once; such was Sartois expertise at keeping him under wraps.

Pierre Sartois had high anxiety about the trip to the foreign north lands, but having Alain Sarda alongside helped to ease some of that trepidation and aided his notion of well being. Sarda would be an ace card. The unknown quantity that would throw D'Angelo and others off guard.

Alain Sarda was a fifty year old monster. He had a frame worthy of the ancient Hercules. More importantly he was a man without remorse, devoid of compassion with a black hole for a soul and an obsidian rock for a heart. There was no humor within him, no thought for the world around him and no reason for what he was.

Sarda would break a man's body or kill on request at the word of Sartois without question. He had no desire to be anything more than what he was and for Sartois he had rubbed out over forty people. Killing was his enjoyment; other pleasures were few and far between.

In the southern underworld, his name sent shivers down every spine. He was never seen at any council of Sartois, so it went that if you ever saw Sarda it would invariably be the first and last time you set eyes upon him.

The underworld needs enforcers and each has their own reputation which echoes fear within their fortified community. Sarda's reputation carried much weight within his mob world, more so because of his frightening silence for he was a mute and had been from birth. There was no medical explanation as to his lack of communication for his voice box, tongue and vocal chords were all intact. It just seemed that Alain Sarda had no need to communicate to the world through words. And though his notoriety was abundant within his southern habitat, to the north lands he was just another name and because Sartois did not venture out of his enclave he could not know that the reptilian killer he took along would have very little affect on the psyche of the northern mob.

At his Plaza hotel suite Sartois talked to the killer Sarda. He offered Alain a glass of water. Sarda did not imbibe alcohol. The big man sipped his water and listened like a school pupil during lecture.

'This business I have with this D'Angelo character is very delicate. These north boys are very strong and have certain lacking manners. After I am finished here I might request for you to stay.' Sartois topped up Alain's glass, who nodded his understanding.

'*Mais*. It will not be a problem for you to operate in this shithole, alone?' Sartois asked to which Sarda shook his head, with the same unchangeable expression that he mostly wore. 'Bon,' added Sartois and checked the time. 'Well, let us go and see this *sacuad*. Let me transform into that which I hate to be.'

Sarda looked at his *podna,* clearly confused.

'Take no notice; I'm old and very foolish. Come come.'

When the two powerhouses finally came together they conveyed upon each other due respect.

'I welcome you to New York Mister Sartois and offer all courtesies during your stay,' Robbie said holding out his hand. Sartois took the offer and shook sincerely.

'I thank you for seeing me in such short notice and congratulate you on your successes.'

Robbie nodded.

'Let me introduce you to my people. This is Silvio,' Robbie stated and Sartois shook hands with the underboss, who nodded and said nothing, but looked deep into the old man's face. Robbie continued, 'And this is my advisor Serge.'

'Ah yes,' said Sartois as if in recognition and Serge stepped forward to offer his hand.

'Welcome. I hope you had a good trip,' Serge spoke. Sartois nodded, then turned his body slightly.

'That's Alain. He's my guide. He doesn't speak; do not take it as an insult.'

Robbie and his crew nodded their greetings. They were impressed with enormity of the man, not overawed though. Silvio was running through his computer of a brain trying to place the man and his name, but he had no records.

'Well, let's go into the other room and get comfortable,' Robbie suggested.

'I'll join you in a minute. I've got to make a quick phone call,' Silvio said excusing himself. Robbie nodded, knowing that Silvio was going to try and get the word on this man mountain that accompanied their guest.

The quartet went into the room and Robbie and Sartois sat across from each other at a table. Alain Sarda stood directly behind the old man like a guarding angel. It made Robbie uneasy to have the massive apparition peering down upon him, but he was not about to ask him to move. Serge took the drinks order and prepared them. After serving he sat at the table, next to Robbie.

'I tell no tales to you Mister D'Angelo,' began Sartois without further waiting. 'I don't want to be here.' His speech was measured which gave the impression he was trying to dispose of his accent. 'As for you and your organization, your progress is impressive. Whether we can do business I don't know. But I come to you as a humble man with many concerns.'

'Well I'll do my best to ease those concerns for you,' interjected Robbie.

'*Bon*. What I find is that a good friend of mine is your enemy, so it seems that I am seen as your enemy,' Sartois took a sip of his brandy, watching D'Angelo closely. Robbie gave out a slight shake of the head. '*Mais*,' continued Sartois. 'We have to find the common ground. I come here today to offer you a service.'

'And for that service you will require a form of compensation?'

'*Qui*.'

'Very well. Speak freely here, for if we cannot reach an agreement let us part as friends.'

'*Bon. Bon.* I need to cleanse my family name. I have a son and grandson and I wish for them to have a fruitful and peaceful future.' Sartois shifted his body as if in discomfort, then took one of his high toxic, rich smelling French cigarettes from the packet and lit it. 'My friend that I have in this city has rage in his heart for you. He feels cheated. Wrong or right he wishes to walk a road that I don't agree with. I can mediate.'

'But you can't guarantee a positive outcome,' Robbie said forcibly.

'In this business, who could?'

'If he was to walk that road you mention, he would not last. The new commission would crush him. So you see I have all the mediation I need.' *The Lamb* was direct never letting his gaze move from *Little Napoleon*.

'As you say it is true, but that does not aid me in my quest for a blank future to hand to my next generations. In this life, sometimes you have to make sacrifices to survive. We both know this. I can lead him to the table or I can take him to his maker.'

Robbie turned to Serge who took a large intake of breath. Robbie moved back into the comfort of his chair and made a gesture with his hand, indicating Sartois to continue.

'We will offer him a way to save his pride. I will entice and seduce him with the word from you that he will get your vote to head the commission next time the presidency arises and that you will persuade the majority to vote in his favor. Power seduces those that need it Mister D'Angelo and my friend needs it. He will know that once he is head of the commission he can move against you with ease.'

'He will never be head of the commission,' Robbie stated with words of iron.

'Of course he won't. But it'll buy time and time has a way of dispelling rage.'

'His rage for me will never go away.'

'Maybe not.'

'So with all respect, you can't guarantee anything and I have the commission backing my arse. What do I need you for?'

'You have the commission backing your arse. I do not. I have managed to keep my land as my land. I have kept those fucking Colombians to a minimum and the Cubans and even you Wops from operating in my backyard. If he carried out what he wishes to do, you and I know there would be a war. I'm a *straniero* to you; you would come for me sooner or later. I could import my Corsican and Marseilles brothers to fight but I'm too old for more war. Either way I will die soon enough. I want the best for my family.'

'You want out?' Robbie asked without emotion.

'I want out. I want to retire. I have certain businesses which are accountable and to my son and grandson they go. When I'm gone it will be open season on my territory, but you have first word and the opportunity to move in before any other family.'

'And your son understands this?'

'He knows they will have a future that is cleansed.'

'And what of your friend, in the final outcome?'

'He might accept but if he doesn't, I can remove him. In my land, where he feels safe. You will be in the clear. I will suffer.'

Robbie sat looking at the old man in studied concentration. 'Let's have another drink,' he said.

After his meeting with D'Angelo the old Frenchman headed for Gigante's territory. He would surprise him and he would put their friendship on the line once he divulged he had met with D'Angelo. It was part of the politics and the old man did not feel easy in his heart, but he wanted a blank future and was willing to sacrifice his comrade.

Gigante was more than happy to accommodate his visitor and insisted on taking Sartois into the city to eat at one of his special restaurants. Sartois declined, he was already sick of this foreign land, but Gigante persisted and eventually he had to capitulate.

With a loss of appetite he picked at the food before him, anxious to explain his reasons for being in New York. Gigante was so excitable though it was hard for Sartois to open his heart. Gigante did not even think to question why his friend was in town.

'Listen, my *podna* I come up north to set our wheels in motion,' Sartois said with a smile and sipped his wine.

'We start to build then and move for that son of a bitch D'Angelo.' Gigante said beaming.

'Let's not get ahead of ourselves my friend. First you have to know I meet D'Angelo,' Sartois explained.

'You met that bastard. What the fuck for?' Gigante's eyes showed anger.

'I have to see if he was the man your people think he is. I need to know what will come upon us.'

'So what did that whore say?'

'Many things. I told him I could mediate, keep you calm. He promised me you would get his vote for the next presidency of the commission, he would use his influence so you could be installed into that position.'

'He said that?' Gigante leaned back into his chair airing his disbelief. 'How can you take that prick at his word?'

'It buys time for us to build our strength.'

'That I like, but you can't trust that fucking piece of shit. Like I told the commission, he whacked out his own boss, so he has no respect for the rules. He wants the world. Ancello in Chicago might be the head of the commission at the moment, but I fuckin' guarantee he takes orders off that *puttana*.'

'That may be, but we know that this commission will be ended once you have the power. D'Angelo will be isolated, patience is the key. He has the power now, but if you can wait, you can strip him. My *podna*, all I ask is that you accept the advice I give you. Forget D'Angelo for now. Let us build.'

Gigante drank his wine, looked his friend in the eyes. 'No,' he said with strength.

'*Bon*. I accept your word. We remove him.'

'I want your Corsicans for this job.'

'Of course my friend. When they arrive I would like for you to meet with them.'

'You know I'll come. I always enjoy your Cajun hospitality and now I like your Cajun girls.'

'*Mais*. They are aplenty for you *podna*.'

19 GOVERNMENT HAMMER

SUSAN RUSHDIE AND HER O.T.C.F AGENCY HAD been in the slow painstaking process of building a R.I.C.O case against the Colombian kingpin Gabriel Vargas. Her investigation had been ongoing, ever since she had had that surprise meeting with her old flame Robbie. She had seen Robbie once more during that period because she could get very little leads on the so called big man Vargas. Robbie had fed her what he knew and after he once more fed her aching body. For weeks after Susan felt ashamed for crossing certain lines, but her strong will pulled her out of it and she threw all her energy into pursuing this Colombian connection.

One of the main reasons why her department could not get into the world of Vargas was because he did not exist. There were absolutely no records on the man until she contacted the C.I.A and was continually stonewalled. She pestered Washington with a zeal that pissed so many people off that in the end she was delivered a file on Vargas.

Robbie was correct; Vargas had indeed helped the C.I.A nail Pablo Escobar and was also responsible for helping his own government wipe out some of the top ranks of the F.A.R.C guerrillas. But like most philanthropists he wore a sheep's clothing to disguise his underlying wolfish nature and soon had taken over both major cartels within Colombia. He increased the exportation worldwide and hid in the sanctuary of a mansion in the hills. He was a faceless head, a man whose name never seemed connected with the cartels because he had structured them with so many bosses that the link to him was a maze. His government refused to cooperate with the Americans on bringing him down, insisting he was an upstanding figure who had served his country with loyalty. For the C.I.A. he was an embarrassment, he had played them at their game and come out clean and finally they had to forget him, for their war on global terrorism began and their resources were stretched.

So Vargas went to the U.S.A for four months out of every year, to quietly oversee a major part of his organization, but mainly to keep in touch with the politicians he had made friends with. Most were out of office now, but some remained and they still liked to socialize with this charismatic enigma that helped win a major battle in the war on narcotics. They all refused to see the accusations that the C.I.A had thrown at him. It was the complex world of politics at its worst.

Nobody in the world would have put money on Susan Rushdie and her department getting to Vargas, but she was a woman who had persistence and fight. She leaned on people in government and threatened those out of office who were friends of Vargas with exposés in the national press if she didn't get what she wanted. She obtained more resources, more employees and more co-operation to go after Vargas. Everyone involved wanted a quiet life and one by one they gave her something. Her pursuit led to the fact that Vargas held American citizenship, therefore qualifying him to be indicted under a R.I.C.O statute and she had enough evidence linking him with presiding over a criminal enterprise to put him away for life. All she needed was for the *Reyes de cocaina* to enter the country.

In politics though, nothing has a straight run to any outcome and Susan had enemies within government halls and Vargas still had powerful friends, who were about to act in a method of self preservation.

The cogs of conspiracy began slowly and churned a protectorate around those who feared exposure. The attorney general summoned her and she dutifully obliged and found herself at a closed hearing, where the attorney general flanked by numerous advisors opened up wounds which she thought she could escape. They attacked fast and hard.

'Miss Rushdie. What is your relationship with Roberto D'Angelo?' threw out a hard faced advisor. Susan was stunned and fought for inner composure.

'I have no relationship with D'Angelo,' she stammered.

'Really. That's interesting, considering you are the head of the Organized Crime Task Force.'

'What's your point?' she snapped.

'My point Miss Rushdie is that D'Angelo is head of a New York crime family and a Mafia commission member, who presides over a sixty billion dollar criminal empire.'

'D'Angelo presides over a criminal empire that has declined and is continuing to decline, their threat is limited.'

To this quite a few members of the room laughed mockingly.

'Miss Rushdie your statement is quite bizarre, considering your organization is housed in New York and for the last eighteen months a war has been waged there. First a crime boss is blown away in the middle of Manhattan; heads of the Russian cartel are slaughtered like something out of the Al Capone days. Irish hoodlums are turning up as corpses and you say the mafia poses no threat. Just what in the hell are you doing in New York?'

'I'm doing my job. We've been chasing the Mafia for years and have made great inroads, but for the recent violence they are not as powerful as you like to think.'

'So because of that, you neglect to investigate further and turn a blind eye to their activities?'

'I'm not turning a blind eye. They'll be brought down like everyone else, but right now I have a bigger fish to catch,' shouted Susan.

'You have bigger fish? Miss Rushdie the department you run is not there for you just to fulfill your own personal aims. It serves the people of this great land and therefore exists to bring to book any and all organized crime syndicates, not just those of your choosing and not to look the other way for those you are in bed with,' said the attorney general with a greasy smirk.

'You son of a bitch. How dare you talk to me that way. I don't have the resources to go after every crime organization in this country at once, I-'

'As I understand, you have increased resources,' butted in an advisor with a raised voice.

'You hypocrites. You know who my department is investigating and you're aiming to protect him.'

'If I were you Miss Rushdie I would choose your words carefully. Any accusation of corruption could land you in libel court and you would not be able to continue in your position while fighting a court case. It could be very easy for you or very hard.'

'This stinks,' Susan said in anger.

'Now we are requesting you to close down your current investigation and turn over any and all files relating to this matter. It will be appropriated to a newly formed department investigating overseas infiltration of the homeland.'

'Just what the fuck does that mean?' countered Susan.

'I would ask you to mind you language Miss Rushdie. Your organization is to close down the investigation, effect immediately.'

'Gabriel Vargas is the investigation and you can't even bring yourself to speak his name. Just what kind of power does he have?'

'That's what we aim to find out Miss Rushdie.'

'This is bullshit.'

'Miss Rushdie. We want to see results regarding the New York crime gangs. There are two men outside who will accompany you back to New York and you will hand over all the relating files. That's all,' the attorney general said and raised himself from his chair, the roomful of advisors did likewise and without saying another word to Susan left her in the room alone, shaking her head trying to figure out in her thoughts, what had just happened.

When she arrived back in New York Susan began telephoning various people in various government agencies, but the wheels were turning and the walls were going up, nobody would take her calls; they were in meetings or out of the office, she was informed. The two men began to lose patience with her and demanded she begin boxing up the files for shipment to Washington. Without demur she eventually obliged and the men accompanied her as she went throughout her department ending the investigation and ordering what they wanted. She was never given a moments breathing space and was forced to hand over everything. She reckoned to herself that she could copy some files, but the chaperones made it impossible. Within half an hour of the boxing of the files a truck arrived and men began loading them for transportation. Within an hour of the truck leaving, she received a telephone call informing her that her extra resources were to be pulled, the final nail was driven home and Vargas was once more a ghost.

Susan became tired of the constant knocks on her office door and the condolences and goodbyes, she took flight from the building on the verge of tears and found a bar where she could hide and drink. The drink would not make the days events disappear though and in frustration she found herself driving, drunk, to Robbie's house. The tiredness and drink made the journey a nightmare, since she had caught the commuter rush hour traffic.

It took a little over two hours to get to Robbie's and she was in no mood to be interrogated by the Sicilian guy at the gates who could barely speak English.

'Listen you fuckin' *ginzo*, justa go an tella da boss dat Susan issa here,' she mocked in a broken accent. The Sicilian realizing that he had a crazy woman on his hands phoned through to the house and soon enough Susan was allowed entry.

'Jesus. Susan, what the hell are you doing coming here?' Robbie asked greeting her at the door.

'We need to speak.'

'Okay. But you're takin' a hellova risk coming here.'

'It doesn't matter anymore, she said enigmatically.

When she sat down and began to calm down she poured out her heart about what had happened. Robbie was stunned, but not surprised, he knew how politics worked and knew it had to have corruption in order to work, but it did not diffuse his disappointment at the fact that Vargas would not be taken down. Susan was wasted and needed some form of comfort. She went off on a tangent about bringing down people in office, she broke down and cried and she raged. She wanted to stay with Robbie that night, but Robbie was meeting Angela. He would not postpone Angela, not for Susan.

'Listen babe, I've got to leave tonight for Chicago. I'll be back tomorrow. What I want you to do is go to my cabin upstate and wait for me, I'll join you. You need some time to calm down and relax. Call in sick tomorrow, don't tell anyone where you are and we'll spend a week together up there to chill and figure this thing out. I'll get someone to drive you up there, so you don't have to worry.'

'I've got no clothes or anything,' she said pitifully.

'I'll give you some money, go shopping tomorrow for what you need, I'll be with you tomorrow, okay.'

'Okay,' Susan said with a nod, she finished off the drink in her hand.

'Go to the bathroom and get yourself together, I'll begin making the arrangements.'

While Susan was in the bathroom Robbie made four important phone calls and summoned one of his Sicilians to drive her giving him implicit instruction on what he wanted. When she returned, he hugged and kissed her then saw her off.

After Susan was driven away Robbie went and poured himself a strong drink. A mood of aggravation cloaking him. It came as no surprise to him that the government had opted to play this way, but it pissed him off all the same. Now they had tied him and Susan together they would make it even more of a desire to come after his organization. Robbie knew he was in a quandary, Susan was the only high ranking government official he could class as corrupted. Don Costello before him had rakes of political affiliations, he was a master at making friends in city hall and that is where Robbie was lacking. When he arranged for the old Don to be blasted from this earth he could never imagine that his political friends would disappear forever, but they did and Robbie did not have the nous for retaining or recruiting sympathizers. In his street world he was a king, a master at manipulating and restructuring. He demanded respect and got it tenfold, he was a true leader.

In the political world he just could not make any inroads and knew that whatever hammer the government was now wielding it would surely have his name upon it. Within the first five minutes of Susan conveying to him the day's events he decided that she was now expendable.

Susan was awoken by her driver a few hours later. Her mouth was dry and she felt rotten as a dehydrated tiredness hung over her. The man opened the door and handed her the key, then said his farewells and drove away. She threw her bag down on a chair then went to the bathroom, stripped and stepped under the warm cascading water of the shower. After twenty minutes she felt better and stepped out, wrapped a towel around her naked dripping body and went into the living room. Instinctively she poured herself a drink, then sat and lit a cigarette. She felt the need to talk to someone but was embarrassed to call anyone. As she sat drinking, smoking and thinking she came to the conclusion that she would have to resign. She was angry with those bastards who had betrayed her and she suddenly thought about something Robbie had said to her once, when he reasoned that organized crime and politics were one and the same. She was drawing upon the same conclusion. No more would she play at their games, tomorrow she would resign.

'Fuck them,' she shouted. Her voice reverberated around the empty home.

Meanwhile outside the Sicilian who had driven her there had returned and was watching her through the window. He played with the key in his hand and bided his time.

Inside Susan drank and cried, drank some more, listened to some music, cried more tears, poured more drinks and finally collapsed in exhaustion on the deep soft sofa. Through the window the Sicilian watched for a few minutes then with stealth moved to the door and quietly opened it.

Susan shouldn't have awoken, but awake she did, just as her assassin clicked off the safety catch on his gun. Her eyes opened wide and she lay staring at him, the man froze, not quite believing, and then suddenly felt a pain in his stomach as Susan kicked out. She screamed hysterically as she leapt up and the man cracked her across the mouth with his pistol. Adrenalin had risen within her and she raked her nails down both sides off his face, oblivious to the pain and blood in her mouth. The Sicilian growled in pain and gave her a straight left jab which caught her flush on the nose, knocking her down upon the sofa, but as if on a spring board she bounced back up and grabbed his hair, using her weight to pull him down, and they fell to the floor at which point she relinquished her grip, jumped to her feet and ran naked towards the door.

The Sicilian fired off a shot and more by luck caught the fast moving Susan, who collapsed face down on the quarry tiled floor. The bullet had smashed into her lower spine causing irreparable damage. She lay gasping for breath, paralyzed, understanding that she would die, and understanding that she had been betrayed by everyone. She could hear the footsteps of the man coming to her across the tiles and then his voice as he said something in foreign. She did not know what he said, but knew he was boiling with anger.

The Sicilian, with his face torn open approached her.

'Fucking whore,' he said in his native tongue and without pity for the stricken woman bent down and fired three times into the back of her head. He put the gun back in its holster then went and washed his face. When he returned he poured himself a drink then dialed a number. The conversation was brief and after he hung up, he sat and waited.

Within five minutes two cars arrived. Vincent Marranzo had been charged with clean up and disposal. He entered with three other men and they took care of cleaning the house and making Susan's body disappear from the world. Vincent drove the assassin away to a supposed safe house. After Vincent dropped him off, the assassin was met by Salvatore Grecco and it was the last person he met in this world. He washed up on Staten Island two days later. He was illegal so untraceable.

Susan's body was driven back to New York and she was unceremoniously buried in the foundations of a new twelve story car parking lot. The night she died, Robbie spent it with Angela, not caring or feeling for Susan Rushdie, head of the O.C.T.F.

20 MILK AND HONEY

ROBBIE MET WITH HIS HIERARCHY THE NEXT morning. He explained the hit on Susan Rushdie and the breakdown of her investigation into the Colombian drug lord Vargas. The OCTF's switch of sights back to their world and anything else Susan had furnished him with.

Serge was first to offer his views. His face did not hide the discomfort and disapproval.

'I told you from the start Robbie that you shouldn't have gone down that road. The government are not to be dealt with. They are worse fucking criminals than us. They can throw out the constitution when it suits their gain; they've ripped off every fucking idea to make money from us. You can never be in bed with them.'

'In Robbie's case that literal,' said Dalla Bonna, making light of the events.

'Very fucking funny Silvio,' said Serge. 'Robbie. You should have consulted with me first on this. I am your consigliere. When you go ahead with things like this without a degree of talk, it makes this organization redundant. '

'I'm the boss,' said Robbie giving Serge a deep stare.

'Yes, you're the boss, but you wanted to boss because you had a new vision. Going ahead without consultation makes you like old man Costello. It's back to those days we all detested.'

'You're right,' said Robbie with a nod, 'There wasn't enough time to call you and discuss it though. She was in a panic; I didn't know what the fuck she was going to do. Had to calm her down, she was at the house; Angela was waiting for me at a restaurant. I had time just enough to arrange it all.'

'You had her clipped at the cabin?' said Dalla Bonna.

'Yeah. It's a clean hit, a communion.'

'When was the last time you had that swept?' continued the underboss.

'I don't know a week, two weeks maybe.' Robbie was aggravated and lit a cigarette. Dalla Bonna sighed.

'Jesus Robbie, you can't be sure the cabin's clean,' added Serge.

'The place is fucking clean. Will youse two stop worrying about it. The fuckin' thing is done 'n' dusted. You know for a little time I would like to forget about all the bullshit with the commission, the government, that old fuck Gigante. You know we got a Marranzo funeral to attend, the second in a year. For a while I wanna know about this family. I wanna know that business is good, the capo's are pulling in green that this family is running as it should. I've been lost in all this high politics crap for what seems like a lifetime. I feel out of touch with the streets.'

'You got no worries there,' offered Dalla Bonna.

'It's on the streets where rebellion begins. You been down there lately?' Robbie said.

'Yeah. I done the rounds. Things are as they should be,' Dalla Bonna said in a stern voice.

'So fill me in.'

'What the fuck is wrong wid youse Robbie? Garbage is in high profits. *Babania* is shifting like candy. Labor unions always come through. Money is coming in through porn like no tomorrow. Everyone of our crews is earning and everyone is kicking up their tribute. There ain't nothing wrong anywhere.'

Robbie turned to Serge. 'The accountants are keeping up on their end?'

'Robbie will you quit worrying. The empire is running smooth.'

'Well that's good enough. I never thought it would be so hard to run this family. Feels like I been doing it for twenty years.'

'Can't tell. You still look good,' Dalla Bonna said.

'No doubt it'll catch up. I got this fear that one morning I wake up, I'm grey, balding, fat and bored.'

'Ain't enough time in this life to be bored. When you gonna marry Ange, have some kids?' Dalla Bonna added.

'Forget personal business. Who wants a drink?'

'It's just about eleven,' Serge pointed out.

'So. If the family is running well, let it run. We'll take a day out. Visit some bars, shoot the breeze. I miss some normal living, friends.'

'I could go watch some girls.'

'Is that all you fuckin' think about?' Serge asked of Dalla Bonna.

'That and money,' he replied with a shrug.

'We should find Serge a woman,' Robbie said.

'Now they cost too much fucking money,' Serge replied.

'Well, if we're going, let's go.'

The trio found their way to some out of town bars, where the clientele was friendly and the girls also. They paid the top dollar entrance and paid through the nose for drinks, but they did not care. They were out of the area, anonymous and in high spirits.

Serge was sizing up the profit margin of the club they were in. He ordered a beer and a whisky chaser from the delectable twenty something waitress, in skimpy shorts and high heels. Robbie ordered the same, while Silvio settled for a vodka and tonic.

'We should open a chain of these fucking places,' said Serge.

'You think?' replied Robbie.

'It's a good and easy source for a lot of income.'

'It's a good source of easy lays too,' said Silvio.

'You and sex.'

'I'm serious Robbie. We should seriously look into it.'

'Okay. Get a business plan together and we'll look at it. I could do with some diversity.'

A selection of girls came and went to the table. Some got large tips; others just got felt up by Silvio, his lascivious juices running high. So high, that he eventually persuaded one of the girls to go out to his car, where he received a blow job and her phone number. Power seduces some women and Silvio was aware of this from his days as a young street punk. While he was gone, Robbie and Serge distracted themselves from the girls and fell into talk about their life.

'This government or any government for that matter is no real different to our thing,' said Robbie.

'That's true. They need a certain level of corruption to survive. How could any government in the world operate effectively without ever breaking the rules they make. Especially in a land like ours. It's ironic that they are the biggest extortionists in existence and there ain't a fucking thing the populace can do about it. They can raise taxes at the stroke of a pen. Who can challenge them? Nobody. They can waste billions, feather their retirement nest eggs, live a life of luxury and spout off crap about how they care, and get away with crass negligence. Politicians are just a bigger version of us Robbie and that won't ever change.'

'It's sickening. I mean think about the things they have stolen from us. The numbers, they legalize it and call it a lottery. Booze, they allow it to be legal and controlled, so they can tax it. Narcotics. They let these giant pharmaceutical companies experiment with drugs and use illegal drugs for their gain, because of their vast monetary gifts. If they ever legalized narcotics, these companies would get the first tenders to manufacture and sell the shit, we wouldn't get a look in. Sometimes I think we're the fools. All we're trying to do is make a living, we've done it through the street, 'cause that's all we know. They persecute us. Joe Kennedy knew this shit, that's why he got out; let his boys get into politics. He knew that's where the real power was.'

'Lotta fucking good it did the boys.'

'The point is Serge, when you're a politician; you're a gangster who gets legally voted to power.'

'Whatchyer gonna do? Take a drink and say fuck 'em.'

Robbie took a drink. 'Fuck 'em,' he said. Serge drank too.

'It's still a land of milk and honey to us though,' Robbie added.

'I'll drink to that.'

Silvio returned and finished his drink. 'So what's the topic?'

'Milk and honey,' Serge said.

'Well, there's plenty of honey,' Silvio said, grabbing the next girl that walked past and hauling her into his lap.

'Jesus,' Robbie said.

21 LEGACY

ANGELA LAY WITH HER HEAD IN ROBBIE'S lap. He rubbed his fingers through her hair and with his free hand sipped his wine, all the while concentrating on the game on TV. Angela lay in a relaxed state, the glass resting on her belly, the wine inside barely touched.

'That's nice,' she said in a low sleepy voice.

'You like that?'

'Umm.'

'Well sorry babe, but you're gonna have to move, 'cause I need a top up.'

'No. I can't.'

'Come on babe. My arm's going dead anyhow.'

Angela sat up with a deep sigh of agitation. She pushed a hand through her hair then shook her head, reached for the cigarettes on the table. Robbie sat up and poured more wine, looked at her glass.

'You're slow tonight.'

'I don't much feel like drinking.' She lit a cigarette and threw the lighter on the table.

'Do you think you'll ever get out of this life Robbie?'

'Everyone gets out eventually,' he mused transfixed on the game.

'I'm serious Robbie. I mean out of the Mafia.'

Robbie gave her a sideways glance and a shake of the head, eyes of stone. 'Why the hell do you have to use that word?'

'What word am I supposed to use?'

'I don't know but why the fuck do you have to start in with this crap again?'

'Don't talk to me like one of your street thugs,' she scowled and stood up began pacing the room.

'I'm sorry Ange, but I can't talk about that life. You know this.'

'It's not that life Robbie, it's your life. It's not separate it is here.'

'It's fucking separate from you and I keep it that way. I don't bring it into your life and I don't bring you into it.'

'Jesus Robbie, you've got a twisted idea of the realms of reality. I'm in your life and every time I'm with you it's with us. There's no over there and over here. It's all one life Robbie.'

'You know what with the shit I have to deal with out there and the mental pressure of keeping my family together you're the one bit of sanity in my life, the one area where I find some peace and now you're going all McMurphy on me. It ain't what I need Ange.'

'McMurphy?'

'Crazy.'

'It's a simple fucking question Robbie. Will you ever get out?' she said in a cold blunt manner.

'I'm the boss of a family. That means I don't have the luxury of retiring or resigning or simply quitting. You wanna change jobs, you just do it, you wanna walk out of your job, you just do it. You wanna call in sick, you just do it.' Robbie tapped his chest. 'I can't do that.'

'And what about if you had a new family?'

'What are you talking about?'

'I'm pregnant Robbie?'

Robbie's eyes narrowed and his mouth became tense for a while as if he was in a void. Then he relaxed and breathed deep through his nostrils, took a gulp of the wine and set the glass down.

'Come over here,' he said all the while thinking about the old man from New Orleans and the conversation they had about legitimizing his blood. He took Angela in his arms and placed his mouth on hers, thinking now about his legacy.

Robbie made love to Angela and after held her strongly. There was confusion running through him. Life was running through Angela. He stroked her belly, tracing circles with his fingers. His eyes transfixed on her stomach, his thoughts on the creation inside.

Reality of new life made him think of his blood family. His mother and sister. His mother had fallen out with him hard when she discovered he was involved with the Mafia. She had disowned him, told him she wanted nothing more to do with him. His sister had landed a job in Seattle and taken their mother with them. Like everything in Robbie's world they were divided from his reality. They were in another life and as much as he loved them, he was detached from their world. His life in organized crime had consumed him and the Mafia was his true love. It was his family and the honour of leading that family could not be measured against anything, until this night.

As Angela fell asleep he gently moved her to the bedroom, lay her in bed, covered her and kissed her forehead, she stirred slightly, but only to turn on her side into the foetal position.

Robbie brewed a coffee and smoked at the breakfast bar. After, he showered got dressed and left. His Sicilian bodyguards, who had dutifully waited all evening, got to their feet as he exited Angela's apartment and took point as they left the building. The streets were empty, but they used caution to assess any potential threat. Satisfied they walked Robbie to the car and only when they were on the road did they relax.

Insomnia invaded Robbie and after an hour of frustrating tossing he raised himself from his bed and opened a bottle of wine. Once he had passed half way the solitude began to hurt and he thought about phoning a friend.

Realization of one's life can come at any time. Life is a kaleidoscope, it is full of confused colors like ideas, startling shapes which mirror our perceptions of just who we are, but when that one instance arrives, when all the colors blend and the shape becomes apparent, sometimes the reality of our existence is just too damn clear for us to accept.

This is what hit Robbie, clean, through his soul. He was a Mafia man of honour, and he had no friends outside of organized crime. He had no childhood friends who were not criminals. He had no friends with which he had a history, someone with which they shared their pain, their pleasures, their philosophy, ideas, had fun with. All the people he knew were Mafiosi. Most of his life had been about business and he struggled to remember anything of fun days as a child. It had been clinically amputated and set off in some ancient filling cabinet, just like his blood family, just like he had been doing with Angela. Everything outside of his criminal world was always, removed, because Robbie had built it that way. Everything outside of the mob was an almost reality.

Robbie poured another glass and held the bottle up. There was still a quarter to go. He set it back down and knew he would finish it, knew he would start a fresh bottle when it was finished, simply because he had to numb the pain of solitude and the pierce of new responsibility that would arrive in the form of his child.

The drinking continued throughout the night. Robbie could not get drunk, his mind would not slow down and the worries would not dissipate. Something other than the news of Angela's pregnancy was tapping the back of his mind; it was the impending funeral of Paulie Marranzo. Robbie felt a great sadness for Vinnie, the eldest of the brothers. The respect he held for the Marranzo's was incomparable, Vinnie had always followed the rules and always earned big and now two of his brothers were dead. Tommy lost to the Irish uprising and Paulie whacked at Robbie's behest.

Although Paulie's card was dealt the minute he began trafficking drugs without permission and had refused to pay tribute, his death did not sit right with Robbie. Inside he felt bad that he could not reason and bargain to save Paulie. He knew Vinnie had done all he could, but it did not make it any easier for Robbie and the thought of standing at the funeral made him nauseous. He had easily stood at Don Costello's funeral even though he had organized the coup; because he reasoned that Costello was old enough and should not have made mistakes to turn his family against him. But with Paulie Marranzo, well he was just a kid who might have learnt in time. Robbie now thought he should have handled it better, with more wisdom and patience.

He had arranged a big wreath and had offered to pay the funeral costs, but Vinnie kindly refused the offer and who could blame him. So now Robbie had to battle against inner demons and watch Paulie put in the ground, watch the tears of his brother, his whole family and then attend the wake and drink to his memory. So Robbie drank, trying to blot out the demons and fears that had suddenly come creeping out of the shadows.

Wine began to taste bitter on his palate and his stomach become a cauldron of acidity. The silence of the house began to bother him and he turned on the stereo and sat before his vast collection of music. The names just glided by him and he got up and with heavy legs made his way to the drinks cabinet, but the heavy spirits did not entice him, he knew he needed a leveler and decided upon a beer, so with heavy legs and heart he walked to the kitchen.

The cold beer in his hand felt good and he placed it against his forehead and sighed. Finally he opened it and the contents fizzed and overflowed, he put his mouth to the tin to try and gather as much as possible, some dribbled down his chin and onto the floor. He took the tin away from his mouth and wiped it with the cuff of his free arm.

'Mutherfucker,' he said, cursing not only the rebellious beer but partly himself.

Back in front of his music collection he sipped the beer and studiously looked across the names of the artists. They all blurred into one entity, nothing jumped out and grabbed him, but he needed the silence to be broken, needed some escape from the self punishing thoughts.

'I love you.' The words came out of nowhere and continued to come into his head. The voice attached to the words was Susan's, clear and precise, the voice of Susan. Robbie shook his head and closed his eyes, tried to dispel it, but it continued, chipping away like a rock hammer. He took a gulp from the tin, heard Angela. 'I'm pregnant.' Like a wave voices smashed into his conscience. Don Costello, 'A man is complete, when he has carried out his life with honour.' His father, 'Don't get mixed up with those hoodlums, have the courage to be righteous.' Mother, 'I don't like your life, but you're my son and I will always love you, but I can never be here for you, you disgrace all of us. So I leave you.' Voices that he couldn't place a name to invaded him. Robbie sniffed hard and took a gulp of beer, lit a cigarette. 'Fuck you all,' he said and pulled a CD from a rack, pushed the open/close button on the player and took the disc from the case and methodically placed it in the tray, pressed play, the disc disappeared into the player and then he turned up the volume. The music blasted out the voices and any other insanity that was lingering around Robbie. More drink filled the inner angst and quelled the violent debilitating thoughts. Robbie continued to drink until that time comes when life gets a total blackout.

Robbie awoke in a start, he knocked over the half can of beer that was next to him and sat up. His eyes were bloodshot and heavy and his face felt clammy. The pounding in his head set in and he groaned.

He went to the kitchen and brewed a pot of coffee, then poured a glass of water, opened a sachet of seltzer, tipped the contents into the glass and stirred it, downed it in one. He perched himself on a stool breathing heavy. Stared at the coffee dripping into the jug.

After three cups of strong black sugary coffee and five cigarettes Robbie took a shower and dressed. Paulie Marranzo was to be put in the ground today and Robbie stared at his reflection in the mirror after doing up his tie. He was the most powerful Mob boss in the country but today he recognized the fear that wound itself around him. The fear of being a Mob boss.

Robbie sat at the back of the church, along with Serge and Dalla Bonna, trying to keep as much distance as was possible in the full church. The mass was given and eulogies spoken for the deceased and although the church was cool, Robbie sweated, his body clearing itself of the alcohol. He fidgeted, tried to get comfortable. When the proceedings came to a close he was glad and outside offered his condolences to the family. He watched the casket carried from the church in silence, studying the faces of Marranzo family members. He wondered where Vinnie got the strength to be a pall bearer to his brother. Then it was on to the cemetery, following way back in the funeral procession.

The wake was no easier, Robbie had to speak with mobsters from all over his New York territories and the conversations grated on him. He was struggling with drink and the endless supply of drinks sent to his table mounted up.

'You okay?' said Dalla Bonna as he brought another tray of drinks over.

Robbie shrugged and picked up a glass, sniffed it. Brandy. He knocked it back in one and felt the burn in his gullet.

'It's a good turn out.' Dalla Bonna sat and picked up a bottle of beer, took a swig then blasted down a whiskey chaser.

'Yeah well,' said Robbie and searched his pockets for cigarettes. He couldn't find them and realized he left them in the car. 'You got cigarettes? I left mine in the car.'

'Help yourself.' Dalla Bonna handed him his packet.

'Marlboro. Why the hell do you smoke these?'

'Better than those English shit sticks you like.'

Robbie gave him a half smile and extracted one from the packet.

'Fuck, a smile, could it be true.'

'It's a wake Silvio. We ain't supposed to smile.'

'Well a little fuckin' cheer won't go amiss.'

Robbie motioned with his free hand, turned his palm upwards and gave out a slight sour look.

'How's Vinnie seem?'

'He buried his brother Silvio, so I guess he's over the fucking moon.'

'Youse don't have to be so fuckin' sarcastic.'

'Well don't ask stupid questions.' Robbie instantly regretted the rebuke. Dalla Bonna gave Robbie a hard look, a killer's look; just for a second, then let it go and picked up his drink and took a long swallow. He looked around the room. It was a vast array of gangsters, mostly from the Cuccione family but there were representatives from some other families.

'You know if the FBI are watching this place they'd have a ball seeing the crop of NY's hoods.' Dalla Bonna tried to lighten the mood.

'They are watching.'

Dalla Bonna turned to face Robbie.

'They gotta be,' Robbie continued. 'It's been a crazy few weeks. Recap on everything. We bust the Irish and Russians, Paulie goes nuts, there's more H in NY than Asia. Pierre Sartois steps foot in our town and requests an audience with me. Susan goes missing. They ain't gonna let all this slide and you can bet your life they'll be building a RICO case against us now they closed down Susan's investigation into Gabriel Vargas. It's only a matter of time.' Robbie picked up another glass and downed it. 'They're coming for us Silvio and I ain't got the power to stop 'em.'

'Come on Robbie. It ain't that fuckin' bad. You beat them in court, you got the top lawyers so beat them. There's always a way to get to a jury, there's always a way to swing these things.'

'Maybe. It's always a long shot though. You can't cover every base in these things.

There's always something that gets overlooked. It ain't prison that scares me Silvio, it's the thought that I won't have enough time to finish this thing I've started. I'm worried that it will all come crashing down. It's a pretty shaky foundation at the minute.'

'The new commission? Nah. It's solid Robbie. Maybe that old fuck Gigante with his bullshit is a spanner, but it's solid. You building a new legacy Robbie. I gotta say I didn't think you could pull it off. Look where we were and look at where we're going, I raise my glass to you.'

Robbie raised his glass in response. 'Thank you. You know there's more than one legacy I've built recently,' he said with a wry smile.

Dalla Bonna looked at him inquisitively then broke into a smile. 'Angela's pregnant?'

Robbie nodded.

'Well let me be the first to offer you my congratulations.' He held out his hand and Robbie took it, Dalla Bonna lifted Robbie's hand to his lips and kissed it.

'Thank you my friend,' Robbie said.

22 WEST COAST BLUES

AL BONDINI HAD BEEN IN CALIFORNIA A month. He had wasted no time in finding out criminal elements. He needed protection. Not for himself, not from his fate, but for his little girl. He knew he would never lay eyes on her again, never hold her, never see her grow into womanhood. Above all he knew he had to leave her something.

The underworld in California was unlike the one in New York. They didn't have the structure like back east, but they still had organization, even though they were fragmented into so many racial groups.

When he arrived in California Al rented a secure lock up and spent two days wrapping up close to two million dollars in cellophane and packing it in boxes. Then he locked up the storeroom. He had negotiated a long term lease for a cut price. The key to the storeroom he mailed to a deposit box. Al kept five hundred thousand, for living and to execute his plan.

He rented a beach front apartment, dressed tidy, but not flashy and begun frequenting bars that were particular to the criminal element. He got noticed. He always had money but he kept to himself. What Al knew from his time of being a criminal was that criminals would always seek you out. They knew, just like gold digging women can sniff out men with money, criminals sense another.

It took a week before Al's scent was picked up in an Oakland bar. He looked out of place, simply because he was constant. It was a black bar mostly but with no air of racial tension. There were always a few white women and now and again the odd white man, but mostly the white men were just working guys who finished their shift and had a few beers. It wasn't a hang out for them, never would be.

So when he kept coming back, drinking, never becoming aggressive, constantly being able to pay for his beer, keeping himself to himself, always dressed smart, it was noticed. It was a sure bet contact would be made.

Al was aware of the crew that was always in attendance. He had spent too much time on the streets not to be. He knew where they sat, began to know their names, their characters. He waited for them and they came eventually.

Contact happened because of a round being ordered. The big guy ordering was shouting back to his crew's table confirming the order when he said to the bartender from out of the blue, 'Get the cracker one too.'

'Same again?' asked the rushed tender to Al.

Al placed his hand on the top of his glass and shook his head. The big guy noticed this and slid down the bar to Al.

'You too proud to accept a drink from a nigga?' The man hovered like the grim reaper.

Al turned his head and looked the man straight in the eye.

'Not at all. I've had enough, but let me get this to show there's no hard feelings. I'll be in tomorrow, if you wanna buy me a drink then, I'll have a drink with you.' He took out a roll and peeled off a hundred, letting the man notice enough of the piece tucked in his waistband. Then he drained his beer and got up from the stool. 'I'll see you tomorrow,' he said and calmly walked out.

Sure enough Al returned to the bar the next evening. He sat at the bar and ordered a drink for himself; he did not have to pay. The bar man informed him that it was all paid for, whatever he wanted, then he motioned his head in the direction of a table. Al turned around and saw a booth with about six men, they were surrounded by women. The big guy from the night before lifted up his glass to Al. Al got off the stool, picked up his drink and made his way over to the table.

The conversation stopped as he approached the table and the men ushered the girls away. Al stood before them.

'Thank you. I appreciate this.'

'Thank you for last night,' said the man sitting in the middle. He wore sunglasses and high priced sports wear. 'Least we can do is return the respect. Sit down.' Al sat.

'Trey,' said the man and offered his hand.

'Al,' he replied and took the hand. Trey introduced him to the rest of the gang.

'You from the East coast,' he said and Al nodded. 'Long way from home, so I figure yer got to be in some trouble o maybe you just wanna clock what's on offer and take some fo yoself.'

'Well, that'd be a sure way to get clipped,' Al responded.

'Maybe you five-o, undercover and all shit.'

'Undercover, that's a million to one bet that even I wouldn't lay money on.'

Trey smiled and lit a cigar. He blew a big cloud up to the ceiling. 'So you got trouble back East and you hiding out in nigga land, ain't a smart place to be.'

'It's been okay so far.'

'You got lucky, if you'd wound up not but six blocks from here you be in Tech-9 country and man, you be in a body bag.' The mention of Tech-9 brought out cussing from all the men.

'Them fools ain't compassionate,' said the big guy, who was named Vaughn.

'Well maybe my luck's returning.'

Trey took a puff on the cigar and blew it out slowly, leaned across the table.

'I'm gonna ask you man to man. What yer want?' he spoke softly.

'If I needed someone to maybe clean some dough for me, could you find me that someone?' said Al with equal softness, lit a cigarette and finished his drink. Trey leaned back in his seat and Vaughn motioned to the bartender for more drinks. Nothing was said until the drinks had been delivered.

'There's always someone who can clean green brother, but their rates ain't cool and then you got ta take care of my percentage. You lose a lot.'

'Money talks,' Al said then took a sip. His mouth was dry, a nervous dry.

Trey studied Al's face, looking for a sign. A sign of nervousness, bullshit or madness.

Finally he told his crew to leave, go join the girls, he wanted some space and he wanted to delve deeper into Al. The men did as they were told and when they were alone Trey removed his shades. He took a puff on his cigar, took a sip of the expensive brandy he drank.

'I can set up this business for you. But I wanna get in my soul some kind of calm first. I don't know you white man and I generally don't have nothing to do with them. I don't like your race and so I guess that makes me a racist. But I gotta a brain, I ain't no country nigga, I'm thinking to myself here's a white man who walks into my bar, dresses good, got money a certain style and no real fear and now he asking for a favor. Say's he comes from the East coast. So I'm gonna ask, what's the story?'

'Okay. I'm Al Bondini and there's people in New York that would reward you for that information, I was a connected man for the Cuccione family. My best friend was Paulie Marranzo and we set up a candy network that net a lot of profit. Only we didn't get it sanctioned. You read the papers, so you know the price Paulie paid. It was only a matter of time until they got to me, so I ran. Now I ain't worried about dying, I know that sooner or later they're gonna find me, but I got a daughter and I got issues with her mother and you know that I can't very well just give her the money, I can't open an account in my daughter's name and deposit large sums, so I gotta clean it and open up some kind of trust fund where she can get the money when she's twenty one and the government can't take it. I need a new identity; I need to stay alive as long as I can.'

Al's story hit within Trey. He also had a daughter and had not see her since she was six, when he was incarcerated and her mother had just upped and left, disappeared despite all his efforts to trace her. His daughter was sixteen now and he thought about what Al must be going through, never being able to see her again.

'You don't have a hook into the candy anymore?'

Al shook his head.

'Too bad, I could use some of those connections out here.'

'I'm sure you got enough of the crack business to be doing okay.'

'Yeah, ain't nothing like a bit of diversity though. Listen if I can set you up with this shit it's gonna cost you a lot. If you wanna cheaper and easier way of cleaning that money I gotta better idea how to put it to use.'

'I'm listening.'

'The music business.'

'The music business?' Al sipped his drink.

'We gotta lot of things out here, lotta drugs, guns, gangs, death and we gotta lot of music. A thriving industry, making billions, legally. Now say you invest in a company, you got say three acts on your books, they sell a few units in Cali, word passes, they get bigger and the big corporations buy you out eventually for big bucks. Or you can just produce the odd artist here and there. I tell you it's a sure fire way to make money.'

'You into it?'

'I dabble.'

'You dabble?'

'Look I ain't telling you for my health cuz. You wanna way to clean your money, I just giving you another option.'

'Well I got be reborn first.'

'I'll start that business tomorrow. New birth certificate, social security number, driving license, passport, credit viability and a doctor's history, you want it.'

'I want the whole shebang.'

Trey nodded. 'Well that whole rewrite is gonna cost close to two hundred thou.'

Al smiled. 'Trey, you do this right I'll throw you an extra twenty thou, but it's gotta be right.'

'Brother, you gotta trust me. You gonna be cleaner than the President.'

'That's a bad example Trey.'

Trey laughed then extended his hand again, Al took it. 'We'll get started tomorrow,' Trey said.

Al was sent on a wild round around town, having his picture taken, signing new signatures, meeting people he hardly knew, he felt uncomfortable but the people he was doing business with didn't want to know his name and were not in the least interested in his personal problems or his business. All they wanted was to get paid.

That day was the start of the rebirth for Al Bondini as he melted into the depths of the Californian underworld leaving his past and waiting for the not too distant day when he could step out into the world again, phoenix like; as Alan Edwards. Unconnected to New York, a clean living viable member of society.

Back east his family would cry rivers over him would make themselves sick with worry and would spend many sleepless nights wondering what happened to him. His ex would turn bitter again, take a new lover, who would become his daughter's dad and would do her best to erase him from the memory of their lives. All this Alan Edwards knew and he also knew that to stay alive he could never again contact them. The day his new life arrived Alan sat in his house alone, with a bottle of whiskey and cried like he had never cried in his life.

23 ANGEL FALLING

THE WEIGHT WAS A HEAVY LOAD FOR Gigante to carry and the desire had now turned into obsession. The Badalamenti family, his family, who were on par strength with the Cuccione family, was still second best. Despite his hard work and his lifetime of commitment, his workability of politics, they still remained the number two faction and it hurt.

Angelo Gigante had not reckoned on the obstinacy of Robbie D'Angelo, did not add up the total measure of his tenacity. Miscalculated his sly mind and his charisma. Life became a bane to Gigante, tiresome and frustrating but he still held in his heart the hate for D'Angelo. His bones hurt and waves of fatigue drowned him. His strong body had begun to deteriorate, his bulk began to diminish and his skin had taken on a grey hue. He slept more than he ever had in his life.

Blood family urged him to see a doctor, but he procrastinated, assuring them he was fine. In his thoughts he laid the blame on D'Angelo and the battle he fought with him, but his reasoning told him it was something more. Finally he went to his doctor.

A week later, after he had given blood, urine and stool samples, been subjected to scans and x-rays the results came back. Gigante took it in then went home and gathered his family and delivered the news. Assured them he would win this personal battle, gave them love and then proceeded to organize a night of celebration. When the new day arrived he ate a full breakfast, read the papers, drank coffee and sucked on a fat cigar. After he met with his other family.

At the private club his underboss Gaspare and his *consigliere* waited for their boss to arrive. They knew of the tests and figured he was going to give them good news. Gigante rode to the club in his silence and despite his driver's best efforts to engage in conversation it was a futile effort. Gigante told him to take the rest of the day off when they arrived.

The old man pulled his coat around his failing body and as the car pulled away from the kerb he turned to look at his particular New York neighborhood. Memories poured into his consciousness and he saw in his mind's eye the changed streets and buildings, the people long gone, he heard the conversations, he saw the hits and battles. He saw the children who had escaped, he saw the children who had become hoods. He saw his life and smiled then turned and entered the club.

'Buon giorno Don Gigante,' said Gaspare rising from his seat.

'Buon giorno. Sit, sit.' The old man took his coat off and hung it on the stand.

'Dov'é Jon?'

'In back, I'll get him.'

'No no. Don't worry, we'll wait. Bring me a coffee please.'

'Sure boss.'

Jon Cirello joined the room and greeted his boss with a kiss, then sat. Gigante sipped his coffee and the silence of the club was only interrupted from passing traffic and the passing talk of pedestrians from outside.

'Well my friends, it's time to be honest and to discuss the future of our family,' Gigante finally said. 'The results show leukemia.'

Gaspare put a hand to his face and lowered his head. Jon's face screwed in tension and he shifted uncomfortably in his seat.

'Don't be concerned. We all have to die eventually. My doctors tell me that chemo will give me a forty sixty chance of beating it, but after some deliberation I have decided against it. I don't want my body pumped with all that shit, so I'm gonna face it and spend the rest of my time with my family. Meanwhile we have some serious decisions to be made. So let us talk openly about what my most trusted friends would like to inherit.'

'I don't know what to say my Don,' Gaspare offered.

'Come on, one of you has got to take the reigns when I'm gone. I have faith in both of you, but I have a dilemma. It's a tough decision to choose between you and I want to make sure that this family will run on a smooth course after I'm gone. I don't want to leave behind any ill feeling, so both of you are going to have to help me. Jon?'

Jon sucked in a deep breath and scratched his neck.

'Forgive me *padrino* but I would bury the hatchet with D'Angelo. This family cannot afford to descend into a war with him or the commission. As much as I don't like the sonovabitch I sense that we would do better to get along with him. I know you have reasons for wanting to destroy him but whatever he is, he is an intelligent and resourceful man. There's no denying that he has made this thing of ours strong again. He has not tried to weaken our family and we have not lost any of our businesses since he played out his final moves in the game.'

While Jon was delivering his opinion, Gaspare chewed the inside of his mouth, holding his peace. He was astonished at Cirello's view. Don Gigante kept his eyes trained on Jon for the longest time and squeezed his hands together as his mind digested what he had just heard.

'Maybe I acted with folly,' he began.

'I'm not saying that-' Jon said but was cut off by Gigante raising his hand and slightly shaking his head.

'Maybe I did let pride get the better of me,' he continued. 'Maybe I have gotten too old to reason in a lucid way. You see my hate for that man blinded me. To this day I still believe that D'Angelo was wrong and broke the rules to suit his own desires. I still believe that I was wronged in not being appointed the head of the commission. But that is by the by now. What's most important to me is that this family survives and that this family suffers not after I am gone. Gaspare?'

'Don Gigante. I have served you loyally for many years. I believe in your judgment always and you have my love always.'

Gigante nodded and smiled at the declamation.

'I don't share Jon's view. I see the commission as a redundant factor in our business. To me D'Angelo broke a rule and he was left unpunished and now he is basically the head of the commission. We all know that Ancello in Chicago is nothing more than a figure-head. Jon say's that D'Angelo has left us alone, but how long will it be before he starts ripping out the core of all the families in New York. I believe that will happen. I can see the Cuccione family eventually eroding us, then the Molina family, Sciorfa and Gennazo. If he is allowed to continue, sometime in the future, there won't be five families in New York, there'll be one and it will be named D'Angelo.'

'So what would you do Gaspare, to stop that happening?' Gigante asked.

'I would make a pact with the Sciorfa and Gennazo families. Combine our strength. The Molina family would not go along with it, but they would not join with D'Angelo.'

'How do you know this?' Jon said.

'The Molina family will stay out of it for as long as possible, they're diplomats. If we made inroads into D'Angelo they would come aboard.'

'And the commission?' Gigante asked as he lit a cigar.

'Ancello would back D'Angelo at first, but in his heart he would know that if D'Angelo went, the position he held would be his for as long as he wanted it. I don't want to embark on a destructive war, but when D'Angelo comes we should be ready. None of us were ready for him before, but we won't make that mistake again.'

Gigante puffed on his cigar, rubbed his eyes. Tiredness hit him from out of the blue. It came like that recently, at inopportune times. He fought it.

'Gaspare, would you bring us all coffee please.'

'Yes boss.' He got up and went to the espresso machine. While he was gone Gigante spoke softly with Cirello. 'What's bothering you Jon?'

'To be honest. I don't really want to take over the family and I can't serve under anyone but you.'

'So retire.'

'I don't want to disappoint you or leave this family without a head that can effectively counsel.'

'You won't disappoint me. You've been a loyal and trusted friend. This family will take the path it must. If you're serious that you cannot have any part to play I give my blessing and I wish you the best.' He reached over and placed his right hand on Jon's, tapped it lightly.

'Thank you Don Gigante,' said Jon. Gigante returned a tired smile.

Gaspare set down the tray, then sat and lit a cigarette. Gigante put two lumps of sugar in his coffee and stirred it continuously, the spoon chinked against the china. He took the spoon out and threw it on the tray.

'Well Gaspare it seems the family will be yours. Jon will retire, so it's up to you to choose a new *consigliere*. I would suggest you appoint Louie Procenzo, but the decision is yours. Jon is to be allowed to retire with grace and respect. You will not call on him for any advice. I trust you understand what I am saying.'

'Absolutely Don Gigante.'

'And I trust you will guide this family well.'

'I will.' He rose from his seat and went to Gigante, kissed him on the hand, then both cheeks as they embraced. The he shook hands and embraced Cirello.

'We will continue this business tomorrow. I am tired. Jon would you drive me home?' Gigante said.

'Of course,' replied Jon and offered his arm to the ailing boss.

During the drive home they talked some more, even though Gigante battled against the storm of tiredness that engulfed him.

'I hope that Gaspare will see some sense and not take this family down that path *padrino*. I would hate to see this family destroyed.' Jon lit a cigarette and lowered the window slightly.

'I'm not so sure. I think he has some valued points regarding D'Angelo. I know you don't approve Jon, but if he is willing to protect this family then so be it. You see we have to give consideration to the fact that D'Angelo has no reason to stop at where he has arrived. Why would he not want to rule the empire of New York? He is young ambitious and talented. Look at the changes he has made in the short time of his tenure.'

Jon glanced at his boss with a curious look.

'Don't be surprised Jon. I do respect the man, I don't care for the way he has done it all and I don't trust his words. He is a man to be feared. If

Gaspare is intent on fighting him, he will need the Sciorfa and Gennazo families and even they may not be enough. Still I will be long gone by that time.'

'I don't want to think about it *padrino*.'

'My friend there's no use fighting it. You will attend my funeral and say your goodbyes. That is a fact. On another matter I think it is time to end our association with Pierre Sartois.'

'Why? He's been a loyal friend for many years.'

'True, but he is moving against me. That visit to New York recently was out of character and to see D'Angelo before me was disrespectful. I let it slide because I needed to think about it in depth. But I've done my thinking and I believe he's setting me up for a hit, on his territory.'

'Can you be sure?'

'Can we be sure of anything in this life?'

'I wouldn't have seen this coming.'

'It doesn't make you a bad *consigliere* Jon. I have always been close to Sartois I understand his thinking more than you could. It's just another example of just how much power D'Angelo is wielding and how much he is feared.'

'I can't believe that Sartois would set you up boss.'

'It's self preservation. He's always been a little unsure about us taking on D'Angelo. He knows that the commission is strong again and that he is an outsider. Hitting me would curry favor with that prick. It's the move of man in a political frame of mind.' He gave out a soft laugh. 'We become that which we despise.'

'What's that?'

'Something Sartois said to me many a moon gone by. So, what will you do in your retirement Jon?'

Jon sighed. 'I don't know. Move down to Arizona or Florida. Go shopping with my
wife in the day, eat well in the evening and most likely drink the night away thinking about the days of old. I might join one of them old folks club's. Play cards and talk about the state of the nation.'

Gigante laughed. 'It won't be that bad. You're one of the lucky one's Jon. Ain't too many who get out the way you are.'

'I never had any intention of getting out.'

'I know. Life has a way of changing the course on us without too much warning at times. You'll be respected Jon, always.'

'You too *padrino*.'

'I'll be forgotten soon enough. Sure my name will get mentioned here and there but the people who are really respected and remembered are the one's like D'Angelo and maybe even Gaspare. Still at least we ain't gonna die in the can; we've got that to be thankful for.'

24 WORDS TO THE WISE

SERGE VALONE MADE A POINT OF TAKING the morning easy. He ate a large breakfast at one of his favorite diners. A quiet one, unknown to mob associates. Through mouthfuls he turned the pages of the morning papers. Took his time on proper news, world events, and the state of his country's economy. The raise in interest for loans and the wiping out of some selected third world country's debt. The irony never ceased to make him smile. The average American man could be sold the dream and buy it, but when things got financially stretched, well, the dream got revoked. A country on the other side of the world, could squander American dollars like no tomorrow, but the good old government would wipe it out with a signature.

There was the usual spread on the topic of the ongoing war on drugs. The governments of the world were losing this one, but Serge read the article with interest. Nothing would change. He washed the last forkful down with a gulp of coffee and then called the waitress to bring him a refill.

The racing section became his next port of call and after checking for winners, he studied the form of the day's favorites. Although he was relaxed, he had uneasy feeling that he was being watched and had been all morning.

The suits that walked through the door were instantly recognizable to Serge. He caught sight of them immediately and closed his paper and sat back, watching them as they walked towards his table.

'Mister Valone,' said the youngest. Serge nodded. 'May we sit?'

'Well you gonna introduce youself first?' his street arrogance rose to the surface as a reflex.

'I'm agent Rani, and this is agent Stannard.' He glanced at his colleague and instantly they both flashed their O.C.T.F credentials.

Serge shrugged and lifted his coffee cup.

'Organized Crime Task Force, New York, Mister Valone. I think you've heard of us. May we sit?'

Serge held out his hand. The two men shuffled into the opposite side of the booth.

'You want coffee?' Serge asked.

'Please,' say the youngest agent.

Serge once again signaled the waitress and ordered the coffee.

'As you know Mister Valone-'

'Let's disperse with the mister eh. Call me Serge or Valone.'

'As I was saying, your organization-'

'What organization are you talking about?'

'You don't have to play games with us Valone. We know you are the consigliere for the Cuccione family. We want you to know that our investigation into the disappearance of Susan Rushdie is bearing fruit and we will take D'Angelo, you, Dalla Bonna and your whole family down.'

'Susan Rushdie?'

'You know who she is Valone. You read the papers. I believe there's a report on page

eight today.' The agent tapped the paper on the table.

'Well I don't. Seems to me you're walking down a dead end alley.'

'Really Valone. You guys think you're impregnable. But we have our ways of getting to the truth, whatever dead end alley we find ourselves in.'

'Then I guess you better go back to it then. This conversation is over and I would appreciate it if you didn't just invite yourself in public again. Next time do it right you wanna talk to me.'

'Like hauling you downtown?'

'If that's all you got, then yeah. Now fuck off and let me finish my breakfast in peace.'

'You guys never leave the gutter, don't matter how big you get,' said the eldest with a smirk as they got up to leave.

'Might be the reason Uncle Sam always come visiting. He gets off on his own kind,' replied Serge staring at the agents.

'We're going to take you all down Valone. You better believe that.'

'Go for it.' Serge let his eyes follow them as they exited, then finished his coffee and demanded a refill.

He sipped his coffee draped in a feeling of ruin for the morning. He folded the paper, set it down on the seat next to him, then looked out across the parking lot. The two worlds that always seemed to be colliding always filled him with a sense of depression. Serge hated the government and their hypocrisy, detested the way they always come across holier thou and wiser than anyone else. It didn't really matter which government it was. The world over they were always the same. All governments were filled with double standards, sleaze, bending of the rules, deceit, crime, collusion, bribery and general disregard for human life, no matter what flowery rhetoric they used. The practitioners of politics were the most mendacious people ever to exist.

Serge paid his bill and exited the diner. As he sat in his car and inserted the key into the ignition he paused before turning it. He cleared his mind, then extracted the key and got out, walked to a boundary wall and sat, lit a cigarette. The car park became busy and he studied the comings and goings, focused on a car where one guy sat alone. He watched him, until a woman joined him with take out coffee and they drove off. After crushing his cigarette on the tarmac, he walked back to the diner and made a call from the pay phone.

Dalla Bonna answered. 'Yeah.'

'Silvio, you with Robbie?'

'Yeah. What's up?'

'I just gotta visit from the G. But I gotta strange feeling, somin ain't right. I need a mechanic to check my car.'

'You think you gotta hit on you?'

'I didn't say that, it just don't feel right. Can you send someone for krisakes?' He could hear Silvio relay to Robbie.

'Ok. Where are you?'

Serge told him the name of the diner.

'An hour. Take it easy.'

'I will.' They hung up on each other.

Fifty minutes later a car pulled up next to his, two men got out. Serge saw the driver was Silvio, the other man he did not know. He threw some money on the counter for his coffee, walked out.

'You ok?' asked Silvio.

'I am now.'

'This is a friend of ours, he's gonna check out your wheels, then he'll drive it back,' said Silvio. The mechanic said nothing, just nodded. Serge handed him the key. Then got in the car with Silvio and they sped off from the diner.

'You seriously think you were up for a hit?'

'I don't know, but I've felt like I was being followed all morning, then the G turns up and they tell me they know about that Susan bitch and their investigation and blah blah blah.'

'They know she's wasted?' Silvio glanced at Serge.

'They're investigating her disappearance in their parlance, and they're gonna put us all away.'

'They got a stoolie?'

'Outside of me you Robbie, Vinnie and Greco who else knows about her?'

'Those that do are at the bottom of the ocean.'

'Exactly. Nothing adds up. They can't tie Robbie in with her, unless she herself was under surveillance, but that don't figure 'cause then they would have stopped the hit. The circus act they gave me was pretty convincing, so they are some fuckin' good actors or they on the level. Either way it's fucked up. If it was a hit, which family they come from and how could they possibly know about Robbie's involvement with Susan?'

Silvio shrugged. 'It don't add up.'

'No it don't.'

Robbie was just hanging up the phone as they arrived.

'Car was clean Serge,' he said.

'Well that's a relief.'

Silvio patted Serge on the back then went and poured three cups of freshly brewed coffee. As they sat Robbie spoke again. 'There's been more developments.'

'Yeah?'

'Old man Gigante got cancer.'

'Is that for real?' Silvio asked.

'It's on the street, the street don't lie.'

'What a day,' Serge said with a heavy breath.

'So we gotta assume this is the beginning. The government will attack again. Those fuckers will win. Nobody beats them.'

'They can't tie you into nothing Robbie.'

'Well, we gotta assume they got something or someone.'

'So what do we do?' Silvio said and lit a cigar.

'What can we do? Apart from get our lawyers and accountants to make sure that everything is legit as it can be. It's a strange feeling to almost reach your pinnacle and find out the view ain't that much different.'

'Me personally. I'd choose this life over anything else,' Silvio said.

'How 'bout you Serge?'

'Well in my next life I'm gonna join a proper crime family.'

'A proper crime family,' Robbie said with a smile, because he already knew the punch line.

'Yeah. I'm gonna be a politician. Have never been such a brotherhood of banditry in the history of mankind.'

'Anyway, we got some serious thinking to do.'

'We got a few punches we could pull. One thing about politicians and judges, they can be corrupted.'

'We need to think circular of them though. We gotta get at the D.A. Wanna know what bag of crap she got under her pillow.'

'Okay. I'll get some research done on her,' Serge said and sipped his coffee.

'Let's get it started then. When they come I wanna have some defense. Right I gotta meet Ange, so I'll see you two at the club later.'

'How's she doin'?' asked Silvio.

'She's good. Being pregnant suits her.'

'I gotta go too. Can you drive me to the city Silvio?' Serge said.

'Sure.'

'Your car is on the way back Serge,' said Robbie.

'Fuck it, let Silvio do some chauffeuring for a change.'

'Screw you. It's all I do lately. Sometimes I forget I'm the underboss of this *borgata*.'

'So do we,' Robbie said smiling and Serge laughed.

'Fucking comedy act youse two.'

'Come on then, let's get moving,' Robbie said with a serious air.

On the drive into the city Silvio sounded out Serge.

'What do you mean?' Serge said and looked at Silvio seriously.

'He's strained. You gotta noticed it?'

'On top of the war and the politics and the internal feuds, having your first child. I'd say that would strain me.'

Silvio grimaced. 'What I mean is that something's not right. There's something that's changed. I can't put it into words.'

'Ain't nothing wrong 'cept all the pressure he's under. You know Silvio; I don't know what angle you're working at here, but a word to the wise. Your talk could be viewed in certain circles as subversive.'

Silvio took his eyes off the road and turned to look at Serge. Their eyes met and a vacuum of silent challenge wedged between them. Silvio took his gaze back to the road and lit a cigarette.

25 PAX ROMANA

NEW YORK SLIPPED INTO AN AUTUMN AND a slumber. The city functioned without front page news of mob killings. The government carried on building their war machine against the mob, while the mob continued their business, taking millions of dollars from the streets keeping their counsel quiet, waiting. D'Angelo watched Angela's belly grow with anticipation of legacy. Gigante grew weak as the cancer ate him away and waited for his release. The five boroughs just got on with being the feasting table for organized crime, without the mayhem and anarchy of recent times.

The Sicilian praetorian, Salvatore Grecco managed his faction in stealth. Loyal still to Robbie D'Angelo and the Cuccione family, his past life in the old country presented itself as someone else's. Salvatore had seen many horizons in his new found land including his own resurrection. His crew of heavy hitters had amassed itself into a round figure of fifty. They were now the strongest and most feared, in all five boroughs. To Robbie D'Angelo they represented his arm of steel. The Sicilians were good earners too. Their importation of heroin was grossing millions, although publicly they weren't sanctioned, privately the tribute was taken.

The Sicilians were unique to the Cuccione family, unique to themselves. They stayed within the confines of their clique, never socializing with their American cousins. Their business was doing well and with the proceeds their own bars and clubs were born. They were totally self sufficient and not a financial burden to Robbie anymore.

Every family throughout America was aware of their efficiency with the gun and they were used as an independent hit mob. For the right money, they would do contracts for other crime factions of non-Italian heritage, also for business corporations who needed dirty work done in multi-million dollar lawsuits and other such underhand dealings. They were the new Murder Inc.

But for all the new power and prestige that Salvatore Grecco had within his grasp he was still fiercely loyal to Robbie. Salvatore had a great respect for Robbie also a love for him. What he had achieved in the new world was beyond what he had ever dreamed of and would be almost impossible in that island in the sun.

Robbie knew his army of Sicilians was now the most powerful crew in the city. Serge as his counselor had continually cautioned him to not let Salvatore build such a big faction. Silvio, underboss, a dreadnought if ever there was one, could never quite fathom the Sicilians. His bloodline originated from Sicily and he liked to talk about the heritage and honour, but he was always wary of them. Made crass jokes about them in the clubhouses. In his heart though he knew that if they caused an uprising it would be a serious problem, one he would be loath to deal with.

The peace that had settled throughout the land and especially New York though was an immense achievement. The Commission had been stripped and had had its renaissance. New Orleans was placated, old man Gigante had succumbed. Chicago was in the bag, the Russians, Irish, the Colombians, the blacks, Chinese and all other outsiders moved back to affiliates. All out war had been averted; Cosa Nostra was back at the head of the snake. Blood had been spilled, some of it needlessly but the end result was the one desired.

Like the peace of the Roman Empire it was felt on the streets. The weight and worry of expectation was lifted and as summer approached New York so did the good mood throughout all the families.

Angelo Gigante, battling cancer and seeing his approaching death passed over the reins to his underboss Gaspare, and prayed to die soon, such was his tiredness. The peace was settling though and it was all down to one man, Robbie D'Angelo and as much as Don Angelo Gigante hated the man, he had to respect what he had achieved. One of his final acts was a request to Gaspare to hit his old friend Pierre Sartois for his betrayal.

The passing of Angelo 'The Black Angel' Gigante solidified the peace. The commission met and inaugurated Gaspare Mateo as new boss of the Badalamenti family. Robbie drank a toast to the departed Gigante and sent flowers to the family. He would not attend the funeral. The government would watch he knew. The days of opulent mob funerals were gone, so was an era, Angelo Gigante was an old style boss; his like would not be seen again. The new empire was at peace with each other, but the war with the other empire was ongoing and would intensify.

Industry profits soared in the new order. Union corruption and the rape of pension funds continued. Extortion of major corporations through waste and recycling collections rocketed without the influx of independent competition. A new expansion to JFK international airport brought in millions through construction union manipulation and sweetheart contracts. Heroin was on the streets in a volume not seen since the seventies; it replaced cocaine as the new fashion drug although cocaine still brought in a vast amount of money. Prostitution and gambling still thrived as old order money makers and new schemes were developing all the time. Internet fraud, which the mobs wrestled away from the eastern European gangs along with credit card fraud. New ventures included high class escort agencies, which catered for the high rollers in business and finance. Ventures like these were legal businesses which gave a legit income worth thousands a year. The pornographic world was growing and growing as people looked for more and more sex to satisfy their needs. Hijacking of trucks with any kind of load did not abate. Anywhere that money could be made, no matter how diverse the mob was there, its hands touched everything, insurance fraud, automobile ringing, counterfeit clothing, perfumes, aftershaves, DVD's, CD's. New York and its surrounding areas once more became a feast for the Mafia.

Robbie who had oversaw all this new rising never allowed his attitude to change. He still met with his captains at least once a week. He managed to keep himself relatively clandestine. Not much press coverage was bestowed upon him. He ate dinner with Salvatore Grecco once a week in upstate New York, away from the bustle of the metropolis. He enjoyed these quiet dinners with his Sicilian hammer, knowing that if any unpleasantness ever surfaced he could unleash this vicious army of zip soldiers, who would keep killing without question. They were his Praetorian guard, silently protecting the new Rome, quietly ensuring the Pax Romana.

Robbie bought a four bedroom house in the commuter belt, nothing too opulent, but big enough for his new life with Angela and their forthcoming first child. He settled easily into this new family life. Angela took on a new found sexiness, being pregnant agreed with her and she radiated warmth and love for Robbie. In her heart she wanted to be married, but knew that Robbie, for all his old fashioned views in some areas was a new breed when it came to matters of the heart. Marriage was not a necessity and he did not view their relationship as living in sin. The baby would take his name, that was understood, but marriage would not be a topic discussed in the D'Angelo household.

Angela wanted to throw a housewarming party, but Robbie was reluctant to agree. He could not have his first family mixing with his new. Plus he suspected the feds would watch, they always would now but he could not discuss this with Angela for he knew it would create tension, so he used his skills to dissuade her and they went about choosing décor for the nursery and shopped endlessly for the things a new baby needs.

On the nights when Robbie could not sleep he watched Angela at sleep in peace and gently stroked her full belly, quite unable to grasp at times that he would soon be a father.

New York never slept, industry continued and the parties continued. The mob's future looked secure once more.

BOOK TWO
ALL IN THE FAMILY

26 THE MARRANZO CREW

VINNIE MARRANZO THE SOLE SURVIVING BROTHER OF the triumvirate sat in the Vesuvio Social Club reading an article in a magazine. Since the loss of his two brothers he had aged somewhat. His dark hair was now specked with grey and lines had formed in his chiseled features. His marriage had hit bad times and his wife was filing for divorce, so he moved into a vacant apartment above the Vesuvio. Absent-mindedly he lit a cigarette, took in a lungful and finished his coffee.

'Tony,' he called to his cousin and now second in command who was leaning on the bar reading a daily.

'Yeah skip,' Tony DiNapoli said looking up.

'Another,' he gestured to the cup, Tony nodded. 'Fucking bullshit.'

'What's that?'

'This fuckin' broad here. She fucks this basketball player and then sells her story. I mean, these kiss 'n' tell times, where's the dignity. Imagine the shit he's gonna have to go through with his wife, his children for krisakes. Fuck being a celebrity in these times, it'll come to a stage where after you fucked a broad you're gonna have to whack her.'

Tony set the coffee down then sat at the table.

'On the subject of women, we could have a situation developing between cousin Benny and a soldier in the Sciorfa mob.'

'Over a piece of skirt. Get the fuck outta here,' Vinnie said, leant back in his chair and rubbed his forehead.

'She's Benny's *goomah* but she's kinda screwing this other guy too.'

'Well she is or she isn't.' Vinnie took a last puff of his smoke and stubbed it in the ashtray, blew smoke out towards the ceiling.

'I guess she is. The two of them had some words the other night in a bar.'

'Just words, no hands raised?'

Tony shook his head. 'But Benny's going round saying he's gonna whack this prick.'

'Un-fuckin-believable. Everything is good again, the streets are without blood and he wants to start it up with the Sciorfa crew.'

'He's got a legitimate beef Vinnie. You don't fuck around with another guy's *goomah*.'

'First off we don't know what the situation is for real, second is it really gonna do any good to whack a made guy over some bitch.'

'Rules are rules.' Tony shrugged.

'Probably a fucking cooz anyway.'

'She's supposed to be a looker.'

'She fucks two guys, two made guys. She's a cooz.'

'Whatever. Something's gotta be done.'

'Fucking women,' Vinnie looked at the magazine article again. 'Okay. Drag his ass in here, let's hear it all.'

'Okay,' said Tony and went out to phone cousin Benny. Vinnie looked at the wall, where pictures of his deceased brothers hung. His eyes narrowed for a second, then he broke into a smile as memories of good times filled his mind.

Cousin Benny arrived an hour later. He wore the look of a man seeking justice. The three cousins embraced then sat. Tony poured three glasses of Sambuca and three glasses of ice water. Benny downed his before the other two had touched theirs. Tony poured him another.

'Okay, so spell it out,' said Vinnie.

'Geraldo Grasso. I'm gonna clip him, this *strunz*.'

'Just fuckin' hold yer horses. You'll whack him when and if you get an okay. That's a fuckin' long way off in time.'

'He fucked my *goomah*. That's an offence punishable by death.' Benny lit a cigarette and threw his lighter on the table.

'You quotin' the fuckin' rules to me?' Vinnie said, drank his Sambuca. Tony instantly poured him another.

'No. But I gotta have some retribution here.'

'How long you been seeing this broad?'

'Three, four months. What the fuck's that got to do with anything?'

'I'm just trying to get the picture, indulge me.'

'Four months, yeah.'

'How long has she been seeing this Geraldo?'

'Seeing, ain't no seeing, he fucked her.'

'What I'm trying to say Benny is, did he rape her?'

'What am I talking Arabic here. Weren't no rape, he screwed her.'

'Do you love her?'

'She's my fucking woman. What the fuck's going on here?'

'Look Benny try and see the whole circumference. How did they meet?'

'I don't know a nightclub or something.'

'Right, so this guy goes up to her asks to buy her a drink, whatever. If she's your girl and she knows she's your girl what the fuck is she doing accepting a drink off some guy, let alone fucking him. See it takes two Benny. Chances are this Geraldo didn't even know she was with you. And if she's acting like that, she's a chippy, whatya gonna do?'

'Fuck this, this is wrong. You don't fuck another man's babe.'

'You're not hearing me Benny so I'll give to you straight. She's a whore; she's got that fuckin' mindset where she knows she has a power. From what I hear she's a real looker and she plays on that. You telling me she didn't know this guy was mobbed up; she's the kinda broad that knows what a mob guy is. She probably only goes out with wiseguys, so she knows about the danger about the money and the flash bravado.'

'You're outta line Vinnie.'

'Shut up a second. Do you seriously wanna whack out another family's made man over some piece of skirt that has disrespected the two of youse? Do you really wanna go down that road?'

Benny swallowed his Sambuca and slammed the glass on the table. Tony poured him another. Benny's jaw was tight and aggressive; he took the shot in a gulp. Tony poured him another. Benny sighed loudly.

'I at least wanna hear his side before I commit then.'

Vinnie nodded. 'Good. We'll reach out and set it up. Now let's have a civilized drink.' He raised his glass and his cousins followed. 'Salute.'

'Salute,' replied Tony and Benny.

After they embraced and Benny had left the club, a little calmer, Vinnie and Tony sat and continued drinking Sambuca.

'He remind you of anyone?' Vinnie asked.

'Just like Paulie,' replied Tony.

'Just like him. *Boun'anima*,' said Vinnie and raised his glass to the picture of his brother.

Vinnie reached out to Geraldo Grasso's captain Willie Moscone. Moscone had heard through the grapevine about the brewing intent and expected a call from Vinnie. They both agreed on a date and time but haggled over the location. Moscone said it should be held at his club. Vinnie strongly disputed this, arguing that since it seemed his soldier had caused the problem it should be on Marranzo turf. Moscone countered that it was Vinnie who was requesting a sit-down, so they should do a courtesy and travel to them. They jousted for about five minutes and finally agreed to meet at the Apple Café, a neutral establishment in the East Village.

Vinnie arose early on the morning of the meet, indulged himself with coffee and bagels while reading the paper. The change to his life over the last two years would be enough to break most men. Losing two brothers and a marriage along with the comfort of home life took its toll for a while. Solace was found in the bottle until his cousin Tony DiNapoli literally dragged him out of the club and made sure he sobered up over a two day period, gave him a stern talking to, telling him that if he really wanted to die he would put a bullet in his head. Vinnie took control of himself and his crew, instantly made cousin Tony his number two. But alcohol had become his crutch.

There were a few hours to kill, so he had a long soak in the bath, sat at the breakfast table in the kitchen, drinking coffee and watching the streets. He watched the cars pull up and various soldiers come and go, the old ladies doing daily shopping at the bakery and butchers opposite, the kids playing stickball in the communal compound gave him much amusement as they rowed about strike outs. He remembered playing in that same park with his brothers as children and as adults when beer had got the better of them and they tried to win money off each other trying to hit supposed home runs. It was in that very park Vinnie got his first blow job and his first introduction to the Mafia through the actions of his uncle.

The Marranzo's uncle was a top capo in the Cuccione mob, though Vinnie never knew this, he watched his uncle talking to three other men on the other side of the street. The seemingly affable talk turned into an argument and the uncle took out a gun from his coat pocket, the other three men froze and Vinnie's uncle shot all three dead. Another man rushed from nowhere and took the gun from the uncle and scarpered. Vinnie watched his uncle calmly light a cigarette and wait by the bodies as the sound of sirens grew closer.

Two squad cars pulled up followed by an ambulance. The policeman hurried from their cars and stopped suddenly to talk to the uncle. One of the policemen walked to the bodies and knelt, checking for signs of life in turn. He turned to his colleagues and shook his head, then joined the rest of them. They all talked to together, then seemed to share a joke, then the uncle took a roll from his pocket and unfolded it, gave some bills to one of the policeman who folded it and put it in his pocket, then shook hands with the uncle, who nodded then walked away as innocent as you like.

The effect on the young Vinnie was immense, he rushed home and told his mother, who told him to forget it and not mention it in front of his father. Vinnie could not forget though. He felt a pride to know that his uncle, whom he had met rarely at the odd family function, could just shoot men and walk away.

At the family dinner he relayed the incident in a torrent to his father who exploded. He cursed and told Vinnie his uncle was a low life, a gangster, a bum, a coward because he wouldn't do an honest days work and he brought shame on the family name and the Italian people. He added that if he wanted to a be bum like his uncle he would either kill him or disown him.

Vinnie was hooked though and formed a street gang. His brothers soon joined and many of his cousins. They started out doing small breaking and entering jobs. Then dealing marijuana. Then they caught a mugger in the neighborhood, beat him to within an inch of his life, took him to one of the rooftops and threw him off. The mugger became a vegetable and the gang got the respect of the neighborhood and the attention of the mob faction that was under their uncle. Vinnie and his brothers suffered terrible beatings from their father until Vinnie decided to take no more, he punched out his father and left the family home, reached out to his uncle, who took him and the rest of the gang under his wing. Two years later the uncle was killed in a power struggle with another Marranzo but Vinnie and his crew were in, they were used as muscle and given certain other jobs. They always kicked up to the capo. Five years later Vinnie's father died of a heart attack. He had not spoken to him since he had left him laid out but he attended the funeral, prayed and shed a tear for his father. Two years later he was given a contract. The contract was fulfilled successfully the crew kept making good money and three years later Vinnie got straightened out, he was finally a made man in the Cuccione family, a part of the Red Hook- Brooklyn faction that had always been a stronghold of the Marranzo family name. Tommy got made a year later, Paulie two years later, just before the books were closed to new members. It was the new Don, Robbie D'Angelo who had re-opened them after almost ten years.

Now Vinnie had to have a sit-down to resolve some bullshit because of his cousin Benny, one of the most recent made men. The new breed who had probably had to wait too long for membership. They were very gung-ho and needed just a bit too much guidance to Vinnie's mind and he understood why Robbie was importing Sicilians.

As Vinnie entered the social club he saw that Benny was already there dressed to the nines. Tony was talking to him.

'Morning,' said Vinnie.

'Hi skip. Want coffee?' replied Tony. Benny nodded towards Vinnie.

'No a glass of water with ice. How you doing?

'Good.'

'You?' he asked of Benny.

'I'm good.'

'Stay that way. You didn't have to dress so formal. It's a minor beef.' Benny did not bite at the slight. 'This is your first as a made man, so you let the capo's open up first, don't interrupt nobody and only talk when you're given the floor, don't raise your voice, don't get into a slanging match with this Grasso guy. You been putting it on the street you're gonna whack this guy so expect this to take some time. You understand all I've said?'

'Yeah cous.'

'You heavy?'

'No.'

'Good. Tony, you go heavy, you'll be outside so they'll expect that.'

'You didn't think I was gonna go naked did you?' he said handing Vinnie the glass.

'To be honest with everyone, I could do without this. I have never liked the Sciorfa's and this Moscone is a first class cunt, he's worn me thin just getting to the table. Last thing I need is this to get out of hand and Benny, you will accept whatever decision us captains come to.'

'Of course.'

Vinnie downed the ice water in one go; set the glass on the table.

'Come on then, let's get going.'

The Sciorfa crew was already waiting at that Apple café. Willie Moscone was sipping his coffee and had already briefed his soldier Geraldo Grasso about what to expect. Moscone's number two sat with them and looked at his watch.

As the Marranzo's approached the café Vinnie ordered Tony to drive once around the block. Tony gave him a glance.

'We'll be late.'

Vinnie nodded. 'Fuck 'em. Let 'em wait.'

'Okay.'

They lost another five minutes trying to find a parking space, and then walked to the door.

'Okay Tony, you wait out here.'

'Sure, I'll take one of these tables. I got a clear view here.'

'You ready?' Vinnie said to Benny.

'Yeah.'

'Good, remember what I told you.' Vinnie pushed the door open and saw the Sciorfa mob, settled at a table near the rear. Vinnie led the way through the café. The three Sciorfa mobsters rose from their seats.

'Sorry for being late Willie, goddamn traffic.'

'It's a bitch, getting worse everyday.' They exchanged handshakes and Moscone nodded to his number two, who walked away and took a table near the door. The four of them sat.

'You want something to drink?' Moscone asked.

'Just water, thanks,' said Vinnie. Cousin Benny shook his head. Moscone called a waitress and ordered.

'Right Vinnie, let's hear your cousin first.'

'Benny,' said Vinnie.

Benny kept his voice at a measured level but did not disguise his contempt and allowed his street talk to fill the table as he explained his grudge. Geraldo Grasso got his turn to make his defense.

'First off I didn't know this broad was with your cousin Vinnie.'

'Get the fuck outta here,' interrupted Benny.

'Hey. You've had your chance. *Sta zitto !*' Vinnie ordered.

'In all respect, I never knew. I mean it ain't like we see each other in the same clubs and stuff and she never said. She told me she was single. I been seeing her for nearly a month.'

'A month? But you knew she was from our neighborhood?' said Vinnie.

'Yeah I knew that Vinnie, but I ain't never met her there and I ain't never took her home. She comes to mine or we meet in the city.'

'Okay but don't you think you should of done some homework on the broad before you started banging her?'

Geraldo shrugged.

'Vinnie's right. You get started with a broad from a wiseguy neighborhood you should do some research,' agreed Moscone. 'That said a rule has been broken, but it seems to me this broad is a cooz and you should both cut your losses here. This doesn't warrant a clipping.'

'I agree,' said Vinnie. Cousin Benny's jaw was tightening and his eyes emitted rage. Vinnie continued, 'But some kind of amends has to be made. I mean it's only right.'

Moscone sighed. 'You suggesting a tax?'

'Nothing too heavy.'

'This is wrong,' said Geraldo.

'You're fucking right it is,' replied Benny through clenched teeth.

'Okay, knock it off youse two,' Moscone commanded. Vinnie took a sip of his water to hide his disdain for Moscone. 'Four grand,' Moscone said.

'Well I guess we got a figure then. I for one don't want to sit here all afternoon negotiating, but it should be a little more.'

'More for what though, ain't nothing really been done wrong here.'

'Come on Moscone. Let's up it at least another grand.'

Moscone gave Vinnie a half smile. 'Five then.'

'Okay. So now it ends here.'

Geraldo held out his hand to Benny who reluctantly took it. 'No hard feelings eh?'

'Whatever,' said Benny breaking the handshake.

'We'll give you a week,' said Vinnie as he got up, then he and Moscone embraced.

'It all okay?' asked Tony as the duo exited.

'Yeah.' They set off for the car.

'Five grand to bang my *goomah*. This is a fucking insult,' said Benny as they walked.

'Will you fucking drop it. There was no way you was gonna get the guy whacked. Listen, you've got a nice payday. Three and half g's and no blood spilt. Take the fucking broad away for a weekend, treat yourself, chill out.'

'Three and a half Vinnie?'

'Hey, I had to arrange the sitdown and use up time for this bullshit. You made money you gotta kick up. Is this something you don't know?'

'Fine,' said Benny and lit a cigarette. 'This fucking broad I should kill her.'

Vinnie stopped in his tracks. 'Well fuckin' do it then it makes you feel better. Frankly I'm tired of hearing you pissing on about all this crap. Go whack out the cooz, give us all a break from your bullshit.'

'I was just expressing a feeling,' Benny said in sheepish manner.

'Okay, so now drop it. Now I gotta go deal with some union business so you can find your own way back.'

'Can't you give me a ride?'

'You know Benny you're a fuckin' ball breaker. I'm goin' uptown, you're a big boy, make your own way back. And I want my fifteen hundred tomorrow.'

'Come on Vinnie how the fuck-'

'Get out there and fuckin' earn it. This is New York cuz. Come on Tone, let's go.'

27 'WE OWN THE STREETS'

EARLY SUMMER SUN WARMED THE SIDEWALKS OF New York and brought joy to New Yorkers who felt they had endured a hard winter. Women searched out their short skirts and flimsy tops, shopped and hung out at coffee shops letting the world know that they existed. Men took the time to notice women again, thinking that the women they saw would be better suited to them than the wives and girlfriends they already had.

Benjamin Santini was one of those men and as he sat outside one of the mob clubs in Red Hook Brooklyn he discussed the various women with his associates. It could be shapely legs, big breasts, a full carved backside or just a pretty face. Whatever raised their desire it brought forth comments and disputes, the odd remark, which generally went ignored. For Benjamin it was a welcome relief from the pent up aggression of the last few weeks. Associates who he hung around with called him by his given name. To the inner circle of the Marranzo's he was just Benny. His street associates knew of his recent trouble with a Sciorfa soldier. Benjamin had been going through the big apple like a whirlwind, his temper arose quickly and a few strangers had felt the pain of his wrath, none more so though than his girlfriend. His anger was fuelled by an imagined assault upon his ego. In normal conversations, Benjamin saw whispers about him, in affectionate smiles he saw ridiculing smirks. Pressure grew in him like a bottle of carbonated water shaken vigorously, and in the same vein if left it would settle, but Benjamin was not capable of that act and the cap was opened. The catalyst was a rumor that his girl was seen in a club in Manhattan with Geraldo Grasso. Finally he snapped. His former girlfriend was beaten savagely and severely cut on her face. She would never look sexy again and she would never bear children. She would never press charges or hang out with mob guys again.

So as the rays warmed the east coast and as the pretty girls walked by Benjamin Santini learnt to enjoy himself again. It was a reprieve but deep inside there was still the damage. He started the motions in his mind and viewed the roads it would take to whack out Geraldo Grasso.

Even in his most inebriated state, when the seething inside would be boiling a voice insisted on telling him that he was taking a wrong direction in his life. Sometimes, he listened, but not for long enough and he would dismiss it. That voice was telling him that whacking Geraldo Grasso would be his doom. Yet the voracious hunger of his ego would not let up. Even after the terrible deeds he inflicted on his ex-girlfriend it remained. In Benjamin's mind, his way was set, so reasoning was beyond him.

On a Friday night in a Brooklyn club, hanging out with various cousins and soldiers and doing too much coke, Benjamin opened the paths of no return. Earlier he noticed that one of the many black street gangs were in the club. This particular gang was called Brook Nines. Their street rep was well known and they had strong ties with a few gangs on the west coast. The Brook Nine's top man was a thirty year old street hood who went by the name Jus Thuggin. His birth name was Justin Love. He was big, bold, and tough, knew the streets and could kill easily.

The crew that Benjamin was hanging with were making plans to go into the city and were starting to drift out. Benjamin made his play, he told the crew he would meet them later, that there was a girl he spotted earlier and was going to check her out first. Some of his cousins said they would wait behind, he told them to go. There ensued some banter and playful insights, regarding the girl and how ugly she must be if Benjamin didn't want them to see her. He played along for a while but eventually told them to fuck off. They got the message and left.

Benjamin went to the bar, a good looking bar girl knew he was Mafiosi and quickly served him, she got a good tip. Without waiting he went directly to the table where Jus Thuggin sat. Gang members made a safe mode, some got up to confront Benjamin, he didn't falter, just looked past them through to the target. To one of them he said, 'I've come to see your man, not fuck around wid youse.' His eyes were serious and deadly calm.

Jus Thuggin sat upright and said aloud, 'Whatchu want guinea?' Benjamin smiled and cocked his head.

'Now that ain't nice. Did I call you nigger?'

'You ain't earned the right to call me nigger.'

'Exactly. You ain't earned the right to call me guinea.'

'You about business?'

'Always.'

'Let the man through.'

Benjamin sat next to Justin as easily as if he was sitting next to his brother. Jus Thuggin glanced at him, keeping his respect for Benjamin's confidence hidden.

'What youse drinking?' Benjamin said.

'Irish whiskey, beer chasers.'

Benjamin leaned and reached into his pockets, pulled out a roll, flipped through them and threw two fifties on the table.

'Get one of your boys to get a bottle of good Mick stuff, your beer, theirs, I'll have a glass of good Italian red wine.'

Jus Thuggin sucked air through his teeth. 'Might not cut it,' he said looking at the money.

'Then make up the difference. Or you can be a cheap black sonovabitch?'

'Ya fuckin' wops!'

'I make no apologies; don't ask for 'em.'

'Ya'll racist fuckers.'

'Just us or the whole fuckin' world?'

'I know who yer wid, but I'm asking myself, should I 'avter take this shit?'

'I ain't givin' it. Let's be clear here. I am what I am. You are what you are. I come to talk business; don't wanna be your bruver, soul mate, even a friend. I need you to do me somin, you don't wanna do it, ain't a problem, we'll walk away, pray to our god's our paths never cross again.'

'You a smooth talkin' muthafucker. You got attitude, like a black man. At the end of the day, youse white, we can't trust the white man.'

'You gonna get these drinks? We gonna talk? Or we gonna bullshit all night?'

Jus Thuggin smiled, sent out the order for the drinks, the money stayed on the table. Justin's show of his power. The drinks came and Benny lit a smoke.

'This is a no smoking establishment guinea.'

'So arrest me and you call me guinea again I'll whack you out right now.'

Jus Thuggin turned his head and stared into Benny's eyes. 'You be sitting at my table, mob guy or not, you talk about whacking me out again us niggas will make you disappear.'

'Well let's do business and stop fuckin' around with all the racist remarks.'

'Ok. Let's talk. Everyone go powder their nose or something.' Commanded Justin. The crew left bar one. He poured whiskey for all three then sat the other side of Benny.

'I'll get right to the point. I need you to smoke someone,' Benny said and gulped down his whiskey, sniffed as it hit the back of his throat.

'You're the mob, why the fuck you want us to do this?'

'That's my business. Can you do this or not?'

'We can do anything. As long as no comebacks and payment is right.'

'Ten large.'

'We ain't field niggas wop mutherfukka. Ten? Get real.'

'You and your fuckin' insults.'

'My insults. You come here, no respect offering me chicken feed for a piece of work. Why you wanna do that?' The malice in Jus Thuggin's voice overrode the music.

'You're right,' said Benny nodding. 'Thirty.'

Jus Thuggin held out his right hand, Benny took it and gripped it tightly. 'I'll give you five now, five in a couple of days and the balance on completion.' He broke the handshake and dug into his trouser pocket, pulled out a roll and counted out five thousand dollars just below the eye line of the table edge, passed it over. Jus quickly viewed it and put in his jean pockets.

'Calls for a celebration, wanna do a few lines?'

'You don't wanna talk anymore business?' asked Benny taking a swig from his wine.

'Details we can work out soon enough, hang out, be cool, do a few lines, there be a party later you wanna go. It's all good friend.'

'Cool. I'll hang out. First I'll get another round in.'

'I'll get this, I insist.'

'Fuck that,' said Benny shaking his head and got to his feet. 'Rack up some lines I'll get the round.'

'You want me to rack up here?'

'Fuck it. We own the streets right.'

'We?'

'Yeah, we.' Benny walked off to the bar.

'This guinea's one crazy fool,' said Justin's second.

'Yeah, but he could make us a lot of money.'

'I don't trust these Italian fuckers.'

'He serious business. Made, most powerful family in the country.'

'So how can you trust him? That's my point.'

'I can't think like that. He came to us, for all his guinea bullshit, you know what this means?'

'What?'

'We do this right, we get affiliated with the Cuccione mob, ain't nothing bigger.'

Benny came back with four bottles of champagne. Jus Thuggin's crew was invited back, more women joined them. The alliance was formed over the usual gangster tastes, fine champagne, good looking women, hard drugs and money.

The party went on all night. Benny hit with one of the girls in the Brook Nine crew. A young twenty year old who was making her own money selling coke and doing very well. She racked up all night for Benny and about five in the morning invited him back to her apartment for coffee, he didn't decline. He said his farewells to Jus Thuggin.

'I'll call you in a couple of days.'

'You going home with her?'

'Yeah.'

'A fine piece of tail, but you gonna be in a lot of trouble.'

'How's that?' Benny said.

'That's pure delight for you white boy, more addictive than that nose candy you been on all night. You're gonna get addicted.'

'You're a real ball breaker. I'll see yer.'

'I'm sure.'

Benny was awoken at two in the afternoon by the gentle caressing of Eloise and her kissing of his chest.

'How you doin'?' he asked, his mouth dry and a fog behind his eyes.

'I'm doin' good honey. Want coffee?'

'What time is it?'

'Just gone two.'

'Jesus. I'm supposed to be at work.'

'And what work is that?'

Benny groaned. 'Feel like I've been in a battle.'

'Well the way you fucked me last night, I feel that way.'

'That good huh?'

'Uum. Never had an Italian guy.'

'Never had a black girl.'

'How was it?'

'Pretty fucking good.'

'So am I gonna get more or was this just a one time deal.'

'I'll be honest with you babe. I like you and I wanna see you again but the circles I move in it's very fuckin' difficult.'

'Difficult, how?'

'Different cultures.'

'Hey, it's a new century.'

'Not where I fuckin' come from. You got any smokes?'

'I think.' She got out of bed and Benny eyed her trim body, her well shaped arse and perfect tits. A body built for the pleasure of man and yes he was addicted.

'Can I ask you something?' he said.

'Anything.'

'You ever slept with Jus?'

'Jus Thuggin. Hell would have to freeze for me to sleep with dat nigga.' She lit two cigarettes and crawled back on the bed; put an ashtray in between them.

'How come?'

'He's a business partner; I don't fuck with those guys anyhow.'

'How the fuck can you survive around those guys, I mean, I just don't get it.'

'What's to get. I buy bulk coke off them and deal it, just like anyone else.'

'Yeah, but my point is you're a girl, how come they don't fuck wid youse.'

Eloise giggled. 'What you think I can't take care of myself?'

'Forget it.'

'So mister Mafia we gonna see each other again.'

'Mister Mafia?'

'Come on I know you're in the Mob.'

'How the fuck you know that?'

'The streets talk baby.'

'The streets are full of shit.'

'Still don't answer my question.'

'Yeah, I wanna, but you gotta understand, I can't introduce you to my people, you can't hang out with us all, so when I'm out with them you won't be.'

'Guinea bullshit.'

'You know I think you people are more racist than us.'

'There's just racism, there's no more or less.'

'So you don't like my race?'

'I don't like some of the crap that goes with your race and it's the same for you. You hung out last night, did coke, danced and fucked but if you saw a bunch of black guys hanging around your neighborhood, listening to loud music in their cars and talking jive you'd say to yourself, Niggers.'

Benny shrugged and stubbed his cigarette in the ashtray.

'I like you, I enjoyed you. I just wanna hang with you, don't have to be serious, we can have fun baby,' Eloise stated.

'I'm cool with that. So do I get coffee?'

'Cream and sugar?'

Benny nodded.

Back on the streets Benny went to work, the last night's exertions causing a slight cloud to overcome him. He worked it off, collecting what he was supposed to from his loan operation and then meeting with other hoods. He chewed the fat and ate a full dinner, then slipped out of the restaurant, called Eloise.

'Hi baby,' she answered.

'How youse doing?'

'I'm good.'

'You busy?'

'Working for the next couple hours.'

'I'll come over after.'

'You sure?'

'If you want.'

'I want. I'll call you when I'm done,' said Eloise with joy in her voice.

'Ok, see ya.' Benny hung up then went back in, ordered a brandy from the bar and rejoined the crew. After he finished the brandy he said his goodbye's then left. In his mind he had made a decision to do some recognizance on Geraldo Grasso. He drove to the bar where he knew he hung out.

Geraldo Grasso was a creature of habit. The bar he sat drinking in was the same one he had drunk in for six nights straight for the last seven years. He wasn't a hard man to find or to track. An hour later he came out and walked to his car. Benny followed him, noting each street he drove. After a ten minute drive Grasso pulled into a dark lot, next to an apartment block. Benny drove on. Benny knew he would follow Grasso for the next three nights. Then he drove home to have a shower and change before he met Eloise.

Satisfied in his mind that Grasso would follow this pattern after three nights of tracking him, Benny set in motion the final touches. Jus Thuggin met with Benny and they talked, Jus suggested he survey the area with Benny, Benny replied he would think about it.

'So how you hitting with that piece o' candy?'

'What?' asked Benny.

'Eloise man. You tapping that arse?'

'What the fuck's that to do wid youse?'

'Conversation man, dat's all.'

'Well, I ain't here to discuss that shit.'

'I know it, but you donwanna talk about this Grasso business, the silence is deafening.'

'Fuck it, you wanna check this fuckin' place out, let's go.'

'Make it easier if I seen the mutherfukka, planning' strategy, yaknow.'

'All I want from you and your nappy head crew is to do it right.'

'Youse a disrespectful guinea at times, you starting to get on my dick. The job'll get done right, you fuckin' wid me ain't gonna make it easier.' Jus Thuggin sipped his Chivas and lit a smoke.

'Fuck it, I'm sorry okay. Got a lot on my plate at the moment. Don't mean to ragging your ass.'

'So is it on?'

Benny bit his lower lip and narrowed his eyes. 'I guess.'

'Then I don't mean to be keeping on, but I gotta get the ball rolling.'

Benny nodded and drained his beer. 'The weekend.'

'Cool. Gives us four days.'

'That enough?'

'Plenty.'

'I mean it Jus, youse can't fuck this up.'

Jus bent his head and looked at Benny through his brow. 'Ain't about to fuck this up.'

Jus Thuggin and his hand picked crew for the job viewed the area for three days. They noted what needed to be noted. Cameras if any, exits from the parking lot. The closest neighbors and their vision of the lot, street lights, a maintenance crew working a block away. Satisfied, they realized that the hit should go ahead without too many problems. Jus picked three of his gang for the job. The youngest was twenty one, but tough and cold. The eldest was thirty five, married with three children, still doing his thing on the streets, always going to be a gang member. The Brook Nines gang and their notoriety veined throughout the streets of Brooklyn. They were the hardest hitting of the black gangs in that borough.

On Saturday afternoon, Jus gathered his hit crew. He treated them to a steak meal and forbade them to drink throughout the meal, even though he worked his way through a bottle and half of wine.

'Donwanna get up yo's dicks, but I want this done right, no mess, a clean take out, can't stress that enough, so make sure youse hearing me' No words came back to him. 'So youse hearing me?' he said with a touch of venom in his voice.

They answered collectively.

Geraldo Grasso was tired. Tired of sitting in the bar and listening to the same old bullshit. The guys were going into the city to a nightclub; Geraldo though was worn out with the idea of clubbing all night. He decided to have another couple of drinks before going home. He told the barkeep to load him up again, add it to the tab. He smoked and sipped, listened to stories with feigned laughter.

The hit squad clocked Geraldo's auto parked near the bar. They had two cars and one went off to the final destination, two shooters. The other car sat, waited. Waiting is hard on the senses; boredom breeds ineptitude, the mind drifts out of focus and leads the individual into mistakes. The young man thought about doing a line of cocaine, but the thought of Jus Thuggin put him off. Close by was a twenty four hour store and he reasoned he could get to that and back before Grasso left the bar. Just as he got back to the car with his coffee Grasso came out of the bar. He threw the coffee into the gutter and got in his car. Then tailed Grasso, while making a call.

'On the way,' was all he said.

At the lot, the two shooters checked their weapons one more time. They got out and one walked into the darkest part, the other positioned himself close to the entrance in some bushes.

Geraldo tired and more than over the limit of responsible driving did not realize he was being tailed, even though the young killer was not subtle. At times the car behind him was just too close, but even though Geraldo noticed all he could manage was to mumble, 'What's wid this prick.' And it was the unprofessional way the young killer went about his business that probably made Geraldo think nothing off it, until that point when he turned into his lot and the tail turned too. He slowed and studied his rear view.

The shooter in the bushes could see the two cars and his first thought was that his colleague was screwing this up by following so close, but if the young driver had not, Geraldo would not have slowed. The shooter stepped out of the dark and aimed straight at the driver's window. Geraldo had caught him in the corner of his vision and realizing screamed out in distraught, 'No.' His voice muffled to the shooter because of the closed window.

The shotgun blast blew out the window and took half of Grasso's face off. His foot had slammed on the accelerator and the car sped into the lot, but with no control slammed into a solid brick wall which cracked and gave way in a section. Bricks, freed from their mortar tumbled onto the hood. The drivers airbag exploded into life forcing Geraldo's injured head back into the headrest. By now the second shooter was upon the car and he unloaded a full clip from his handgun into Geraldo's body. Then he dropped the gun to the floor, took another from his coat pocket and leaned in and from close range put four into the already deceased's head. This gun he dropped into the car. The tail car had already turned around and the two primary shooters got in and with car wheels burning rubber sped away. They went in a full circle of four blocks, left the car. The driver caught the subway the two shooters drove in a clean car, getting snarled up in the traffic caused by the hit they had just made. They had not screwed it up.

Anthony Lascelle

VESUVIO CLUB, BROOKLYN

The morning was wet. Vinnie's mood was dark like the skies over Brooklyn. He rocked into the club like a hurricane. Only cousin Tony was in attendance, head down at the bar in the paper, cigarette in hand, glasses perched on the bridge of his nose. Tony looked up and then turned to the coffee pot.

'Give it to me black,' commanded Vinnie.

'You got it.'

Vinnie sat at the bar, turned the paper around. The page was already open at the story. *Reputed Mobster Hit* ran the heading. Vinnie screwed his mouth up and began reading. Tony placed the cup before him.

'Incredible. Fucking incredible,' Vinnie said, in low audio.

'They got a witness, say's it was Zulu's.'

'I can read,' Vinnie said without looking up. 'Be the Brook Nine's.'

'You figure?'

'Dose fuckers be the hardest crew. It's a money job, ain't no way they go round rubbing out made guys over business. They hard but they ain't got the muscle for a war. And I'll lay a grand that it's Benny that hired them.'

'Come on Vinnie.'

'He ain't got the fuckin' smarts to think any other way. It's so obvious that it won't take the Sciorfa two minutes to work out. You can bet that prick Moscone will be on the line soon.' He lit a cigarette. 'Once the word is out, then Dalla Bonna will be down here. I'm gonna have to eat more crap and once more I'm gonna look like a guy who can't control my crew. How much do you think the guy on the throne is gonna let go. All the problems seem to keep coming from here. If it was me making the call,' he inhaled on his cigarette, 'I'd have to go.'

'Vinnie, these beefs happen all the time. There's a thousand guys who have been whacked over bullshit, it's the life.'

'But what do they want? The streets quiet, no heat. The commission needs to function; the guy wants no grief from New York. Just say the Sciorfa go off, what then?'

'They ain't got the balls for that, not over some low level prick. Why would they?'

'A made man, hit without an ok. You new to this?'

'Jeez, Vinnie all I'm saying is that it don't make no sense. Start a street war over this shit. The Sciorfa mob wouldn't dream of taking on us.'

'But it's a card to play with Tone, get Badalamenti or Gennazo families on their side, you got division, you got war and anarchy and then you got the commission and it's all fucked up for D'Angelo, just 'cause some whore opened her legs and some guy lost his head.'

'Ego,' said Tony nodding.

'Ego. Fucking ego.' Vinnie shifted on his seat and peered through the small window in the door, rain still fell on Brooklyn.

CAFÉ ROMA, QUEENS

Willie Moscone ordered a bottle of wine. He had arose early, ate a full breakfast. It was only eleven, but he wanted a drink. His two next in command were with him.

'Well, Grasso's gone. Here's to him,' he raised his glass.

'You spoke to that piece of shit in Brooklyn yet?'

'Fuck him, fuck all them Marranzo's. Let him stew a while,' Moscone said.

'Hiring niggas to do a piece of work. Just don't sit well wid me,' Number two said.

'Yeah well, I'm gonna see the man today. Going by the book on this one.'

'If he doesn't wanna play, what then?' Number one said.

'The game those Marranzo's play we can too. There's a thousand young punks out there who will pick up a gun for the green. Unconnected to us, then they'll disappear unlike those moolies they used.'

'That way there'll be no escalation.'

'Exactly. Just be another fucking footnote to the history of this thing of ours. Nobody gonna lose any sleep over it. But Benjamin fucking Santini is gonna go, that's the end of this story,' Moscone growled and poured himself another glass. He looked at his watch. 'Gotta meet the throne in an hour, gonna finish this bottle, one of you can drive me up there, decide among yourselves. Now let me be until then.' The two gangsters nodded and got up without a word, walked to the other end of the café.

ELOISE'S APARTMENT

Benjamin Santini awoke late, the alcohol from the night before still ran through his blood, his brain pulsed, enough for him to hear in his ears, hot waves crashed over his forehead and down to his chest. Looking at the ceiling he drew in a chest full of air, and then let it out in a resigned way. He moved his left hand and felt the heat of human flesh, Eloise's flesh. She had her back to him and he ran his hand up and down her thigh, across her arse, then over her hips. Benny shifted and wrapped his right arm over her, letting his hand feel the fullness of her breast, then pushed close, his morning semi nestling in the crack of her arse.

'Don't even think you're getting any,' mumbled a half awake Eloise.

'I'm too fuckin' hung-over anyways babe,' he replied.

'Uh huh. You're making coffee,' she said.

'Yeah right.'

'Well you better be, I sure as hell ain't moving.'

'So much for romance.'

'Told you last night, if you don't fuck me, you're making coffee in the morning. And mister, you didn't fuck me 'cause you spent all night wid your head in a bottle.'

'Jesus. Why you gotta talk so crude?' By now his semi had gone.

'Just go make coffee wiseguy.'

'I seriously doubt I can move.'

'Uh huh.'

Then his mobile rang again. It was still in his trouser pocket on the other side of the room.

'That fucking phone has been ringing all morning,' Eloise complained. 'That has to be the most annoying ring tone. Why don't you change it?'

'Why don't you shut up?'

Eloise gave him an elbow in the ribs making him cough and tense up. It was a good hit. When his coughing fit finished he said, 'That ring tone is from a great film.'

'Like I give a fuck. Can you at least put it on silent when you're with me?' There was annoyance in her voice. Then the music stopped. 'Thank the lord.' The only sound in the bedroom was their breathing, tired, alcohol sodden breathing. Two minutes passed and Benny's phone began its annoying alert once more.

'Jeeesus,' shouted Eloise. 'Seriously, can you fuckin' answer it, turn it off, do something.'

'Yeah, yeah, yeah.' Benny unwrapped himself from her and slid out of the covers, he sat for a second or two on the edge of the bed as the blood drained from his brain and little white spots formed in his vision. He rubbed his temples, then stood and walked to his trousers. Upon seeing the caller identity he rejected the call, then switched it off and made his way to the kitchen, to make coffee.

While waiting for the coffee to brew Benny lit a cigarette and looked at the empty bottles of beer and the near gone bottle of vodka, the residue of racked lines on the worktop. He brushed the grains onto the floor. He could taste the alcohol in his mouth, stale, bitter. Yet that was the least of his worries. He knew the mob world knew about Geraldo Grasso. He knew that the phone calls were a summons. He turned back to the coffee pot, watching the water filter through.

HIERARCHY

'I'm saying it loud and clear,' shouted Silvio Dalla Bona.

'I hear yer, but Grasso is just a low level soldier...' Serge Valone could not finish.

'He might be a soldier but he was whacked out by the Marranzo's and in turn that means us, the Cuccione family.' Silvio was standing over the sitting Serge and pointing at him, his rage filled body solid like a marble monolith.

'What I'm trying to say to you is, it's the streets, this shit happens all the time.'

'And what I'm saying is the fucking Sciorfa family will use this as an excuse. This ain't about some nameless hard on getting whacked, it's about an excuse to rock the boat. You're a fucking street man, you know this or did you really spend too much time in prison your brain's gone slow.'

'Fuck you Silvio. The Sciorfa mob won't even think about rocking New York. You wanna know why?'

'Fuck you and your reasons,' Silvio turned and walked back to his chair.

'Because everyone, everyone in this fucking city is making money, because the commission is solid, because Ancello in Chicago is tight with Robbie and simply because like you said, Grasso was a hard on, nothing ain't gonna change what's been built.'

'Guys, guys. Jesus. What are we arguing about this for?' Robbie finally interjected while there was a moment of calm. Serge shrugged his shoulders. Silvio shook his head with a look of distaste in his mouth. 'To be honest I can't have a meet with Vinnie. This cousin of his, what's his name?'

'Benjamin Santini,' said Silvio.

'Ok this Benjamin, he's gotta be disciplined, no question of that. But Vinnie, well, Serge?'

'Whachyer gonna do. From what I hear, this beef that started with his cousin and this Grasso character was straightened out about a month ago. There are no guarantees it even was Benjamin that whacked out Grasso.'

'No, it was that black crew call themselves the Brook Nines. But Benjamin has been running around with them, partying doin' a little coke wid em, even banging one of their fucking whores. Benjamin Santini, using outsiders to whack a made guy from another family, without an ok.' Silvio said all this while looking at Serge, not Robbie.

'To be honest, all this fucking street grief is not on my agenda. The streets are just a cog in this machine, a money maker. Granted, I don't want all this kinda crap in the news bringing attention upon us, but sometimes these things are unavoidable. What we have worked so hard for in the past few years is to rebuild this thing of ours, take us out of public view. I know the way I done things brought us into the spotlight, but sometimes I had no choice. The public have known about us for forever, the government ain't ever gonna get off our arse, we're realists, we know this. But I want us to be so deeply embedded, so quiet now. Ain't been easy and won't ever be easy, but the streets have to know this ain't no good. Serge I believe you when you say everyone is making money, so who is gonna rock the boat? But Silvio has a point. What if the Sciorfa mob wanna go for it. Small ripples like this have escalated into all out war in the past. We gotta contain it.' Robbie lit a cigarette and sat for the first time near his consigliere and underboss.

'What I hope we are working for, and I don't want to keep sounding tiresome with this, is insulation. This was how our thing always survived. If you are on the streets, you take the heat. Me, you, the captains, this is the hierarchy; this is where the insulation keeps us out of the uncle Sam's reach. We still have a lot of work to do. I am nowhere near where I wanted to be of reconstructing political allies and I wanna make sure we keep all our enemies down. They gotta earn of course, but we can't allow all those outsider factions to rise to our level again. Which got me thinking about a recruitment drive.' Robbie sucked on his cigarette and let this last statement hang in the air with the smoke.

'Making more guys?' Silvio said deeply. Robbie nodded.

'Robbie we got close to three hundred soldiers now, with connected guys five. Not including Salvatore's Sicilian mob,' added Serge in a measured voice.

'I know and we got five families in this city and as much as I detest this so called boss of bosses crap, they do see me in that role.' A silence fell upon the room.

'Say what you mean to say Robbie,' Serge said with strength.

'Just a consideration. Build this family to a strength not ever seen before.'

'Well what do you mean Robbie? Assimilation of the other families or just being boss of bosses.' Serge had a scowl draped across his face.

'I'm just talking about making the Cuccione family bigger than it's ever been.'

'It fucking is Robbie. For myself I'm proud to be counsel to this family and I will be ever thankful that when I came out, you reached and offered me this position. And you should be proud of your achievement; yes there is much work to do still. But if you want to pursue a road to one New York family and being the only boss, you are gonna do it alone. The commission will definitely line up against you. I will not be around to witness it and you can whack me out, because Robbie, that ain't gonna work and you'll destroy us.'

'Underboss that I am, loyal to you Robbie and this borgata, I'm with Serge on this. I love power as much as the next guy, but what you're talking about will bring about an end.'

Robbie smiled and leaned back into his chair.

'It's okay,' he said. 'I was just testing. Sometimes I gotta know that my true friends would give me reason, just in case I ever lost mine. The only thing I was serious on was expansion.'

'But making new guys is a pain in the arse process. The other families have to vet them; they will see it as a threat if we went on a major expansion. They might go to Ancello in Chicago; he in turn might get jumpy. You could go with maybe letting the Sicilian mob expand, but you give Salvatore too much power, you got more problems. In all honesty Robbie, we are fine as we are,' Serge said.

'Silvio?'

'I'm with Serge on this one Robbie,'

'Settled then. Now this recent business, what we gonna do about it?'

'Well, ain't no way in hell Moscone gonna let Benny walk from this. He has whacked out a made man without a go ahead. He's a loose cannon, no respect for his cousin Vinnie, no respect for the Cuccione family. He's gonna go,' Silvio said, lit a cigarette, then poured himself a beer.

Serge nodded, 'He can't be saved, but Vinnie has got to get that crew in line. I trust Vinnie but he has to be tougher.'

'It's hard losing two brothers. Do you think he's got the stomach for it still?' Robbie got up from his chair and walked to the window. He watched the traffic flow through Manhattan.

'I think he's solid,' Serge answered.

'Flip a coin as far as I'm concerned. You know my feelings. I would have removed him after the fiasco with his heroin dealing brother. But, those fuckin' Marranzo's do earn,' Silvio stated.

'Yes they do. But how many more blood relations of Vinnie think they are above the rules of this family?' Robbie returned to his seat.

'How about restructuring them?' Serge said.

'Will that cause more divisions though?' Robbie questioned.

'You could make Vinnie take in some of Salvatore's zips, that'll make 'em tow the line,' Silvio added.

'Then I undermine Vinnie. Nothing worse in this world than a guy who thinks his loyalty is being questioned. Silvio, you go see Vinnie, you make him understand the position of this family. Make him understand this is the last time. Any more crap from his crew forget about it. And give the Sicilians the contract on this Santini.'

'Sure Robbie. What about this Brook Nine mob.'

Robbie sighed. 'It's Vinnie's mess; let him fucking clear it up. I'm gonna meet Angela for lunch. Serge, I need to meet you later. We gotta discuss our politics in this city.' Serge nodded.

'What about me?' Silvio said.

'You go see Salvatore. Then Moscone.'

'I gotta sit down with that prick?'

Robbie looked at Silvio with eyes of impatience.

'I'll go sit down with that prick.'

'Glad to hear it,' Robbie said with a smile.

28 SILVIO VISITS

THE PISTOL WALKED INTO THE MARRANZO'S CLUB in Red Hook unannounced. Vinnie was already through a bottle of wine. About ten of his crew were in attendance, playing cards before they hit the clubs and bars of Brooklyn.

Silvio sat without an invite. Vinnie called for another glass and told his crew to beat it. Cousin Tony stayed, it was understood and he poured a glass for "The Pistol" Dalla Bonna.

'*Grazie,*' said Silvio.

'This about fucking Benny?' said Vinnie and lit a smoke.

Silvio nodded, took a sip. 'And other things.'

'Well you can tell the chair that I'm gonna take care of it.'

'We know that. I ain't here for re-assurance of that though. Besides our Sicilian cousins are gonna sew that matter up. Vinnie, you are drinking at the table of the last chance saloon. There's gonna be no more of this shit. You was told after Paulie. This *borgata* is destined to survive, with or without the Marranzo's. So you gotta start reining them in. One more fuck up, wild west show, anything that goes beyond what I'm telling you now, fuggedaboutit. You go. This whole crew goes.' Silvio delivered this in a flat low voice that managed to reverberate through the Brooklyn streets. It was power.

'Mister Silvio, people like Benjamin sometimes don't wanna listen, no matter how hard...'

'And that's the fuckin' point. As skipper of this crew, you should have made sure this shit don' happen. You gotta discipline your crew harder. Look back over the last few episodes. Your crew started it up with the Irish which resulted in Tommy getting blown across this city. Paulie who decided the rules don't apply and now your cousin. It's yer crew all the way down the line.'

'What the fuck I'm supposed to do, in all respect Mister Silvio. Maybe the boss set this all off when he began breaking rules.'

'Youse drunk?'

'Hardly.'

'Then maybe youse losing youse fuckin' mind. Youse gonna question your *borgata*?'

'All I'm saying is it get's very difficult to make a guy understand you can't break the rules when you got a boss who does.'

Silvio sat back in his chair, took a sip of the wine and sighed.

'I'm gonna give you a minute to think about what you said. Then I'm gonna listen again to what you say.'

'I'm tired.'

'Come again.'

'I'm tired, of being a skipper, of trying to follow all these rules, trying to keep guys in line, of killing, of making money, of this fucking mob life.'

Silvio Dalla Bonna sucked in air, and then drained his glass, set it down. He looked at Tony and to his glass. Tony frozen by his cousin's words broke out of it and poured more wine for Silvio. Silvio put the glass to his mouth, drained a large portion of it, set it down; then reached inside his jacket and pulled out a piece, rested his hand on the edge of the table, the gun pointed at Vinnie.

'If it's clarity you want, we can set it all straight now.'

Tony pushed his chair back from the table, his breathing so hard it overrode all other sounds.

'If that's what it takes to get me out, let's go. I've got no energy left for this. I ain't got my brothers, ain't got no respect. I'm done Mister Silvio. And you can tell Robbie I wish it was another time that he came to the throne. I'm loyal to him, he has my respect always, but I can't do it anymore. So let's get it done.' Vinnie picked up his glass and raised it in toast, then drained it.

Silvio Dalla Bonna was in a state of check mate. It was not the response he had envisaged. He picked up the glass with his free hand and drank. Set it down.

'Vinnie you can't talk this way and I know you donwanna go. Youse a mob guy. Youse don't go out like this. And as far as respect goes, you got a lot of respect. Why the fuck d'yer think yer didn't go when Corsini and Shapiro went? You're a captain in the Cuccione family and youse brothers would be sick to their stomachs if they could hear yer today.'

'My brothers are dead, because of this fucking life.'

'Don't mean you have to go the same way. You've always earned, done the right thing, this ain't the way to go Vinnie.'

'Ain't the way to go? What the fuck should I do then? Keep on like this, going from one trauma to the next. I am tired Silvio, I'm a skipper and I have held it together for too fucking long, my mind can't take the pressure no more. Couple years ago, I was still in love with the life, but all I do now is wake up in dread. I spend my days working it through alcohol, sitting in this fucking clubhouse in a haze listening to soldiers bitch about street shit and bringing me scores for my approval, just for fucking money. This is a prison, this fucking life ain't glorious Silvio and I'm beginning to see that,' Vinnie finished his glass of wine, 'Go open another bottle Tony.'

Cousin Tony was still in a fearful trance, he looked at Silvio for assurance; Dalla Bonna nodded, put the gun away. He offered a cigarette to Vinnie, who took one from the pack; Silvio took one out for himself, lit it and threw his lighter on the table casually. He looked at Vinnie.

'So what now?' Vinnie asked. Silvio sighed.

'You lay this shit on me, ain't what I was expecting I can tell you that. You got responsibilities to your crew, this family. You gotta shape up, quit fuckin' drinking. You wanna go in a programme, somin, I'll put it to the chair. You take a break, let cousin Tony run things for a while, get your mind straight. But you gotta get cleaned up Vinnie; this ain't no good, no fuckin' good. We can't have it. You understand what I'm saying, right.'

Vinnie stared at Dalla Bonna, through him. Tony returned with the wine and refilled the glasses, took one himself, the shake in his hands still evident.

'Go into a programme.' Vinnie sipped his wine. Dalla Bonna shifted forward and lent upon the table.

'Vinnie, one way or another youse gonna realize how fuckin' serious this situation is.'

'I realize. I don't think you do. Take a break maybe. I'll go down to Florida for a few weeks.'

'I'll square it away, but first you gotta take care of this black crew that whacked out Grasso.'

'I have?'

'It's the Marranzo's mess, you gotta clear it up.'

'To be honest I donwanna get involved with this.'

'Well fuckin' involved you are. It was a Marranzo member that hired them to whack out Grasso under the banner of the Cuccione family. Now you're gonna tidy this shit up before they start in with their rap shit about how they affiliated with this family. They gonna be made an example and youse gonna do it. And it's gonna be a confirmation. Then you gonna get yourself straight and come back to work clear. You got it.' Dalla Bonna's face appeared chiseled from marble, the eyes a deathly cold, reaching to the soul of Vincent Marranzo, grabbing hold of it as if to steal it. Vinnie sat up, sobriety swam over him.

'I got it Mister Silvio.'

'Good,' he looked at his watch. He picked up his glass drained it, set it down and looked at Tony.

'I got an hour. Let's finish this bottle have a few hands. Whatdyer say?'

'Sounds good,' said Tony filling the glass.

'Sure,' Vinnie said in a despondent air.

'It's been a while since I been on the streets with the troops. Feels good,' said Dalla Bonna, lighting a cigarette.

Bang on the hour, Dalla Bonna walked out of the Vesuvio. He stood on the sidewalk and lit a cigarette, breathed in the smoke and the Brooklyn air, then made his way to his car. He made a call.

'Yeah,' said the voice on the other end.

'Silvio. Where's he at?'

'He's at Mansion Brewery on Bowery.'

'Ok.' Dalla Bonna hung up. Started the car and eased out into traffic, back to the city.

At the Mansion Brewery all the gangsters looked at Dalla Bonna with fear and hate. The Sciorfa captain Moscone was sat at the bar, he turned to look at Dalla Bonna, but he had no fear, just disgust. Dalla Bonna made his way over to him and took up a stool to Moscone's left.

'Well, this social or business?' said Moscone, his body still in a half turn, his eyes hard.

'Business.'

'What you drinking?'

Silvio turned his body so as to rest his left arm on the bar. 'Moscone I ain't gonna drink wid yer, I'm here to tell you one thing. You keep yourself in check. Benjamin Santini is gonna be dealt with by the Cuccione family, no one else. Your crew don't go near him or any of the Marranzo's.'

'He whacked out a made man on my fuckin' crew without--'

'Close yer mouth. We're gonna deal with it. I ain't here to discuss it or reason about it. I'm telling yer.' Dalla Bonna stared into Moscone's face. Waiting. Moscone returned the hard look, but could not hold it for long, his lids opened and his brow furrowed.

'Ok,' he said. 'Sure you won't have a drink?'

'I'm busy,' Dalla Bonna said and lifted himself from the stool and walked from the bar to the door.

Silvio walked down to Little Italy, got himself an espresso and a slice of cheesecake while having a friendly conversation with the owner. It was a small break from his visits which were tiring him. Next he had to go see the Sicilian Salvatore and he knew that he had a pain in the arse drive before him.

Salvatore Grecco waited alone for Silvio. He had worked his way through a pot of coffee and half a pack of cigarettes, reading the Italian papers. Though he could speak English he had difficulty reading the language of his adoptive country.

Silvio arrived and the two killers shook hands.

'How yer doin'?' asked Silvio.

'Ima good. You?'

'Yeah yeah.'

'You wanna coffee?'

'No, give me something stronger. Scotch.'

Salvatore called to the guy behind the bar in his foreign dialect of which Silvio did not understand and a bottle of scotch was brought to the table and a pitcher of water. Silvio poured himself one.

'Got a job for your crew. Guy named Benjamin Santini, from the Marranzo crew in Brooklyn. Gotta be a confirmation. Done as soon as.'

'Datsa no problem Mister Silvio.' Salvatore reached into his pocket and took out a roll of money and slid it across to Silvio. Silvio picked it up, looked at it for second then pocketed it.

'Business is good then?'

'Yes, good,' replied Salvatore.

Silvio swallowed the last of his scotch then stood up.

'I gotta get back.'

Salvatore stood up and the two men shook hands. When Silvio had departed Salvatore called to the bartender then made a phone call.

Benjamin Santini was high on drink and cocaine, delving into the pleasures of Eloise. Worry was abandoned, fear buried as he slide into the sanctity of Eloise. His mouth glued to hers, their tongues searching out the depths of passion.

The first bullet went through the base of Santini's spine, exiting his pelvis and entering Eloise's lower abdomen coming to a halt as it shattered her hip bone. The searing pain made them suck the breath from one another and their eyes met as they opened. A deep fearful confusion.

The shooter placed his muffled weapon into the base of Benjamin's skull. This fatal second bullet ripped through his head exploding out from the bridge of his nose, missing Eloise and sinking into the pillow. Bone fragments and sticky blood mixed with mucous and brain fluid covered her face. There was no breath for her to suck in and her heart raced to dangerous levels. She was paralyzed with fear and pain. Her eyes blinked furiously as they tried to clear the obstructions to her vision. In her head was a high pitched drone as her blood pressure rose. Upon her right temple she could feel something cold being pressed into it. The shooter delivered her fatal bullet, then he turned to the back up shooter.

'*Andiamo,*' he said.

'She looka lika nice peecova ass,' said the back up shooter.

'*Stuppaghiara.*'

Jus' Thuggin and his Brook Nine crew were still partying on the back of their success. Smoking a wiseguy surely had boosted their ego and their street ranking. They could not know of the Mafia politics, the inner sanctum was a shut out. The maelstrom gathering for them they could not know of. So they continued to party, feeling safe, affiliated, untouchable.

Vinnie Marranzo reached out to Jus Thuggin, arranging a sit down with the pretence of discussing their business affiliation. The Brook Nine crew could do nothing but agree. Big time was beckoning.

Vinnie put two of his cousins in charge of the hit, he would not be there. The two cousins took five hitters with them. They greeted Jus Thuggin and his lieutenants at the motel on Long Island. They went to the room.

'Where's Vinnie then?' Jus demanded.

'Just running a bit late. We're gonna have a drink while we wait.'

'Ain't this a bitch. Drag my ass all the way out here, can't even be on time. Nigga hate to wait on line yer know.'

'He apologizes, couldn't be helped. We got a cooler full of drink, whad'yer want?' Vinnie's cousin replied, convincing Jus Thuggin not to think anything out of the ordinary.

'I'll have Irish whiskey.'

'Shit, no Irish.'

'Greasers gotta be kiddin' you know this nigga likes Irish.'

'Oversight. Ain't a problem.' He called out to the door. 'Joe.'

Cousin Joe pushed open the door and stepped in, 'What?'

'Got no fuckin' Irish whiskey, go to the liquor store, get a bottle.'

'Youse fuckin' serious, take J an B like a man.'

'Hey, be fuckin' nice. It's bad enough Vinnie's late, he wants us to take care of these guys, go get the fuckin' Irish.'

Jus Thuggin was looking at the mobster at the door and even though he wore sunglasses, his look was still serious.

'Sure, I'll go,' said the second cousin then walked out. The first cousin asked the other Brook Nine crew what they wanted. One declined, said he would wait for the delivery. The two others asked for beers and vodka chasers. They were accommodated.

Seven men shared the room. Four Brook Nine top men. Three Marranzo crew. They shared jokes and every now and again a straight up derisive comment. It was obvious to both factions that they disliked each other, but they had to tolerate each other.

Soon enough the whiskey arrived. The Brook Nine's began to relax. Vinnie phoned his cousin, then he passed the phone to Jus Thuggin.

'Yo Vinnie, you missin' the party nigga,' said Jus. Then he laughed as Vinnie said something to put him more at ease. 'Donchya worry, it's all good, see ya when ya get here.' He handed the phone back to the cousin, who also took Jus' glass to refill it.

Entering through the door came two Marranzo mobsters, with pump shotguns. Jus Thuggin got the first blast; it blew it him across the bed and into the wall. One of his lieutenants who was sitting got a cartridge from close range which just about took his head off. The blood sprayed another Brook Nine, frozen in fear; he squeezed his bottled beer so hard the glass broke. He was hit in the chest which fused him into the chair. The fourth member battled, with a reflex he threw his bottle of beer at one of the shooters and tried to rush them. He was shot in the back with a .45 and fell to his knees, breathing hard and cursing his double crossers. A point blank head shot silenced him.

Jus Thuggin was injured badly but it was not fatal. Vinnie's cousin who had plied him with drink went to him.

'Thuggin, who hearin' me.'

'Fuck ya, ya double crossin' guinea.' He breathed hard.

'Listen good. Yer whacked out a made man. Good as yer mob were, ain't somin yer can walk away from. Just for future reference.'

'It …was ya … man.'

'Benny Santini. Our cousin. He's gone too. Yousall nearly started a war wid this shit. But it all ends today.'

'Fuckin' guineas. Ya niggas ain't shit.'

'Vinnie says goodbye.'

'Tell him I'll see him in hell.'

'Too fuckin' tough Jus.' He put his .45 to Jus' head, ended it. All other Brook Nine gangsters received another shot to the head, to make sure. The guns were thrown on the bed, the gangsters left.

Vinnie met with Dalla Bonna. Dalla Bonna had squared it away with Robbie. Vinnie was sent to Florida for a two week vacation. When he returned he would seek help for himself. Vinnie Marranzo would clean up. Vinnie Marranzo was Mafia; it was an oath that could never be broken. Not even in the WPP. You might be an outcast but it was an oath till the day you die. Mafioso just do not walk away, quit.

29 BIRTH

ANGELA'S WATER BROKE AND SHE WENT INTO heavy contractions early on a Saturday morning. Robbie tried to calm her whilst grabbing the pre-packed bags. Angela just could not be calmed though, she screamed at Robbie to get her to the hospital. Screamed at him to call her mother and father. Robbie just picked up the bags, took her arm, led her to the car, and drove like hellfire to the hospital.

Angela went through a difficult delivery. But there were no major complications and she gave birth at four in the morning to a six pound baby girl. The baby was healthy although had a touch of jaundice, but the doctors assured both parents that there was nothing to worry about and the jaundice would disappear within a few days.

Angela's hair was bedraggled and had lost its natural shine and bounce. Her eyes were heavy, with deep dark circles that resembled bruising and her olive complexion had turned pale. But when she was given her baby the joy rose above all this and tears fell from her eyes as mother and daughter connected.

Robbie sat next her, kissed her forehead and took his baby's tiny hand, the small fingers tried to grip and found her father's index finger and clung on. Robbie smiled and Angela took his other hand, gripping it tighter.

'I love you,' she said.

'I love you,' he replied and they kissed.

'Rosa Maria D'Angelo,' she said.

Robbie laughed.

'What?'

'It's traditional. I was worried you was gonna call her Rainbow Sky or something.'

Angela smiled. 'I wouldn't inflict that on a child of mine. It doesn't bother you that she has your mother's name.'

'No.'

'Don't you think it's time you reached out to her and your sister?'

'I'm disowned. She always told me after my father died if I got mixed up in his thing, she would never speak to me again. She's been good on her word.'

'Family Robbie, no greater bond. Call her, see how it goes. If it works out we could visit them in Seattle, we both need a vacation.'

Robbie pulled away from Angela and Rosa, stood up.

'You're moving too fast Ange. Let's enjoy this moment for now.'

'Only if you promise me you'll think about it.'

Robbie nodded.

'Say it Robbie.'

'I promise to think about it.'

'Now come back here you.'

Robbie leaned to her and they shared a long loving kiss.

'You gonna be okay for a while. I'm gonna grab a coffee and a smoke.'

'You said you'd quit when baby was born.'

'Yeah well.'

Angela shook her head and gave him a smirk. 'Go, we'll be fine.'

Robbie bent to kiss Rosa's forehead, then got up from the bed and left the room.

Outside the hospital entrance Robbie lit a cigarette, sipped his coffee and placed the cup on top of a wall. Took his phone out and dialed Serge.

'Serge, is Silvio there with you? Yeah, it's a girl, six pounds, all well. We're gonna call her Rosa Maria. Ange is fine. Couple of days we'll all wet the baby's head. Yeah sure. I'll call you in a couple. See ya.' He took a drag from the cigarette, exhaled, picked up the cup and took a mouthful, set it back down. Then dialed.

'Mum, it's Robbie, please don't hang up,' he said, took a long drag of smoke and dropped the butt to the concrete, crushed it. 'Mum, you're a grandmother; you got a baby granddaughter, called Rosa Maria. Mum, please don't cry. Yes it's true. Please stop crying and slow down, I can barely make out what you're saying.'

When he finished the call, Robbie picked up the cup, but the coffee was stone cold and he spat out the mouthful, then tipped the rest away, dropped the cup into a bin and looked up at the sky. The night sky was clear and he peered into the vastness of stars, sighed deep, rubbed his temples, and made his way back to Angela and Rosa.

He stood at the door and stared at Angela and his baby, smiled. Angela was looking deep into their baby, in awe, mesmerized with the love of creation. A look of indescribable happiness cast into her face. She looked up and saw Robbie, then burst into tears. Robbie went to her.

'What's wrong babe?'

'I'm just so…I don't know. I'm.. I feel euphoric, like this isn't real and yet it is, does that make sense?'

Robbie had picked some tissues from the box on the bedside table and began to soak up the tears. He wiped her nose.

'It all makes sense babe. And it's all real. You're right, we both need a break. We'll go see my mother and sister, but first, we should see your family.'

'My mother and father, brother and his wife, my sis and her husband will be here soon.'

'Your old man gonna lay off me?'

Angela gave him eyes. 'Why you gonna start? I don't understand why you two can't get along.'

'Because he always wants to take me fishing or shooting or some crap that I just cannot do Ange.'

'It's natural to spend time with your in-laws Robbie.'

'Even if you're an outlaw.'

'Why do you have to spoil a perfect day?'

'I'm sorry okay. I just don't think you really understand the life I'm in.'

'I choose to blank it out. I can't understand it Robbie, I don't want to.'

'Look, let's not talk about this tonight, eh?'

'Okay.'

Robbie took a back stage while Angela's family fussed over the new addition. Then his father in-law asked if Robbie wanted to go and have a smoke with him, Robbie agreed.

'Brought some cigars, to celebrate,' he offered one to Robbie, who naturally accepted. 'Also brought this along, the wife don't know, but it's an occasion right.' He pulled out a hip flask from his jacket, unscrewed it, took a swig. 'Umm, to the bambino. That's good, twelve year old.' He handed it to Robbie.

'Thanks,' said Robbie, took a hit. Handed it back.

'I gotta say something to you,' said Angela's father.

Robbie nodded. 'Go ahead.'

'It bothers me, that you are what you are. I detest the fuckin' mob; you know that, I'm guessing. I hate the entire aura that goes with you guys, I hate the way you treat decent people. And I hate the bad rap Italians get on the back of you guys. I worry constantly about my daughter, simply because of you. I always prayed she would fall out with you find another guy, a legit guy. But fate is fate. Ain't gonna stop me worrying, but I'm gonna have to live with it. All that aside, I respect you for keeping the low profile you do, but Robbie you're very young, I mean really, how long do you think you can last before, shit, I don't know what I'm trying to say.'

'I think you said it. Mister Napoli.'

'My granddaughter's beautiful,' said Angela's father and puffed on his cigar.

'Like her mother.'

'Like her grandmother.'

They both laughed. Then took another hit from the flask.

'You know Angela prays that you will get out Robbie. I've overheard her talking to my wife, she prays a lot.'

Robbie nodded. Shrugged then sighed.

'Well let's hope God is listening to her.'

'I'm a realist Robbie; I know you're in till you die. You make a pact with the devil, that fucker don't let go.'

Robbie looked at his father-in-law. Dropped his cigar to the ground.

'I'd better get back.' As he moved, Angela's father grabbed Robbie's arm.

'Wait up Robbie. I don't mean to be getting at you. I just don't want to think about Angela having to live a life visiting you in prison or being a young widow.'

Robbie looked down at the hand on his arm, Angela's father released his grip.

'Stop thinking Mister Napoli. It's my daughter's first day in the world.'

Two days later Robbie sat in an expensive restaurant with his underboss and *consigliere*. They were celebrating Rosa Maria's birth. All three were in high spirits. Serge had brought good news with him. For the last year they had retained the services of a prominent lawyer and he was on the cusp of delivering to them a police captain and a high ranking official in the Mayor's office.

Robbie was happy that they could finally make some inroads to the political elite. He knew he needed political muscle.

'These people won't be cheap Robbie, but it's a start, the next batch will be less expensive.'

'What is cheap in this country anymore?'

'The lawyer is a good investment I think,' said Serge.

'He's got his finger on the pulse it seems.'

'A lot of contacts.'

'Can we stop talking about all this faggot crap,' said Silvio.

'What do you want to talk about?' Robbie asked.

'That three hundred million contract that's coming up for the maintenance on the Brooklyn and Williamsburg bridges.'

'Knew it wouldn't be long,' said Serge and smiled.

'Well that's why we need some political allies; make sure we get some sweet contracts out of it.'

'We can't miss out on this,' Silvio persisted.

'We won't. Anyone got an idea who's gonna bid strongest for rubbish removal?' Robbie asked.

'I would say that big firm from Jersey.'

'We can get to them?'

'We can get to them,' Silvio said with force.

'And concrete, tarmac, painters,' added Serge.

'Well, you two start putting the word out. Now let's have more drinks, we're supposed to be wetting the baby's head,' Robbie commanded.

'You out all night?' Silvio said.

'For a good while.'

'Gives you a break from diaper changing eh?'

'Fuck you,' Robbie said and they laughed. 'More champagne.' He summoned a waiter and ordered.

'In a couple of weeks I'm going to Seattle, gonna take Ange and the baby to see my mother, patch things up, I think. So youse two are gonna have to mind the store. I'm gonna send Ange back with the baby, then drop into Chicago, so Serge I want you to meet me out there. Silvio, you can look out for this city for a few days yeah?'

'Yeah, sure.'

Come the day of the flight to Seattle Angela was overcome by worry. About the baby being too young to fly, about meeting Robbie's blood. About being away from New York for a while, though why she didn't know, about whether she had remembered to cancel the papers, turn off what electrical goods they wouldn't be using, and the water at the stopcock. Endless amounts of worry. All of Robbie's reassuring did not assuage her and just before they were called to board she began to cry. Robbie comforted her and the women working in the first class lounge offered help. Robbie took Rosa from her arms and Angela went to the bathroom to compose herself. During the flight though Angela began to relax.

Their hotel was right in the heart of the city, close to the space needle, with wondrous views of the skyline. Baby Rosa, was sound asleep, gave them no trouble the whole journey. Robbie put her in the cot and Angela began to draw a deep bath, full of bubbles and moisturizing mixture. Robbie opened a bottle of wine, poured two glasses, called in to New York, then his mother.

Angela was drifting into deep relaxation; her wet hair fell about her neck as she rested it back on the bath end. The warm soft water caressed her skin and her muscles eased into a calm state and a tingle surged through her bones.

'Babe,' said Robbie disturbing her from heaven.

'Jeez Robbie, I was just about to drift off.'

'It's bad to fall asleep in the bath.'

'Who says?'

'It's in all the medical journals.'

'Bullshitter.'

'Thought you might like a glass of wine.'

Angela raised herself and took the glass from him.

'Rosa okay?'

'She's fine,' said Robbie, looking at her. 'So are you.'

Angela gave him a devilish smile and raised her knees, opened them slightly. Robbie sat on the edge of the bath, put a hand on one of her legs, stroked it. Angela moaned through half closed her eyes; Robbie let his hand slip under the water line, rubbing the inside of her thigh.

'You getting in,' she said in a hoarse lustful voice.

Later as they lay together on the bed, sharing the wine, baby Rosa awoke.

'Our daughter is very considerate,' Angela said getting up and throwing a robe on.

'We're very lucky,' Robbie responded.

'I suppose you're just going to finish the wine.'

'When she goes back to sleep I thought we'd both finish it.'

'I bet you did,' she smiled and went to the cot.

In the morning Robbie stood watching Angela feeding Rosa. He had just got out of the shower and a towel was wrapped around his waist, he sipped his coffee.

'Are you going to get dressed?' she asked.

'Soon,' he took a cigarette from the packet and grabbed his lighter, walked to the balcony.

'Are you nervous,' she said. Robbie shrugged. 'Everything will be alright,' she added, Robbie nodded, closed the door to the balcony after him. Being a mob boss seemed easier than meeting his mother, he knew he would have to take some chastisement and feel like a young boy again, then he stared at the city, thinking.

A warm day engulfed the environs and while driving to his mother's house at a stop light a car drew next to them, the occupants were street thugs, that much was obvious to Robbie, the bass from the boom box made Robbie's rental shake. He looked across at them; the bandana wearing passenger looked back and blew Robbie a kiss. Robbie gave him eyes. The volume decreased.

'Problem?' growled the passenger, his voice carrying across the short void between them.

'Kinda loud, you're waking my baby. That aside, no problem.'

'You know it.'

'Both of us know it,' replied Robbie, and then felt Angela's hand on his leg. The music resumed reverberating though the street. The passenger kept staring at Robbie, nodding his head to the beat. The light turned green and the thug car spun wheels as it pulled away.

'Pricks,' said Robbie.

As they drew up to his mother's house Robbie took a deep breath, just looked at the door. It opened and his mother stood there, dressed in her widows weeps. Robbie noticed her aging, sat frozen for a second; Angela was already out, waving at the stranger, getting Rosa out of her baby seat. Robbie moved himself, got out, then walked to his mother who instinctively held out her arms.

Mother and son embraced, the years of silence, grudge and despair rolled away. Rosa Maria cried and kissed her son's face repeatedly, holding his head between her hands, words choked in her throat. Robbie had placed his hands on her hands and he fought back tears. He looked up and could see his sister standing at the door; she seemed to be clutching her chest, holding her heart in. Robbie pulled away from his mother who put a hand in his.

'Mum, this is Angela and this is your granddaughter.'

Angela stepped forward and was embraced with warmth and intensity, baby Rosa was kissed upon her forehead and Robbie's mother put her hands together as if in prayer, then she put her hands to her mouth, covered her nose as another hurricane of emotion overcame her and he tears poured. Angela put an arm around the old woman as a few tears fell from her eyes too. Behind them brother and sister had found each other and gripped on tight, as if in fear of losing each other again if they let go. Robbie's sister Sarah buried her head in her brother's chest, her tears soaking into Robbie's shirt. After a while she broke off and looked into her brother's eyes, snot and tears streaming down her face.

'I've missed you,' she said.

'Me too sis,' he said with tears. 'Come meet your niece.'

Sarah wiped her face with a palm, then wiped it on the seat of her jeans. Nodded. Robbie led her by the hand. Sarah embraced Angela and kissed baby Rosa.

'Can I hold her?' she asked Angela who smiled and passed the baby to Sarah. Sarah cradled her and stared at her. Tears fell again.

The house was filled with talk as each person spoke over one another. Sarah's husband had arrived, plus Robbie's aunt and some of his mother's closest friends. Robbie did not think this was strange; it helped break all the tension that he perceived was there. A cold spread was laid out along with bottles of wine. Robbie drank cold beer from the fridge, grabbed Angela when he could, just to give him some gravity. Every now and again his sister came and held him. His mother talked with friends as if the world was about to end, the topic was invariably baby Rosa and her son.

It was late evening when Rosa's guests left. Sarah sat with her husband, holding the baby, who slept giving no trouble to the world about her. Sarah rocked gently talking to Angela who sat with a glass of wine, totally relaxed for the first time in the weeks since she had given birth. She knew she had found a new friend in Sarah.

Robbie's mother put a shawl around her shoulders, poured herself a glass of wine, then took her son's hand, led him to the garden. Robbie had been gearing up for this one on one, knew it had to come at some point. They sat on the swinging hammock. Rosa would not let go of her son's hand.

'So many years,' she said in Italian.

'It doesn't matter mama,' replied Robbie in English.

'It matters Robbie,' she continued, reverting to English. Took a sip of her wine. 'It was hard for me when your father died, but you grew up quick, took his reins, I could not see it, but you was just trying to be the figurehead, just as your father had taught you. You was such a quiet child, you always had your head in a book, always history and biographies. You should have been a lawyer, politician, teacher. I just don't know how you became what you are.'

'Mum, I didn't, I don't need judgment.'

'Hush, my child. I am not judging you no more. I'm just trying to tell you that if your father did not pass on when he did, another path you might have walked.'

'Life is what it is mum. I never caused you trouble, I just found a way into a life that made sense to me. To you it's an anathema. To me its family, just as you and Sarah are.'

Rosa laughed. 'There you go with your big words again. I don't know these words.'

'Anathema. It just means something that is detested.'

'Tell me how you manage to keep all those street hoods in check with big words Robbie. You were never a violent child. How is it you can play those two worlds and survive?'

'I never thought of it like that. I don't see two worlds mama. It's just my world.'

Rosa nodded. Then lent into Robbie. He slipped his hand out of hers and placed it around her shoulder.

'I'm sorry,' she said.

'You have nothing to be sorry for mum. I am sorry that I didn't make you proud.'

'Today I am the proudest woman alive.' She moved away took Robbie's arm from off her shoulder, placed her glass on the decking, then took his hand between hers.

'Forgive me son. I will never forsake you again. Please be careful though and thank you.'

'Thank me. For what?'

'For my beautiful granddaughter and for reaching for me, breaking the spell.'

'You're my blood; you don't have to thank me. I love you.'

'I love you son.'

BOOK THREE
ROBBIE'S FINALE

30 OUTFIT COUNTRY

SERGE MET ROBBIE AT THE AIRPORT THEN they travelled straight to see Ancello, who greeted them at his restaurant, which he had closed for privacy. The meeting was to be one of informality, the time had passed quickly and Ancello's tenure of president was to be ended. Robbie needed some clarification as to who they should elect next. During the last few months, Ancello had become vague with Robbie. But the machine was working, well oiled, the country was theirs.

'Congratulations,' he said, holding out his hand. Robbie took it and they embraced, then Ancello produced a box of Cuban cigars.

'*Grazie*,' Robbie said and took the box.

'Come on.' He led them to a table in the middle of the floor, spacious and filled with starter courses, bread and a few bottles of wine. He poured four glasses, and they waited for his underboss who was en route.

'*Salute*,' said Ancello and held up his glass. Robbie and Serge responded. 'Seems like an age since you been in my town.' Robbie said nothing, just shrugged. 'What's on your mind?' asked Ancello, Robbie said nothing, just sipped his wine.

His underboss arrived, greeted their New York cousins, and then took a seat next to his boss. Robbie began immediately.

'Well, it's over a year now.'

'Is that the thing?'

'You know it is.'

'Robbie. Things have not been as smooth as what we could have imagined. Still a lot of work to do.'

'You're talking about Detroit and Cleveland.'

'We have problems with them.'

'We have problems because you've been eating into Detroit's drug trade and Cleveland's trucking scams.'

'Robbie,' Ancello poured himself another wine with a half smile.

'Robbie nothing. You wanna bring this thing down before we set the foundations.'

'As I see it, it's all running as it should. Your family is the most powerful in the east. Our organization is strong in the mid-west.'

'With all respect you're breaking rules with this shit you're pulling in Detroit and Cleveland. This ain't what we agreed on.'

'Detroit and Cleveland ain't the fucking issue. Those families are still disorganized; they need a strong hand to guide them.'

'You ain't guiding you're taking.'

'And what about building secret factions does that go against our rules? Your Sicilian army in New York is striking fear through the streets. An army you created to carry out discipline and intimidation.'

'We got five families out there. Ain't as stable as this city. I needed an edge.'

'Listen Robbie, us playing politicians with this new commission is all very well, but we gonna both sit here and bullshit each other. At the end of the day, we're about making money and gaining power. It's what we do.'

Robbie shook his head. 'We agreed. If you don't relinquish the helm, either the commission is gonna remove you or it's gonna dissolve and we'll be back to square one.'

'Remove me. Of the twenty odd families in this country I have the support of sixteen; Detroit and Cleveland will support me, for concessions of course. How much support would you get even in your own city? You're the man who blew away his own boss remember. This thing of ours don't forget easily.'

Robbie said nothing, lit a cigarette.

'This is what politics are Robbie.'

'Well there's nothing more to say then. I gotta get back to New York.' He stood up. Serge stood up. Ancello and his underboss stayed sitting.

'Stay and eat something,' Ancello said.

'Ain't got the appetite to eat your table Ancello.' Robbie and Serge walked out of the restaurant into the Chicago streets and hailed a taxi.

'What's our next move boss?' asked Ancello's underboss.

'We don't need one.'

'Why don't we hit him while he's here?'

'Very fuckin' smart. The whole world will know I ordered it. D'Angelo is a smart man, once he understands that the majority of families will line up against him, he'll go along. The commission is mine, nothing can stop that now, we'll give him a week or so to get his head around it, then we'll tell him of our plan. Political muscle is everything and D'Angelo don't have of that yet. Chicago holds the power and he'll understand the bigger picture soon enough.'

In the taxi Serge wanted to talk but knew Robbie was raging inside, so he looked out the window at the passing streets. Robbie mumbled something.

'What Robbie?'

'How the fuck I didn't see this coming,' he broke off.

'How could anyone see this coming?'

'What's his game Serge?'

'I honestly don't know Robbie, but whatever it is; it's bigger than our thing.'

'All these old timers, it's always about power, selfish power. This commission was my dream. Now I'm gonna be an outcast.'

'We gotta find out which families are backing him,' Serge said.

'If the four New York mobs line up against us Serge. I don't know.'

'Maybe we should strike first.'

'Maybe that's what he wants. Whatever his plan is, you can be sure a commission gathering will be called very soon. They're gonna hit me Serge.'

'Ain't got a reason to do that.'

'Ancello said it, whacking out a boss. Some people don't forget and less forgive in our life.'

'What's our move then?'

'I don't know, but we gotta make sure New York stays calm. I need some time.'

'Let's get out of this fuckin' city,' Serge said.

'Nothing's gonna happen here; Ancello's too smart for that.'

'Even so, never felt comfortable here.'

'I can't take another flight. Gotta freshen up, rest a while. We'll just hole up at the hotel, have a few drinks, and fly back tomorrow.'

After checking in at the hotel, having a shower and phoning Silvio, Robbie met Serge at the bar. He had a light dinner then followed it with a cold beer.

'I had some thoughts,' Serge said.

'Oh yeah.'

'Ancello has a lot of political clout; maybe he's angling all this to unite the two.'

Robbie looked at Serge, drank a mouthful. 'You mean to try and elect another president?'

Serge nodded.

'Sonovabitch. Always Chicago. How comes we in New York could never get that

close?'

'We had a hand in the last time we did it.'

'And we ain't supposed to talk about it.'

'That's 'cause it turned into a cluster fuck, went bad for a lot of people and this country as a whole.'

'Yeah none more so than old man Kennedy. Can't imagine losing two sons, fuckin' heartbreaking,' said Robbie with pity.

'The old man played gangster when he was young, played politics in his middle years, washing all his sins away going legit, then he reached into the mob again, played us. Guy danced with the devil all his life. Should have convinced his sons to be in the movies, kept 'em away from politics, away from the mob.'

'Hmm. Still a lot of good people went during that craziness.'

'Yeah. America lost its innocence and lost its way, carrying a broken heart for too many years, being angry at the world, trying to mould everything in our image. We fucked it all up.'

'Jesus Serge,' said Robbie, gulped down the last of his beer the summoned the bartender.

'Yes Sir.'

'Two more beers with two J and B's please.'

'Okay.'

The drinks were served and Robbie motioned for the bartender to take the money from the pile before him.

'And to this day no one knows who the shooters were,' Robbie said, sipped the whiskey.

'I heard a long time ago..' Serge cut himself short. Robbie turned his head to look at him. Serge gulped down his whiskey then followed it with a gulp of beer.

'Finish what you was gonna say. You got permission,'

'I heard that what conspired against him in Dallas that day wasn't a planned strategy, it was just fucked up fate.'

'How's that?'

'Just what I heard.'

'Don't leave it hanging then.'

'Well, no one in our world had actually given an okay, there was talk of course, but fuck, hit the president. Chicago was relying on Marilyn to fuck him up. But of course the fucking broad fell in love with him, which is why Giancana raped her at Sinatra's place. You heard that story right?'

'Who hasn't?'

'So Momo being what he was, raging, suggested the hit. Well, nothing was decided, people wanted rid of him, were angry at him, Meyer Lansky contacted the old man, told him to reign in his boys, the old man told Lansky to go fuck himself, you know, blah, blah, blah. The commission though, never agreed an okay. But there was this kind of unsaid mist dawning. If it happens it happens, no one crosses no one collaborates.'

'For fuck sake Serge, you gonna get to it.'

'I'm getting there. Could do with a smoke. You wanna go on the terrace?'

'Sure. Barkeep,' Robbie called out.

'Sir.'

'We're just going on the terrace. Serve another round and keep you eye on this? Robbie said motioning to the money on the bar.

'Sure thing, take your time.'

The evening was mild and they both lit up looking across the deserted golf course. There were a few couples outside but the hotel was not busy.

'So,' continued Serge, 'Chicago sent a two man team to Dallas. New York reached out to "Little Napoleon" and he imported hitters from Corsica. And nobody knows who got him that day, it's just history now.'

'Where's Oswald fit in?'

'Who the fuck knows? Primed by another faction, certainly nothing to do with us.'

'Jack Ruby?'

Serge laughed. 'Ruby,' he said with a shake of the head. 'Ruby was supposed to just harbor the Chicago shooters, and then whack 'em. But for who knows what fucking reason he went half crazy, done Oswald, created this whole conspiracy theory on that day.'

'But he was poisoned in prison.'

'Fuck yeah. Same with the Corsican shooters. They never made it back to their home. The Chicago shooters were disappeared soon enough though. Then the edict came down that we never talk about that mad period.'

'That's some fucking story Serge.'

'Robbie, it's just what I heard. You see all these history documentaries, they talk about C.I.A conspiracies, Oswald acting as a lone gunmen, Oswald being a fall guy for a free Cuba movement, Russian infiltration, Castro, stories are stories, they get added to thrown through a kaleidoscope of insanity and everyone has a specialist opinion. I ain't saying all this shit I told you is true, I'm saying it's what I heard. The only thing that is true is that we got that bastard the presidency and he set about fucking us up and Chicago was the main player in his tenancy. Those are facts.'

'And Ancello's gonna go for it again, you reckon?'

'Makes sense. He's a politic player, so I figure this is his angle now. He wants to retain the chair, get it in motion. If he does have the backing like he say's we got no option but to go along. Besides Robbie, what have we got to lose?'

'Nothing I guess, but it's the disrespect Serge. He could have come to me with this. I'm reasonable right?'

'For sure. But Ancello fears you. Ain't nobody done what you have since the days of Luciano, Genovese and Lansky. Unifying the country into a strong commission again. Takes a lot of balls Robbie. I don't figure they gonna hit you, unless you go against 'em on this.'

'Maybe. I'm fucking worn out.'

'Well I'm gonna have a few more nightcaps.'

'I didn't say I was going to bed.'

As they sat at the bar with more drinks, Serge turned the conversation to family.

'So what about your mother? It all go good?'

'Yeah. We had a lot to put away, but my mother has got wise.'

'And Angela and the baby?'

'Good. My mother is over the moon. I'm glad that my sis is ok with me though. It's fucking crazy how time passes and a void happens.'

'Family. What can you do about it? All this Italian bullshit about family bonds never break. It does no more than any other race.' Serge lifted the drink to his mouth with a scowl.

'You ever reached out to your blood.'

'No. They're all scattered. Got nobody real close anyway. This is my family.' Serge fingered the pinky ring he wore.

Robbie nodded. 'We all in it.'

'Ain't that the truth.' Serge lifted his glass. *'La Familia.'*

'Familia.'

31 EMPIRE STATE

ROBBIE AND SERGE RETURNED HOME TO BE met by Silvio with some disturbing news.

'When I called in you said everything was kosher,' Robbie said.

'This just cropped up,' replied Silvio.

'So tell me.'

'The four families want a sit down.'

'Regarding?'

'Didn't say. But it weren't a request Robbie, it was a demand.'

'Who called first?'

'It was just one call from the Badalamenti family.'

'So it begins,' Robbie mumbled.

'What the fuck's going down?' Silvio said.

Robbie sighed, lit a cigarette. 'I need coffee.' Serge set about pouring three cups.

'The Cuccione family is gonna be thrown off the commission Silvio,' Robbie said.

'Bullshit.'

'No bullshit. It's what's going down.'
'I don't get it, for what?'
'Politics.'
'But the commission is solid. You said it.'
'Well I was wrong. Chicago has played the ultimate game and I have made a major misjudgment. All the hard work we have done has handed all the power to Ancello.'
'Fuck it. Let's hit 'em all.' Silvio exploded.
'That's impossible,' Serge said.
'We're the strongest mob in the country. Ain't impossible,' Silvio responded.
'It's impossible and fruitless. Whatever way we go now the commission is gonna line up against us. The battle now is to keep this family intact.'
'This family is solid.'
'Now. When they start squeezing us and our people ain't earning, then we got trouble.'
'Let's take out the Badalamenti mob, it will all fall into place.' Silvio lit a cigarette and paced the floor.
'That's one cog Silvio. We cannot take on the whole damn commission.'
'I don't fucking believe this.'
'Well you're gonna have to, because I need you calm, this family needs you calm.'
Serge handed coffee to Robbie and Silvio.
'Gotta go for the sitdown Robbie,' Serge said, 'If you don't they gonna figure you ready to go to war.'
'Yeah.' Robbie put his cup down. 'Set it up. I'm going home, need some time to think.'
'Okay Robbie.'
At home Angela was cooking. Baby Rosa was lying in the cot. Robbie came behind Angela, put his arms around her and kissed her neck.
'Umm, that's good.'
'Something smells real good.' He kissed her again, broke off. 'I'm gonna hold Rosa.'
'Awe Robbie, she's just gone down. Don't wake her.'

'Stop your worrying mother,' he said. Angela shook her head with a half smile, turned back to her cooking.

Robbie lent into the cot and picked Rosa up gently, then cradled her to him. She stirred but did not open her eyes, just moved into the comfort of her father.

'Shush,' Robbie sounded, then walked back through the large lounge to the kitchen and stood at the French doors.

Angela turned to watch him, she could sense he was whispering to Rosa, but could not make out what.

'You okay honey?' she asked.

Robbie turned to her, nodded.

'You sure?'

Robbie nodded again but Angela could sense the undercurrent of anxiety within him.

'I'll pour some wine. Okay?'

'Sure babe,' Robbie replied then turned back to the scene of the garden, gently rocking his baby daughter. Angela watched him for a second with a look of dismay. Then she took two glasses from the cupboard and chose a bottle of red from the wine rack, uncorked it, let it breath, turned her attention back to Robbie.

Robbie kissed his daughter; put her back into her cot. So at peace was Rosa she barely moved when transported back to her world of comfort. Robbie went back to the kitchen, opened the French doors and went out onto the oak decking. Sat at the table and lit a cigarette. Angela joined him, placed a glass before him.

'I know something's wrong,' she said. The strength in her voice could not be masked.

'I don't bring my business into our house. You know this Ange.'

'Fair enough. But something is deeply troubling you. I can sense it and our baby will sense it, so you are bringing it into our house, even if you leave it unsaid.'

Robbie took a drag from his cigarette and a gulp of wine.

'I want you to go to your parents for a while.'

'No. I need to know Robbie. I am not going to my parents in a state of anxiety. I want to know what's wrong.'

He shifted in his chair and looked at her, took another suck of poisonous smoke then stubbed it out.

'I've got problems in my world. Big problems. I don't want it to spill over into this world.'

'But it is Robbie, it is. All this crap, one world don't mix with the other. It's all bullshit Robbie. I've told you before, you are twinned with my life and our life now has Rosa. It's all one life Robbie.'

'Listen. It's all arranged if anything happens to me-'

'Shut up. I don't want to hear it.'

'If anything happens to me, you get the houses, a trust fund is set up for Rosa that she cannot get access to until she is twenty one. There is more than three million in a Geneva account for you. Totally washed and legitimate money that can never be taken from you by the government. There are two fashion businesses that will go to my sister, goes without saying she will support my mother.'

Angela shook her head, tears in her eyes.

'I just want you. Rosa wants you.'

'Angela, I have very little control over what is happening now. I held it all in my hands,' Robbie illustrated the point with a gesture. 'But I have no control now; I cannot stop the storm that is coming. This is why I want you and the baby away from it.'

'This is insane. Why can't we just go away together? If you have all this money, we can just--'

'Hide. Angela I'm Mafia. A man of honour, I don't hide. I face up. I've told you numerous times, you don't walk away from this life. I am not going to debate with you. This is an order.'

'Fuck you,' Angela screamed jumping up from the table and run back into the house.

Robbie finished his wine, then went into the house. He turned down the stove to prevent the saucepans boiling over, went in search of Angela.

She was on their bed, laying face down, sobbing. He sat next to her and rubbed her back. 'Angie. All that I told you is just the worst case. It's just that I want you to be prepared.'

Angela turned over and wiped her face

'We are just beginning on our journey. We have a beautiful baby. How do you think I feel? Having to think about you lying in a coffin. Rosa without her father. What do you think is going through my heart?'

Robbie pulled her close, kissed her with all the power he held in his soul. Then broke from her, looked into her eyes.

'I will do everything; to prevent that.'

'Promise me.'

'I promise.'

The meeting was set. The Cuccione family captains were told to be on their guard for trouble and to make their members know that they must keep going about their daily activities, but with caution. Salvatore Grecco was commanded to arrange security for the meeting and if anything happened, to attack with extreme violence. His group of Sicilian killers were hid well, come the day of the meeting.

On the morning the three top men of the Cuccione family met for breakfast. After they sat drinking coffee, saying little. It had been agreed that the meeting of the five mob factions would be conducted with all three representatives from each family. A move suggested by the Badalamenti family. In the history of the Italian mob, this had never happened. It took much negotiating and the deliverance of a five million dollar bond per family, to be held by the Buffalo mob until all members at the meeting returned safe.

In his thinking Robbie knew that Buffalo was being kept in the dark. If a hit was going down, there was no way they could deliver that money to the offended family, notably his. The four families would wrestle that money from them.

'Silvio. You're not going to the meet.'

'What?' asked Silvio of Robbie.

'You're staying.'

'What the fuck you talking about?'

'Robbie. You figure this will be it then?' Serge said. Robbie nodded.

'Yeah.'

'You think their gonna hit us? After all the fuckin' negotiating and Buffalo and that crap,' Silvio said with venom.

'Silvio. The moment I go into that meeting, you're the boss. If we don't come out, you have to guide this family. You understand what I'm telling you.' Robbie said this in a quiet directive which cannoned into Silvio's consciousness. Serge Valone said nothing, stared into his coffee. The realization that this could be his last day began gnawing at him. He was thinking about his life.

Robbie continued. 'You have to pick your own consigliere. But Salvatore must be your underboss. You can't fight them Silvio, so you're gonna have to negotiate. You're gonna have to keep as much territory as you can and play hard ball when they demand you cut the size of this family. They will go after the Sicilians first, but you got to keep them on the leash and hide them throughout the country, say they have been shipped home. There is gonna be some harsh times coming for this family, you have to keep it together.'

'Fuck Robbie, you..'

'I have complete faith in you and Salvatore. I figure they will throw this family off the commission. During the exile you will have to rebuild, quietly. But you can never show what strength you have. They will renew this family to the commission when they are satisfied you pose no threat, so pose no threat. Be humble.'

'Humble you say. I mean fuck..'

'Silvio,' Robbie said through clenched teeth. 'If you want, come to the meeting. Phone your family and say goodbye. If not, take the advice I am giving you.'

Silvio nodded, said nothing, but his eyes were squinted as his brain took on board the reality. Robbie looked at his watch.

'Okay, we got an hour. Let's have a drink together, see if we can't think of anything else.'

'I can't think of anything,' Serge said, his voice hoarse.

'I apologize to you both for where I have led you.'

'No need Robbie. I'm a grown man, I could have said no to you when I come out. But I wanted the life, I chose it,' said Serge.

'Robbie, I came along too. Let's have that drink.'

They shared a few glasses, some jokes, talk of times past. The future was not mentioned. Near time Robbie raises his glass.

'To the Cuccione family.'

'Salute,' said Serge.

'Cuccione,' said Silvio.

They shook hands, embraced each other, and then Robbie gave one last look to Silvio. No words were spoken. Robbie nodded, Silvio nodded back, then Robbie and Serge left, to greet their fate.

FINAL SITDOWN

Serge drove. There was nothing said between him and Robbie as they headed for midtown, close to the area where Robbie had begun this journey with the assassination of his boss. The traffic snarled up and they both lit cigarettes. Robbie watched New Yorkers begin the rush home. He looked at the buildings of a city he loved, his city, his empire. Whatever feelings were running through him, he hid well.

The meeting was held at a well known restaurant. It had been hired for a private function, so no members of the public were in attendance. They were met at the entrance by representatives of the Sciorfa mob, searched and allowed to enter. Robbie had a sour taste in his mouth. He viewed it as disrespect.

There was a large conference table, with jugs of water, wine and glasses. Bowls of olives, cold meats, vegetables, grapes, bread and cheeses, condiments and cutlery. The five families were all represented now Robbie and Serge had arrived.

The Badalamenti family was headed by Gaspare Mateo. The Sciorfa by Dominic Lupe. Molina family boss Jack Agostini. Gennazo mob boss Frank Gattuso. All four families had their underboss and consigliere present, as per agreement.

Gaspare Mateo was the first to greet Robbie. They shared a tentative handshake. Then the rest of the bosses shook hands with Robbie. Gaspare suggested they sit. All bosses sat with their underboss to their right and consigliere to their left. Robbie whispered to Serge to sit at his right.

'Well first off, thank you all for coming. If no one has any objections, I will chair this meeting,' proposed Gaspare. There was no objections. Robbie shook his head, while pouring himself a glass of water. He noticed that behind the doors leading to the kitchen were some mobsters. He knew that on the streets, his Sicilian guard were waiting, just like the hidden guard in the restaurant.

'It seems that the Cuccione family is under represented,' said Gaspare.

'I won't give you my reasons, but Silvio could not make it.'

'But it was agreed,' said Dominic Lupe, Sciorfa boss.

'Well, apologies,' Robbie said with nonchalance.

'And your consigliere sits in the place of your underboss,' Lupe added.

'In the absence of Silvio, he is my underboss. No more so than your consigliere.'

'Forget about it,' interjected Gaspare. 'Let's tend to the business in hand.'

'Fine,' said Robbie, sipped his water.

'The commission is going to sanction Don Ancello in Chicago to continue as head for the foreseeable future.'

Robbie smiled. Serge gave Robbie a look then took his gaze back at Gaspare.

'Something funny in that?' said Lupe.

'Funny that it has already been agreed without a commission session.'

'Well this is part of that session. Don Ancello thought it prudent that the New York families will chair their own meeting. He will chair the mid-west session,' continued Gaspare.

'And the other families?'

'Many have been consulted and have agreed to go along.'

'So the commission will meet but it kinda won't.'

'With respect Robbie, this is the best way to meet. In these dangerous government surveillance times, you understand that it's risky for us all to be caught together.'

'I understand,' said Robbie. He fidgeted in his chair, lit a cigarette.

'Don Ancello has a plan of breadth and depth that will only help this thing of ours,' said Gaspare.

'To put a president in office,' Robbie interrupted. A silence then swept through the meeting. The Sciorfa, Molina and Gennazo bosses looked at Gaspare. Gaspare was caught off guard as much as the others.

'How do you know this?' he asked.

'It's the obvious game. He is playing the commission. He has more political weight than any family in this country. He figures that by getting a president into office he can twist you to back him, and you have. He will stay in power till his death, creating a Chicago based commission. He will be your new boss of bosses.'

'And surely he should be rewarded if he delivers our safety.'

'If you believe that.'

'Robbie, you have to realize the magnitude of this. If you do not go along, you risk your family being thrown off the commission.'

'This family rebuilt the commission,' Robbie said sternly.

'Yes and destroyed a commission, said Gennazo boss Frank Gattuso.

'Clipped a boss without a fuckin' commission okay,' added the Molina boss. They had lined up just as Robbie predicted.

LITTLE ITALY

Silvio Dalla Bonna sat in his clubhouse, drinking whiskey. Salvatore Grecco sat next to him.

'All of them in place?' Silvio asked.

'Sure.'

'Let's pray to God this all goes right.'

Salvatore nodded, said nothing, lit a cigarette, and looked at Dalla Bonna who gulped down his whiskey, poured another. The phone behind the bar rung and the soldier behind the bar answered it.

'Skip,' he called out, holding up the phone.

'Who is it?' he shouted back. The soldier shrugged, just placed the phone on the bar. Silvio got up and walked to the bar, picked up the receiver.

'Yeah, Silvio.' He listened, looked at his soldier, then over at Salvatore.

'I got it,' he said into the receiver, hung up. 'I gotta go across the street to the phone booth,' he announced.

'You wanna me to come?' asked Salvatore.

'No no, you stay here.'

Rain began to fall across New York, Silvio jogged across the street. Tucked himself into the booth, loaded the phone with change, dialed.

'Silvio. Well I ain't. That's no fuckin' business of yours,' he said then listened. 'Fuck you.' He searched for his cigarettes, cradled the receiver between his shoulder and craned head, listening. Lit the cigarette, returned to a normal position. 'Well I tell youse now, ain't gonna fuckin' happen. You think I'd let that happen,' he said in a raised voice. He smoked. 'Listen, if I did, ain't no way there's time to do it.' He sucked in more smoke. 'That long huh.' He listened while looking along the street, the rain grew heavy and he tried to move more of his bulk under the booth. His eyes were transfixed on something not visible as if looking back in time. For an age, he said nothing.

'I ain't interested,' he finally said, jammed the receiver back into its cradle. Spat on the sidewalk, finished his cigarette. He looked at the clubhouse from across the street, thinking, lit another cigarette. Phoned the number again. 'Okay,' he said, hung up then crossed back to the club. Ignored the soldier behind the bar, walked straight to Salvatore. Standing he poured another whiskey. Salvatore looked up at Silvio.

'Call 'em back,' Silvio said.

'Call 'em back,' repeated Salvatore, his voice resonating with surprise.

'That's what I said. Ain't going down.'

'This is what Mister Robbie says ?'

'It's what I say. Now call 'em off.' The menace in Silvio's face would frighten most men. The Sicilian though saw deeper than fear.

'Okay Mister Silvio.' He took out his phone, pressed the speed dial. Silvio sat, gulped down the whiskey, poured another. Salvatore sighed.

'No service. I try again.' He hit speed dial again, then spoke his regional dialect into the cell phone, hung up.

'It's done,' he said.

'Good. Let's have a drink.' He poured two glasses of whiskey and pushed one to Salvatore. The Sicilian shrugged, picked up his glass.

'Salute,' said Salvatore.

'Salute,' said Silvio.

SITDOWN

'New York will remain a powerhouse, but all five families will have to be on a more equal footing,' Gaspare proposed. Mafia politics had always been about deception. This was deception. What Gaspare meant was the Cuccione family would be stripped of power to make the weaker families stronger. The Badalamenti family would arise as the phoenix, stronger than ever. Equality never existed in New York.

'So what do you wanna take from us?' Serge asked.

'You have not been given permission to speak here Valone,' Gaspare said. It was a rebuke which served to ridicule Serge and push home the point that Gaspare was now the most powerful boss in the empire. Robbie stood up and placed his hands on the table. 'Serge is my underboss. He has my permission. You disrespect the Cuccione family again, we walk. And if you and your fuckin' puppet master in Chicago want to settle this in the streets, so be it. This family will go all the way.'

'Robbie, sit down. I apologize.'

'Okay,' Robbie said and sat.

'A war would not be good for anyone. You could not win and it would be an act of childish destruction.'

'Fuck you Gaspare.'

'Robbie. You have to concede. Your family will be outcasts; you will bring about your own demise. This plan is good for all of us.'

'We are all Cosa Nostra here. I believe in Cosa Nostra. All we have achieved in the last few years is removing one boss of bosses for another. They say history repeats itself. Some of you here think that I killed my boss simply to be boss. But I did it because I could see what we had become, our core was being eroded, the respect we once carried was spat on. I wanted to take us back to the days when we had this country sown up. When we were the mob.'

'Which is just what Don Ancello wants,' interjected Gaspare.

Robbie shook his head. 'If you can't see it, I can't make you see. I'm not about to bring destruction to my own family. So what do you want?'

Gaspare poured a glass of wine for himself, smiled.

'You must send your Sicilian army home. You must not make any new members to your family, and some of your interests must be shared with the other families.' Gaspare sipped his wine.

'And for this the Cuccione family stays on the commission?' Robbie said taking a plate, proceeding to fill it with food.

'You have mine and Don Ancello's word.'

Robbie nodded, continued filling his plate without looking up. When he finished he sat back.

'I'm gonna eat this and discuss it with my underboss, before I give you a definite answer.'

'Okay,' Gaspare said, and then got up. As if it was their cue the other representatives of each family rose and left the table. They blended into various sects, intermingling and conversing. Serge sat back and sighed.

'They're gonna keep us here as long as possible, to carry out their plan,' Robbie said.

'You still think it's a hit?'

'Let's just agree to everything,' said Robbie.

'Everything?'

'If they don't hit us today, they have planned it for soon.'

'So what's our move?'

'Our move has been made,' Robbie said. Serge looked at him quizzically. On getting no response, he poured a glass of wine for himself.

'Pour me one too,' said Robbie.

'Sure,' replied Serge in a whisper.

Anthony Lascelle

LITTLE ITALY

Silvio kept pouring glasses of whiskey and passing them to Salvatore. The Sicilian, not being a big whiskey drinker was getting drunker by the minute. His spirit was high; he laughed and told Silvio stories of his time in the old country. Silvio laughed along with him. Kept him on the track of reminiscing by asking questions.

Salvatore knew. It was instinct. He had lived through many troubles in his native Sicily and he knew. So he did not fight. In his heart he was satisfied that he had served his boss loyally. He had lived by the Cosa Nostra code all his life and he was satisfied he had been true till this day.

'Get another bottle from the bar you crazy zip,' said Silvio, laughing.

'Me?'

'Yeah you. I wanna make sure you can still walk.'

'I can walk.'

'Yeah right.'

'I prove it.'

'John, grab another bottle place it on the bar. Gonna give this zip here a sobriety test,' he shouted to the soldier behind the bar.

'Sure,' replied the soldier and placed a bottle on the bar.

'There it is. Sure you can see the bar?' Silvio said.

'See de bar,' said Salvatore.

'Yeah as in your vision, you know,' said Silvio gesturing with hands.

'See de bar.' Salvatore laughed.

'Go get the fuckin' bottle.' Silvio laughed.

'Okay,' Salvatore said getting up; he slumped back into the chair.

'Here we go. You Sicilians can't drink for shit.'

'Fuck you Mister Silvio. I show you.' He got up, grabbed the table, and steadied himself.

'How's the view up there?' said Silvio, still laughing.

'I okay. I go.' He let go and began staggering to the bar.

'There youse go,' said Silvio getting up too. He reached into his waistband, took out a snub nose, and followed Salvatore. When he was close enough, he raised it and fired a shot into the back of his head. The Sicilian as if grabbing for the bottle fell into the bar, his body hit the polished teak and bounced back, lifelessly fell to the floor. Silvio bent down and fired another shot into his head.

'Fuck skip,' said the soldier.

'Yeah. Find somin' to wrap him up in. And get a mop and bucket.'

The soldier just leaned across the bar and stared down at the dead Salvatore.

'Today'll be ideal,' said Silvio with impatience.

'Sure.'

SITDOWN

The talk continued. Robbie wanted repeated which of his industries the families desired to eat into. They laid out construction, the new drug venture of heroin he had. The credit card and internet fraud he had wrestled from the eastern Europeans.

Robbie agreed to the drugs and credit/internet fraud. Construction he would not unleash. Another round of negotiations resumed.

'Okay,' Robbie said finally. 'How about first I get something as an act of faith.'

'Like what?' Gaspare asked.

'How about you send off those guards you got tucked away in the kitchen, those out front. It's just me and Serge, we got no pieces. They don't need to be here.'

Gaspare looked at Robbie closely. He noticed the tiredness in Robbie, the look of defeat. He nodded. Sent out the command for all of them to leave.

'Thank you,' Robbie said. His voice humble, he continued. 'I agree to disband my Sicilian faction. The construction industry will be shared, the details of what goes where I will let you decide.' He stood up. 'I want to say to all of you. Let us not forget our history. Let us hope that we can survive what is about to happen, let us begin with new strength.' He lifted his glass of wine. 'Cosa Nostra.'

Everyone raised their glass. They all repeated Cosa Nostra, drank, then applauded. Robbie left his place and went to Gaspare. They embraced. Then Robbie embraced the heads of the other families.

A time was set for discussing details of the carve up of Cuccione interests. The New York commission meeting was adjourned. As they all gathered their coats, Robbie calmly walked to the door, entered the street. The pavement was alive as usual, a New York alive. He looked around, saw what he needed to, nodded, and walked back into the restaurant. The congregation was near the door, he stalled them by shaking hands, slipping through them to Serge. When he reached Serge he grabbed his arm, led him to the kitchen.

'What the fuck Robbie?' asked Serge in confusion.

'Walk,' commanded Robbie.

As they got into the kitchen, the service entrance opened and in piled killers. Determination etched on their faces. They pushed past Robbie and Serge without a glance of recognition.

At the entrance, after Robbie's nod to New York, a Sicilian who for five hours had been watching the restaurant moved through the crowd and with his duplicate key calmly locked the restaurant doors. He pulled on them to give the impression he didn't really believe the restaurant was closed to the public, even though a prominent sign said so, and then blended in with the crowd of the city.

Robbie led an astonished Serge through the alley behind the restaurant to an awaiting car, which drove off without drawing attention. The carnage they left behind was a message. A message from Robbie D'Angelo to Chicago, to New York, to the commission. The Cuccione family could never be beaten, be removed.

In the car Serge was sweating. His head was banging, his heart pumping. He looked at Robbie who portrayed nothing.

'What the fuck Robbie?'

'Serge. I figured Ancello would call a hit. Could not be sure they would do it today. His puppet Gaspare would lead me into concessions, to make me feel that if I went along, I would survive. This family would survive. They gave me nothing at the sitdown. I told Salvatore to stay with Silvio. I had no intention of bringing him to this meeting and everything I said to him this morning I meant. But on this phone,' he said pulling it out from his jacket, 'Which no one but Salvatore has the number of; I got a missed call during the meeting. It was on silent vibrate in my pocket. I told Salvatore to ring once and hang up if anything strange happened. When I went outside, I saw two things, a car with four men in, the hit team for us and the zip across the street that I and Salvatore worked out. If I gave the signal, it was on. Serge, if I never got the missed call this wouldn't have gone down.'

'Jesus. Not Silvio.'

'I hope not. Two things could've happened. Either Silvio and Salvatore have been blown away, or Silvio has hit Salvatore. If he has it's a smart move on his part. Ancello ramps him up, for a day he's the boss, this thing is what it is. Your friends turn into your enemy, sometimes your enemy becomes your friend.'

'Sometimes I wish I never got in,' Serge said.

Robbie looked at him, gave a half smile, nodded.

'Now what?'

'We gotta meet the Sicilians. If Salvatore ain't there then Silvio betrayed me. Then we'll deal with him, sit back, and see what Ancello's next move is.'

'The four families?'

'They'll be in confusion. They'll all have a massive power vacuum. There'll be no revenge. We'll reach out to their strongest captains in a few days. First we gotta get the Sicilians organized. If Salvatore is gone we need to stabilize 'em.'

Serge said nothing.

'You okay?' Robbie asked.

'I feel I've let you down.'

'How so?'

'I didn't have the vision for this. I should have been setting this up as your consigliere.'

'You're no longer my consigliere. You were a good one, but this was a last minute plan, acted on instinct. If I never had the Sicilians I could never had managed it. Now you are my underboss.' Robbie held out his hand. Serge took it and a firm handshake ensued.

'Thank you Robbie.'

'Thank you, for your loyalty.'

CHICAGO

Ancello had no word from New York. He was becoming increasingly agitated. He puffed on his cigar and paced the room. His underboss brought him a *demitasse*. He took it from him, laid his cigar in the ashtray, then using the remote flicked through the channels to alleviate his angst. It was here he got news from New York. He turned up the volume.

The news reporter was standing across the street from the restaurant. It was cordoned off and the road was filled with cars and ambulances, lights flashing. Policeman stood at the entrance and others in suits flashed badges and entered the restaurant, the camera paned into the doorway, but the door was quickly closed barring any close ups, the camera pulled back to the reporter.

'All we know at this point is that around six this evening gunfire was heard from inside the restaurant. The restaurant had been closed to the public, but eyewitness reports say that the people seen entering the restaurant earlier in the day were well known mob figures in New York. The police have not confirmed this at this time, although one officer did tell me it looks like a contract killing. Now we don't who or how many people are dead in the restaurant but have heard people leaving describing it as a bloodbath. This is as close as any media is allowed right now. The police, forensic teams, FBI even representatives from the mayor's office have descended upon this crime scene, which indicates to this reporter that this is a major development in the New York underworld. Back to you in the studio Guy.'

Ancello switched channels. It was news on other stations, but there was no more information than what he had just heard. He sipped his coffee, turned to his underboss.

'That's that then,' he said.

'Seems that way. That fuck Silvio held up then.'

'He wanted to be boss. Now he is.'

ROBBIE'S HOUSE

Angela was holding baby Rosa, rocking her in her sleep. Like the rest of New York she was watching the news. Her heartbeat raised and she stopped rocking Rosa, picked up her phone and called Robbie's. It went straight to voicemail. She rang again, same result. The phone fell from her hand and she stood transfixed on the news report until the emotion erupted from her. Her tears exploded like a pyroclastic flow, she sunk to her knees, the grief too strong for her to fight.

CLUBHOUSE

Silvio Dalla Bonna believed like most other people, that Robbie was dead. He was alone; the body of Salvatore was being disposed of. He didn't smile or gloat at the news reports, just believed Robbie D'Angelo was now just a name mob history. He went to the bar poured three shot glasses of Sambuca. Raised one to the television.

'Robbie. Rest in peace.' He downed the Sambuca, slammed the shot glass on the bar upside down, picked up the next one.

'Serge Valone. Rest in peace.' He repeated the process and picked up the third glass.

'The Cuccione family.' He blew heavy after the final shot. Turned off the TV. Locked the clubhouse, made his way home.

THE STREETS

In every gangster clubhouse, bar and restaurant in the city, hoods were transfixed on the news. All were eager to find out who had been hit. The rumor mill began in earnest. False reports filled the streets of the empire state. No one knew the truth. All five families were in a state of chaos. Paranoia began to grip. Captains throughout the five boroughs thought they would be next. Soldiers, mostly the younger generation talked of war.

THE SICILIANS

By the time Robbie and Serge got to the Sicilians, Robbie knew that Salvatore was gone. He had been constantly ringing him, but got the standard service provider message telling him the number he was trying to reach was currently unavailable and to please try later. Needless to say, Salvatore was not at the meeting place.

Robbie explained everything to his army of killers. They said nothing to the news of their fellow countryman's death. Robbie appointed their new leader; ordered them to find Silvio Dalla Bonna, but not to kill him. The new leader sent out the army, then embraced Robbie and Serge.

SILVIO'S HOUSE

Silvio arrived home to an empty house. He found a note from his wife telling him she had taken the children to her sisters for the day, would be home late and there was some cold pasta in the fridge. He went into the fridge, disregarded the pasta, and grabbed a bottle of beer, switched on the television to check if there had been any developments. Tomorrow he would attend to restructuring his family. He flicked to the news channel. The story was still running like fury. The reporter relayed the news that the authorities had released the names of the deceased. She began reeling off the names. Silvio stared at the TV, his eyes had become lifeless. The bottle slipped from his hand and smashed on the quarry tiled floor. He grabbed his keys and rushed from the house.

EPILOGUE

A YEAR HAD PASSED SINCE ROBBIE'S TRIUMPH. He lay on the floor in his house playing with Rosa, who giggled and climbed over her father. Angela stood in the doorway watching them, her belly swollen. Her eyes were dark and weary, aged beyond her years, worn out, defeated.

Robbie lifted Rosa in the air, and then brought her back down again.

'Okay enough. Daddy's got to go now,' he kissed her and she giggled again. Robbie got up leaving her on the floor and walked to Angela. He kissed her cheek and she shied away, he put his hand on her belly.

'I think it's a boy,' he said.

'You know it's a boy.'

'Yeah,' he smiled and kissed her again, walked away, grabbed his jacket from the back of a chair.

'Robbie,' she said.

'Yeah.'

'How long do you think?'

'Stop worrying.'

'But I am Robbie. What's gonna happen to us?'

'It's gonna be fine.'

'You always say that,' she said and squatted down to pick up Rosa who was tugging at her dress.

'And I'm always right,' he said, then moved back to her, kissed her lips then Rosa on the head.

'Gotta go,' he said and walked out.

On the driveway, Serge waited in his car. The ashtray was overflowing with butts and as he put one out, he lit another. Robbie opened the passenger door and got in. They said nothing just nodded at each other. Serge shifted into drive and pulled out. After ten minutes Robbie broke the silence.

'We can beat it Serge.'

'How? How you gonna stop that fuckin' rat Silvio spilling his guts? A fuckin' RICO. How Robbie?'

'We'll beat it. If we don't, we don't. We're Cosa Nostra. We'll take it. Like men of honour who took the oath should.'

As they hit the city Robbie felt a surge in him. Pride. Pride flowing through his body as he looked at the city bubbling with life, industry, money making. New York City. Robbie's city. Robbie, head of the most powerful Mafia family in the country. The family that now bore his name, D'Angelo.

Printed in the USA
CPSIA information can be obtained
at www.ICGtesting.com
LVHW050223011223
765449LV00006B/15